DEDICATION

This novel is dedicated to my wife, Dietlinde, as I would not have written it without her constant encouragement and good advice over a period of several years. My wife is a native German speaker, and I have been humbled by her ability to read and understand my English text and offer very cogent advice about my composition.

AGAINST ALL ODDS

Volume One –
Jason Smiley Stewart – My Life Story

A NOVEL BY

John Milton Langdon

Tate Publishing, LLC

Jason Smiley Stewart–My Life Story by John Milton Langdon

Published in the United States of America
by Tate Publishing, LLC
127 East Trade Center Terrace
Mustang, OK 73064
(888) 361–9473

This novel is a work of fiction. Names, descriptions, entities and incidents included in the story are products of the author's imagination. Any resemblance to actual persons, events and entities is entirely coincidental.

ISBN: **1–59886–14–7-6**

ACKNOWLEDGEMENTS

I would like to thank Mary Godwin, Curator and Archivist at Porthcurno Telegraph Museum at Porthcurno for her help and advice concerning the development of the telegraph system between Britain and India and also Frau Katharina Ferris for preparing the illustrations that are included in my book.

Many relatives and friends have offered suggestions and words of support. There isn't space to mention everyone individually so I hope that a global thank you will be acceptable.

CONTENTS

PREFACE

My novel is fiction based loosely on fact and all the characters, companies, and events described are figments of my imagination. Any resemblance to persons living or dead, companies extant or closed, and historical events are coincidental.

Pickworth, Lenton, London, Liverpool, Bombay and so on, all exist in the real world but are simply the backdrop to my story.

I have to admit that I was astonished to find that Pickworth, the name I thought I had invented for Jason's birthplace, does actually exist. The Ordnance Survey maps for 1891 identify two villages named Pickworth located about twelve miles apart but with the prominent buildings differently disposed. Only one village remains today and any resemblance between Pickworth today and my imaginary village are again due to coincidence.

ONE
Formative Years

"Thank you, Nurse" I said politely.

Then much less politely, I thought, I wish she wouldn't keep pushing dollops of that awful, foul-tasting medicine down my throat.

It's later. I know it's later as the sun shadow on my bed has moved. I try to find a comfortable position in the bed, and as I wriggle, I hope that my end is not too far away. I know why I'm confined to bed. The nurses know why I'm here and so does my family.

So why does everyone pretend it is otherwise? Are they protecting themselves from grief or trying to protect me from the truth? It's a waste of time if they are considering my feelings as I know I'm dying. It's not if but when.

It happens to everyone eventually but to some it happens earlier than to others, as I know to my sorrow.

I had to take another dollop of that awful medicine, and I wake to find the sun has moved some more. I'm sure it's the medicine that's making me so sleepy.

The priest was here earlier wearing his funereal black clothes and celebratory red face. He was full of false enthusiasm and "You'll soon be up and about Jason," comments as he mentally revised the date and time for my interment. I felt like saying, "I'll tell you when I'm ready to go, Vicar," but restrained myself as he would have given me a long lecture about my life being in God's hands and not mine.

I said I would write my memoirs but never found the time. I wonder where I would start if there was time to begin. Probably at the beginning, I thought profoundly.

Later!

I've been to sleep again. Now what was I starting to think about? Oh! I remember. The memoirs I have never found the time to write. It's a pity really, as I have lived quite an interesting life.

The doctor came and examined me.

"I don't need anything, thank you, Doctor," I said in response to his enquiry, then added "Good night, Doctor. I'll see you tomorrow," as he left the room.

I reclined back against my pillows and as I started to drift into sleep, a picture of the village where I was born came into my mind.

I was a typical village child. A dirty kneed, snotty nosed little ragamuffin, who was alternately laughing and squabbling with his peers in the dirt outside the smithy where my father laboured each and every calendar day except Christmas.

I was not allowed over the threshold of the smithy in those early years after I had learnt to walk. My parents, but particularly my mother, thought it was a much too dangerous place for a mischievous and adventurous infant to be, so I had to stand in the entrance and peer into the exciting gloom from the sunlit doorway. I could see the ruddy glow of the hot coals. I could see the showers of bright sparks that flew up the chimney in time with the wheeze and pant of the bellows as my father's sweating helper pumped industriously. My father would stand at the side of the forge watching and turning a piece of metal as it heated in the glowing coals. When he judged it had heated enough, he would grasp the red hot metal with a pair of long handled tongs and carry it swiftly to the anvil. There, with practised swings of his hammer, he would shape the glowing metal and then just as swiftly return it to the forge to be heated again.

I grew up with the clang of hammer on iron and the sputtering hiss of steam as red hot metal was quenched in the water trough. The smell of hot metal and the throat grabbing reek of the smoke from the forge were omnipresent. And there was always the smell of horses mingled with aroma of sweating men. I remember seeing the beads of sweat in my father's black curly hair. As a small child, I recall being entranced at the way they used to sparkle when he happened to pass through a stray beam of sunlight as he walked from forge to anvil and back.

Even today, if one of my senses detects one or other of those sounds or smells, my memory conjures up a picture of the forge and my father. It's as fresh and as clear as if I was seeing it now and not over the passage of more years than I care to remember.

I wish I had a portrait of my mother or even a brief but accurate description, but I haven't.

I know she had golden hair but my abiding, small child memory is of someone I looked up to. She seemed to be always silhouetted against the light. She was just a dark shape with a bright edge. I should be able to picture her as she was just before she died when I was about ten years old but cannot, much to my regret.

I do not remember now who it was, but someone told me she was the daughter of a rich farmer who had gambled away the family fortune and then killed himself. The little education she had received was of no real value to a suddenly destitute young woman. She had gone into service with the vicar of the adjacent and much bigger parish of Lenton and stayed there until just before she married. It was only a small household and even when the brother of the vicar's wife came home from the navy, her duty was not onerous. There was time for improvement and the vicar's wife obviously recognized my mother's potential and took it upon herself to teach her all she could absorb about poetry, cooking, botany, and so on. My mother had also learned something of arithmetic and geometry from the vicar's wife. These are not normal accomplishments for a lady, but apparently the vicar's wife had been taught by a series of male tutors who had been engaged to tutor her brothers while she was growing up. Clearly my mother had learnt skills that were normally taught only to boys. These she tried to pass on to me, but with limited success.

My mother didn't speak like the local village people as a result of her experiences in Lenton and tried to make me emulate her example, but the constant influence of the village vernacular was too strong for her to have much success.

My Mother, may God rest her soul, is responsible for my Christian name. At some stage during her confinement, she had read about the voyages of Jason and the Argonauts in a volume our local vicar had loaned to her. Apparently, he told my mother that it would be good for her to sit and read so she did and thought the name Jason had a nice ring to it. I believe she was secretly attracted to the heroic nature of this mythical man. So she blessed me with his name. I often cursed that choice during my childhood as children can make cruel sport of anything unusual, and the name Jason was excuse enough in our small rural world.

That and auburn hair. Ginger Jason followed me everywhere during my youth.

My Father was a big, broad shouldered, dark haired, heavily muscled man. He habitually wore a homespun woollen shirt and trousers with a well worn, scarred, brown leather apron to protect the front of his clothing. On his feet he wore big, clumpy, wooden soled shoes, with leather uppers nailed to the edge of the sole with big, round headed, copper nails. He had a round cheerful face and a hooked nose. His ears were quite normal in shape but one was slightly bigger than the other, not that it was very noticeable to a casual glance. He had a habit of pulling the larger ear when he was thinking through a problem and I wondered if he had been born with a big ear or developed it over years of thinking and absent minded tugging. His eyes were very dark brown, set back under bushy black brows. Remarkably, his face was almost devoid of wrinkles except for the crow's-feet at the corners of his eyes.

During my early years he was a cheerful individual who lived up to his name. He was also an industrious man and he was well liked in the neighbourhood because he was a good craftsman who charged a fair price for excellent work.

I remember as a small child being picked up and thrown repeatedly into the air like a feather. All the time I wished he would stop and equally strongly hoped that he would not. His deep voiced laughter mingled with my shrill voice as I screamed with fear and enjoyment. He was strong but gentle. I remember that he was able to work with wood with the same facility as he fashioned metal. He made, and later had to mend, the wooden toys he fashioned for me. But he did so with loving care and never blamed a small boy for clumsiness. As I became older and grew bigger, his attitude started to change towards me. But he was always gentle and polite and his chastisements, when I transgressed, were never more than a warning of worse to come if I failed to take heed of his strictures.

His relationship with my Mother always seemed to be happy and mutually respectful. It never seemed to change, but as a small boy, I might not have been aware of any strains that could have existed in their private relationship.

But he changed slowly and steadily from a cheerful man to a miserable one. As the years passed, he became dismal and dour, and by the end of his life, he was never content with anything he produced, whether it was made from metal or flesh.

By then a man less suited to the name of Smiley would have been hard to find.

I was at least partially to blame for the deterioration in his spirit. I was a disappointment to him when he realized I would have my Mother's auburn hair, blue eyes and slim physique and not his burly blacksmith's frame. When it was clear I would be unsuited physically to follow in his footsteps and worse, had evinced no interest in spending my life slaving in a forge for a pittance, he started to lose interest in me. I think his inability to father another child while my mother lived and to find another wife after her death compounded his problems and his cup of misery overflowed continuously during his later years.

I was sent to the village school as a matter of course. The school was financed by the local gentry as they needed somewhere for their own children to be taught and this was a much cheaper option than a governess or a private tutor for each family. I started to attend the school as soon as I was considered to be big enough, but I was already able to hold a piece of charcoal and write my name. I had learnt so much from my mother that I was well ahead of the other children of my age with the three R's and this added to my unpopularity.

The bleak stone built school had two rooms. The larger room contained all the children who were in the school to learn except for the very oldest who spent their time with the curate in the smaller room. In the bigger room the elder children taught the youngsters the rudiments of reading and writing that they themselves had learned from an earlier group of older children. The curate then tried to polish the rough diamonds the system had created.

Looking back I'm certain the curate was quite a normal, God fearing and deeply religious man, but he was a frightening figure for all of us small children.

He was as thin as a rake and looked as tall as a tree. He dressed in unrelieved black and had a face as pale as whey crowned with mouse brown lank hair. He sniffed through a perpetually runny nose down which he looked with undisguised distain at the lesser mortals at his feet. Looking back, I realize that he knew very little about useful subjects but a great deal about the Bible and penance.

I remember that the number of older children attending the school on any one day fluctuated in accordance with the demands of the seasons and reasons such as "picking potatoes" or "turning hay" were regular excuses to explain absences from lessons. Even the beadle appointed by the Parish to ensure attendance at the school could not overcome the economic demands of the age. When it was time for planting or harvesting, parents were obliged to use their children as free labour on the farms as they could not manage otherwise.

Even as a small boy, my mother encouraged me to always seek to better myself. Whilst she walked God's earth she often said to me,

"Jason! Whenever you are presented with a chance to learn

something new you must grab that chance with both hands. If you do as I say, then you will always know at least as much as but probably more than the peers who will be competing with you."

This is a philosophy that I have embraced wholeheartedly all through my life, and I commend it to my readers as enthusiastically as I have recommended it to my children.

My desire to learn soon outstripped the teaching ability of our curate and this left me with no outlet for my desire to better myself. The curate was too unimaginative to see my frustration and think of finding more advanced lessons for me to learn in his school, or elsewhere for that matter so for years I didn't advance at all.

When I look back on those days, I can see what an extremely frustrating period in my life this had been.

While I was attending the school, I did discover that I had a gift for mimicry, but the discovery proved a mixed blessing. I could reproduce faithfully the sniffing, complaining voice that the curate used when he addressed one of his students. In fact my mimicry was so accurate that I could walk up behind another schoolchild and say quickly and in a loud, complaining voice, "Sniff! Wretched Boy! Sniff! Sniff! That's all wrong. Sniff! Bend over and I'll see if a beating will wake up your ideas." And I would whack a stick on the side of a bench for extra affect. The unfortunate child would be bent double before you could say knife much to the amusement of the other children who were in on the game. It didn't endear me to the victims of course.

The curate, when he happened to witness one of my performances, was far from amused and inflicted three full blooded strikes of his cane on each hand for my insolence. I didn't cry, although the pain was bad enough. I gritted my teeth and when no one was looking tucked my stinging fingers into my armpits and hugged them. He made a point of taking me home that day so that he could make a formal complaint to my father about my lack of discipline and rudeness to a man of the cloth.

It is a pity that modern parents do not follow the old practices, as the world would be a better place, but in those days "spare the rod and spoil the child" was an adage every parent lived by and mine were no exception.

My father took off his thick, broad, leather belt and bent me double over the anvil. As he gave me six stinging smacks across my backside he said "This is for being caught being disrespectful to your elders," and I was sure that there was a slight emphasis on the word "caught" not that the thought lessened the pain.

I ate my supper standing up and slept on my stomach when the pain from hands and bottom allowed some repose.

I wasn't beaten often, so I couldn't have been much worse than the rest of the children with whom I played and studied.

Life proceeded in tune with the seasons, and the daily routine of the house and family seemed to be unshakeable. Then in 1853, when I was about ten years old, my mother suddenly died and my life was irretrievably altered. She had been untiring in her efforts to feed and clothe us and to keep the little cottage beside the forge clean and tidy. The cottage garden that decorated the front, back, and one side of the cottage was my mother's pride and joy. She spent many hours there. They were happy hours I believe as she was always humming and smiling as she gardened—planting, weeding and picking the fruits of her labours as they came into season. I remember the hollyhocks and other bright flowers that grew between the rows of vegetables.

She was also very proud of her herb garden and was always able to provide the appropriate medicine to ease my childhood ailments. I think she was quite a knowledgeable herbalist although I have no idea where she gained the expertise unless it was from the wife of the vicar of Lenton. It certainly wasn't gained from anyone in Pickworth as all our neighbours came to my mother for help.

She dried and preserved as much of her produce as possible ready for the inevitable shortages of winter. By the end of each autumn, the larder was full and every available inch of shelf space in our tiny cottage was stacked with bags and boxes and crocks full of essential things. She made and mended my clothes and didn't scold me too much when I came home with torn and dirty clothes following a rough and tumble in the field in front of the school house.

I took her presence for granted, as all young children rather selfishly do and when she stayed in bed with a fever one morning, I went off to school with neither a backward glance nor a second thought. She had been ill for some time, I realized later, although she tried very hard to conceal the fact. She had become pale and weak, but I didn't understand that she was actually dying from some disease until it was too late and she had gone from my life.

My father came to the school later that morning and beckoned the curate outside where they had a short conversation. I could hear their voices and not the words, but I could sense the seriousness of their talk by the calm measured tone of the curate. My father beckoned me outside and said, through teeth clenched with barely suppressed emotion,

"You must come back to the smithy. Your mother has been called to heaven!"

I didn't understand what he meant immediately and when I did I could not believe the misfortune that had befallen me. I was inconsolable for a long time despite the kindly efforts of neighbours. I couldn't think of anything or anybody but myself. I rejected my father's attempts to console me even though he was almost prostrate with grief himself, and at the same time, I did nothing to help my father in his loss. I know now, of course, how selfish and unreasonable my attitude was, but I felt he was responsible for my mother's death and would do nothing to comfort him. After the funeral and as time passed, I stopped blaming him, but we had grown too far apart during the long months of grieving for a comfortable coexistence to re-establish itself.

Time passed slowly, and soon I could no longer go to school as there was nothing left for the curate to teach me except about religion, which was a subject in which I had no interest and less aptitude.

My father would not pay another man to keep me out of mischief during the day and as I was physically big enough and no longer attending the village school, he dismissed his helper in the forge and I took his place. I worked the bellows in the smithy for him and held one end of long pieces of red hot metal in tongs as he shaped the other. I practiced forging small metal items often enough to learn something of the blacksmiths trade, but I wasn't really interested.

I was mentally and physically unsuited to follow my father's calling and none of the other village trades attracted me. I had absorbed so much from my mother's teaching that I knew too much to be content with the simple life of a farm hand. Equally, the possibility of an apprenticeship in the local mill or bakery was as unattractive as the thought of living in the confines of the same village for the rest of my life. But there seemed to be nothing I could do to escape from the daily routine of life at the forge and the miserable, frustrated outpourings of my widowed blacksmith father.

Sometimes a person's life is changed forever by the chance happenings of fate. Mine was, one bright day in the early summer of 1860 when I was just passed my seventeenth birthday, although it was some time before the reality of that fact impinged on my consciousness.

Late in the afternoon a man on a large chestnut horse stopped in front of the smithy and dismounted stiffly. He stretched and walked over to my father after looping the reins around the hitching rail. He said in a cultured, deep, commanding but polite voice,

"Good day to you. What is your name?"

"Smiley Sir."

"Well Smiley. My horse cast a shoe a mile back and needs to be re-shod. Check the other shoes and replace any that are worn or loose. Is this young man your son?"

"Yessir."

"Can he take my baggage over to the inn?"

"Yessir," said my father, and then turning to me he said "Take the gentleman's baggage to the inn, Jason and come back immediately."

As I turned and went towards the horse my father asked, "Shall I send the horse over to the inn after it's shod, Sir?"

"Yes. I will stay the night in Pickworth and go on in the morning."

The stranger untied his luggage and passed it to me. Carrying the luggage is my usual role in these circumstances, and I shouldered an old leather portmanteau and carried two polished wooden boxes, one by its handle and the other tucked under my arm. This was all that was packed on the back of the horse and it seemed very meagre luggage for such an important looking person.

He was a tall, broad shouldered man and dressed like a gentleman in a black top hat and tailcoat. His dark blue trousers had braided seams and his tan coloured riding boots were or rather had been, highly polished. The boots like the rest of the stranger's apparel wore a coating of dust and suggested a long hot day in the saddle. His demeanour and the quality of his clothing spoke of wealth. He carried himself with the erect posture of an army or navy officer accustomed to being in command of others. He had a tanned, weather beaten face, curly fair hair and bright blue eyes surrounded by the crow's feet of a man accustomed to looking at distant horizons in strong sunlight. He appeared to be the sort of man who had lived and would continue to live an interesting and adventurous life. I gazed with awe at this stranger who had touched my life so unexpectedly and for the first time in my short life, I was conscious of the fact that I had met someone of whom I was immediately and unashamedly very, very envious.

When we arrived outside the Blue Bell Inn I was unusually clumsy and nearly dropped one of the boxes. For this carelessness I was roundly cursed at a volume that made everyone in the vicinity stop and look to see what was happening. Red faced and stammering, I bowed and apologized as humbly as I knew how and waited to receive the kick or clout that would normally follow quickly on the heels of the curses.

To my amazement nothing happened and he turned away from my apology with a nod of his head, in order to speak to the innkeeper who had arrived red faced, jowls aquiver, fat, hot and panting from somewhere in the depths of his house.

Whilst the innkeeper wiped his hands on his not so white apron and nodded or shook his head as appropriate, the stranger arranged for the collection of his horse from the smithy, the stabling of his horse and then for a room and a meal. When the Innkeeper had bustled away to get everything ready, he turned and instructed me to carry his baggage upstairs with a bloodcurdling description of what would happen if anything were damaged, which he completed by saying, "If you drop anything, you clumsy young jackanapes, I'll have you keelhauled and sent to Davy Jones locker, before you can say 'Sorry Sir.'"

As you will imagine everything was carried upstairs as if it was made of the most delicate eggshells. Although, I had no idea of his meaning at the time, the warning had been issued in such a strong, stern voice that an appointment in Davy Jones locker did not sound an attractive proposition.

Two pretty young chambermaids were in the passageway outside the captain's room.

They curtseyed as he passed and simpered, "Good day, Sir," and the looks they exchanged after he passed them indicated how attractive the stranger was to both young women.

He returned their greeting quite civilly, but the quick glance he gave them suggested he had not noticed how very attractive they both were. In my seventeen-year-old state of unrequited lust, I could not imagine how he could have been so unaffected. To me, they looked the essence of desirable feminine company, and I did not understand how he could not have felt as I did.

With the wisdom of passing years, I came to understand.

Once in the room he directed me where to place the baggage. When that task had been completed, I started to sidle towards the door so that I could return to my tasks at the forge. It was customary for me to hold the horse's head and keep it calm whilst it was re-shod. As my hand found the door handle, he picked up the box I had nearly dropped and my "By your leave I'll go back to the forge, Sir," died in my throat, as his threat still rang in my ears. I wondered if I would now receive the punishment I had escaped earlier.

Captain James Stewart, as he had announced himself to the inn-keeper when we arrived on the scrubbed doorstep of the inn, turned to me, box in hand, and said in a quiet but commanding voice, "What is your name, boy?"

"Jason Smilcy, Sir," I replied sounding very much calmer than I felt.

"How old are you, Jason?" was the next question.

"Just over seventeen years, Sir," I answered, beginning to wonder why this obviously important and wealthy man wished to question the son of the village blacksmith.

"I knew your mother. She was a lovely woman. I was truly sorry to learn of her death," he said in a matter of fact voice.

It was a most unexpected admission, and I didn't know what to make of it.

I was still trying to understand why this man should have known my mother when Captain Stewart asked, "Would you like to see what is in this box you nearly dropped?"

I was so amazed that I could barely stammer out a "Yes, please Sir."

The thought of looking in a box this mysterious man thought important was as exciting to me as having a Christmas or birthday present.

The box was made from a reddish coloured wood, mahogany I

later learnt, and shone as if it had been polished with great care for many years. It was not a big box. I estimated that it was about twelve inches square and six inches deep and not heavy as I knew from carrying it. Captain Stewart placed the box on the table, reached into his pocket and took out two keys attached to a metal ring. I noticed now that the box had a brass lock set into one face and brass hinges. There was a name-plate set into the top, but I could not see what was inscribed there.

Captain Stewart selected one of the keys, unlocked the box, and opened the lid. Inside was an unusually shaped object resting on padded supports. It appeared to be made of polished brass and shone warmly. I noticed that even the lid had shaped supports and clearly, when the lid was closed, the object contained in the box was held in place between the top and bottom supports so that it could not rattle around.

He lifted out the object quite carefully although obviously with very great familiarity, and I could see that every surface that was in contact with it was lined with green felt.

"This was given to me by my Father in 1835 and has been a constant companion ever since," he said and added enigmatically "It helps me know where I am and how to get to where I wish to be."

He held it out to me and said "This is called a sextant. You look an intelligent youth, so I want you to describe what you see and try to tell me what it is for."

I reached out a tentative, frightened hand and was scolded for my lack of courage.

"It doesn't bite," he said and showed me the small handle attached to the back of the instrument that I had not previously noticed. I took hold of the handle, lifted it and was immediately surprised by how light it was.

I was awed by the perfection of the workmanship. I had crafted small items out of brass or copper and worked on small wrought iron items myself and thought them to be at least acceptable. I had seen the work of those known in the area as craftsmen, like the clockmaker for instance, but this was craftsmanship beyond anything I had seen or even imagined. I saw my beginner's efforts in their proper perspective and was almost struck dumb with awe as I turned and twisted the object so that I could look at every feature from as many different angles as possible.

But I could feel the captain's eyes upon me and I knew I would have to say something quickly or find myself parted from this beautiful object.

It was quite thin and approximately triangular.

"It looks like cast brass that has been polished," I said tentatively. No response.

"One edge is curved and there are short lines marked along a raised strip along this edge. Some of the lines are slightly longer than the others and have numbers written above them rather like a ruler; but not like any ruler I have used."

"There are small "O's" written above and to the right of the numbers" I added. No response and still those eyes watched me.

I noticed a strip of brass on the front. It was finely made like the rest of the instrument and seemed to be pivoted at the end where the two side pieces of brass came together at a sharp angle, but I was unable to move the arm. I tilted the instrument so that I could look at the curved edge and noticed that it was toothed like a gear wheel. There was a little wheel on the bottom edge of the arm. I turned the wheel tentatively and noticed that the whole arm moved freely across the ruler. I turned it back and the arm moved in the opposite direction.

"Good," said the captain, who had by this time settled into one of the armchairs so that the boot boy could pull off his riding boots. More exactly the boot boy grasped the boot between his legs and held tight with both hands whilst the captain exerted pressure on the boy's backside with his other leg. The boy staggered across the room as one boot came off very quickly after some stubborn resistance. It looked so comical that I almost laughed out loud but fortunately was able to stifle the guffaw.

"It looks as if it is used for measuring," I said without any idea what it could possibly measure—nothing within my knowledge, I was sure.

"Better," said the captain, who now had his feet up on the second easy chair and looked very comfortable. A pot of ale with an overflowing head of white foam had appeared on the small table at his elbow, but I had not seen who had brought it, as I was too busy with my examination. I heard a girlish giggle from outside and assumed one of the chambermaids had delivered it.

This was confirmed when I heard one of them say "He pinched me bum," followed by another giggle.

I looked more closely at the face of the instrument and saw that a small circular object was attached to the side of the instrument. Half of it was a mirror and the other half clear glass. There was another mirror higher up attached to the top of the moveable arm and a small telescope. I put the telescope to my eye. Through the clear part I could see the captain or part or no captain depending on how accurately I pointed the telescope.

"Very good!" he said "and now if you rotate the little wheel" and as I followed his instruction he said "No! Turn it the other way!"

As I turned it, the captain's form appeared in the mirrored part and by carefully aiming the telescope I could make two separate half captains appear. One half was in the mirror and other in the clear glass. I could not understand how this could happen, and it seemed so like magic that I almost dropped the instrument for the second time in one day.

The captain's dinner arrived. He retrieved the sextant, replaced it in its box and locked it then sent me on my way with a cordial, "Well done Jason. Next time I see you, I'll ask you again what the sextant is for. Good evening to you."

"Good bye, Sir," I replied and left his room and the inn.

My father was not pleased with my long absence. When I reached the smithy, I found he was having great difficulty fitting the new shoe to the horse's hoof on his own. The horse had become skittish because of the bangs and clangs and strange smells emanating from the smithy. It was tied to the hitching rail and kept dancing about as there was no one to stand by its head and keep it calm. It looked so nervous that I was surprised that it hadn't given my father a good kick.

As I went to the horse's head and started to calm it my father said angrily, "Where have you been you lazy ragamuffin? You know I need you here to help. No! Don't waste my time trying to tell me now. Just keep the blasted horse steady so that I can fit this shoe." As soon as the horse was calmer he pulled the horse's hoof up between his legs and there was the familiar burst of smoke and the stench of melting horn as he planted the red hot shoe in place, then removed it to check the bearing. My father went on with his task without another word, and I spoke calmly to the horse and patted his neck.

When the horse had been re-shod, I told my father about the sextant and launched into an excited description of the workmanship in this marvellous instrument I had been privileged to handle, but he could not or would not envisage what I described with such enthusiasm.

Clearly he was not happy that the captain was present in our little village and even less happy that I had spent so much time in his company, but he would not give any reason for his opposition. He was not averse to taking the captain's money, however, as an ostler came from the inn at supper time to collect the horse and pay for the new shoe.

The next morning I had nothing to do in the smithy as my father had gone to the market in Grantham so I walked over to the inn to see if I might have the good fortune to see Captain Stewart again. I only saw one of the chambermaids and she was polishing the brass door knocker. She told me the captain had paid for his board and lodging early in the morning and ridden out of Pickworth in the direction of Lenton, then added, "He has gone to Lenton to visit his sister and brother-in-law. He's the Vicar of St. Peter's Church"

"Do you know if he will return?" I enquired.

"I've no idea," she said and went on with her polishing.

I could not understand why I felt as if I had been deserted. Travellers pass through our village often enough on their way to or from Boston or King's Lynn, so I should have been used to it. But there was something about Captain Stewart that made him seem more important than just a passing stranger.

TWO

Invitation to Learn

I spent many hours puzzling over Captain Stewart's "What is it used for?" question when I was mindlessly pumping air into the forge, but no matter how much I wracked my brains, I could not deduce what possible use the instrument he showed me could have. I was certain that the beginnings of an answer lay in the markings on the bottom edge of the instrument. Was there some clue in the triangular shape of the instrument I wondered? I could feel something stirring in my memory but no matter how hard I tried, I could not bring it to my consciousness.

Following the surprise interruption caused by Captain Stewart's visit the weeks passed slowly and uneventfully following the seasonal rhythm of the countryside. On many occasions I saw a horseman on the road from Lenton, but it was never the captain, much to my disappointment.

One Sunday after Church I had to take a newly shod shire horse back to its owner so that it was ready for work the next morning. As I was walking back to the village, I decided to go a little out of the usual way and pass through a small copse lying beside the track so that I could pass the millpond. I did this as quietly and secretly as if I was going poaching, as I had heard that some of the maidens from the village came to bathe on a warm Sunday afternoon. I wanted to see, but did not want to be heard or seen.

The breathless anticipation of seeing these young women bathing with no clothes on made my heart race as I crawled furtively through the long grass from the copse to the edge of the pond. I reached out and parted the long coarse grass at the water's edge slowly and carefully, peered out and there was–nobody to be seen!

I collapsed back into the long grass and wept copious tears of physical and mental frustration. As I wept I remembered that the last time I had indulged in such unmanly behaviour was whilst my mother was alive.

Then it was the frustration of not understanding about angles, and suddenly my brain remembered what had been stirring in my memory.

Triangles and degrees!

My mother had used the small 'o' symbol when she wrote down degrees as she described the angles of a triangle.

How that helped me understand what the captain's sextant was used for continued to elude me, but most of my frustration had evaporated as the tears dried on my cheeks. I consoled myself with the thought that there were many untouched Sunday afternoons to come when I could try to see the maidens bathing. I crawled back to the edge of the copse and walked quietly through it. After making sure that no one was about I stepped out of the trees onto the track and started to walk back to the village, hoping that no one had seen my diversion or would notice the mud on the knees of my breeches.

As I walked, I tried to remember what my mother had shown me, but it was too many years before and at the time I was not interested enough to try to remember something I had not really understood. I was sure that if I could understand why the slide moved over the curved side with the markings on it I could answer the question.

My 'Brown's Study' was suddenly and startlingly interrupted by a loud voice demanding,

"Good day Jason. Well! What is it for?" and there was the captain.

"The maids don't go to the millpond any more. Too many peeping toms," he added as he matched his pace to mine.

I was struck dumb by the question but much, much more by the revelation that he knew where I had been and why and my cheeks flushed crimson with embarrassment.

He repeated in a voice that allowed for no delay "Well! Have you an answer?" and I said the first words that came into my mind,

"Measuring angles, I think, Sir"

"A good answer," he said, "did anyone tell you?"

"No, Sir, I had to puzzle at it."

I can only imagine that sub-consciously my brain had recognized the markings on the curved edge as degrees. Since the markings were in a line like they are on a ruler which is used for measuring distance, the instrument probably measured angles. How it did that I could not imagine.

The captain looked at me and smiled with pleasure and said, "Very well done, Jason. You have done well to deduce so much from such a short acquaintance with a sextant. You are obviously as bright as I would have expected the son of my friend to be." We walked on in silence for a few steps, side by side. Then,

"Would you like to learn how to handle a sextant correctly and understand what it is used for?" he asked unexpectedly.

I was so eager to learn that I could barely articulate the words, "Yes please, Sir."

"Come to Lenton vicarage next Sunday afternoon after lunch. Good day, Jason," and with that he turned into a side path and strode away.

Except in one respect the next week passed much more slowly than usual as I had something interesting and exciting to look forward to for the first time in my life. I couldn't understand what prompted his attitude but clearly my Father was not pleased that the captain was taking an interest in me. I am sure he would have prevented me from going to Lenton if he could have thought of a good enough reason.

When I said, "Captain Stewart has offered to teach me all about a sextant. You should just see it, father. It's beautifully crafted from brass. You would appreciate the workmanship."

He said gruffly, as he turned away to prevent further discussion, "What use is a sextant in a hayfield or blacksmith's forge? You're wasting your time learning about it as you will never need to use one."

"But it's knowledge. I can learn something new," I said to his unresponsive back and that was that. It was never talked about again.

The comment about knowledge and learning reminded me that there was another subject that I was intensely curious about, but I didn't know of anyone that I could discuss it with. Even the thought of such a discussion made me hot with embarrassment.

I lived in the country, so there was no mystery about the ways in which the farm animals reproduced themselves. But at the same time I had no idea what happened between a man and woman when the bedroom door was closed. This nocturnal activity was the subject of much lurid speculation with my male peers and because the girls were closely chaperoned, we couldn't learn anything through our adolescent contact with them. Consequently we had many misconceptions that our elders and betters did nothing to dispel.

This rudimentary knowledge was of no comfort as I grew older and the desires of my developing body demanded a release that was impossible to achieve.

To my eager, adolescent eyes, all the village girls seemed very shapely, and I only needed a nice smile from one of them to cause a tingling sensation and a rapid increase in heart beat.

My knowledge of the female of our species was improved immeasurably one afternoon during the week that I waited to go to see Captain Stewart for the first time and many of my preconceived notions were turned on their heads at the same time. Thank God!

One afternoon, just to get away from the forge and my father's dour mood, I volunteered to ride a newly shod horse back to a farm a few miles west of Pickworth. I rode into the barnyard of the farm half an hour or so later, dismounted and called across to the buxom young woman who was standing there feeding grain to some chickens.

"I'm Jason Smiley from the smithy in Pickworth. Where should I tether your horse?"

She put down the bowl of grain and walked towards me, "I'm Bessie Pollack. My mother and father are up in the meadow," she waved her hand in a vaguely northward direction and continued, "I'll show you Fanny's stable."

She walked beside me to the barn and then opened the door whilst I held the horse still with the bridle. I had already been aroused by the swing of her hips and the movement of her breasts when, with Bessie beside me, I walked the horse into the barn. Inside there was an area fenced off with some wattle panels that was used as a stable for the horse.

I took off the bridle and handed it to Bessie to hang on a peg on the barn wall just beside her shoulder, but she managed to drop it on the dusty, straw-covered mud floor of the barn.

We both stooped to retrieve it, but she was just a little quicker than me. As she bent forward the front of her dress opened. I gasped with amazement and pleasure. She heard me, saw where my gaze was directed, and as she straightened up, she showed no sign of embarrassment.

I was powerless to speak at that moment. A sight that I had dreamed about since the moment I realized that a woman was different had been presented to me at a most unexpected moment. I wished she would bend down again, so that I could feast my eyes on her breasts once more and considered taking the bridle from her and dropping it again, but I was too scared to take such a step.

"Do you think they're too small?" she asked a little plaintively.

With my pulse thundering in my ears, I gasped out enthusiastically "No! No! Your breasts are beautiful. I've never before seen such a wonderful sight."

"Haven't you ever seen breasts before?" she asked incredulously, as if it was an everyday occurrence for a young man to see such a breathtakingly exciting vista.

I admitted sadly, "No! Never!"

"Poor, Jason!"

She looked at me with a strange expression in her eyes, then took my hand and led me out of the stall to the back of the barn where there was a thick layer of hay lying on the barn floor. It was soft, dry and sweet smelling and rustled as she climbed up onto the level top of the mound. I didn't know what else to do so I climbed up after her. She sat down, then reached for my hand and tugged it until I sat beside her. A moment later we were lying side by side and passionately kissing each other. Very soon afterwards we were fumbling with the fastenings of each other's clothing.

As I lay sweating and panting in the hay I wondered why I had been so worried about not knowing what to do. It seemed as if nature provided the necessary guidance when the time came, and I was amazed how easily I had managed to lie with a woman for the first time.

Much, much later I realized that Bessie had used the chance occasion and my obvious desire to satisfy the demands of her own young body, but at the time, however, the indescribable sensations that flooded my body as she led me from innocence to carnal knowledge left no room for anything more than the joy of the moment.

When we had recovered from our exertions we dressed, picked bits of hay from each others clothing and then strolled out of the barn with innocent faces. We said a decorous farewell in the yard and parted.

I walked home with a stupid grin on my face and the urge to dance every step of the way, I was so happy. However, my mood alternated between ecstasy, about what had happened and abject terror about what might occur when I realized that she could have conceived.

The thought of a forced marriage loomed very large in my mind as did the public disgrace of being in such a position.

Although I behaved as normally as possible, I had a very worrying time of it. Some weeks later, when Bessie's father appeared at the forge and had an altercation with my father, I thought my worst fears had been realized but it turned out to be something else altogether.

Fanny had cast one of her new shoes!

I made as many excuses as I could think of for visiting the farm again, and whilst Bessie was always friendly towards me, there was never an opportunity for me to improve my knowledge as we were never alone. My frequent visits prompted some comment in the village and this must have come to my father's ears as one day he said, "You're too young to be courting, Jason. You're making a fool of yourself mooning about after that Pollack girl. You'd better stop going to the Pollack's farm unless I send you. Until then go and dunk yourself in cold water and cool your ardour."

"Yes, Father," was all I could say, and as Father didn't have a reason to send me there I didn't see Bessie again.

However, I digress.

A few days after my chance encounter with Bessie, the day on which I was to meet Captain Stewart, dawned with clear bright skies and the promise of a beautiful day in prospect. After an interminably long sermon, the theme of which I had forgotten five minutes after the vicar blessed the congregation, I had a solitary lunch of bread and cheese and then set off to walk the five miles to Lenton.

The track was deeply rutted from the passage of farm carts during the rains of the last winter. In between the wheel ruts and on both sides of the track as well, grass and wild flowers grew in profusion. An earth bank and tall hedge lined both sides and as I walked I could hear the rustling of small animals in the bottom of the hedge. Birds burst out of the hedges with squawks of alarm and agitated wings as I passed by. I could hear a lark singing above me, but it was too high in the sky to be seen. Rooks and crows were abundant and as always, noisy. I could hear the harsh cawing of the birds echoing across the quiet Sunday countryside. The cows in the nearby fields munched steadily on the new green grass, and in the distance white blobs of sheep bleated, as they wandered about a meadow following first one leader, then stopping to crop some grass before adopting another.

The meagre remnants of last autumn's bulging haystacks and ricks of straw bore a mute testimony to the hard winter and wet spring just passed. I thought to myself that it was lucky that the weather had improved recently, as a few more wet weeks would have found the farm animals out in the fields regardless of weather conditions, as there would have been no fodder or bedding left.

I wondered if the farmers who had been thanking God so fervently for the sunshine during this morning's service would be praying for rain just as fervently in a few months time if the dry spell continued.

I walked quite briskly and could soon see the parish church of St. Peter across the fields. The road curved round to pass beside the church and lead directly to the vicarage. The church, which exists to this day, is made of local dressed stone and has a pleasingly proportioned spire with a wonderfully melodious peal of bells. At that time the Lenton bell ringers were a very proud group who practiced conscientiously several times a week to maintain the reputation of the parish.

It is many years since I have heard them, and I wonder if they are as good now as they were all those years ago.

I reached the vicarage just before two, and as I approached the garden gate, I wondered if I should go to the back door, which would have been normal for us village people, or ring the front door bell as I had an appointment with the captain.

I opened the gate, entered the vicarage garden and found that the decision had been made for me because a housemaid was there cutting some flowers.

I said "My name is Jason Smiley. I'm from Pickworth and I have an appointment with Captain Stewart."

She stared at me as if I looked familiar and then said "Wait here Mr. Smiley and I'll go and see if the captain is at home." She collected the flowers and disappeared into the house through the open front door.

She reappeared after a few minutes walked across the garden to where I waited and said "Please follow me." She turned, led me to the house and made sure my boots had been thoroughly cleaned on the boot scraper before allowing me over the threshold.

The floor of the short hall leading from the front door towards the back of the vicarage was made of oak planks. These had been polished so energetically, over so many years, that it was possible to see a reflection of one's self in the surface. It was also a trap for the unwary as it was rather slippery. Up to the dado the walls were covered in dark coloured, almost black, oak panels carved in a linen fold design and above the dado, in white, lime washed plaster. There were several pictures of religious scenes that I did not recognize hung on both walls. The ceiling, like the upper part of the walls, was also coated in white lime wash. There was a polished mahogany semi-circular table just inside the entrance. On it was a small cut glass vase of freshly cut spring flowers set upon a crocheted doily in the centre near the back of the table. Beside it was placed a small silver tray for visiting cards. Inside the doorway against the wall was an empty hat and coat rack made of oak with a large brass container for walking sticks. There were three doorways visible from the front door, two on the left and one on the right. In the middle of the hall on the right hand side was a staircase leading to the upper floors.

The maid led me along the hall and knocked on the right hand door.

A cultured lady's voice called out "Enter!"

The maid opened the door and announced me. "Mister Jason Smiley has come to see Captain Stewart, Ma'am."

The maid stood to one side as I entered the room and I saw the captain standing beside a chair in which a lady a few years older than the captain sat. The door closed quietly behind me but the maid had not been dismissed so remained by the door. Mrs. Perceval looked up, said to her brother very quietly after she had stared at me for a few seconds, "I think you may be correct," and then with a beaming smile she said, "On behalf of the Reverend Perceval and myself, I welcome you to Lenton Vicarage, Mr. Smiley."

"Thank you Ma'am," I said.

"Good afternoon, Jason," said Captain Stewart in quite a friendly voice.

"Good afternoon, Sir," I said.

Mrs. Perceval closed the book she had been discussing with her brother and stood up. She was a tall, fair-haired woman with sparkling blue eyes. She had a small turned up nose, a peaches and cream complexion and small regular white teeth. She was dressed in the long, sombre and demure clothing expected of the wife of a cleric. Even so, there was no hiding her very feminine curves from my eager, adolescent eyes.

She said quietly, in a soft, musical voice "Captain Stewart has informed me that he is going to instruct you in the use of a sextant, Mr. Smiley. Whilst you have your lesson, I will go into the garden and enjoy the sunshine after our long wet winter."

With that brief comment she moved gracefully towards the door, which the maid opened for her, but she hesitated and turned back to face the captain and me.

She said, "May I call you Jason?"

"Yes, Ma'am."

"You can read, I imagine." It was more a statement than a question and I nodded my agreement.

"What books do you have at home?" she asked.

Mrs. Perceval shuddered slightly as I said in my broad village accents "We don't have no books, Ma'am, 'sept Bible."

"No, Jason. You should say, 'We don't have any books, except for the Bible.' Please try again."

As I repeated the sentence again, I remembered my mother's frustration as she tried to make me imitate her pronunciation, but Mrs. Perceval was clearly pleased with my effort, as she said, "Very well done, Jason."

She went on "We have a large number of books here by some good authors. When you and my brother have finished the lesson with the sextant, perhaps you would like to come to the library here and I will help you choose a book to read. You can practice reading out loud so that I can help you to pronounce the words accurately. Would you like to do that?"

"Yes Ma'am," I said remembering my mother's good advice.

"Good. I will see you again in a little while," and she turned, glided back to the doorway and disappeared from view as the maid followed her mistress out into the hall and closed the door behind them.

Captain Stewart who had been a mute onlooker up to now cleared his throat and said, "Wait here Jason and I will go and get the sextant from my room."

While he was gone, I had the chance to look around me. It was a calm and peaceful room with leather upholstered, wing back chairs grouped around a low table in front of the fireplace. They looked very comfortable and inviting. The fire had not been lit but was laid and the cast iron surround had been newly coated with blacking. Apart from the door and window openings, the walls were covered with bookshelves and the books themselves were arranged in an ordered manner. The bindings were generally of green leather with the titles in gold but there were some in red leather and some in cloth. As in the hall the ceiling was simple white lime plaster. Clearly the room was used as a place for quiet study, and I noticed other books lying open on a big table in front of the window.

I was very tempted to look at them but decided it would be more polite if did not. After all they could have been of a private nature, and I couldn't establish that without examination.

The captain returned during my moments of indecision and apart from the sextant box, he had also brought a long cylindrical leather container. He stacked the books on the corner of the table and then took a roll of something that looked like paper from the leather container. This he spread out and put a book on each corner to stop it from rolling up again.

He pointed at the rolled out sheet of paper with his finger and said, "This is a chart. Charts like this are used by seamen to find their way from place to place over the oceans of the world. This one shows the area known as the Wash and includes the seaports of Boston and King's Lynn and the adjacent coastline.

"Every chart has a grid of imaginary lines printed on it," he continued and pointed some of them out to me. One set of lines is for measurement of longitude and the other for latitude. When a ship is out of sight of land a navigator can only determine where he is by reference to the sun, the stars and knowledge of time. I will tell you how time and the stars are used another day. The sextant is the instrument that is used for measuring the angle of the sun in relation to the horizon at midday. It has other uses as well, but shooting the sun, as the noon measurement is often called, is the main one."

He unlocked the polished mahogany box and lifted the sextant out of it with the same practised ease that I had remarked before. He pointed to and named all the parts for me and as he named them he explained what they were used for. For example, he showed me a small lever near the toothed wheel that I hadn't noticed when I first examined the sextant and demonstrated how it could be used to release the toothed wheel and allow the central arm to move freely from one end of the scale to the other. He also pointed out how the scale was graduated in degrees and how each degree interval was subdivided into three.

He paused for a few moments and then, sextant in hand, started to question me about what I had been told. I think he was surprised by the amount of information I had retained. I know I was and I also think he was quite pleased although he didn't show it.

He said "I think it is time for some practice" and led me into a part of the garden remote from where his sister was sitting in the sun and handed me the sextant. He instructed me how to check that the sextant was zeroed so that it read accurately and then after putting the dark glass lens in front of the mirror how to measure the angle of the sun. I repeated this exercise a number of times over the next thirty minutes and wrote the angles down on a piece of paper the captain gave me.

"Now Jason," he said, "you have measured the angle between the sun and the horizon several times in the past thirty minutes. Look at the angles you have written down and tell me what you can deduce from them. Remember that you have stood in the same place all the time."

I noticed that each angle was less than the one preceding it. As it was afternoon, I realized that I was measuring the reducing angle the sun made relative to the horizon and I said, "Each angle is smaller than the one preceding it, so I must be measuring the movement of the sun as it gets closer to the horizon."

Captain Stewart corrected me.

He said, "It's not the sun that is moving. It is the earth that is rotating relative to the sun and you have been measuring the movement of the earth as it rotates on its axis through the north and south poles."

I had never before considered that the solid earth I was standing on was moving and the revelation made me suddenly very quiet.

As we went back in to the house at the end of the lesson I thanked the captain for his patience.

He responded warmly, "Not at all Jason. You learn very quickly and more important, I believe, is the fact that you want to learn. If you would like to continue the lesson next Sunday I should be very pleased to see you."

I was overjoyed to be asked to return and said, "I should be very happy to come again Captain if you can spare the time."

"Of course," he said.

In the library Mrs. Perceval was sitting in one of the wing back chairs reading, and when I entered, she laid the book to one side. She said in her gentle voice, "I expect you know all about the sextant now, Jason, and you're eager to study some English."

"Yes Ma'am. No Ma'am," I stuttered, and then as I saw her eyebrows start to rise in surprise, I said, "What I mean, Ma'am, is that I don't know all about the sextant, and I would like to study some English if you can spare the time"

"Yes, Jason, I can spend half an hour with you this afternoon, and I think that the best course is to see how well you read out loud."

Mrs. Perceval rose from her chair and moved gracefully to one of the bookcases. She didn't appear to take steps. It was as if she was on wheels her movement was so smooth. She looked at the titles of several books; took one down and opened it. She read a little then closed and replaced it and selected another. It was a slim volume bound in green leather with gold lettering on the spine. She brought it to where I was standing and gave it to me.

"This book will do very well," she said, "It's by Charles Dickens and it's called *A Christmas Carol*. He is a very good contemporary author." She sat down in her chair again and I stood before her.

"Now Jason" she said, "I want you to just open the book anywhere and start to read from the top of the page."

I did as Mrs. Perceval instructed and was amazed at how easily the pages parted. It was clearly a well read book. I opened the book somewhere near the middle and tried to read the first few sentences. It was a disaster. It wasn't a complicated text, I remember, but of the first twenty words, I recognized about fifteen and made a complete hash of pronouncing anything more complicated than 'perhaps' and 'maybe.'

"Oh dear!" said Mrs. Perceval, "You definitely need some practice at reading out loud, Jason, but do you understand what you have read?"

"Yes, most of it" I responded, "There are some words that I don't know."

"Which are they?"

I moved to stand beside her chair and was suddenly aware that Mrs. Perceval was wearing a very attractive perfume. It was very faint scent, but I found it more than a little distracting. I collected my thoughts and pointed out the unknown words, and she told me how to pronounce them and also what they meant. She showed me how to use a dictionary and I was pleased that I could still remember the alphabet. The half hour passed very quickly, and when it was time to leave, she handed me the book and a small dictionary.

"Try to read the first page and use the dictionary to find the meanings of the words you do not know. When you come next week you can practice reading out loud the text you have studied."

My father was scathing when I returned home proudly clutching the book and dictionary. I won't bore you with a repetition of his comments, but in a nutshell he believed reading books was a complete waste of my time as I would never be able to use the knowledge in the village. He was a successful blacksmith and didn't have any need to read books—and so on and so on.

Many years later I realized, that on that Sunday afternoon, I had taken the first step on a long path that turned a semi-literate village child into an educated gentleman. As time passed and my speech moved away from the patois of the villagers and closer to the educated tones used by Captain Stewart and his sister, old friendships started to die. I think they felt uncomfortable because they could see the Jason Smiley they knew but not hear the familiar accent and words.

"Aping your betters," was a common criticism levelled at me both by my father and my friends.

Only one person in the parish of Pickworth supported me and that was our vicar. I don't know how he came to know that I was going to Lenton, but shortly after I went for the first time, he stopped me outside the church one Sunday morning.

He said, "I hear that you are going to Lenton for lessons from Captain Stewart and his sister. I'm very pleased that they wish to help you, Jason, and if you think I can assist you in any way, please come and see me."

"Thank you Vicar," I said, "I will certainly do so."

Over the months, my boring weeks in the forge were punctuated by the absorbing task of learning about navigation and getting to grips with the English language and more particularly with the literature of our country. My mentors also took time to start teaching me better table manners and some of the other social graces, which I soon realized were sadly lacking.

True to his word, the captain had explained how time was important and showed me the beautiful chronometer he had been given by his father. Very soon I was able to calculate the latitude and longitude of the pergola, where I had my tuition if the weather was fine and also the church porch and the yard beside the Bluebell Inn amongst other places. Captain Stewart had a large number of books about seamanship and navigation and similar subjects and if he was too busy to teach me, I was able to sit down in the library and read about the subjects that interested me. He always made a little time to question me about my reading and to make sure that I had understood the text. Like his sister, he took pains to ensure I could pronounce new words accurately.

One Sunday a uniformed messenger arrived with letter for the captain. After he had read it, he folded it up and put it back in its envelope. After a short pause, during which Mrs. Perceval and I both held our breath in anticipation, he said "I have to go to Liverpool to take over my new ship. I will have to leave this evening if I am to be there in time for the launch."

The vicarage became a hive of activity as Captain Stewart packed his belongings with the help of the maids and readied himself for a rapid departure. I noticed that he was taking away much more than he had packed on his horse when he arrived at the forge in Pickworth.

He said "Goodbye, Jason. No more lessons in seamanship for a time."

And suddenly the horse and trap were at the front door, the Reverend Perceval made one of his rare appearances, wished Captain Stewart "Bon Voyage," said "Good afternoon, Jason," to me and disappeared back into his study to polish the sermon he would deliver later.

Captain Stewart climbed into the trap and rattled away.

Mrs. Perceval and I walked back to the study rather sad and deflated after the frantic activity of the last few hours.

After a while she said "I should be very pleased if you would come and continue to study English with me. I enjoy reading, and it has been very pleasant introducing you to some of the literature of our country."

"Yes, of course I will," I said with enthusiasm.

And so every Sunday afternoon and often during the week if there was nothing to do in the forge, I walked to Lenton to see Mrs. Perceval. Whether it was because she had no children of her own, I don't know, but she started to mother me which was a very pleasant experience, as I had been starved of affection since my own mother had died.

I didn't know why they had decided to single me out for special treatment, but I did know how much I was enjoying the easy friendship as well as the tuition they were giving me so freely.

I think my mother would have been proud of my efforts if she had been alive to see them.

THREE

The Message

Now that Captain Stewart had gone to take over his new ship, I no longer had his guidance about the order in which to study maritime subjects, and after a time stopped reading about the sea and ships. But as the weeks and months passed, the time I would have divided between Captain Stewart and Mrs. Perceval was utilized solely for the study of English. Not only reading but composition and discussion started to fill the available hours.

I really did enjoy the time I spent studying with Mrs. Perceval, but if I'm honest, I have to admit that I enjoyed tremendously the undivided attention of a mature, intelligent, and attractive woman after so many years without the companionship of my mother.

Even so, the months following Captain Stewart's departure were a test of my patience. I did not realize how much I had enjoyed the intelligent, quick wits of my captain tutor and the theoretical and practical knowledge he provided, until he went away. Studying English in all its many guises was a poor substitute for the technical knowledge I preferred to master.

And with my frustration I was forced to endure the dour, ill humour of my father without respite. Sunday morning was particularly bad because we attended church together and sitting shoulder to shoulder on a cold, hard, wooden pew on a wet morning did nothing to improve the ill humour of my father or to lift my flagging spirits. I went to church with as much good grace as I could generate, not because I had deep religious feelings, but because I was expected to accompany my father. To do otherwise would have set the village tongues chattering, and I didn't want to be the source and subject of idle gossip.

Late one Friday afternoon a small group of horsemen with several heavily laden packhorses arrived. They took rooms at the inn and unloaded the packhorses into an empty stable. Early the next morning they unpacked their bags and boxes in front of the inquisitive gaze of a group of villagers who had nothing better to do. I was one! They had chains with brass handles at each end, poles with alternate red and white bands, several things with brass tops that stood on three legs and two boxes that reminded me of Captain Stewart's instrument boxes because of the size and shape.

Clearly they all knew exactly what was required of them as they set to work with the minimum of discussion. A little later I watched from the entrance of the forge as some of the men started measuring all the buildings and the unoccupied spaces in between. I also saw the remaining two men carry one of the boxes, one of the three legged objects and some other items to the top of a low hill at the back of the village.

My father had no blacksmithing work to do, so I was free to fill in the hours as best I could without getting into mischief. I was sure that whatever was inside the box would be of great interest so I decided to follow the two men to the top of the hill. I arrived just as they started to unpack the equipment they carried. I walked up to the man who seemed to be the leader of the group. I thought he must be quite old as he had a long white beard. His face was weather beaten and in his big boots, green canvas jacket and black moleskin trousers, he could have doubled for one of the local farmers.

He glanced at me and said uninvitingly, "What do you want, Ginger"

"I am interested in what you are doing, sir"

"You're only a village kid and wouldn't understand what I told you even if I did waste my time telling you. Go away. We're busy."

I responded rather indignantly. "I'm sure I would understand what you tell me, sir. I know how to use a sextant," I added proudly.

He laughed out loud at that and called across to his mate, "Did you hear that Jeb?" Scornfully he added, "This boy, from a village in the middle of the English countryside, knows how to use a sextant. I see no ships around do you?"

Jeb laughed because his leader laughed, but clearly he was unsure what he was laughing about.

"Look Ginger," he said impatiently but not yet unkindly, "I don't want you to waste any more of my time. You may have heard the word, but I don't believe you know what a sextant is and I'm certain you would be unable to use one if I put it into your hands. Now be off with you. I have to work and not indulge in idle chatter."

I was rather desperate by now, as I feared he would become angry and really order me to go away so I said as firmly and politely as I could "Sir, Captain Stewart has been teaching me about the sextant. I do know how to use a sextant for sun sights, and he has started to teach me navigation."

He looked at me quizzically then passed me a notebook which he opened to a clean page, then a neatly sharpened pencil and said bluntly, "Draw a sextant and name the parts," then he turned away and busied himself with his equipment.

After about five minutes I handed the book and pencil back to him. He looked at the sketch I had made and whistled in surprise.

Jeb, who was looking over his shoulder at the sketch, said "What's that?"

"That, Jeb, is a sextant."

"I've never seen anything like that before."

"That's not surprising Jeb. I have been a surveyor for thirty years and I have seen a sextant only once before. I've never used one. He may be a village lad, but he knows what a sextant looks like," he admitted, as he pointed to the sketch.

In a more friendly tone of voice he said, "I can see from the sketch that you know what a sextant looks like, but how do you know that it is reading accurately?"

He had posed a simple and astute test of the depth of my knowledge and I answered him quickly and accurately by saying, "If the real horizon and the reflected horizon are in a straight line when the sextant reads zero it's reading accurately."

"Very good," he said, and he sounded impressed even if he didn't admit as much. "What are you interested in?" he asked.

"Everything," was the only word that flashed through my brain and larynx.

"That's a big subject," and he laughed gently. "If you would like to work with me I'll teach you as much as I can," he offered.

"Thank you, Sir," I said. "I should be pleased to help you if I can."

He started to turn away then turned back and said, "What is your

Christian name lad? I cannot go on calling you Ginger."

"Jason, Sir," I replied and added, "Thank you, Sir," because I didn't really like my nickname even although it was apt.

"Very good," he said. "My name is Mr. David, and I am the surveyor in charge of this team. Jeb, there, is a chainman. Down there," and he gestured over his shoulder at Pickworth, "is my assistant surveyor and two more chainmen."

"Well Jason, you had better watch what I am doing as the first lesson has begun. This is a tripod," he said as he indicated one of the three legged objects. He turned away and started to assemble on top of the tripod, an instrument that he took piece by piece from the box.

All the time he smoked a pipe. It was a curved pipe that he said was called a "mersham" and it gurgled disgustingly when he sucked on it. I do not know what tobacco he was using and certainly the odour defied polite description. It stank! I have smelt burning compost heaps that have been much more aromatic. As far as it was humanly possible, Jeb and I stayed up wind at all times and watched the smoke drifting away from us with some relief.

As he deftly fitted the parts together, he explained in detail how the instrument, an Engineer's Transit, was set up, operated, and what it was used for.

"The instrument has to be exactly level before it can be used accurately," he said as he showed me the spirit level mounted on the base plate and the four levelling screws between the underside of the base plate and the top of the tripod.

"Would you like to try and level it?"

An easy task I thought, as I understood how the levelling screws should work. Not easy I found, as I manipulated the screws and alternated between making the screws too tight to move or so loose the whole instrument wobbled on its mounting. After a frustrating few minutes at the end of which I was no nearer levelling the transit than I had been at the start Mr. David came to my aid.

"Not as easy as it looks, is it?" he said with a smile then added, "There is a simple knack that all surveyors have to learn."

He stood behind the instrument and adjusted each levelling screw until it was just tight. He turned the instrument until the spirit level was lined up with two opposing screws and then with a few, deft, practiced movements of both hands it was levelled in one direction. In a few more swift movements the instrument had been turned through ninety degrees and levelled again.

"How did you do that?" I asked in amazement.

When he realized that I had not understood what he had done, he demonstrated how to adjust the levelling screws so that they were just tight and then how he rotated them in opposition to each other so that they remained tight, but the instrument tilted one way or the other.

"It's quite easy when you know how," the surveyor said with a grin. "Move your thumbs towards each other and the transit will tilt one way. Move them apart and it will tilt the other. Try it," he said and took a pace away from the instrument.

I did and it worked. When I stood in front of the transit with a thumb and finger on opposite levelling screws, I could see my thumbs, and if I moved them together it tilted one way and the other if I moved them apart.

"You can write, Jason? Neatly I mean?"

"Yes Sir," I answered wondering why he wanted to know.

"I am going to measure the angles between this station," and he gestured to a peg driven into the ground immediately under the transit, "and those church spires. You can book the angles for me as I call them out. The angles will be in degrees, minutes and seconds. You already know about degrees and minutes from your work with the sextant, but did you learn about seconds"

"No Sir."

"For now write down or book what I tell you and I'll explain about seconds when we finish."

"Yes Sir," I said rather apprehensively as I ventured a little further down this unknown path. I was afraid I would do something wrong and annoy him.

He sighted on the spire of Lenton church then tightened two thumb wheels on the side of the transit. He looked at the graduations on the degree ring through a little telescope mounted on a moveable arm and called out the angle which I wrote down under Column 'A' as he directed. He looked at the scale on the opposite side of the transit and I wrote down this angle under Column 'B'. He loosened the upper thumb screw, rotated the instrument and sighted on the spire of Sapperton church. Again he read out the angles and I wrote them down as he dictated. He then sighted on Newton church and called out another set of angles for me to record. I should mention that Mr. David had drawn a table in his field book, as he described it, that gave the names of the churches in order and I filled in the blank spaces in the table as he called out the angles. He then took another set of readings for Face "B" as he called it. With the sextant I only made one measurement and here we were recording four angles each time. I was mystified.

"Why do you take so many readings each time?" I asked.

"That's a good question, Jason. The answer is simple. Accuracy! The instrument is really very accurate but there are minor defects in the machining of the graduations. By taking all four readings I am using different parts of the graduated ring and by averaging the readings I minimize any error."

That makes sense I thought and said, "Thank you, Mr. David."

"By the way," he added, "a second is one sixtieth of a minute which is, as you know, one sixtieth of a degree."

"Thank you, Mr. David," I said again.

He sat down on the instrument box and started subtracting one angle from the next and averaging the results. He seemed satisfied.

"Good, he said. Now Jason I can spare a little time so I want you to try to measure one or two angles."

I stood behind the instrument sighted on Lenton Spire, locked the plates and tried to read the angle at which the instrument was set. I could read the degrees and minutes, but he had to show me how to read the seconds with the vernier scale.

A little while later he said, "I think that is all we have time for this morning, Jason. Well done."

We packed up all the equipment, and as I helped carry it back to the village, he asked, "Are you interested in what we have done and the reasons for doing it, Jason?"

"Yes, of course I am Sir," I said with eagerness. "I did say I wanted to know about everything."

"So you did," he admitted with a grin and started to talk as we walked down the hill.

"I'll give you a little history first. In 1841," he said, "Parliament passed the Ordnance Survey Act. The act requires the Ordnance Survey to prepare detailed maps of England and Scotland, and I am in charge of one of the survey teams collecting the information in the field."

He paused and relit his pipe, which mercifully had been extinguished for some time, and added, "No one expects the survey to be complete until the end of the century. So I have a job for life if I don't get drunk and lose it."

After a pause for polite laughter from Jeb and me he went on, "Now Jason, you will have to use your imagination to understand what we are doing. It is simple enough to measure the buildings, the duck pond, church and so on in their correct positions relative to one another. I can draw this information to scale on a sheet of paper and call it a map. I can do the same in every town and village in the county very easily, but before a useful map can be prepared, it is necessary to know where each town and village is located relative to one another."

He looked at me searchingly then said, "Is that clear so far?"

"Yes Sir. Except that I don't know what you mean when you say scale."

"It's not immediately important Jason, and I will explain about scale later."

"You will know from your captain what a triangle is I'm sure." I nodded agreement.

"Then try to imagine the whole of England covered by an imaginary network of lines making triangles. Then try to imagine that the base of the first triangle is a line nearly seven miles long on Salisbury plain. It was measured very accurately by an officer in the British army called Mudge as I recall."

"That sounds similar to the lines of latitude and longitude that I've seen on a chart," I interrupted. "They're imaginary also. Captain Stewart showed me a chart when he started to teach me about the sextant," I added.

"Yes, but they have different purposes," he said and stopped to take out his field book. On a blank page he drew a group of connected triangles. At the apex of two adjacent triangles he wrote in Sapperton Church and Newton Church. He wrote Pickworth village at the apex of a triangle joining those two churches and a line from Pickworth to a point that he labelled Lenton Church.

"This is how the survey framework is built up. It's called triangulation."

Mr. David went on with his explanation, pointing at the different places on the diagram and explaining what we had been doing during the morning. He was a good and enthusiastic instructor, and I understood the concepts quite quickly.

Later in the day he showed me how to use a level. As before he took the readings and showed me how to book them and check that there were no errors by summing the foresights and back sights. Then I was allowed to take some readings myself and accidentally provided some amusement at the same time. I turned the level until it was lined up on the staff the chainman was holding then bent down a little to look through the eye piece. I reached for the focusing knob, turned it and jumped back in alarm as something poked me in the eye. There was a loud chorus of delighted chuckles from the other members of the survey party who had all been anticipating such a reaction.

A smiling Mr. David said, "That happens to everyone until they get used to it," and he demonstrated how the eye piece moved in and out of the telescope to change focus.

The day was over before I knew it, but I had learned something about land survey and I hoped to be able to continue my education the following day, but that depended on my father and work in the forge.

God smiled upon me every day for the next week because there was no work in the smithy that needed my help and my father seemed to be quite content to be on his own. Each morning I joined up with the survey party and helped wherever I could, and all the time Mr. David gave me instruction and information. What was equally important, I think, was that each new aspect of the work provoked questioning about what I had learnt? When necessary Mr. David gave me further instruction until he was sure I had completely understood not only what to do but also why it should be done in a specific way. He responded to my eagerness to learn and seemed to enjoy imparting his knowledge to me. One morning I helped the assistant surveyor and learnt how to measure with the chain and use survey arrows on the flat and up or down slopes. Although this work is essential for filling in the detail on either side of the main survey lines, it was not as much to my liking as working with the instruments. Instrument work required much more concentration and expertise to be accurate.

One day, it must have been the fifth or sixth day that the surveyors had been in the village, the assistant surveyor was ill.

"Too much ale," said Mr. David in an unusually bad tempered voice, "Stupid man never learns. Drinks ale or scrumpy until he cannot stand and then wonders why he feels like death in the morning."

It was bad luck for the assistant but good luck for me as I was entrusted with a chainman and a small area to survey. Suddenly I was putting into practice all I had learned during the previous days. It was a marvellous feeling. I was suddenly responsible for something and felt ten feet tall.

"What happens to all these measurements, Mr. David?" I asked late that afternoon.

"I send all the field books to our main office in Southampton and the draftsmen there plot all the details to scale." Then he added, "I did say I would tell you about scale, didn't I?"

"Yes Sir," I responded. Although I have to admit that I had forgotten about it. There was so much else to absorb.

He said, "Simply put a scale is the ratio between the information on the map and the information in real life. A scale of one to one means that a map of Lincolnshire is as big as Lincolnshire. It would require a very large sheet of paper that would be difficult to handle in a wind and consequently is not very useful."

I laughed when I visualized this enormous sheet of paper flapping in the wind.

He went on, "A scale of one to fifty thousand means that one foot on the map is fifty thousand feet in the field. This gives a piece of paper that is a manageable size but contains a lot of information. Is the principle clear Jason?"

"Yes Sir. Would it be possible for me to go to Southampton to see them drawing the measurements we have taken?"

"I'll see if that can be arranged, Jason."

Day by day the work progressed and took the surveyors further and further away from the village. At the end of one afternoon, when it was clear that the survey party would move on the next day, Mr. David took me to one side and said quietly,

"Jason, I have been very impressed by the speed with which you learn and the accuracy of your work when you are on your own. I think you could become a very good surveyor if you continue in the same way. If it would be of interest to you, I can arrange for you to become one of my assistant surveyors."

"I should like that very much, Mr. David," I said quickly, "but you will have to speak to my father and get his permission."

"I understand that and now that you have agreed to the idea, I will visit Mr. Smiley this evening and ask his permission to employ you." What could I say except "Thank you, Sir," to this saviour who had presented me with a way out of village life?

When I returned home I told my father that Mr. David wanted to see him and why. Only a dog with two tails could have been happier than me at that moment.

"This is really a good chance to better myself and I'm so pleased that Mr. David wants to continue teaching me," I gushed with happiness. But my cheerfulness started to evaporate when my father said nothing and I saw that the expression on his face was not encouraging.

Mr. David came to the cottage by the smithy in the early evening. He was greeted cordially enough by my father but not invited to sit down.

Mr. David took a deep breath. "Mr. Smiley" he said, "I have been very impressed by young Jason here. He is a strong, well set up young man with a pleasant manner. Much more important is Jason's willingness to learn and his quick grasp of technical matters that would be totally beyond the comprehension of every other village child I have met. It has been a pleasure to have his company this past week, and I think you must be very proud of him. Jason has said that he would like to be employed by the Ordnance Survey and learn to be a surveyor. I would like your permission to make arrangements for Jason to join my team as an assistant surveyor."

I held my breath hoping for good news but, remembering the expression on my father's face, fearing the worst.

Father had already made up his mind I think, because he didn't pause for a second before saying firmly "No! I am not allowing Jason to go wandering about the countryside with a group of surveyors. There's no telling what mischief you'll let him get into. Besides I need his help here."

"I would certainly not allow Jason to come to any harm if he was put in my charge, and I'm sure there is a good future for him as a surveyor," Mr. David said with some heat. I am sure he had been offended by my father's behaviour.

Bluntly and rather rudely, my father said "My answer is the same. I will not permit Jason to go with you and that is the end of the matter. I wish you goodnight, Mr. David." My father turned away to prevent further discussion.

Still irritated by my father's attitude Mr. David, said stiffly, "I'm very sorry to hear that Mr. Smiley. In my opinion you are doing your son a great disservice. I wish you goodnight, Mr. Smiley," and in a more friendly tone, "Goodnight, Jason." He turned and marched out of the cottage. I closed the door on Mr. David and my future. I went sadly to bed without any understanding of my father's attitude.

The next morning I walked over to the inn to say goodbye to the surveyors. They were all packed and ready to ride on to the next village, but each one took the time to shake my hand and wish me well.

I really appreciated their unexpected courtesy.

Mr. David said, "If your father changes his mind and you still want to join me, I have written down the address of the Ordnance Survey office in Southampton so that you can write. They will forward a letter to me. I'm gratified that you are interested in surveying, Jason, and I wish you well for the future." Then he gave me a sheet of paper with his name and address on it.

"Thank you for spending so much time with me, Mr. David," was all I could say.

"It has been a pleasure to have someone like you for company, Jason," he responded.

The survey party all climbed onto their horses, took up the reins of the pack animals, and rode away to start the next section of the survey without a backward glance.

As I watched this group of self-reliant men leave the village, I could not have imagined how valuable my casually acquired knowledge would be in tragic circumstances some years later.

The next day I went to see Mrs. Perceval again and told her what had transpired. She said simply and very practically "Remember, Jason, when one door closes another door often opens. So for now let us carry on with your reading practice."

It was fortunate that there was no urgent or large work in the forge during the days after the surveyors left. If there had been, I would have been required to assist my father and I think we were both glad to be in different places. I know I didn't wish to face him after he had refused to permit me to accept such a good offer.

My days returned to their monotonous routine with only my visits to Mrs. Perceval to brighten my existence until one day in late August a tired and dusty uniformed messenger rode up to the door of the forge and dismounted. My father went out to meet the messenger, exchanged a few words with him, and received a letter. He threw it carelessly onto a bench in the smithy and went on with the work he was doing. The messenger walked his horse across the common to the inn where he handed the reins to a stable lad and disappeared inside.

Trying to appear helpful, but in all honesty also bursting with curiosity, I said to my father, "Shall I help you read the letter the messenger brought?"

He went red with rage and shouted at me "Don't you dare try your airs and graces on me. Remember who you are boy!"

He collected a piece of red hot metal from the forge and carried it to the anvil where he picked up his hammer, and his next words were punctuated by the violent, angry blows of his hammer.

"When," clang "I," clang "want," clang "you," clang "to" and so on until he had completed the sentence, "read my letters for me, I'll tell you." By this time the piece of metal had cooled, cracked under the violent assault he had made with the hammer and was thrown into the corner as useless. The angry outburst and spoilt metal did not improve his temper one iota, and he picked up the message and stamped out of the smithy.

I assumed he had gone to find the vicar so that the letter could be read to him. I could have done this simple task for him, but clearly he did not want me to know the contents of the letter until it suited him to tell me. When he came back to the forge he volunteered nothing about the letter, and I had to contain my curiosity, as he would not respond to my questions except with, "Be quiet damn you!"

It was difficult being silent because letters were as rare as hen's teeth in our village community, and to have one hand delivered by a uniformed messenger was previously unheard of. In my view it was an event to celebrate, not to be taciturn over, but my father clearly thought differently.

Some days later, when I was just setting out on an errand to a neighbouring farm, I happened to meet our vicar as he was on his way home from a service in our local church.

At that time the incumbent was the Reverend Daniel Daly. He was a short stout florid complexioned middle-aged man with no wife or family. Looking back I'm sure he must have had a private income to supplement the thirty or forty pounds a year he received as his stipend as he really lived too well for it to be otherwise. He existed for the members of his congregation. Everyone in Pickworth and the surrounding area for that matter, held him in the highest regard. His only fault, as far as I was concerned at the time, was his apparent desire to make his Sunday morning sermons of record length and unbelievable complexity.

But perhaps that was only the judgement of an impatient youth.

It was a hot sunny day and the vicar was starting to perspire by the time he reached the gate in the churchyard wall. He stopped beside me and said, "Good day Jason. I understand you have been offered a rare opportunity to better yourself. When do you expect to leave Pickworth?"

My silence and totally blank look must have spoken volumes because he said, "So that's how the land lies." Then he turned and left me standing beside the gate set in the stone wall of the churchyard. He started to march across the common towards the forge, little puffs of white rising from the dusty footpath at each footfall. Like a latter-day St. George, armoured in his black suit, dog collar and black hat, about to do battle with the dragon blacksmith.

For a few moments I was motionless with surprise. Then, abandoning my errand, I turned and followed the vicar as I didn't understand what was happening. Father had obviously seen the vicar coming and hurried out of the smithy to meet him. A few moments later I came up to them and heard the vicar say to my father in very direct and uncompromising tones, "Now Smiley, why haven't you told the boy about the opportunity he has been offered? It's the chance of a lifetime! Do you intend to ignore it and consign your son to a life of a blacksmith? Do you expect him to hammer hot steel as you have done since you were a young man when he has the chance to better himself and bring credit to you and everyone here?"

"I need Jason here to help me," my father said by way of explanation.

"Absolute rubbish," said our vicar. "Any idiot can pump up the forge. You don't need someone with Jason's ability to do that. He doesn't even do the blacksmithing work. You do that. Jason is simply a convenient, unpaid labourer and he deserves better from you."

I was mightily impressed. I had thought our vicar was a mild mannered man, except on Sunday when he gave fire and brimstone sermons, but here he was laying down the law to my father on my behalf. Secretly and silently I cheered him on, although I had no idea what this was about.

My Father's head started to droop and was hanging in shame by the time the vicar finished his comments because he obviously had intended to let the offer, whatever it was, lapse and keep me in Pickworth. My Father said nothing.

The vicar turned to me and explained the enigma. "Captain Stewart has written to your Father and told him that he has taken over his new ship. The owners have agreed that Captain Stewart can take one young man as a Cadet for training as a deck officer. The ship will load its first cargo in Liverpool and is due to sail on the first of September."

He paused to draw breath. "If you wish to be considered for this opportunity, Jason, and in my opinion it is an exceptional opportunity," said the vicar with enthusiasm "You must go to the Hornby Building in Liverpool where the Gold Star Line offices are located. The captain wrote that the offices are in Water Street and near to the Town Hall. You will be interviewed by Captain Downing, the Marine Superintendent and if Captain Downing forms the same high opinion of you as Captain Stewart, then you will be appointed the first Gold Star Line cadet. Captain Stewart wrote also, that he did not expect you to have any difficulty with your interview and after it you should go to Victoria Dock to meet him and join the ship's crew. After you sign on you will be provided with uniforms and food. I understand you will also receive a small allowance."

The vicar paused for breath again, looked from my father to me and waited expectantly for one of us to say something. I was speechless with surprise, but my father took one look at my face, which must have been radiant with pleasure at the thought of leaving the drudgery of a blacksmith's life and said, "Go then. Abandon your father," and walked away into the forge and started noisily hammering a piece of metal on the anvil.

The vicar took command of the situation and said, "There is very little time to spare, Jason. You must be ready to leave the day after tomorrow at the latest. I will help you as much as I can as I'm sure your father will not."

Next morning I ignored my obligation to help in the smithy and instead walked as quickly as I could along the lane to Lenton in order to see Mrs. Perceval and tell her about her brother's offer. She looked very surprised when I was shown into the study and her first comment reflected her concern.

"You're here to see me very early in the day, Jason, is something wrong?"

"No Mrs. Perceval, nothing is wrong," and I explained about the letter Mr. Smiley had received and the vicar's intervention.

"That's very good news, Jason," she said warmly and then added what I thought at the time to be a rather strange comment. "It will be good for you and my brother to spend some time together." She elegantly indicated a chair and said, "Now, Jason, please sit here for a few minutes whilst I go and pack a few things that my brother left behind. I must also write a short letter for you to take to him if you will."

"Of course I will take whatever you wish, Mrs. Perceval."

"Thank you, Jason," she said as she glided from the room with the maid following in her footsteps. Soon afterwards I could hear their voices from an upstairs room as they looked for the forgotten items. Much more than a few minutes had passed before she returned with a carefully wrapped package which she gave to me. She went to the desk, sat down and after a few moments thought started to write to her brother. The letter was soon finished and sealed into an envelope which was also put into my care.

As I stood up to leave Mrs. Perceval said, "Wait a few more minutes, Jason, please," and she went to one of the bookcases and selected several leather bound volumes which she also gave to me.

"These are for you to read when you are not on watch, Jason. When you come home on leave you must come and see me and change them."

"Thank you, Mrs. Perceval, that is very thoughtful of you, and I will take good care of them."

"I wish you every success in your new life as a sailor, and I will pray for your safe return, as I pray for my brother's."

"Thank you, Mrs. Perceval," I said, knowing it was an inadequate response but too consumed by the emotion of the moment to have the wit to think of anything else.

We walked to the front door, and just as I was shaking her hand and saying goodbye, the Reverend Perceval shot out of his study and came to the front door,

"My wife has told me of the offer her brother has made you. You are a very lucky young man, Jason."

"Yes Sir, I know."

"I'm sure you will do well, and I will pray for your success. Goodbye and good fortune, Jason."

He shook my hand and went quickly back to his study. Mrs. Perceval and I said our goodbyes, and I left the Lenton vicarage and walked back to Pickworth as quickly as I could with the good wishes of Mrs. Perceval and her husband ringing in my ears. I left the books, letter and package on my bed in the cottage by the smithy and then went to find Reverend Daly. I needed help. I had never been more than about five miles from Pickworth, and suddenly I had to make a journey of several hundred and didn't know where to begin.

At the cottage that Reverend Daly used as his vicarage, I knocked on the front door. It's strange how little things stick in your mind, but I remember that it was a big, highly polished brass knocker shaped like the head of a dragon. It made a very satisfactory noise and the door was opened quickly by the Reverend's maid, who said before I could utter a word, "Please come in Mr. Smiley."

She led me down a hallway and ushered me into a room which appeared to be the vicar's study.

"Please sit down, Mr. Smiley, and I will tell the Reverend that you are here. Can I get you something to eat or drink?"

"No, thank you." I was hungry and thirsty but far too agitated to eat or drink or sit down for that matter. I paced about the room for several minutes unable to settle and look at a picture or the view from the window or the books in the bookcase. But suddenly the door opened and Reverend Daly erupted into the room.

"I'm very pleased you have come to see me Jason as I was just about to start looking for you. I met Jeremiah Smallwood in the village earlier this morning, and when I told him of the opportunity you had received, he immediately offered to loan me his horse and trap so that I can drive you to Grantham tomorrow morning. You remember Jeremiah?"

"Yes," I said. "He has a farm on the Sapperton Road. My father has shoed his horses for many years. How can I thank him for his generosity?"

"He will bring the horse and trap here early tomorrow morning, and we will take him back to his farm on our way to Grantham. You can thank him then. Do you have a bag you can use for your clothes, Jason?"

As I shook my head, he said, "I thought as much. You can borrow this one" and he handed me a leather bag–a valise I think it would be called now. "You can return it when you come home on leave. Now you had better go home and pack your clothes. You can travel in what you are wearing but you must carefully pack your Sunday clothes for your interview."

He stopped and thought for a moment then said "At Grantham, tomorrow, you will have to get a train to Retford on the Great Northern Railway. At Retford you will have to change to the Manchester, Sheffield & Lincolnshire Railway to get to Manchester and then the London and North Western Railway to Liverpool. Here's a little money to help you on your way. You can repay it when you are earning, Jason." He handed me a small purse that chinked as I took it.

"Thank you, Sir," was all I could say.

I think the money came from the poor box in the church, but as I had no support from my father, I suppose the vicar was right to consider me a deserving case. I have repaid it many times over since that day, so the vicar made a wise investment. He also gave me a letter of introduction to a clerical friend who lived in Liverpool near to the main station.

I walked back to the cottage by the smithy in the late afternoon and went directly to my room. There was no activity in the workshop and no sign of my father in the cottage.

In my room I laid my meagre selection of clothes on the bed then carefully packed them into the valise together with the package and letter for Captain Stewart. The purse and the letter to Reverend Daly's friend, I put into the side pocket. I even remembered to clean my boots.

I ate some bread and cheese that I washed down with a small glass of cider and went to bed. As I lay there waiting for sleep to come, I looked around the room I had used for so many years of my life and wondered if I would miss it if all went well with my interview and I joined Captain Stewart's crew. But I went to sleep before coming to a decision.

In the very early morning next day I was up and dressed by the time the vicar brought the pony cart to the forge.

I put the valise under the seat as he said cheerfully "Good morning, Jason. It's a lovely morning, now isn't it?"

"Good morning, Sir," I responded "It really is a nice morning. Where is Mr. Smallwood?"

"He's at the vicarage eating a large portion of ham and eggs my maid has cooked him. We will pick him up as we pass."

I was just about to climb into the trap when my father came out of the cottage. He said a grudging goodbye as I left, but there was no feeling or emotion in his farewell. He probably added "and good riddance" under his breath. He had become such a miserable man.

The vicar glowered at my father because of his continuing ill humour.

I said "Goodbye, Father," but received no response.

The vicar and I climbed into the trap and drove away without a backward glance. We clip clopped to the vicarage where Mr. Smallwood was waiting for us. He gave the vicar a small package wrapped in a cloth napkin and climbed up into the trap.

"Good morning again Vicar," he said. "Your maid cooks the best ham and eggs I've tasted for sometime." Then, he turned to me, "Good morning. You must be the Mr. Smiley who is about to conquer the world."

"Good morning, Mr. Smallwood. I don't know about conquering the world, but I must thank you for allowing the vicar to drive me to Grantham. It would have been a long walk otherwise."

"Pleased to help," he said briefly, and then he started talking to the vicar about the coming harvest which prompted the Reverend Daly to start a discourse about the next Harvest Festival. I felt a sudden pang of regret as I realized that I was going to miss the festival for the first time in my life as well as a stab of panic at the step into the unknown I was taking. After a short drive, the vicar steered the horse and trap through the narrow gateway into the Smallwood farm yard, and as soon as the trap stopped moving, Mr. Smallwood jumped down.

"Good fortune, Mr Smiley," he said, and with a wave to the vicar, he disappeared into the cowshed.

The journey to Grantham, along the dusty country lanes and through the sleepy villages of Sapperton, Ropsley, and Old Somerby, took under two hours, but it was starting to become hot by the time we arrived at the station.

Grantham was a small town then and one of the places on the Great North Road where stage coaches changed their horses and the passengers refreshed themselves. Historically it was quite important for that reason, but the vicar thought that the town would start to expand now that the railway station had been built.

"I'm sure the railway is going to attract many people from the surrounding areas, Jason, and they will bring their produce to sell in the market to traders who come to the town on the railway. It will be good for the whole area."

As we drove into Grantham, the vicar pointed out the 14th Century Parish Church of St. Wulfram and particularly the steeple.

He said in a rapturous tone, "Isn't that the most perfectly proportioned steeple you have ever seen, Jason?"

"Indeed yes, Vicar," I said.

To me it was really just another church steeple, but I couldn't spoil his pleasure by saying so, and clearly it did give him much pleasure to look at it. He rotated on his seat as the pony and trap passed by, so that he could keep it in view as long as possible.

Even in our little village we had heard about this wonderful new invention, the steam engine. We knew that railways had been built, but apart from the vicar, who used the railway when he had to make his periodic visits to see the Bishop, no one in our village had ever seen one, let alone travelled on one. I viewed the idea of this railway journey with mixed feelings composed of a natural fear of the unknown and my desire to learn more about the outside world.

The vicar and I stood on the platform waiting for the train after I had paid for my third class ticket to Retford. I would have to buy another ticket at Retford for the journey to Manchester and a third one in Manchester for the journey to Liverpool as all the railway companies operated independently of each other. Another drawback, as I was to discover later, was that some towns had railway stations belonging to competing companies in different parts of the town. Consequently changing trains could involve a long and tiring walk, particularly if you had luggage and couldn't afford a porter.

I looked about me and was a little disappointed as there seemed nothing remarkable about the raised platform we were standing on, nor the two shiny topped strips of metal fastened to cross pieces of wood.

"Those are the rails the train travels over," said the vicar in answer to my question.

The rails disappeared into the distance in both directions and there was no indication that they were an integral part of this new almost magical form of transport people talked about.

We had been very fortunate with the timing of our journey from Pickworth as we only had to wait a short time for the train I had to catch.

Its imminent arrival was heralded by a sudden increase in activity on the platform as uniformed railway employees appeared and busied themselves carrying bags and boxes from a storage shed and placing them adjacent to the platform edge. I noticed how agitated some of the other passengers appeared as they checked and rechecked their pieces of luggage as if they were afraid they might mysteriously disappear as the train arrived. Suddenly, I took an involuntary step back as the black monster of a locomotive passed in front of my eyes, clanking and steaming and smoking. Then the whole train came to a halt with a screech of brakes and the metallic clashing of buffers.

The vicar ensured that I found a seat in one of the open sided carriages, thrust the package he had been given by Mr. Smallwood into my hands and said quickly,

"Fortunately my maid thought of the inner man and packed some food for your long journey. I have to confess I had forgotten how long you would be without food."

I pushed the package of food into the valise and the valise under the bench I was sitting on. "Thank you, Vicar, and please thank your maid for me. That was very thoughtful."

After a pause I said, "When I can, I will write and tell you how I am. Perhaps you would tell my father. He cannot read so there is no point in writing to him."

"If I get a letter, I will certainly tell your father what you are doing," he answered with a sceptical note in his voice that suggested that he didn't really expect a letter from me. He was a good judge of people I'm afraid because I never did write although I had intended to and often thought about starting one.

"Good luck, Jason, come back safely and tell us about your adventures." Then with a quick wave of goodbye, he was back on the platform.

Moments later there was a shrill whistle from behind me followed almost immediately by a sudden, loud hoot from in front that made me jump in fright. For a moment nothing happened, and my eyes roamed from place to place and person to person in an attempt not to miss anything and also to make sense of this totally new experience. One or two of the passengers looked quite unconcerned, as if travelling by train was an everyday affair, but most of the passengers sitting around me appeared to be anxious about something; as if they were not sure what was to happen next and feared the unknown.

There was a bellow of escaping steam from the locomotive, followed by an increasingly noisy sequence of bangs and clangs as the couplings between the wagons snapped tight and we jolted into motion with a suddenness that snapped my unsuspecting head back to crash into the wooden wall behind me. By the time I had recovered from the shock, Grantham station and my vicar had disappeared from view and we were rushing through the countryside at an unimaginable speed wreathed in smoke, steam, and smuts from the locomotive. The wagon swayed erratically from side to side and jolted up and down so violently that most of my fellow passengers clutched the seats or window frames in order to keep their seats. Their look of apprehension was a little more apparent now as they realized how unnaturally quickly the fields were rushing past. And all the time there was an incessant rhythmic clack,

clack noise from below me and the howling of the wind through the openings in the sides of the wagon assaulting my eardrums. I should have shared the fear, but I think I was too fascinated by what was happening around me to be frightened.

We seemed to be making such a commotion as the train sped past woods and pastures, sometimes high above the fields and sometimes below them, but the cows we passed seemed unconcerned and grazed stolidly on. Occasionally, one of them would raise its head and eye us for a moment, but nothing stopped the rhythmic grinding of their jaws.

The sheep, on the other hand, rushed about in a fearful turmoil, and I imagine they were bleating as hard as they could, but I could hear nothing over the noise of our passage. I noticed that the panic ceased as soon as the locomotive passed and they immediately resumed nibbling the grass.

Always curious, I looked around at my fellow passengers. There were several small families surrounded by bags and cloth wrapped bundles and a number of men travelling alone.

I felt immediately sorry for the woman who sat directly in front of me, as she tried to hold on to her bonnet as the wind tried to snatch it from the grip of her hat pins; hold on to her children as they refused to sit still; hold on to the side of the wagon as it lurched about and at the same time keep hold of a bag perched on her ample lap. The man with her, whom I assumed to be her husband and the father of the children, seemed to be oblivious of his wife's situation until one of the children fell off the seat following a particularly violent lurch of the wagon. He picked up the squalling child, smacked its bottom, dumped it back in its place, said something to his wife with a facial expression that looked unpleasant in the extreme and returned to his solitary contemplation of the passing world. The woman took a handkerchief out of her pocket, dabbed at her eyes and redoubled her efforts to keep everything in its place.

Illogically, given the way he had behaved towards me of late, I was suddenly quite proud of my bad tempered father, as I knew he could never have treated my mother so cruelly when she was alive.

Sitting on the bench opposite to me was a heavily bearded, reasonably well dressed and probably middle-aged man. I realized he had seen me staring at the family group I have just described and had looked in the same direction just in time to see the man's actions. He turned back, leant toward me and said quietly in my ear in strongly accented but educated English.

"That's no way to treat a wife."

Much later I learned the accent was specific to Liverpool, where it was known as Scouse, and more particularly, that when it was uttered by an ill-educated person the resulting speech was barely intelligible to the intended listener if he was not a Scouser himself.

"No Sir," I said. "My father would never have treated my mother so."

"Are you going far?" he asked.

"I'm going to Liverpool, Sir."

"That's quite a long journey. I am going to Liverpool as well. I work there," he volunteered. After a pause he asked "Are you going there to work perhaps, or to visit relations?"

"Neither. I am going for an interview for a position as a deck officer cadet with the Gold Star Line, sir."

"I don't know anyone from that company personally, but they have a good reputation in the port."

Port was a word I'd never heard before and since the man had spoken so politely, I felt emboldened to say "Excuse me Sir, but what is port, please?"

"A port is a safe place where a ship can load cargo before sailing and unload cargo when it arrives." He must have seen my expression change to puzzlement at the word cargo for he added, "Cargo is the word used to describe every thing that is put on board the ship. It could be wool or cotton, timber or coal, or any other commodity that needs to be transported from the seller to the buyer. Do you understand what I mean?"

"Yes. Thank you Sir. I understand"

"Would you like to know more about Liverpool and the port?" he asked. "It will make the journey pass more quickly if we talk."

I didn't respond as quickly as I should have done, as I was thinking over what he had already told me and was a little ashamed of myself when he repeated,

"Would you like to hear about Liverpool?"

"Yes please, Sir," I agreed with alacrity.

Because of the noises made by the train our conversation, apart from our first few words, had been conducted in quite loud voices, and to make further conversation easier, he came to sit on the bench beside me. He was quite a big man with curly black hair, a broad unwrinkled forehead and dark eyes beneath thick black eyebrows. He was wearing a long black coat and had polished black boots on his feet. I noticed that he had long slender fingers, and more particularly, that the nails on both hands were clean and carefully shaped. His hands didn't carry the damage caused by manual work and I wondered what occupied his time in Liverpool.

He spoke close to my ear and it was soon apparent that he knew Liverpool very well indeed, as he came from a place called Bootle which was about five miles from the Liverpool town centre, to the west. He was very proud of Liverpool and talked at length about the development of the docks. He worked for the Mersey Docks and Harbour Company as a draftsman preparing drawings of new port structures in the office of the Civil Engineer and Superintendent. He seemed to be equally proud of the Superintendent who was a man called Jesse Hartley.

He told me that Hartley had been born in a town called Pontefract, which I had never heard of and he had been working as a master stonemason in Pontefract when he was selected unexpectedly for the post of Superintendent at Liverpool. He went on to say that Hartley was a very energetic man, and under his leadership, the area of Liverpool docks had been increased and the docks themselves made bigger and deeper in order to accommodate the largest ships then at sea.

"Have you heard of the steamship named 'Great Britain'?"

"No Sir." Actually I had no knowledge of the sea or ships. It was a subject about which I was totally ignorant, although I was reluctant to voluntarily admit the lack to this stranger. The nearest I had been to a ship was a painting of a ketch under full sail in the Wash and that had adorned one of the walls in the taproom of the Blue Bell.

He said, "The steam ship Great Britain was built in Bristol by an engineer called Brunel and when it was launched by Prince Albert, in 1843, it was the biggest ship in the world. Because Liverpool has such big docks, this huge ship sails regularly from Liverpool to New York."

Even with this explanation I was really no wiser, as my imagination could not envisage any sort of steam ship regardless of size, and silently I wondered where New York could be. It sounded important.

He went on to describe some of the docks that had been designed and built by Hartley and told me about Victoria Dock as I had told him that Victoria Dock was where Captain Stewart and my ship would be if I could pass the interview.

Many months later I chanced upon an old copy of the Liverpool Recorder and learnt that Hartley had died at his home in Bootle a few days after my conversation, and I wondered how my fellow passenger was dealing with the death of his hero.

Fortunately, my travelling companion chose to accompany me throughout the whole journey, and his help and advice when we had to change trains was invaluable. I wonder now how I would have managed without his help and imagine I would have fared badly in all probability.

We eventually arrived at the terminus in Liverpool. The station is known as Lime Street and is approached through a deep cutting and a long, dark, smoke filled tunnel. My companion stood and picked up his bag.

As he shook my hand he said, "I wish you every success with your interview young man."

"Thank you, Sir, and also for talking with me," was all I could say.

As the train halted, my companion stepped down and with a casual wave of his hand disappeared into the crowd. I picked up my bag and stepped down after him. I found that I was under a glass roof supported on iron columns and arches. It was such an unexpected and amazing sight for a country boy that I kept stopping in open mouthed awe and was bumped and cursed as got I in the way of hurrying passengers who were too busy or blasé to share my wonderment.

Just outside the station in the forecourt, I noticed a well dressed man who was standing just to the side of the stream of passengers and obviously watching for someone to arrive. I walked over to him put down my bag and said,

"Excuse me, sir."

"What is it?" he responded in a gruff but not unfriendly voice as his eyes continued to scan the passing people.

"Can you direct me to Clayton Street, please sir?" I asked. "I believe it is near here."

"Yes, it is," and he told me precisely how to get there on foot.

"Thank you, sir" I said. I picked up my luggage and set off to find the vicar's home in Clayton Street.

I walked out of the station forecourt into a sunny August evening and was greeted by the sounds and smells of Liverpool. To someone accustomed to the clean air of the countryside Liverpool stank in the shimmering heat. It was a mixture of soot, smoke and steam from the railway behind me, but mainly it was the smell of the town in front of me. A pungent odoriferous scent compounded from rotting refuse and the dung that had been dropped by the horses pulling the many carts and carriages that clip, clopped and rattled past and now lay baking in the sun.

I picked my way across Lime Street more carefully than I would have walked across a pasture at home and then continued down St. John's Lane past a monumental building that I learnt later is called St. Georges Hall. On my right, as I walked down the incline, was the church of St. John's and at the end of the street, I turned into Old Haymarket. I crossed William Brown Street and walked into Byron Street.

The directions I had been given were concise and accurate and I was soon able to turn right from Byron Street and walk between the terraced houses that lined both sides of Clayton Street. Half way along the street, I arrived outside a house that would have been indistinguishable from the rest, but for a highly polished brass plate fixed on the wall beside the door that proclaimed in raised lettering 'Vicarage of St. John's Church' and beneath, in a smaller script, the name of the present incumbent; Reverend Daniel Evans.

I tugged on the bell pull, but there was no audible response. I reached out and was about to give the bell-pull a much harder tug when the door swung open and there, framed in the doorway, was a tall, thin, black clothed woman whose physique and superior eye reminded me instantly of the Curate who had taught me in Pickworth and mercifully remained there. I couldn't help looking for the dewdrop that had always trembled on the end of the Curate's nose and was very relieved to see that it was not visible. She said something that was totally un-intelligible. Her accent and pronunciation were so strange I could not be sure she was even speaking the Queen's English. She spoke again, more sharply this time, but again I did not understand a word of what she said and in desperation I handed her the letter from my vicar.

She stepped back into the hallway. Perhaps she was afraid I would follow because she swung the door to with such violence that I jumped back in alarm, but she closed it with only a gentle click. I stood on the footpath in front of the door feeling a little foolish.

With the door shut and my letter of introduction on the other side behind it, I began to wonder what I should do. As I stood in my indecision the door reopened and a small rotund, red-faced man dressed just like the vicar in Pickworth appeared in the doorway. He greeted me like the prodigal son. Then he fired off a series of questions in a loud pulpit voice with such rapidity that even though I could understand what he was saying, I could not completely articulate an answer to one question before the next arrived and rattled my eardrums. I managed to interject a few "Yes's" and "No's" in response, but for detailed explanations there was no time. Evidently my letter and minimal comments satisfied him to some extent because when he eventually paused for breath he stepped back into the hallway.

"Come in please, Mr. Smiley," and he beckoned me into the vicarage, led me up a flight of narrow stairs and showed me into a small first floor bedroom at the front of the building overlooking Clayton Street.

"I expect you would like a wash after your long journey," he said indicating a wash stand on which stood a red rose patterned bowl with a matching soap holder and water pitcher.

"Come down stairs when you have freshened up, and Mrs. Jones will give you some supper," he added.

I did as the vicar advised and went downstairs after a good wash. He hadn't said where I should go, but I followed my nose. Quite literally, I let my nose direct my footsteps towards the delicious aroma I could smell and found myself in the kitchen.

The housekeeper, who had met me at the front door, was washing a pot in the sink when I walked into the kitchen.

"Good evening Mr. Smiley," she said. "Please come in and sit there," and she pointed to a place at the scrubbed wooden kitchen table which had been set with knife, fork and spoon. As soon as I had sat down, she placed in front of me a big plate of Irish stew, or so the vicar described it later. It was mutton and delicious and just what a tired, ravenously hungry young man needed. Unfortunately, the vicar chose not to eat with me and was able to question me without the hindrance of chewing. On the one hand, I had to find a way to satisfy my hunger for food and on the other the vicar's thirst for information without losing my newly acquired table manners.

He said, "I would like to provide you with appropriate help, Mr. Smiley, but I need to know more about your intentions than is given in the brief introduction written to me by my old friend the vicar of Pickworth. He simply says that you have a very good opportunity to better yourself and asks me to give you a bed for the night. I can accede to that request with pleasure, but I would like to know more about why you are here and how long you will need to stay."

I swallowed hastily, and as I wielded knife and fork to prepare the next mouthful said, "Sir, I have been befriended by a sea captain who lives in the next village. He has offered me a position as an officer cadet on his new ship, on condition that I pass an interview tomorrow morning. The interview is with the Marine Superintendent of the Gold Star Line at the Company's offices in Hornby Building."

I hastily stuffed a fork laden with mutton, potato and carrot into my mouth and chewed industriously as I started to prepare the next fork full.

The vicar said, "I don't understand why you only expect to stay one night here. Surely you will have to stay in Liverpool until the result of the interview is known and arrangements are made for you to join ship. I hope you understand that you will be very welcome to stay here as long as you wish."

I swallowed quickly and said, "The letter written by my vicar is essentially accurate in its request for a bed for only one night. If I am successful I will join the ship immediately, and if not then I will return to Pickworth and the life of a blacksmith. I shall catch the first available train from Lime Street."

The vicar thoughtfully waited whilst I consumed more of the delicious stew and then said "I understand your situation much better now, Jason, and I will be pleased to provide you with a bed and a hearty breakfast too."

"Thank you Vicar" I said gratefully as I had no idea what I would have done if he had taken a dislike to me and refused to help. After mopping up the rich, fat marbled, gravy that lay in a succulent pool on my plate with a doorstep of new white bread, I said, "May I ask for your help with another matter please, Vicar?" and when he nodded his assent I said, "I have no idea where Hornby Building is located and if you could give me directions tomorrow I would appreciate your help."

"I would have been happy to escort you there personally, but I have to officiate at a service tomorrow morning. However, I will be happy to give you directions before you leave."

The vicar, like most of the clerics I have met during my life, was extremely curious about people and places. When I had finished eating, he ushered me from the kitchen and sat me down in a wing back chair beside the fireplace in the small room I took to be his working room. He took the opposite chair and we conversed across the dead embers of a recent fire. He asked many questions about my life in Pickworth and my parents and about the Reverend Daly and life in the village.

The calm discussion with this patient and kindly man was extremely beneficial and when the questioning stopped, I went to bed thankful that a day of emotion and travelling was at last over.

Even to this day I get a cold empty feeling in my stomach when I look back and remember that the letter from Captain Stewart had stood in full, tantalizing view for more than two weeks. It had been propped on the mantle over the hearth, and but for a chance meeting with the vicar, I would have missed the opportunity that made me the man I am. I would have been destined to follow the trade of a blacksmith all my days. My father never said one word to explain his extraordinary actions and at the time I didn't ask.

I had what I had dreamed about. I had an opportunity to escape from the drudgery of village life, and I intended to grab hold of it with both hands.

FOUR

The Interview

I slept well under a light blanket on a comfortable bed, and when I woke I momentarily enjoyed revelling in the peace and tranquillity of my temporary room. Then the reason for my presence came back to mind and my stomach churned at the thought of the testing time I was soon to be subjected to. I was more than a little frightened that August morning and hoped that the clear bright start to the day would be a good omen; that the weather was smiling on my enterprise.

I got up, took hold of the handle of the pitcher, poured cold water into the washing bowl and then washed thoroughly with a strong smelling soap. I dressed carefully in my Sunday best clothes and long before anyone else in the house was awake, I was ready to start the day. The trouble was that I was so early and had so little to occupy my mind that I started to panic. As soon as it was decently possible, I went downstairs and into the breakfast room to wait for the housekeeper to provide breakfast. Normally the smell of frying bacon would make my mouth water in anticipation, but this morning it simply made my stomach feel more unsettled.

Mrs. Jones came bustling in from the kitchen with a plate piled high with hot food.

"Here you are, Mr. Smiley," she said with a beaming smile as she placed a plate in front of me that was overflowing with bacon, eggs, sausage, black pudding and fried bread. "This will give you a good start to your day. A young man like you needs feeding up." I was amazed when I realized that I had understood almost every word she uttered. The accent was still the same as the night before, but my understanding was much improved.

As Mrs. Jones hurried back to the kitchen, I picked up my knife and fork. It certainly was a substantial meal and in keeping with her philosophy. I tried the bacon and found my mouth was too dry to swallow it and had to drink some water to get it to go down. I cut into the egg and as the yoke spread in a viscous yellow pool onto the plate my stomach heaved and all appetite disappeared. I toyed with my breakfast but was unable to eat more than a few mouthfuls.

Mrs Jones came back from the kitchen and her cheerful face crumpled into a mask of worry when she saw how little I had eaten.

"Was there something wrong with the food, Mr. Jason? You have not eaten enough to keep a fly alive!"

"I'm truly sorry, Mrs. Jones. The food is delicious, but I have no appetite this morning."

"Are you worried about the interview?"

"Yes!" I said, "Very!" and I wondered how she knew about it. Perhaps the vicar had told her after I went to bed. It was true however. My normally healthy appetite had disappeared as I realized that today was the day that would shape the rest of my life. All depended on one short interview, and I imagine that the prospect was daunting enough to affect anyone's appetite.

"When you've finished at Hornby Building," she said, "you will have to come back here for your bag. When you do, I'm sure your appetite will have returned and I'll get you something to eat," and she took away the almost untouched plate of food.

After my meagre breakfast, the vicar escorted me out of the vicarage and on the pavement outside, he gave me explicit directions to the Town Hall and then how to find Hornby Building.

As he shook my hand, he said, "It has been a great pleasure to meet you, Jason, and I wish you every success in your new career and a safe return to your loved ones when your voyages are finished." Then he added, almost wistfully I thought, "I could almost envy you your chances of adventure. Goodbye, Jason."

He went back into his little house and closed the door, and I stood on the pavement feeling again the loneliness of facing an unknown future.

As I was not prepared to give into my fears and return ignominiously to Pickworth where I would have to face the sneers of my unhappy father, I had no option but to put as brave a face on things as I could. So I squared my shoulders, straightened my back and set off, back the way I had come the previous evening. However, instead of crossing into Old

Hay Market, I turned right into Dale Street. After about fifteen minutes walk and where Dale Street became Water Street, I passed the Town Hall on my right. A little way down Water Street and on the opposite side of the road, I could see the Hornby Building where the Gold Star Line offices were situated.

I crossed the road and in a fever of fear and indecision I walked past the entrance instead of going in. After a few minutes, during which I berated myself for being such a coward, I turned and retraced my steps. I almost walked past the entrance again, but this time I managed to steel myself and walk up the marble steps towards the entrance instead.

I pushed open one of the big, mahogany framed, half glazed, double swing doors and entered a large cool, dark and unfurnished hall. Immediately in front of me was a wide marble staircase with moulded mahogany handrails on wrought iron balusters leading to the upper floors. The floor was of a dark varnished wood that looked like oak. The walls, above a deep, dark brown varnished, moulded skirting, were of smooth plaster painted a pale colour. It could have been a pale blue or green, but my eyes had not adjusted from the sunlit exterior to this gloomy interior and I couldn't be certain. The ceiling had been finished in the same way, but there were elaborate plaster cornices painted in a slightly darker shade of the same colour around the perimeter of the hall where wall and ceiling joined. If there was lighting I did not notice it. On both sides of this ground floor hallway, there were big imposing doorways, each with a highly polished brass plate mounted in a hard-wood frame fixed to the wall beside the doorway. The main staircase rose to the half landing at the far end of the hall and then became two staircases, one each side of the hall, for the flight up to the next floor. On the wall, to the right of the entrance doors, was a notice board giving a list of company names with the associated floors and office numbers in gilt letters on a black background.

It was uncomfortably silent and so immaculate it looked as if an army of cleaners had finished dusting and polishing only moments before I pushed open the door. I walked to the notice board to find out which office I should go to and was so concerned at the noise my foot-steps were making in this cavernous hallway that the last few paces were made almost on tip toe.

I saw that the offices I needed were on the first floor, and I walked as quietly as I could to the foot of the marble staircase and started to ascend. No matter how hard I tried to be quiet my footsteps echoed in the stairwell and I reached the first floor with an oppressive feeling of insignificance in my heart due to the silent, opulent grandeur of the building.

With some trepidation I knocked on the door beside the polished brass plate bearing the name "Gold Star Line" and there was no response. "There's no one there so now you can go home," said a tempting inner voice.

After a suitable pause, during which I defeated my cowardly inner self, I knocked again, but harder and heard a muffled voice say something. I didn't hear clearly what was said but took it as an invitation to enter. Inside the room there was a clerk sitting at a big, mahogany, roll top desk busily writing in a ledger. There were many other ledgers on the desk and on shelves beside his work place.

"Wait," he said.

He carefully completed an entry in his ledger in the neatest handwriting I have ever seen. O's as round and as regular as carriage wheels and uprights that were as vertical and regular in height as the balusters in a railing. There was not a blot or smudge to mar the perfection of this man's work. He gently closed the hinged brass lid on the inkwell, wiped the nib of his pen on a piece of linen and laid it carefully on the rack beside the inkwell. He turned to me, looked me up and down from my boots to my hair and back again and sniffed.

He said, "Well young man, what do you want?"

"I wish to see Captain Downing, Sir," I said and handed him the letter that Captain Stewart had sent to my father.

He took it and read it, very slowly and then read it again, equally slowly. As he read I could see his eyes following the print from side to side across the page and his head slowly lowered as he read down the page. It was the same both times he read the letter. He took off his glasses, put them on the desk, rolled down the tambour front of the desk to close it and said again "Wait!"

He went across the room to a door in the far wall and knocked.

After receiving a thunderous, "Enter," from the other side of the door he opened it just wide enough to insinuate himself into the inner room and left me alone in the outer office as he closed the door after him. I have no idea what was said of course, but after a short time the door reopened and the clerk came back to his desk where I still stood.

"Captain Downing will see you now, Mr. Smiley," and gestured towards the still open door. I walked into a spacious, well-lit office, and the clerk, who had walked across the outer office behind me, closed the door as soon as I crossed the threshold.

"I am Captain Downing, Marine Superintendent for the Gold Star Line," said a tall, weather beaten, bearded but balding man from his chair behind a big, mahogany, pedestal desk, "and you are the Jason Smiley that Captain Stewart has recommended to me, I believe?"

"Yes sir," I said.

"Please sit down Mr. Smiley. I have to finish these papers, but it will only take a few minutes."

I sat down in front of the desk in one of the visitor's chairs Captain Downing had indicated, and for a few minutes, whilst Captain Downing meticulously dealt with some papers on his desk, I was able to glance around.

Captain Downing was wearing a Merchant Navy uniform with the four gold rings of a captain on his sleeves, a starched white shirt and black tie. In his lapel was a small, gold, star shaped badge. His uniform cap rested on a side table. A copy of Mercator's Projection of the world had been mounted on the wall behind Captain Downing together with four, gilt framed, oil paintings of sailing ships under full sail in rough weather. The paintings had been so well executed that I could almost smell the salt and hear the sounds of the sea and the ships as they rode the waves.

The top of the desk was covered with tooled dark green leather and was the same colour as the leather in the button-backed chair the captain sat in. I noticed that it creaked as he moved. The visitor chairs also had green leather upholstered seats but a hard wooden backrest. There were two big bookcases in the room and they were full of books bound in brown or red leather with titles in gold print. They gave the office an opulent and studious air.

Apart from an inkwell and some pens the only other item on the desk was a small glass fronted instrument on a circular brass stand. I could see two of the four faces suggested by its shape. One face was obviously a clock, but I couldn't determine what the other was for. The name on the face was 'Sewills, Established 1800 Liverpool. The clock face was a pale creamy coloured material that I later learnt was ivory, with beautifully formed black numbering around the edge. The hands were also black, simply shaped but functional. Although the bevelled glass front to the instrument was square the face of the clock was rectangular. On each side of the face was a narrow, fluted sidepiece in polished brass. It was an elegant instrument, and as I was to discover on a later visit, the other three faces were equally attractive as well as functional.

Captain Downing picked up the last piece of paper from the pile that had been on his right, laid it on the desk in front of him, read it, made some mark or other with his pen then added it to the pile of papers on his left. Apparently unbidden the clerk appeared silently by the desk, picked up the papers and departed with them. The office door closed with a click.

Captain Downing put down his pen, not as carefully as his clerk I noticed, looked at me in a considering way and said simply, "Tell me about yourself."

I described my origins and what I had been doing in my life so far, and I could see that he was not at all impressed when I told him that my father was the village blacksmith and my education only from the village school.

He stopped me after a few minutes and impatiently, but still politely said,

"Mr. Smiley, by your own admission you are the son of the village blacksmith in Pickworth, a small remote village out in the country near the Wash. You have a little education that you have gained at the village school, but you have no knowledge of the sea or ships. There is, apparently, not even a remote family connection with the sea. I do not understand how you have become acquainted with Captain Stewart or why he has decided to sponsor you as the Company's first officer cadet. He must know something about you, or see something in your character, that has escaped me up to now, and I am usually a good judge of men."

There was silence in the office for several minutes. There was nothing I could say to counter Captain Downing's accurate but irrefutable assessment of my status. He stared at me for several minutes whilst he decided what to do next. He was, I think, torn between respect for Captain Stewart's request and his own inclination to bring the interview to a close. Fortunately for me, he decided in favour of Captain Stewart.

"Are you related to Captain Stewart?" he asked.

"No sir" I said.

"How does Captain Stewart know of your existence then?"

"I nearly dropped his sextant, sir"

"How do you know it was a sextant?"

"At the time I didn't." I said too quickly.

Captain Downing made a sudden move in his chair that made the leather squeak in protest and gave a snort of impatience at my short, accurate, but unhelpful answer, and I realized that if I did not give a satisfactory explanation very quickly my chances of a cadetship were over. I could almost smell the red hot charcoal and feel the weight of the hammer in my hand as my chance of betterment started to evaporate.

I said quickly, "Captain Downing, sir! Please let me explain. The sextant was in a box I nearly dropped when I carried Captain Stewart's baggage to the inn when his horse went lame just outside Pickworth. The captain opened the box to show me what I could have damaged with my clumsiness. Because I was interested in the sextant, not only because of the craftsmanship but also as an instrument, he offered to teach me about it. On Sunday I used to walk over to Lenton vicarage, where the captain was staying, and he taught me how to use the sextant. He started to teach me about navigation before he took command of his new ship. Captain Stewart's sister has also taken an interest in me and is helping me improve my knowledge of English."

I was thankful to see that Captain Downing's frown of irritation was being replaced with a more interested expression. He got up from his desk and strode out of the room. He came back after a few moments with a sextant box that he put carefully on his desk. He took out the sextant and handed it to me.

In a stern voice he commanded, "Now. Mr. Smiley. Quick as you can. Name the parts and demonstrate how it is used, if you please."

When I had finished answering his question, he was clearly impressed with my knowledge and I had obviously ceased to be a total country bumpkin in his eyes. He questioned me further and was interested in my experiences with the Ordnance Survey. I think the fact that I had wanted to learn was at least as important as the knowledge itself.

He sat back in his chair and considered me for a few moments and then said,

"Captain Stewart is also a good judge of men, and I agree with his recommendation that you are appointed as the company's first cadet. Please wait in my clerk's room whilst I prepare the orders for Captain Stewart."

The clerk appeared so quickly, I was sure he had been listening at the door. I suppose Captain Downing could have had one of the new electric call bells to summon his clerk but I didn't see or hear anything. With barely time to draw breath, let alone say thank you to Captain Downing for his trust, I found myself once again in the anteroom. I could not believe what my ears had told me.

I had been successful, as Captain Stewart had expected and my father doubted. A new life, unlike anything I had ever dreamed of, was open in front of me, and now I had to have the courage to explore it and learn everything there was to learn. I could have cheered I was so happy but didn't think such high spirits would be appreciated in the staid surroundings of the Gold Star Line offices.

A short while later I was ushered from the clerk's room and down the stairs to the pavement outside the building holding a letter for Captain Stewart and a pass for the gateman at the entrance to Victoria Dock. The directions to Victoria Dock the clerk gave me as I was leaving were extremely simple.

"Go down Water Street to the Mersey," he said, pointing down the hill towards the River. "Then turn right towards Waterloo Road. Victoria Dock will be on your left. The gateman will point out where the 'Earl Canning' is moored when you give him the pass."

With that I was once again alone in the world and heading into the unknown, but this time there was an objective in my sight.

Initially I ignored the clerk's instructions and set off in the opposite direction towards the vicar's house in order to collect my bag. I realized it was now late morning, and my stomach was crying for food after such a poor breakfast. I hoped Mrs. Jones would not forget her promise and walked along with my fingers crossed to be on the safe side. I knocked on the vicarage door and after a short wait it opened and there was Mrs. Jones framed in the opening.

"Congratulations Mr. Smiley," she said with a broad smile, as she beckoned me into the hallway and shut the door.

"How did you know?" I asked in wonderment, because I couldn't imagine how she had found out so quickly.

"It's no mystery, Mr. Smiley. I had only to look at your face to know that you have been successful. I am very pleased and the Reverend will be delighted. I imagine that you are now hungry, Mr. Smiley."

"Yes! Very hungry Mrs. Jones," I responded.

"Come along then and I will see what I can do to fill your empty stomach," she said as she led the way into the kitchen and sat me down at the table.

With my nerves gone and my appetite fully restored, I was able to eat with great relish. I remember there was a rich vegetable and mutton soup followed by ham, cheese and home made pickles accompanied by freshly baked wholemeal bread.

When I was replete, I said to Mrs. Jones "That was a meal fit for a king, Mrs. Jones. Thank you very much for the food and for your kindness since I arrived so unexpectedly yesterday."

"It was nothing, Mr. Smiley. I was pleased to help you as much as I was able."

I got up from the table and went upstairs to collect my bag. The vicar had not returned so I asked Mrs. Jones to say thank you for me. I thanked Mrs. Jones again and then I was on the pavement and heading for my destiny.

I retraced my steps to the Hornby Building with my bag slung over my shoulder by the strap and then walked on down Water Street towards the River Mersey. On the river between the houses I caught my first views of masts with sails spread and ships with their funnels belching smoke. At the end of Water Street I turned right into The Strand opposite what I discovered later was George Dock. A little way along on the right, was St. Nicholas's Church and just beyond the church the road became New Quay and then Bath Street, before Waterloo Road started.

I walked along beside a high boundary wall that blocked out all signs of the ships and cargo movement that was taking place, except where I passed a gateway and could see into one of the dock areas. The boundary wall was constructed of stone; 'Kentish Rag' was how my recent travelling companion had described its appearance and it was crowned with a semi-circular stone coping about twelve feet above the pavement. The road was very busy and very noisy in consequence.

There were many teams of sweating horses dragging heavily laden drays along the roadway. I could hear the groaning of the wooden framework of the drays mixing with the creaking of the horse' harnesses and the grinding of the iron rimmed wheels as they passed over the stone sets which paved the roadway. Pony carts and carriages sped past with a rattle of wheels and the clatter of iron horseshoes on stone ringing in the air. It was a cacophony of sound punctuated by the crack of whips and the shouts of the carters. The agricultural sounds and smells of horses and harness and hay and manure were as familiar to someone bred in the country, as the smell of steam, hot oil and coal smoke were alien. Also infiltrating the air were the smells of the cargos being loaded and unloaded on the other side of the wall; some exotic and attractive but some made even my nose wrinkle.

Just before I reached the entrance to Victoria Dock I passed the Waterloo Railway Goods Station and crossed the railway tracks leading from the goods yard into the dock area. The rails had been polished by the passage of many iron wheeled wagons and reflected the rays of the sun with a brightness that dazzled my eyes. On both sides of the entrance to Victoria Dock, the boundary wall ended in a big round buttress and in the centre of the opening was a massive gatekeeper's house made of the same masonry as the boundary wall. Both sides of the entrance could be closed with a sliding gate that was as high as the wall and constructed of very heavy timber with bolted iron frames and stiffeners. I think it would have taken a big charge of dynamite to get in without permission when the dock was closed but today the dock was working and the gates wide open.

At the entrance to Victoria Dock I had to dodge through the horses and carts to find the gatekeeper. I waited whilst he finished a shouting match with the driver of a big, overloaded dray and then gave him my pass from Captain Downing's office. He looked at it without interest and I wondered if he was able to read, when he asked "What do you want?" in the thick accent I was starting to recognize as typical of the Liverpool area.

"I have come to join the crew of the 'Earl Canning,'" I told him and asked "Where is it?"

"She!" he said. He must have seen the dumbfounded expression on my face because he added, "Ships is 'She', not it! SHE's over there.

Your first ship is it?"

It was really a statement not a question, but I nodded anyway.

He pointed towards a huge black object that dwarfed everything in the vicinity said something incomprehensible like "Gangway's midships" and turned his attention to someone else.

I walked towards it with my mouth hanging open in surprise and awe. How could a mere man control such a monstrous object? Certainly my ambitions and possibly my daydreaming life could have ended at that moment, as I started to take a step that would have taken me onto the railway tracks and in front of some loaded wagons a steam engine was pushing across the entrance. I had neither seen nor heard anything, but an alert stevedore grabbed my collar and yanked me back in the nick of time.

"Be careful, Wack," was all he said and he went on his way leaving me shaking with fright and looking down at the oil stain an axle box had left on my trouser leg as it brushed past. I had never been closer to death than at that moment and in my imagination the agony of that steel wheel slicing my body in half against the steel rail made my stomach heave.

The memory still makes me shudder.

I stood rooted to the spot for some minutes, but gradually the noise and press of people brought me back to my senses and I set off towards the 'Earl Canning' again but this time keeping a very careful lookout in this alien and dangerously noisy place.

The ship was moored in the corner of the dock with I learned later, its rounded stern facing me. I could see the name "EARL CANNING" and underneath "LIVERPOOL" painted in white on the curved black painted hull plates. As I approached closer I could see the lines of rivets that stitched the ship's iron plates and frames together. I skirted around an iron post that held one end of some ropes that drooped down from the ship and walked along the ship's side towards an inclined walkway I could see about half way along. It seemed the only place at which I could get from the road onto the ship.

All around me was the bustle of a ship being loaded.

From the gloomy interior of a big building opposite the ship, men were carrying or wheeling on carts, a multifarious selection of bags and boxes and then stacking them on nets on the paving outside. Big machines were picking up the filled nets, swinging them across to the ship and then lowering them out of sight. They seemed to be following the hand signals given by a man standing at the railing that ran most of the way along the ship's side.

I walked on oblivious to the possibility that something could drop on my head and managed to arrive unscathed at the foot of the gangway.

There was no one there, so after reading a notice saying 'NO VISITORS' pinned to a board attached to the end of the walkway at the shore end and then waiting about five minutes for someone to help me, I decided to ignore the notice as I wasn't really a visitor. I climbed up to the top and then stopped. Apart from the two or three men guiding the crane drivers there were no other people in sight.

In front of me was a low metal wall that was surrounding an opening in the iron floor the end of the walkway rested on. From the shouting and swearing I could hear from the void beneath my feet it seemed as if there were a large number of men down there. A bulging net on the end of a long rope from one of the machines disappeared down the hole under the silent, watchful guidance of the man who was using hand signals to communicate with the machine driver and I noticed that he had now moved from the railing to the side of the hole. I   noticed that the volume of noise increased as the net disappeared out of sight but couldn't distinguish any words that would have explained why.

No one appeared to take any notice of me, so I jumped down onto the metal plate below me and looked around.

A voice from above shouted, "You down there! Visitors are not allowed. Can't you read?"

I looked up and there above me I could see the head and shoulders of a man dressed in a white shirt, with a black tie and wearing a peaked cap with a gold star badge above the peak. I shouted back above the noise and said, "Yes, I can read and I'm not a visitor. I have a letter for Captain Stewart from Captain Downing."

"Come up to the bridge," said the man and withdrew his head and shoulders from view.

I looked all around me, but I had no idea which way to turn to satisfy the instruction. Fortunately the man guiding the crane driver, a banksman I later learnt, had been attending to me as well as his work and he gestured towards some steps that I hadn't noticed. He indicated that I should go up them. This I did and came out on a small landing with a half glazed, varnished wood framed door to my right. There were white painted railings on my left and ahead of me to enclose the landing. The door opened outwards towards me, and the man I had spoken to looked out and then gestured for me to come in.

"Now what's all this about, youngster?" he said.

I gave him the letter and said, "My name is Jason Smiley, sir. I am to be Captain Stewart's cadet. Captain Downing said I was to come and join the ship, sir."

"Welcome on board, Mr. Smiley. I am John Evans the third officer. I'll take your letter to the captain. Wait here," and he disappeared down an internal staircase.

I was left alone to examine my surroundings and realized at once that there were many, many things for which I would have to learn the names as well as uses. Starting with the big wheel with extended spokes near the windows looking out over the deck of the ship towards? Towards what I didn't really know and the short column surmounted by a brass drum with a handle mounted on one side, to everything else I could see both inside and outside.

Mr. Evans returned quite quickly and said, "Captain Stewart is busy and will see you when he can. In the meantime he has ordered me to start your education as a deck officer."

He drew a big breath and said, "As you know, my name is John Evans and I am the third officer on this ship. Senior to me is the Second Officer, the First Mate and then, totally responsible for the ship and everything and everybody on board, is Captain Stewart. I am twenty-five years old and I have been at sea for ten years. I have as many years of sea time as you have minutes of experience on board a ship. My father was the master of the East India Company Ship 'Broxbournebury' and my grandfather was lost at sea when the 'Calcutta' sank off Mauritius in 1809. I was at sea with my father as a child in a short trouser."

He paused, took another deep breath and went on, "You have a lot to learn, Mr. Smiley. You will meet the other deck officers and the Chief Engineer when they are on board and have time to teach you about their duties, but for the present recognize that you are the most junior officer on the ship. Even the seamen know more than you. You address the other officers in person as 'sir' and you refer to them by using their rank and name, or as Mr. Evans, except for the Captain. When you are given an order by a superior officer you say, "Aye, Sir." You then act upon it immediately AND WITHOUT QUESTION."

After a momentary pause he said, "Is that clear, Cadet Smiley?"

I started to say, "Yes, Sir" and as Mr. Evans drew in a big breath with which to shout at me, I managed to change my response to, "I mean, 'Aye Sir'."

"This area," he said, indicating what he meant with a wave of a hand, "is called the Bridge and no one is allowed here without the permission of the Officer of the Watch or the Captain. I am the Officer of the Watch at the moment. The ship is controlled from here."

He said, "This ship was built in Glasgow and is totally constructed of iron plates riveted to iron frames. It is two hundred feet long, has a beam of forty feet and a laden draft of twenty feet.

"What are the ship's main dimensions, Cadet Smiley?" Mr. Evans questioned suddenly, but I could not remember what he had said as I had been gazing in fascination at the activity outside. Clearly Mr. Evans had noticed and his irritation at my inattention showed in his tone of voice, "If you are going to have any hope of a successful career at sea, Cadet, you will have to pay attention at all times. Do you understand?"

He repeated the ship's dimensions and went on, "The ship has two masts with yards for square sails and we can also set fore and aft sails on both masts. The ship is equipped with a steam engine that can propel us at ten knots in a calm sea."

He gestured in appropriate directions as he said, "The bow is there and the stern there. That is the starboard side and that the port side."

"This," he said, indicating the big wheel I had noticed earlier, "is the ship's wheel and is used for steering the ship. When the wheel is turned clockwise, the ship will turn to starboard," and he pointed to the right. He then pointed to the left and said, "and to port when it is turned in the opposite direction. Steering the ship well is one of the skills you will have to master Cadet Smiley.

"This is the binnacle," and he pointed at something in front of the wheel I hadn't noticed before. I stood behind the wheel and looked down into the white painted interior of a big, brass tube. Inside was a compass. I recognized it because there had been one under the telescope of the Transit used by the surveyor.

"I know this is a compass sir, but I haven't seen one mounted like this before."

Mr. Evans said, "It is necessary to keep the compass as level as possible so it is mounted in gimbals to counteract the pitching and rolling of the ship." This last piece of explanation was accompanied by some graphic gestures that not only made me feel slightly nauseous, but also I hoped, had been exaggerated.

"Now Cadet Smiley, what are the main dimensions of the ship and what does the wheel do."

This time I was able to answer with very little hesitation and was rewarded with a terse, "That's more like it, Cadet."

He then pointed to two balls about the size of turnips mounted on short columns and fixed by a nut and bolt arrangement to a slotted rack on both sides of the binnacle. One was red and the other green.

"These are to compensate for the ship's magnetism," he said mysteriously and without further explanation.

We moved a few yards from the wheel to the other object I had noticed earlier. Attached to the handle was a pointer and on the side face of the drum words were printed. "Full Ahead" was at one end and "Full Astern" at the other. Other words were printed in between but had no meaning for me at the time.

Third Officer Evans explained, "This is the engine room telegraph and is used by the captain to instruct the engineer to change the speed or direction of rotation of the propeller."

At that moment Captain Stewart came on to the bridge, acknowledged Mr. Evans salute and said, "Good afternoon, Cadet Smiley."

"Good afternoon, Sir."

He said to Mr. Evans, "Cadet Smiley will use the spare bunk in your cabin and work the same watch as you. Show him where he will sleep and then bring him to my cabin."

We said, "Aye Sir," almost in unison as the captain turned and walked out to the port side bridge rail and started to watch the stevedores stacking cargo in the forward hold.

Evans and I went below. His cabin was very small. Two bunks, one above the other, were fixed to the bulkhead to the right of the door, which opened against the foot end of the bunks. A small closed porthole was located in the middle of the wall immediately opposite the doorway. Fixed to the wall were two cupboards that extended from the floor to the ceiling. One was in the corner to the left of the porthole and the other in the corner to the right. There was a narrow writing shelf fixed to the wall under the porthole and in between the cupboards. The ceiling was painted white and the walls a very pale green. The floor was covered with something that looked like woven rope.

Evans saw my glance and said, "Coconut matting. You can use that cupboard opposite the door Mr. Smiley," as he pointed to it.

I noticed that there was just room to open the door and pass between it and the closed cupboard. It was a hot, stuffy little place that afternoon and full of unidentified and not very pleasant odours.

Evans noticed me wrinkle my nose and said, "When we are at sea the ventilators work better and we get outside air coming into the cabin."

"That's good," I said with some feeling, relishing the thought of clean, cold air, but Evans remarked, "You should reserve judgement until you have experienced the tropics."

I was to use the top bunk and before putting my bag on the straw palliasse to get it out of our way, I took out the letter and package from Captain Stewart's sister.

"Captain Stewart's sister gave me these to bring to the captain," I explained to Third Officer Evans.

"Do you know them well?" he asked.

"Not really," I said and continued, "Mrs. Perceval, the captain's sister, lives in the next village, and I met the captain there." I decided not to say more than the minimum as I didn't know Mr. Evans well enough yet.

"I see," said Mr. Evans but he sounded quite impressed.

We left our cabin and went up one level to the captain's cabin where Evans knocked on the door and waited. After a short wait we heard the captain's voice call out, "Enter."

Naturally, this cabin was much bigger than the box Evans and I had to share and contained a desk with a set of office chairs, a chart table, a pair of leather clad wingback chairs and a big bookcase. Through the doorway leading to an inner room I could see a bunk bed with storage cupboards built in beneath the bed base together with a clothes locker and a washbasin to complete the furnishings. There were several open portholes and none of the bad odours I had smelt in Evan's cabin.

"Sir," I said, "Your sister asked me to give these to you," and I passed over the letter and package that had been entrusted to my care.

"Thank you Mr. Smiley," he said, and then turned to Third Officer Evans "That will be all, Mr. Evans."

"Aye Sir," said Mr. Evans as he left the cabin to resume his watch.

"I am pleased to welcome you as one of my crew" said Captain Stewart. "In the personal letter that accompanied Captain Downing's official orders, he expressed the opinion that you are intelligent enough to become a good officer. That is also my opinion, but intelligence will not be sufficient on its own. To succeed, you will need to work hard at every task you are set and obey immediately and without question the orders you are given. My officers and I will give you every opportunity to make a success of the career you have chosen, but it will be due to the effort you make over the next several years that will determine whether you are a mediocre officer or an exceptional one in this demanding and dangerous profession."

Captain Stewart opened a drawer in his desk and took out a foolscap size cloth bound book and passed it to me. It was about an inch thick. He said "During the course of every day from now on, I expect you to record what you have experienced. Good experiences or bad, successes or failures must all be written down in sufficient detail to allow me to read and check on your progress. It will be good practice for the time you become a captain in your own right and have the ship's log to maintain."

"Thank you for the opportunity you have given to me, Captain Stewart. I will do my best to meet your standards," I responded in as serious voice as I could manage.

"If you honour the trust I have given you that will be thanks enough," Captain Stewart responded and was about to add something else when he was interrupted by a knock on the cabin door.

He called out, "Enter," and a rotund, red-faced man wearing a blue pullover and with work stained trousers tucked into leather sea-boots opened the door and stumped in.

He saluted the captain then glanced at me, then the captain, then back to me again.

Apparently without noticing the glances, Captain Stewart said "Bosun, this is Mr. Jason Smiley and he has joined the ship as the Company's first cadet. He will bunk in Mr. Evans cabin and share the same watch. To begin with he is here to learn."

With that he turned to me and said, "Cadet Smiley, this is Mr. Willis the Bosun. I would advise you to listen carefully to everything he tells you about seamanship as he is the most experienced seaman on board."

I reached out to shake his hand but the bosun quickly stepped back and saluted. I didn't know what to do so I did nothing and my confusion brought a slight grin to the captain's face.

Willis turned back to the captain and said, "I have checked the manifests, sir, and we should finish loading in three days as scheduled."

"Very good Bosun, thank you. Carry on," responded Captain Stewart.

After exchanging salutes the bosun left and Captain Stewart completed what he was about to say before the bosun interrupted him,

"Until the First Mate and the Second Officer return from leave you will accompany Mr. Evans when he is on watch. When all my officers have returned and after we have sailed, I will arrange for you to start regular lessons on all aspects of the life of a sailor. Very well, Cadet Smiley, you can go to the bridge and re-join Mr. Evans."

I stood to attention, said "Thank you, Captain," and left his cabin. On the bridge Evans greeted me in a more friendly fashion and started immediately to question me about what I had learnt earlier and then to give me more information about the ship.

When I climbed into my bunk at the end of my first, admittedly shared, watch I slept regardless of the sounds and smells that permeated our cabin. The straw in the palliasse was hard and lumpy but didn't spoil the sleep of a tired but very contented new cadet.

FIVE

My First Voyage

Early the next morning, whilst I was waiting for Evans to finish washing, the bosun came to the cabin with a pile of uniform clothing draped over his arm

"Been raiding the ditty box, Bosun?" asked Evans

"Aye, sir. Can't have Mr. Smiley looking like a passenger," he said as he dumped the clothes on Evan's bunk. "These are about your size, Mr Smiley. They're old and used but they're clean. Try them on; keep what fits and bring the rest back to me. They'll do until your uniforms are ready," and he saluted and left.

With Evans help and some hilarity when I tried on a jacket that we could have both worn simultaneously, we selected a uniform shirt, jacket and trousers that were much more in keeping with my new status as a cadet than the clothes I had worn the previous day. That said, I still looked like a badly dressed scarecrow beside Mr. Evans tailored perfection.

On my first morning, Donovan, the captain's tall, thin steward walked into the mess as I was finishing breakfast with John Evans.

"Good morning, gentlemen. The captain wishes to see you in thirty minutes, Mr. Smiley," he said without the slightest change of expression on his lugubrious face and walked out again.

After Donovan had left the mess and before I could begin to express my curiosity, Evans said, "Donovan's a strange one. He must have a Christian name, but no one seems to know what it is. He seems to be quite happy to be called 'Donovan' by everyone from the captain down. When he joined the ship, it was rumoured that previously he had been the butler at the country residence of some lord or other but had been dismissed. Apparently he was enamoured of a servant girl the said lord had his eye on. She was more interested in Donovan than the lord, so Donovan had to go."

"How did Captain Stewart find him?" I asked.

"The captain's previous steward was getting on in years and wanted to give up his life at sea. Captain Stewart heard about Donovan's situation somehow and since Donovan was a highly trained servant he decided to give the man a chance and let his old steward retire. This will be the second voyage that Donovan has taken in order to look after the Captain. What ever the rights and wrongs surrounding his dismissal, he is an excellent servant and devoted to the Captain's welfare and that is very good for all of us."

I realized then that my first and puzzling impression had been accurate. Although he was wearing the same uniform as the other sailors, the expression on his face and the way he moved suggested he should be carrying a tray or being otherwise subservient.

I knocked on the door of the captain's cabin punctually. It was opened almost immediately by Donovan and following Evans instructions I said, "Cadet Smiley reporting to the captain as ordered."

Donovan stepped back and gestured me into the cabin. I stepped smartly up to Captain Stewart's desk and stood at attention waiting for his attention to transfer to me from the papers he was frowning over.

After a few minutes he put the papers aside and said, "Good morning, Mr. Smiley. I have written a letter to the company tailor instructing him to prepare uniforms for you to wear when you are on duty on board and when you go on shore."

He stood up and with a warning note in his voice said sternly, "You should understand that Gold Star Line takes great pride in the appearance and maintenance of its ships, which are all less than ten years old and on the demeanour and dress of the men who sail the ships. I will take action against any member of my crew who brings my ship into disrepute. Collectively, we act as ambassadors for the company and our country, particularly when we are in foreign lands."

His homily delivered, the captain handed me a sealed envelope, which I saw had been addressed to a Mr. H. Dasher, Gentleman's Tailors and Outfitters in Little Howard Street and dismissed me with, "Go and find the Second Mate, Mr. Smiley and tell him, with my compliments that you have my permission to leave the ship to visit the tailor."

I said, "Aye, Sir" and left the captain's cabin to look for the Michael Judd the Second Mate who had just returned from a short leave.

When I found him on the bridge a little later he was deep in discussion with the bosun about the best way to load a particular piece of cargo. I didn't like to interrupt and waited until he noticed me standing beside him.

"What do you want, Mr. Smiley?"

"The captain's compliments, Sir, and he has instructed me to go ashore to get uniforms from the company tailor."

"Very well, Mr. Smiley, report to me on your return."

Then, perhaps recollecting that I was a stranger to Liverpool, he asked "Do you know how to get to the tailor?"

"No, Sir."

"I see. Go out of the dock gate, cross the road and turn left. Turn right into Oil Street, then left into Great Howard Street. The tailor is across the road on the corner of Great and Little Howard Streets. I will expect you back in one hour." Then he added with a grin that was echoed by the bosun "That allows you thirty minutes to walk there and then back, fifteen minutes to be measured and fifteen minutes for a country boy to get lost in the big city."

I checked the time on the bridge clock and said, "Aye, Sir," as I saluted and turned away to go on my errand.

I found the tailor's shop without difficulty, introduced myself and handed over the captain's letter. As my clothes had either been made by my mother or were serviceable hand-me-downs and my Sunday suit had been made by a travelling tailor, I had never seen the inside of a tailor's shop before and embarked on another learning process. The tailor was very business-like and immediately caught hold of the tape measure that was hanging around his neck. He opened a big ledger and carefully recorded each one of the prodigious number of measurements he took of every part of my anatomy.

"Come back at this time tomorrow for a fitting and every thing should be ready for collection by evening the next day. That's the night before you sail, I believe," said the tailor, who clearly knew more about the ship's schedule than I did as a humble new cadet.

"Yes, Sir," I said and left the shop to return to the ship.

I found the Second Mate after being absent for less than fifty minutes. He saw me and checked his pocket watch,

"Very good, Mr. Smiley, you didn't get lost I see. Go to the bridge and report to Mr. Evans."

"Aye, Sir," I said and did as I was ordered.

The next three days were very busy indeed as I learnt as much as possible about my duties, the ship itself and the officers and men who ran it.

I ate in the officer's mess, which was a room without portholes under the bridge and I recollect that the food was not at all bad. The crew ate in the forecastle and since there were few complaints I imagine the food the cook prepared for them was also acceptable. The captain ate all his meals in his cabin which made the atmosphere in our mess a little less formal.

As the days past the slightly relaxed attitude of a crew waiting for loading to be completed was replaced steadily with the more purposeful air of seamen getting ready to face the power and unpredictable nature of the sea. The first line of the sailors hymn, "Those that go down to the sea in ships see the wonders of the Lord" was in everyone's mind after the service the captain had held on Sunday.

Mr. Edgar Richards, the first mate, came back from a short leave a little more than a day before we were due to sail. There was no doubt that he had arrived. As he was getting down from his cab he saw something that displeased him and even as he climbed the gangway he made his presence known in language that would have made a navvy blush.

I met the Engineer in his hot, oily, steam wreathed engine room as he lovingly prepared the engine for departure. Like most ship's Engineers, he was a Scot from the Clyde where the ship and its engines had been built. He was dour and uncommunicative except during a discussion about his engine and then his whole demeanour changed and the ignorant would believe he was talking about a favourite child or even a lover. I was fascinated by the latent power of the engine and a little awe struck that this small, oil spattered man could control it.

I went back to the tailor as he had instructed and tried on my best uniform. The tailor tugged at the collar and a sleeve and made mysterious marks with a piece of white chalk on the pristine blue material of the jacket. My working uniforms and other kit were all ready finished except for minor adjustments to suit my slightly broader than average shoulders.

And all the time I was being instructed about my duties on board my first ship and the lore of the sea that my superior officers thought I should know.

"This is a new type of ship," the proud third officer informed me, when we were on the bridge on my second day and he was proudly talking about "Earl Canning," "It carries sails on two masts and also has a steam engine to drive the propeller. We can use the sails if the wind is right or the engine if it isn't."

On this occasion the captain happened to stop beside us, listened to Mr. Evans for a few minutes then took the opportunity to lecture us both about naval history based on the theme Mr. Evans had embarked upon. He said,

"When ships with steam engines were first built they had paddle wheels. This arrangement was effective but had two disadvantages. The weight of the engine was very high in the ship and this made it roll easily in rough weather. This is very uncomfortable for the passengers and can be dangerous if the cargo starts to move at sea. Another problem was that the engines lacked power, but the sails could not be used at the same time as the ship always listed when it was under sail. The list caused the paddle on the downwind side to be deeper in the water than the upwind paddle causing an increase in drag on one side that forced the ship down wind."

Warming to his lesson, and I noticed that Evans was also listening attentively, he went on,

"In 1839 a unique ship was launched. Instead of paddles she had a propeller and was named 'Archimedes.' This form of propulsion proved to be very efficient and the Admiralty then built two sister ships, the 'Rattler' and the 'Prometheus'. The 'Rattler' had a screw and the 'Prometheus' traditional paddle wheels but in other respects they could be considered identical. In trials the 'Rattler' was found to be the more efficient design. It thus became possible to combine the advantages of steam power and sail power as the propeller has none of the disadvantages of the paddle wheel and the weight of the engine can be lower in the ship making it more stable."

Captain Stewart then added proudly "'Earl Canning' has been designed and built following this new principle and I look forward to showing the owners what we can achieve."

That evening I went back to the tailor for the last time to collect my uniforms. The tailor had packed all the working uniforms into a canvas bag and gave me my best uniform on a hanger. I took the hanger from him, picked up the bag, said, "Thank you Mr. Dasher," and turned to leave the shop.

"No! No! Mr. Smiley. You cannot go on board carrying your number one's. You must change."

I demurred, but he insisted that it was company policy for me to wear my best uniform back to the ship. With great reluctance I accepted his word and adorned myself in my brand new No. 1 uniform. I put on the cap with its small gold star emblem and at the tailors insistence, I looked in the mirror he proffered. He was pleased with the result and when I recovered from the shock of seeing in the mirror, Jason Smiley in a naval uniform, I had to admit I looked very well.

And so it came to pass that Cadet Jason Smiley marched proudly up the gangway of the SS Earl Canning to the cheers of the few off duty sailors on deck and not a few ribald comments along the lines of, "Now he's all dressed up, we'd better find him a nice girl to impress."

The morning of 01 September 1861 dawned cold and wet. A strong westerly wind was blowing and even in the shelter of the docks the ship moved to the extent allowed by the moorings. It was the first strong wind I had experienced since coming on board and whilst the movement was not great it was disconcerting to my landsman's conditioning. It brought home to me the realization that this enormous iron structure, which had seemed so massively inert, was actually floating and being blown about by the wind. It hardly seemed credible.

All the hatch boards had been carefully placed and covered with tarpaulins and these had been dressed down the sides of the hatch coamings and securely wedged in place. The Blue Peter was flying and we only waited the arrival of the pilot and the tugs that would guide the ship into the River Mersey.

In some trepidation I stood in the bows with Mr. Evans and four seamen. We all wore our working uniforms. We officers wore dark blue trousers, reefer jackets with a small gold star on the breast pocket and uniform caps again emblazoned with the company insignia woven from gold wire. The men were dressed in dark blue trousers and woollen pullovers with the ship's name across the breast in white. There was an air of tension about the ship and many sad faces as well. Many of the men were leaving wives and families and I had overheard one grey bearded old sailor say to a younger man, "It doesn't get any easier saying goodbye, no matter how many times you do it," and his companion nodded a silent agreement.

Something that I have subsequently found to be a regular occurrence is that there are always some of the men who celebrate too well the night before they sail and regret it for some days following our departure. Today was no exception and the ship's crew contained a big proportion of pale faced, head holding, ex-revellers who clearly would have preferred their beds to a cold, windswept deck.

I thought back to the short meeting with the officers Captain Stewart had held in his cabin early the previous day. After we had all found seats around his desk he said, "Good morning, gentlemen. We sail tomorrow at eight bells in the morning watch bound for Bombay. En route we will call at St. Vincent and Cape Town amongst other ports to discharge cargo and bunker ship, and if there is any cargo waiting we will load it for Bombay. After discharging our remaining cargo in Bombay, we will trade in the area until the cotton crop is on the Green. We will load and return to Liverpool as quickly as the weather permits. Ensure that the men under your control know the sailing time and preferably arrive for duty sober tomorrow morning if they have shore leave tonight."

His final comment, as he closed the meeting, was simple and to the point, "If you all do your duty, and I am confident I can rely on you all to do so, this will be a successful voyage. That will be all Gentlemen" and we all stood, saluted and went back to our respective duties.

Evans told me that Captain Stewart made a practice of informing his officers about his plans for the ship, but as I discovered later, this was not a common practice amongst other captains. Some captains believed they held a position second only to God and consequently did not allow the officers to know what was planned until the order was given and never gave an explanation for their decisions.

I remembered, as well, the only incident that had marred the hitherto smooth loading of the ship. Mr. Evans and I were on watch and supervising a small group of dockworkers who were stowing some crates into the after hold. We suddenly heard crackling noises above us just like fireworks exploding followed by excited and alarmed voices on the quayside below shouting, "Look out!" and "Keep clear!"

We looked up in time to see the last strands of rope in part of a cargo sling snap with a resounding crack and the whole net seemed to unravel and burst open. Four large boxes fell out and started a speedy descent to the quayside. They smashed open on the granite sets with the crunching, crashing sound of shattering timber and breaking bottles and amber liquid started to drain across the quay.

"Whiskey," said Mr. Evans sniffing the aroma that drifted across the bridge. "What a pity!" he added, "There will be a little less for the raj to get drunk on now," but he did not look at all unhappy at the prospect of their impending thirst.

It was the only mishap we suffered during loading for that voyage. Later I wondered if the net had been weakened deliberately, as mugs and other suitable containers were evident almost before the echoes of the breakage had died away, and the stevedores collected the remaining liquid content presumably for their future private consumption.

As I was thinking back over the events of the past several days the pilot arrived, climbed the gangway, and made his way to the bridge. The gangway was raised, brought inboard and secured. Side by side two squat black tugs raced along the dock towards us and separated to stop at bow and stern with much thrashing of the water with their paddles. Towlines were passed down onto the after decks of both tugs and made fast to the towing hooks. The pilot reached up with his hand and pulled on a rope above the bridge.

As the steam whistle mounted on the front of the forward funnel suddenly burst stridently into life, I jumped violently. It was louder than anything I had heard in my life and totally unexpected. My companions on the forecastle clearly knew the whistle was going to be sounded and just as clearly they had anticipated what my reaction to the sudden noise would be.

Evans said tersely, "Stand back and watch carefully what is being done. Do not try to help unless you are specifically asked to do so. At the moment you don't know enough to be useful."

"Aye, Sir," was all I could say and moved away from the group to give them more space.

Captain Stewart shouted down to Evans, "Let go forward, Mr. Evans," and Evans released the tension on the bow mooring lines so that a man on the quayside below could pull the bight of each of the ropes off the bollard. They dropped into the water, and Evans seamen started to haul them in and then coil them on deck as quickly as they could. The bow tug gave an answering blast on its whistle, moved forward slowly and the dripping towrope slowly lifted from the water. It straightened and water streamed down as it creaked tight as the tug started to take the weight of the ship. Suddenly the frantic activity ceased. At the stern I imagined a similar ballet had just ended and the ship moved slowly away from the quayside and along the dock under the command of the pilot and towing power of two tugs.

I moved over to Evans, who was standing at the rail carefully watching the bow tow rope and said, "Please Mr. Evans what is all the whistling about?"

"The Pilot is signalling to the tugs," he answered.

He obviously realized that this wasn't a sufficient answer as he went on to say "The pilot has to tell the captain of each tug what he must do and to avoid the tugs acting on the wrong signal he has arranged to signal the bow tug using the steam whistle and the stern tug with a mouth whistle. The captain of each tug answers by repeating the signal using either the tug's steam whistle or a mouth whistle at bow and stern respectively. He has also arranged the sequence of whistles necessary for each manoeuvre. For example, one blast to pull ahead, two blasts to stop pulling and so on. Do you understand?"

"Aye, sir," I said

As we talked the ship was moving towards the far side of the dock and just as I started to worry that my first voyage was going to end with a disastrous collision with the very solid masonry wall opposite, the bow tug started to move to port and pull the bows around in the same direction. The stern tug pulled in the opposite direction and very suddenly and without any fuss at all, the ship had been turned through ninety degrees and we were gliding along beside the river but many, many feet higher.

Mr. Evans said, "We are going to lock down into Prince's Dock Basin through Waterloo Dock Lock."

"Aye sir," I responded, but I must have looked as mystified as I felt because my only previous experiences with a lock had been on the forge door. What possible connection there could be between that lock and Prince's Dock Lock I could not imagine?

He saw my expression and said patiently, "I will explain as we go along, but you must watch what is happening and try to understand it."

"Aye, sir."

The semi-bascule bridge at the junction between Victoria and Waterloo Docks was raised, and we headed for a strip of water that looked impossibly narrow for the ship to sail through, but we passed under the bridge with plenty of space to spare on both sides. The tugs stopped pulling us ahead as we came through the passage and as soon as the stern was clear, they started to pull us sideways into Waterloo Dock. In no time at all it seemed we were lined up on another narrow passageway.

Evans gesticulated forward over the bow and said, "That's Waterloo Dock Lock," then turned away to order his men to get the mooring lines ready before I could comment.

The tugs pulled us towards the entrance to this next narrow strip of water, but from my elevation in the bows the water appeared to merge with the river beyond which was impossible as there was such a difference in level between the dock and the river as I had just seen for myself.

His preparations completed Evans explained about locks. He said, "Do you know anything about tides?"

"Aye sir," I answered, because Captain Stewart had told me about them although I chose not to mention that to Mr Evans. He didn't need to know unless he asked a direct question.

He then went on to say, "The tidal range in the River Mersey is more than twenty-five feet, and it is impractical to moor a ship and move cargo when the ship is rising and falling so much. To avoid this difficulty the docks in Liverpool have been built so that the water level is kept nearly constant at about high tide level. Other ports with similar tidal difficulties have been built in the same way," he added.

He went on, "To enable ships to get into the dock from the tidal river, and out again of course, a lock is required. They are common on the canals and although they are much smaller in size, they have a similar function. Have you seen one, Mr. Smiley?"

"No sir," I had to admit.

"A lock," he went on, "is a narrow, water filled chamber fitted with one or a pair of gates at each end and is connected to the dock at one end and the river at the other. The inner gates have been opened," he said pointing ahead and down below the bow. "As you can see the water level is the same in the lock as it is in the dock. When we are moored inside the lock the inner gates will be closed behind us and the water in the lock will be allowed to run away into the river. When the water level is the same in the lock and the river the outer gates will be opened and the ship will be towed out of the lock by the tugs. Now I must get ready to tie up in the lock."

I watched in amazement as the ship and the tugs squeezed into the lock. Men on the lock side took our mooring ropes and dropped the ends over the waiting bollards. When all was secured and the ship unmoving, a man on each side of the lock near the entrance from the dock, pulled over a big lever. Nothing seemed to happen at first, but as I looked back along the ship's side, I could just see a black object start to appear from a recess in the side of the lock. It wasn't very high out of the water and as I watched it became longer and longer until the end disappeared from view. Evans had seen me staring and said the inner gates were closing. Below me other men pulled some more levers and again nothing seemed to happen but suddenly I realized that the men were getting closer. One minute it seemed I was looking down on the men and the next we were nearly on the same level.

"What's happening?" I said. "Are we sinking?" I asked Evans trying not to panic. I was concerned about the imminence of death by drowning but at the same time I was marvelling at the calm demeanour of the men around me who were clearly going to suffer the same fate.

Evans laughed and said, "It's just as I explained to you, the water level in the lock is being lowered to bring the ship down to the level of the river. Look there."

He pointed and ahead of the ship and towering above me I could see the black coal tar painted outer gates. I hadn't seen them when we came into the lock. The water level in the dock had been unusually high and water was running over the top of the gates and hiding them from view. Very quickly, it seemed, the gates swung back and the tugs manoeuvred us into the Prince's Dock Basin where they turned us ninety degrees to sail into the muddy, choppy River Mersey and then a further ninety degrees to face the river mouth and the Irish Sea.

The tugs cast off and scurried back inside the lock to return to the docks and the ships that were now high above us. The tall, narrow, black, outer lock gates swung slowly closed and the tugs were gone from my view, and another of the hundreds of first experiences that had come to me during the past few days came to an abrupt, silent end.

I heard the telegraph ring on the bridge and the answering ring from the engine room and felt the vibration from the engine as it started to turn the screw. The mooring party in the bows coiled up and stowed all the mooring lines and the towline. When everything had been completed to Evans satisfaction the mooring party were dismissed to go to their normal duties. Evans and I were off watch now and when he went below to our tiny cabin I stayed in the eyes of the ship and looked around me and started to savour my first experience of a sailor man's life.

As we steamed down the river we soon passed the last of Jesse Hartley's new docks and industry gave way to mud flats and fields and small towns in the distance. The town of Liverpool in the County of Lancashire and Furness was left behind. On the opposite side of the river the shipyards and small town of Seacombe had been replaced by open country. Bidston lighthouse was clearly visible and the sails of a windmill stood out black and solitary on the ridge of high ground lying nearly parallel to the river.

I could soon see the advantages of steam power over sail as we pushed on into a breeze that would have prevented us from sailing if we had been reliant on sails.

We soon reached the Mersey Bar, made a lea for the pilot cutter and the captain saw the pilot over the side with a word of thanks. The pilot swarmed down the Jacob's ladder with the practiced ease of a monkey climbing down a tree and disappeared into the cabin on the cutter, which turned away and headed for an incoming ship he was to pilot into port.

We were soon steaming purposefully out into an unusually calm Irish Sea. I found the gentle pitching of the ship quite pleasant but soon went down to the cabin as the wind was quite chill. Evans went on watch as required and I followed like a faithful shadow. At the end of the day I wrote up the first page in my journal and slept like a stone

The next morning we passed Anglesey, turned towards the south, stopped engines and set sail as the wind was favourable.

The motion of the ship changed dramatically as soon as we set course to the south. It started to roll from side to side as well as pitch up and down as we quartered across the oncoming seas. With the engine stopped, I was able to appreciate the quiet beauty of a big ship under sail and I quite enjoyed this new sensation. Having to keep one hand free for myself and remembering to balance to the movement of the ship was a task in itself for my landlubber legs.

I was quite busy helping Evans with the daily tasks of our first watches at sea and enjoyed the sunlight on the water and the distant views of the coast of North Wales. The visibility was good and Evans pointed to a mountain on the horizon. He said in a rather wistful tone, "That Mountain is called Snowdon in English. In Welsh it's called Yr Wyddfa."

It was just a mountain shining in the sun, as far as I could see, but I was pleased he had taken the trouble to point it out.

We went off watch and straight to the mess for a meal. I was ravenously hungry after many hours in the fresh air and with great enthusiasm tucked into the bowl of beef stew that was offered by the cook. I noticed that the table had been fitted with fiddles since morning and on occasion the motion of the ship would have sent my bowl to the deck if it hadn't been so restrained.

For the first time, Evans and I had time to start finding out more about each other. We had already developed a friendly relationship, which was just as well, considering how closely we had to live together as well as work in harmony.

"I was born in a north Wales town called Caernarfon. It's on the Menai Strait" John Evans remarked that lunch time, "and I grew up with the scent of sea air in my nostrils whether I was at home or at sea with my father. My mother always worried about my father's safety. Losing her father, my grandfather, at sea made the dangers seem much more personal I suppose, and she was not at all pleased when she realized that I would go to sea as well. The greater strength and better maintenance of ships in fleets like the Gold Star Line have let her sleep more easily, I think, but she is a much happier lady when my feet are on dry land."

He paused for a moment and I noticed that the smell from the remains of our lunch didn't seem quite so appetising any more.

John Evans went on, "I have no brothers and only one sister. She is about your age, Jason and as pretty as a picture. I have a miniature of her in my cabin. It doesn't do her credit, but I'll show it to you one day. She ought to be thinking of getting married, but she hasn't met anyone who attracts her in the slightest degree and our parents would never arrange a match for her with someone she didn't care for. There are not many young men in and around Caernarfon who would be considered eligible by my parents any way, and none of my shipmates have been attractive to her. A great pity really, but she could end up on the shelf."

I noticed that I was starting to feel hot, but my skin felt strangely clammy. My stomach felt a little uneasy as if I had eaten too much. Although it was impossible to see what the sea was like, it felt as if the ship was pitching and rolling much more than when I had been on the bridge.

Evans said, "One of the main reasons she is unmarried is that we became involved with the Temperance Society and as we agreed with their aims we signed the pledge. As a result my sister doesn't want to become involved with a man who does not hold similar views."

"What does 'sign the pledge' mean," I asked, but my interest was feigned, as I thought that it would be much nicer to lie down on my bunk rather than talk before I went back on duty.

John Evans said "Signing the pledge means that we have sworn not to drink alcohol, and we try to persuade those who do drink it to sign a pledge swearing that they will not take alcohol again. It doesn't make us very popular with most people, particularly the eligible young men of my sister's age. They are more interested in showing their manliness by drinking larger quantities of beer or cider than anyone else. And that is particularly so in the heat of summer. Since they prefer beer to thoughts of marriage, my sister has never had a serious suitor."

I yawned and suddenly found my mouth full of saliva. I swallowed, yawned again and suddenly the urge to lie down seemed irresistible. The mess room had become very confined and stuffy and my stomach was beginning to feel very unsettled. I noticed that Evans was looking at me with some concern.

He said solicitously, "You look a little pale, Jason, perhaps you should go up on deck for a while and get some fresh air. It might help to steady your stomach."

"I think I will go back to the cabin and lie down," I replied, feeling a little giddy.

"As you wish Jason, but I think the upper deck would be better for you."

I stood up with difficulty and because of the roll of the ship I staggered to the mess room door. My legs felt weak and my stomach rumbled and churned as I made my unsteady way along the passage, opened the door to my shared cabin and climbed gratefully into my bunk.

Shortly afterwards Evans came in, lay down on his bunk and calmly started to read a pamphlet.

Now that we were at sea the air in the cabin smelt of the oceans, but in the closed unstable confines of the cabin, I started to feel more and more uncomfortable until my overwhelming urge to vomit could not be delayed and longer.

As I climbed from my bunk in order to rush from the cabin as fast as my weak, unstable legs would carry me across the heaving, pitching deck, Evans looked up called out "Lee side" and went back to reading his pamphlet.

I was sick. Oh dear! I was so sick. Then I was sick again and then a few minutes later I wanted to be sick and heaved and heaved and nothing came up. I held on to the ship's rail with a grip that whitened my knuckles and heaved. I grew cold and wet and wished that the uncontrollable urge to vomit would stop. I was empty and each heave felt as if my stomach would come up and disappear over the side. And all the time the ship kept up its unfeeling, regular, monotonous, nauseating motion. Bow rising at knee buckling speed, rolling to port, bow falling like a stone with a sharp roll to starboard.

I staggered back to my bunk some time later feeling unbelievably weak and chilled and believing that I couldn't possibly be sick again. There couldn't possibly be anything left in my body to vomit could there? It felt as if everything I had eaten for days had been dredged from the depths of my body and ejected overboard. I was wrong! Each time I returned to the cabin, and no sooner was I horizontal which was an inexact description considering the pitching and rolling of the ship, than I had to leap off my bunk and run to the heads or the ship's side depending on the urgency of the heaving of my stomach. The heads were at least inside the ship and out of the wind and spray, but they didn't smell very pleasant as other new crewmembers had been sick as well. The rail was closer, but meant being soaked in cold sea spray as I heaved dryly over the side and this added to my discomfort.

In everyone who is severely seasick and who also knows that the ship is not going to stop its nauseating motion in the foreseeable future, is borne the desire for the miracle of a swift and painless death to end the agony. The misery of the next hours and the amusement my shipmates could derive from the reaction of my stomach to a solicitous, "Shall I get you a nice piece of fat bacon from the galley?" is best glossed over.

Some did try to encourage me by saying, "You'll soon have your sea legs, Jason," but they were very definitely in a minority.

Mr. Evans woke me from an exhausted sleep and said "You're on watch in five minutes, Cadet Smiley. You may not have official duties yet but you must be on watch at the appointed time whether you are sick or not," and walked out of the cabin.

How cruel and unreasonable I thought, but I swung my legs off my bunk and stood up to comply with Mr. Evans instruction. Although I felt and probably also looked a little like death warmed up, I reported to the bridge feeling too weak to stand and not sure for how long my stomach would leave me in piece. As it turned out, I started to recover as soon as I was in the fresh air again and busy.

My appetite was a little slower to fully recover!

The days passed steadily. The weather varied from good to bad but was never very severe and I didn't suffer another bout of sickness. We progressed under sail as much as possible, but as soon as it died away or blew from an adverse direction, Captain Stewart ordered the boilers to be fired up and we resumed our course under a cloud of smoke and steam and vibrated towards the distant horizon.

The temperature steadily became warmer as we headed south but it was nearly another year before I realized that the benign temperatures I was experiencing now would be replaced by the searing summer heat of India and the Oman.

We sighted Madeira and anchored in St. Vincent for six incident free days. We took on coal, discharged some of our cargo and loaded a small consignment for Bombay. Some days after we sailed for Cape Town, I was on the bridge when the captain and mate took the noon sights. After comparing their readings the captain said,

"I calculate that we will cross the line tomorrow about midday. We have three novices I believe."

"That's correct, sir," answered the Mate, and then asked, "Will the arrangements we had on our last voyage be acceptable, sir?"

"Yes," answered the captain and left the bridge.

The next morning I was about to leave the cabin to go on watch, when a stern faced Evans opened the door and walked in. He said that I had been relieved of duty by the captain and I was to stay in the cabin until called for. With that he turned on his heel walked out and closed the door behind him. I hadn't recovered from the shock he had given me with this unexpected order when I heard the key turn in the lock. I had been locked in.

As far as I could remember I had done nothing remotely wrong that could have caused the captain to turn against me and order Third Officer Evans to lock me in the cabin. I realized that I would just have to wait until an explanation was forthcoming.

As far as I could judge the door was unlocked about an hour later, and Evans walked in accompanied by two brawny seamen.

"Why did you lock me in?" I demanded of Mr. Evans but he ignored my question and still looking very stern, said simply, "Come with me. The court is ready."

Before I could say another word Evans turned away and with one seaman in front and the other at my back we marched out of the cabin. I tried to stop, but the sailors were so big and so close that the gesture was ineffective.

We marched to the portside entry and then forward along the main deck towards N0.1 hold. The crew was lined up on the port side of the ship and we halted between them and three chairs, the middle one being big enough to be a throne. We were just in time for me to see a blue robed, but burly figure with a flowing beard, a gold coloured helmet and a trident being helped over the bows by two acolytes dressed in similar blue robes. I noticed that the ship had slowed down and looked back to the bridge where the captain and mate, both in full dress uniform stood at attention. They saluted in unison and as I turned forward again, I saw the figure in the bow raise his trident in an answering salute.

"Welcome aboard, King Neptune," said Captain Stewart in his 'all hands on deck on a stormy night' voice, "I hope all is well in your Kingdom below the waves?"

"Thank you for your welcome, Captain. All is well in my kingdom below, but you have three pollywogs on board who have not paid their dues to my court. They have committed misdemeanours and must be tried and punished before they can be accepted."

"I understand, King Neptune," answered the captain, in stentorian tones, "Please make your court on the forward deck and try the miscreants."

I started to move and was immediately grabbed by the two seamen. Effortlessly, it seemed, they held me still. I opened my mouth to shout and a big hand covered my mouth.

Evans leant towards me and said very, very sternly "Keep still, Jason. Be quiet and above all, whatever happens you must behave like a man. I will explain as much as I can about what is happening. Do I have your word that you will do as I say?"

"Yes," I said, but very unwillingly and totally forgetting that I should have said, 'Aye sir'. He turned to the sailors and told them to release me.

By this time the three persons I had seen in the bow were sitting down surrounded by people in strange costumes.

Evans indicated with a glance where I should look and said, "In the middle of the group is King Neptune and on his right is Davey Jones, his Chief Assistant. On King Neptune's left is the Royal Scribe and to his left is Her Highness Amphitrite."

I couldn't believe my eyes when I looked where Evans directed. Clad in a long bright red dress was a woman with long blonde hair. She had the voluptuous curves that every deep-sea sailor dreams about! Most of the rest of Evans description fell on deaf ears but I do remember reference to the Royal Physician, the Royal Barber and the Royal Dentist amongst other luminaries.

The Royal Scribe stepped forward, waved a sheaf of papers at the crew and shouted, "Officer of the Guard bring the prisoner Jason Smiley forward."

The two seamen assigned to escort me took no chances about my obedience and picking me up by my elbows, carried me forward and then forced me to kneel on the deck in front of King Neptune. My hands were tied behind my back and my escort retired.

I tried very hard to behave like a man, but I didn't know what was happening. I was scared witless and the urge to pee or worse where I knelt, almost became uncontrollable.

The Royal Scribe then said in a loud voice, "Jason Smiley you are charged with the most terrible crimes imaginable. They are listed here in full and lurid detail" and he brandished the papers in the air.

The crew said, "Ooohhhhh!" in unison.

The Chief Scribe waved his papers in the air again and said in a voice that I could barely hear over the noise made by a crew who seemed to be half for and half against me.

"Jason Smiley, there are two charges against you. First you are charged with 'Attempting to steal the line' under the provisions of the Unlicensed Burglar Act and secondly you are charged with 'Attempting to thrive on ship's provisions' under the Indigestion Act. Under the powers invested in me by the Royal Judge you have been found guilty on both charges. It only remains for me to pronounce sentence, under the penal code established in King Neptune's Kingdom"

I knelt on the hot deck in the sun and have never felt as alone as I did at that moment. My knees were hurting as if they were on fire and my hands had started to go to sleep from the pressure of the ropes they were tied together with.

Nothing happened for what seemed an interminable time whilst the Royal Scribe consulted other members of the court.

Then he addressed me in a voice that could have been heard a mile away. "Jason Smiley. You have been tried in absentia and as you have been found guilty on every charge the court convened here by King Neptune has decided to impose the most severe penalties permitted under our penal code."

I knelt on the deck in the sunshine and my bowels turned to water as I tried to rationalise what I was seeing and hearing and relate it to my scant knowledge of the sea. King Neptune is a myth, isn't he? I'm not really guilty of any crimes. Am I? They cannot punish me for things I haven't done. Can they? The realization that I was on my knees with my hands tied lead me to the inescapable conclusion that they could do exactly what they liked, and as the captain was still on the bridge looking down on the proceedings, they probably would. My imagination suggested that death was imminent. Behaving like a man was a waking nightmare.

The King's Scribe said, "The King's Doctor will examine you to ensure that you are fit enough to survive the sentence lay down by the court. Call the King's Doctor" and various voices echoed the command from behind me.

I was dragged to my feet by two of King Neptune's supporters and held firmly as the King's Doctor slowly approached and walked all around me. I tried to watch him but my guard wouldn't permit me to turn my head.

Suddenly my captors turned me to face the King's Doctor who had positioned himself so that I had to squint into the sun to see him. He looked in my hair, in my mouth and under my tongue and seemed disappointed that my ears didn't rotate. He pulled up my shirt and prodded my stomach with bony fingers and then pulled down my trousers. After looking at my nether regions and sorrowfully shaking his head, he pulled them up again. He made a gesture to the crew that indicated that mine was less than an inch long, which provoked howls of laughter from everyone but me. I felt too humiliated to do more than stand in stunned silence.

He said, "He's fit to take his punishment."

The Royal Scribe shouted, "Let the punishment begin."

The King's Doctor stepped forward, held my nose until I had to open my mouth to take a breath, popped in a large pill and then held my lips together so that I couldn't spit the object out. It was soap and I seemed to have no option but swallow it. Another man stood in front of me and lathered my face with a mixture of flour and water and then tried to shave me with an enormous mock wooden razor. He scraped at my face and it felt as if my skin was being detached with the paste. This done, I was pushed backward into a large pool of water where I lay blowing bubbles but unable to move as my hands were still tied. I really thought I was going to die at that moment and I was terrified. After what seemed a lifetime, but was probably only a minute or so, I was dragged out and unceremoniously dumped on the deck to cough and splutter back to verbal coherence.

I was just gathering strength to give vent to the feelings of terror and humiliation I felt, when Evans appeared, untied my hands and knelt beside me. He said, "Well done, Jason, I'm proud of you."

I opened my mouth to shout out something but Evans laid a finger across my lips and suggested I count to ten.

Before I could respond in any way he started to count out loud himself in order to encourage me. He said "Een, Dai, Tree, Pedwar, Pimp."

I interrupted him and said, "What are you saying?" which was not at all what I had in mind a few seconds before.

"Sorry Jason, it's Welsh. In the excitement I forgot my English. Now, you must go to our cabin and when you have changed your uniform the captain wants to see you on the bridge."

He helped me stand up and escorted me back to our cabin. I squelched, blew bubbles when I spoke and felt sore and humiliated. More than anything else I was bewildered by what had happened and more importantly why. I changed and went to the bridge where I was greeted warmly by the captain and mate.

Captain Stewart said, "Cadet Smiley, it gives me great pleasure to present you with the Shellbacks Certificate. You have behaved like a true sailor."

He held out a sheet of thick paper in his left hand and shook my right hand with his. The mate also warmly shook my hand. I glanced at the paper and noticed it was richly decorated around the perimeter with whales, dolphins, sea serpents, sea shells and sea weed. Written upon it in ornate script was.

SHELLBACK CERTIFICATE

To all Mermaids, Sea Serpents, Whales, Sharks, Porpoises, Dolphins, Skates, Eels, Lobsters, Crabs and all other living things of the sea.

We solemnly declare that in Latitude 00.00 and Longitude 30.15 our shipmate

CADET JASON SMILEY

Has been found worthy to be numbered as one of our trusty Shellbacks, has been gathered to our fold and duly initiated into the solemn mysteries of the ancient order of the deep,

Signed: King Neptune
First Witness: Davey Jones
Second Witness: Captain Stewart Master of SS Earl Canning
Date: 21st September 1861

I said, "Captain, Sir, I do not understand."

Captain Stewart looked at me with an expression of surprise that changed to one of understanding and said, "I had forgotten that you have no knowledge of the customs of the sea, Jason. You have taken part in a ceremony that has its roots in ancient history. Even the Vikings had similar ceremonies. It is a ceremony of propitiation to appease the Sea God Neptune and ensure the safety of all sailors. All the crew who officiated in our ceremony have crossed the line, the Equator, on past voyages and are called Shellbacks. You are now one of them."

He turned and looked over the bridge rail at the ceremony that was continuing on the fore deck. One of the new seamen was being initiated and was screaming and weeping in fear and this seemed to make his punishment worse.

Captain Stewart turned to me and said, "You faced the unknown and behaved with courage, Mr. Smiley, and the men respect that. As a result your initiation was not pleasant, but it will be much worse for that young man. He's behaving like a coward. The experienced men use this ceremony as a test to see who can be relied upon in an emergency. Go and get something to eat and then report for your next watch."

"Aye, sir."

The ceremony lasted most of the day and then the ship's routine was re-established and we sailed on to Cape Town, where we bunkered the ship again.

Chippie, as every ship's carpenter seems to be called, made a frame for my certificate and this was presented to me with due ceremony by the bosun. I really started to feel that I was being accepted by the crew.

Each day I had tuition about some aspect of seamanship and the duties of an officer and found that I was taking watches with Mr. Evans but also receiving tuition from the first mate when he was on the bridge at the same time. The bosun taught me about the sails and rigging and gave me lessons in signalling and splicing. He made sure I had a basic knowledge of mooring and towing techniques.

Following Captain Stewart's philosophy that an officer must be able to do anything a subordinate could do, I had to help set and furl the sails when we were not using the engines. In my previous life I had never been higher off the ground than the lowest branches of an apple tree, so I will never forget the gut wrenching fear I experienced the first time I stood on a footrope high above the sea and fought with the bucking, heaving canvas on a yardarm. I fought and won both battles, and thereafter I was able to go aloft whenever it was necessary. Captain Stewart had watched me that day and whilst he said nothing, I sensed he was pleased I had conquered my fear.

My knowledge of the sea and ship management grew day by day and as it grew I realized how much more there was left to learn. Most lessons were serious but one, in retrospect, was quite hilarious. The mate had come to the bridge and sent Evans off on some errand or another. The helmsman had been fidgeting for some minutes and eventually requested permission to get a relief helmsman so that he could go to the heads.

The mate looked carefully around the horizon with his glass, then turned to me and said, "You haven't had a lesson on the helm yet, Mr. Smiley. You take over the wheel."

With that he told the helmsman to go below and, "Be sharp about it." The helmsman gave me the course to steer, which I repeated and then took his place in front of the wheel. The ship maintained its course for a few minutes and then the bow started to drift to port. I turned the wheel a little to correct the swing and nothing happened. I turned it some more and the bow started to track back to starboard. I centred the wheel as we came back on course but to my horror the bows kept swinging out to starboard. I turned the wheel to port and stopped the swing but I was too slow and the bows swung rapidly out to port again and much further than the first time. I continued to swing the wheel frantically back and forth and the ship heeled and swung one way then heeled and swung in the opposite direction. I was soon sweating from my exertions and full of anger and frustration at my inability to control the ship. The helmsmen always made it look so simple and the wake was always ruler straight.

The helmsman came back looked out over the stern and was about to make some comment when he noticed the mate glaring at him. He changed his mind and took over the wheel without a comment.

The mate said quietly, "Now that he has written his name in the water show him how he should steer, Stubbins."

"Aye sir," said Able Seaman Alf Stubbins.

I looked back and could see the contorted shape of the wake left by my effort at steering the ship being replaced by the usual ruler straight wake left in the sea by an experienced helmsman. I took over the wheel again and my lesson continued under the watchful eye of the mate. Stubbins showed me by example how to make small corrections with the wheel and more importantly how to cancel them quickly enough to maintain the chosen course without over steering. Like most skills it looked so easy when performed by an expert!!

After Cape Town we rounded the Cape of Aquinas and sailed up the west coast of Madagascar.

A good development as far as I was concerned was the increasing regard that Evans and I developed for each other during the remainder of the voyage. I was pleased that he didn't try to persuade me to sign the pledge and as far as I could see he didn't push his views on the other officers. We talked a great deal when we were off watch together and I came to appreciate his wide knowledge of subjects other than the sea and his sense of humour. In one of those discussions I was astounded to learn that there were another native languages in Britain apart from English.

Evans said bluntly, "The Welsh language is spoken extensively within the Principality of Wales but particularly in those areas in the north and west that have not been dominated by English speaking Britons."

In order to demonstrate that he was not misleading me, as initially I was openly sceptical, he produced from his locker a Bible in Welsh and read the Lord's Prayer and showed me the written language to prove what he was saying.

Ein Tad, yr hwn wyt yn a nefoedd,
Sancteiddier dy Enw,
Deled dy deyrnas—

This is all I remember of what he showed me, but when I understood that there was an area of my country that spoke an antique language that was much older than English, it made a profound effect. Evans also told me the little he knew about the language used by the Cornishmen and the Gaelic of Scotland and Ireland.

On another occasion he showed me the portrait of his sister and insisted that it was a very poor likeness. Even allowing for the rosy-eyed view of a devoted brother who thought the picture not good enough, I was entranced by the beauty of this young Welsh lady and accepted with unseemly haste an invitation to visit the family home when it could be arranged. I wondered sometimes why Evans and I were compatible, as our backgrounds were so very different, but it doesn't pay to question good fortune, and I listened and learnt from a very willing tutor. If I had been blessed with a sister, I should have been delighted to introduce her to Third Officer John Evans and mortified if she had rejected this very knowledgeable and presentable gentleman.

We passed Assumption Island and the Seychelles and over the next weeks we made good time to Bombay. Wherever we anchored, we discharged some cargo and took on some new boxes and bales consigned to Bombay and as a matter of routine we refilled the coalbunkers whenever there was an opportunity. Over the years I grew to hate the smell, feel and taste of the coal dust which permeated every space during coaling.

In Bombay we unloaded the cargo in the ship's holds and then, as soon as space became available, we stuffed those spaces as full as we could with the Indian produce destined for England. Bale upon bale of cotton, consigned to the mills of Lancashire, were hoisted up the ship's side from barges and lowered into the holds where it was stacked and shored into place. When loading finished we sailed and I do not believe I stepped onto the shores of India for a moment on that first voyage. Bombay remained an enigma for a very long time.

SIX

Maturing

When I was selected to be the Gold Star Line's first company cadet and joined the crew of the 'Earl Canning' I was extremely proud of my achievement. My first voyage did nothing to dent my pride and I was too callow to recognize that the crew, from Captain Stewart down, were carefully guiding my over eager and often premature actions.

If I had known how difficult the next four or five years were going to be, I think I would have terminated my career as a deck officer cadet immediately, but I didn't and so I continued to follow the path I had embarked upon.

I thought I was grown up and an adult ready to take control of the world. I thought I was superior, but in reality I was ill educated and inexperienced. I had not yet lived independently in the real world so had no yardstick against which to measure myself. I did not realize how much I had to learn about the custom and practice of being a sailor or how much I had to mature to become an adult.

Maturing was a long and painful process.

I must have been about eighteen years old when I returned to Liverpool after that first voyage to Bombay and over the following years we made many such trading voyages. I won't bore you with an account of each voyage, as it would become a repetitive and uninteresting narrative, but I will highlight the events that had a lasting affect on my development

The first of these formative events occurred not long after we tied up at the end of our second voyage, at what was our normal berth in Liverpool docks. I was on the bridge, sitting by the chart table and writing up part of the official log from the notes made by the officer of the watch.

Captain Stewart walked across the bridge to where I was working, checked what I was doing and then asked, "When did you see your father last?"

"Just before I joined the ship as your cadet, Captain."

"There is time for you to make a quick visit to Pickworth before we complete loading. If you wish to make the trip you can leave tomorrow morning after six bells, but you must return in five days."

"Aye, sir. Thank you sir," I responded. I wasn't sure I wanted to make the journey. After the way my father had behaved when I left home to join Captain Stewart I didn't think he would be very interested in a visit, but filial duty demanded that I should make the effort.

At dawn the next morning and resplendent in my best uniform, I walked quietly down the gangway and left the ship and my colleagues to return to Pickworth. I carried the Reverend Daly's valise and inside I had placed a small bag with a few clothes and toiletries.

I walked to Lime Street Station, a little bigger and stronger than I was when I had arrived in the town and used the railway to return to Grantham. The journey seemed to take much longer than the previous one but that was probably due to the lack of an interesting travelling companion to help pass the time with.

I started to walk to Pickworth but was fortunate to get a ride on a farm cart. It was only a little quicker, but it was much less tiring than walking. On the way, the carter started to regale me with some of the local gossip, but as it did not concern any of my narrow range of acquaintances in the area, it was not very interesting and I was too tired to pretend to listen. When he realized eventually, that he was talking to himself he became quiet and left me to my thoughts. I wondered what I would say to my father and whether he would show any interest in what I had been doing for the past months. He could hardly bother to get out of bed to see me depart on a new and unknown life, and I suspected that my homecoming would be just as unemotional as my departure.

The farm the carter was going to was outside Pickworth and I walked the last mile to the village and went to the forge. It was locked up and weeds were starting to grow in the area outside the door where my father had tethered the horses when he fitted new horseshoes. The little house alongside was also locked and the garden was overgrown. Weeds were sprouting where my Mother's vegetable garden had been.

It was starting to look very neglected and rundown and I could find nothing there to indicate what had caused the Smithy to close. Not knowing what else I could do, I went to the vicar to find out what had happened. The Reverend Daly did not recognize me at first. I was bigger than he remembered, tanned and wearing uniform, and I had to repeat my name twice before his memory returned. I was sorry to see how much he had aged in the short time I had been away. He had obviously had a seizure because his mouth was pulled down on one side and his speech had become much less clear.

The vicar said indistinctly, "I'm very sorry Jason, but your father is dead. It's a tragic homecoming for you."

"What happened?" I asked, stunned by the unexpected news.

"Your father had been fitting a new mould board onto a plough. Do you remember old Jeremiah, Jason, from Stone's farm? No? Well he often laboured for your father after you went to sea. On this day he was helping your father by holding the plough. Your Father was using a big sledgehammer to fettle a bent piece of metal when he grunted and dropped to the floor of the forge. Old Jeremiah came running to the vicarage to get me. We thought your father had suffered a seizure, but it seems a piece of metal had broken off the plough and gone through his eye directly into his brain. He just dropped dead on the spot." After a pause, to wipe up the spittle that had dribbled down his chin on the paralysed side, the vicar went on, "We buried your father in the churchyard next to your mother, Jason. I hope that's all right. You were away at sea, so we had to take what seemed the correct decision in your absence."

"You definitely made the right decision, Vicar. It's what I would have requested had I been here."

"I'm very sorry that you have returned to such bad news," he said.

"Thank you, Vicar," was all I could find to say.

This was so much worse than the poor reception I had anticipated that I felt nothing and stood rooted to the spot until the vicar broke in on my muddled thoughts,

"If there is anything I can do for you Jason please come to me and tell me what you need."

"Yes, of course, Vicar," I said, then "Good night, Vicar," and I walked away from the vicarage in a daze. I went to the Blue Bell to get food and a bed for the night.

I could barely believe what the Reverend Daly had told me of my father's untimely death. I walked and talked automatically; without apparent thought. My body dealt with the routine necessities of living, whilst my brain grappled with the unexpected and unwelcome intelligence that I had become an orphan.

I found myself at the Bluebell Inn and arranged a room for the night, but a few moments later could not have said whether the innkeeper or his wife had arranged the room for me. I do not remember climbing the stairs to the room, but I must have done, as I remember going down them after dropping the valise on the bedroom floor. I should have given it to the Reverend Daly, I thought inconsequentially.

Downstairs a buxom young waitress came to where I sat in a quiet alcove, away from the ingle nook and the inquisitive old timers drinking ale or cider there. When I asked for something to eat she said, "We have a nice piece of roast pork with apple sauce and fresh vegetables for dinner. Would you like some?"

It had been a long time since I had last eaten and I ordered a big portion with lots of crackling, thinking as I did so, that this was my father's favourite meal and wouldn't he have enjoyed it tonight as a celebration of my homecoming. The realization that I would never ever enjoy roast pork with my father again caused the dam that had been holding back my grief to break.

I rushed from the dining room trying desperately to get upstairs to the privacy of my room so that I wouldn't be seen weeping in public. In my haste I almost knocked over the waitress who was bringing in my dinner and I vaguely heard her outraged voice shouting after me, "Don't you want your roast pork, then?" But I was already on the stairs and moments later I had slammed shut the bedroom door.

I had not parted from my father on the best of terms. But I had returned home with the anticipation and belief that he would have been proud to learn of my experiences and achievements. Now he would never hear about them. In fact there was no one to hear about them and that made my sense of loneliness seem much more acute and harder to bear. The night dragged slowly past. I may have slept a little but I have no recollection of waking from a sleep, only of lying awake and knowing that there was no one in the world that I could call family. Discovering that one is an orphan is a very frightening experience and I believe it is so much worse when one is alone during the first long night of bereavement. My distress seemed to continue all night. I wept for the memory of my mother and father but also for myself as I realized that I was suddenly alone in the world.

Next morning I sat in my room in the inn still stunned by the news but no longer weeping with the emotion of bereaved loneliness. I was once again functioning as a human being but even so I wondered why the fates had taken away my remaining parent. I realized very quickly that there was no need to stay in Pickworth as I had no family ties to bind me. I decided that the most sensible thing to do would be to go back to the ship as soon as I could and rejoin my surrogate family on the Earl Canning. I packed my small bag, paid for the bed and the food I hadn't eaten and then went to see the vicar.

He must have seen me walking towards the vicarage as he came to his front door and greeted me with a mumbled "Good morning, Jason."

I responded with, "Good morning Vicar."

I was thankful that this hardworking and kindly old man still seemed to possess all of his faculties and went on to say, "I have decided to return to my ship as there is no reason to stay now I have no family here. I will never come back to work the forge so it is better if it is sold. If someone wishes to buy the forge and cottage for a fair price, I should be grateful if you would sell them both. Please keep the money for me until I return to Pickworth after my next voyage. I must also return the valise you lent me when I left. It has travelled a long way and been very useful. Thank you for your thoughtfulness all those months ago."

I turned away and walked to the church where I left my bag in the porch and went into the churchyard. I knelt down between the old and familiar grave, in which my mother had lain for many years and the newly turned ground where my Father now lay at peace. At least I hoped he was now at peace after so many unhappy years. I said a prayer for both of them and thanked them for my upbringing. I wished them peace in their eternal life together and shed the many lonely tears only a new orphan can shed over his parents.

I have no idea how long I knelt there in my abject misery and was only vaguely aware of the sound of a carriage stopping at the church gate and then the sound of footsteps approaching. Until I felt a hand on my shoulder the rest of the world had ceased to exist.

I turned and looked up into Captain Stewart's serious but kindly face, and he said, "Come away lad, you can do no more here." How he came to know I was in the churchyard, I never discovered, but I was very pleased to see a familiar face.

I stood up and brushed the dirt from my knees, turned away from the graves of my father and mother and followed Captain Stewart out of the churchyard. I climbed into the carriage and sat down beside him. The coachman had already put my bag in the boot and we set off.

"We will stay at the vicarage with my sister for a few days," was all he said and he settled back in his seat with a thoughtful and rather worried expression on his face.

The short journey passed in silence, apart from the creaking of harness and the clip, clop of the horse's hooves as both of us remained wrapped in our thoughts for the whole of the journey.

At the vicarage in Lenton, Captain Stewart's sister greeted us at the front door. Her first words were, "Mr. Smiley, I was so sorry to learn about the unfortunate death of Mr. Smiley," in a voice that suggested he had been simply an acquaintance, rather than my father. She went on, "I have prepared a room for you. Please stay with us for as long as you wish."

The captain and his sister ushered me into a small sitting room where we all sat down, stiffly and silently, all of us ill at ease. The maid brought tea and after she had poured it and handed each of us a cup and saucer she went out and closed the door.

Captain Stewart was looking very uncomfortable and fidgeted in his chair as if he was sitting on pins. He cleared his throat several times, as if he was about to speak, but uttered not a word. It was a very strange phenomenon considering how confident and loud he sounds on the bridge of the ship.

His sister looked at him several times as if to urge him to speak then said, "My brother has news about your past that we both believe it is important for you to know. We also have a suggestion for your future."

Captain Stewart took a deep breath "Shortly after you left the ship I received a letter from my sister giving me the news of Mr. Smiley's death. As I was instrumental in persuading you to leave Pickworth, I believed I should come here to help you overcome your grief. I handed over to the first mate and came the same day as you but on a later train. I was so late I hired the carriage in Grantham so that I could get here quickly. I have decided, after discussing the matter with my sister, to tell you about something that happened about twenty years ago."

He paused, went to a small walnut escritoire inlaid with fine brass strips, unlocked it and took out two old letters. He carried the letters across the room, resumed his seat and said, "Both my sister and I know from personal experience how very painful the loss of a parent can be, and you have our sympathy, Jason. Following the death of my father and a serious argument with my elder brother, I had no family home and when my sister married the vicar of Lenton he very kindly agreed that I could use one of the spare rooms in the vicarage when I was not at sea. I was very grateful for his generosity as I had nowhere else to go, and so I lived here for long periods."

He stopped for a moment to drink some tea, and I wondered where this conversation was going to lead me.

He put the cup and saucer carefully on a side table and said, "As you know your mother worked here at the vicarage, and because she was such an intelligent person, my sister started to teach her about the things a lady should know. Over a period of several years I came to appreciate your mother's charm and intelligence, and when she asked me a question, I was pleased not only to give her an answer, but also to have her company whilst I did so."

He paused again to consider his next words then said, "Over time our relationship changed from that of master and employee to that of equals with a very great regard and strong affection for each other. Although we fought against the desire we had for each other there came a day, just before I was to leave and rejoin my ship, when I could not resist the temptation to kiss this lovely and desirable woman. Her initial, surprised attempt to push me away was very quickly replaced with a desire as strong as my own as she returned my kisses. We couldn't help ourselves and in moments we were lying together on a chaise-longue."

Captain Stewart's face had developed a strong pinkish tinge and he was clearly much discomforted to be relating such a tale in front of his sister. I wondered why he thought it necessary to tell me. In the pause that followed this revelation I glanced at his sister, but she obviously had prior knowledge of these events and her face gave no indication of her opinion or feelings. I didn't know what to think.

Captain Stewart said simply, "We knew we were doing wrong but we were unable to stop. I would have married your mother then and there if that had been possible."

He went on, "The next day I had to leave to join my ship, and twelve months later I received this letter," and he handed one of the two letters to me and urged me to read it.

I opened the envelope and took out a single sheet of paper written in my mother's very familiar handwriting. When I looked at it, I could not stop the tears flooding my eyes and had to wait for a little composure to return before I could see what was written.

The captain and his sister waited patiently for me to compose myself, and this is what I read.

The Vicarage
Lenton
15 October 1842

Lieutenant James Stewart
East India Ship 'Endeavor'
King's Lynn.

Dear James

I write to tell you that I am with child.

I am happy that our love has been blessed and I am confident that you would marry me if you were in Lenton and not somewhere on the high seas.

My Dearest, you will understand the pressures I will come under if I remain unwed and my condition becomes known, particularly as I live in the vicarage. I have to take measures to give the child a father as I do not know when you will return to make an honest woman of me.

It is with a very heavy heart that I tell you that I will wed John Smiley, the blacksmith from Pickworth in a week. He is a good man and has asked for my hand several times in the past and been refused. He may suspect the reason for my sudden change of heart, but I am sure he will provide well for our child and me.

By the time that you read this I will be married and I implore you not to seek me out nor try to contact our child. It will be better for our child to be unaware of the truth about his parentage.

With all my love and devotion
Emily Tanner.

The captain then handed me the second letter and said, "Both the letters were waiting for me when I arrived back in Liverpool from a voyage to India. Please read this one as well."

I took the second letter and read it.

The Vicarage
Lenton
20 August 1843

Lieutenant James Stewart
East India Ship 'Endeavor'
King's Lynn.

Dear James

I am pleased to tell you that I have borne a healthy son and only wish that his true Father could see him.

I beg you to allow him to grow up without knowing the truth about his parentage. One day if by chance you meet him, you will recognize your features in his face and if you are in any doubt he has a small dark round birthmark on the small of his back.

Your Sister guessed the truth very quickly and has helped me as much as she is able. I bless her for her kindness to a servant in her husband's employ. She has allowed me to write what will be my last letter to the only man I will ever love and will see that it is posted.

If the vicar of Lenton knows, I cannot say, but he has given no sign of disproval.

With all my love and devotion
Emily Smiley.

Captain Stewart, after a glance at his sister, went on, "I knew that your Mother had married Mr. Smiley, as much to protect me as herself, and I did exactly as she requested. I desperately wanted to see your mother again and hold our son in my arms, but I honoured her wishes until long after my sister told me of her death. In fact I did not come here again until last year after an absence of some seventeen years."

He looked as if he was close to shedding a tear himself and surreptitiously wiped his nose and eyes with a large handkerchief he took from his sleeve. He said in a voice thickened by emotion, "I did not intend to go to Pickworth last year. I planned to go directly to Lenton, but my horse went lame. Chance brought us together and once I met you, I could not resist the temptation of knowing you better. Now that Mr. Smiley has died and no one can be hurt by the revelation, I would like to acknowledge you as my son, if you will accept me."

We all sat in silence wrapped in our individual thoughts. I noticed that the room was suffused with a rosy glow from the setting sun, but it did not lift my troubled spirits. The death of one father and the birth of a second all in the space of a day were a little difficult to assimilate.

The captain, and I was surprised at how much more easily the title 'Captain' fitted this man than 'Father' in my mind, was offering me his name and a measure of security that I would find difficult to achieve on my own. He was my natural father and it would certainly explain the similarities in appearance that people had noticed and sometimes remarked upon. I certainly had a small mole on my back.

On the other side, my mother had married John Smiley out of necessity not love and if he didn't know she was carrying another man's child at the time, he must have known when he saw how little I favoured him in colouring and eventually, stature. Even so, he had treated my mother and me as well as if I had been his own son and he taught me much about how to live a Christian life. Whether my mother had been unable to bear another child, or had been unwilling to try because of her love for the captain, was a secret she took with her to the grave. Mr. Smiley had much to be unhappy about I realized belatedly, yet he never treated either of us badly. As my mother had written in her letter, he was a good man and he had demonstrated the truth of her comment over the years.

I turned to the captain and his sister and without really consider- ing my words said simply, "I understand that you are my natural father, Captain, but the Jason Smiley that people meet and know is the result of the upbringing I was given by my mother and the man I believed to be my father. Mr. Smiley was a man who did his best for both my mother and me even when he must have known that I wasn't his child. I think it is best that I remain the man I have been for the past twenty years and retain the Smiley name. I hope that you will accept my deci- sion and not think badly of me."

It was a decision that I would come to regret in time, but it seemed the correct course of action at that moment.

Captain Stewart was visibly shocked by my decision and said, "Jason, I am really disappointed, but I understand and respect your decision. I hope you will always feel you can rely on me for advice and support when you need it."

In the circumstances I suppose I should not have been surprised by his next question but I was. He asked, "Do you wish to remain part of my crew? I will arrange for you to be transferred if you wish."

My reply was immediate and sincere. "Of course I wish to stay with you, sir," and he gave a little smile and nod of pleasure.

Mrs. Perceval had said very little during the afternoon but now turned to me and said, "I'm very sorry that you have turned down my brother's offer, but I will respect your decision. In public you will always be Mr. Jason Smiley and one of my brother's officers. In private you will always be my nephew, the son of James and Emily. I hope that will not be a source of difficulty for you, Jason."

"No of course not," I responded.

Captain Stewart went back to Liverpool and his duties soon after our discussion but for me the next few days passed quietly. I enjoyed the peace of the vicarage as I reconciled myself with the fact that I was publicly but not privately an orphan. Almost everyone loses their parents eventually and it is part of growing up to overcome the grief and loss that is felt so strongly. By the end of the second day I was in a much better frame of mind and starting to look at the books and papers that were in abundant supply in the study.

On the morning of the third day the vicar of Pickworth sent a message to Lenton saying succinctly, "I have a buyer for the forge and cottage. Come at once,"

This was very good news, and I was glad to go to Pickworth to meet the prospective purchaser. The price offered was fair and so without any haggling at all, I agreed to sell everything to a blacksmith from a village about twenty miles away. He desperately wanted to leave his Father's forge and set up on his own and be independent of the interference he was receiving from his aging parent. He bought everything, forge, anvil, tools and even the furniture in the house and suddenly I was no longer penniless. I repaid the money the vicar had provided for my journey to Liverpool and then gave him the same amount again as a practical way of saying thank you and perhaps helping someone else change their life.

I went to Lenton and said a quick goodbye to Mrs. Perceval with a promise to visit her as soon as I came back.

I managed to get a ride on a farm cart as far as Grantham market and then caught the train back to Liverpool and my floating home. I paused in Liverpool only long enough to deposit the money I had received from the sale of the forge in the Mercantile Bank in Water Street. The Reverend Perceval had loaned me a thick, strong, leather money belt and insisted that I wore it under my shirt. I was very thankful to be rid of the bulky, uncomfortable thing strapped around my waist.

When I returned on board, the mate greeted me in a kindly fashion. He said simply, "I was very sorry to learn from Captain Stewart that your father died whilst we were at sea. It is very hard to arrive home and receive such news, But as you know life must go on."

"Aye, sir. Thank you, sir," I said.

After the mate had given me my orders for the next few days I went down to my cabin as my first watch would not start until eight bells in the afternoon.

I entered into my work and training with as much energy as I could muster and the pain of Mr. Smiley's passing diminished as people had said it would. The ship was soon fully loaded and we made the now familiar exit down into the River Mersey and set off on another voyage to Bombay.

About a year after my father died one of those events that shape you as a man took place. It was a hurricane in the Indian Ocean of a severity, we discovered later, that had sent many well found ships to the bottom of the sea with the loss of all their crews to sharks or drowning.

It happened like this.

We had passed Madagascar several days earlier and had been steaming calmly through a gentle swell with a slight head wind on a direct bearing for Bombay. We were nearing the end of another voyage and as the realization that we would be able to go ashore in a few more days percolated through the ship there was a general lightening in the mood of everyone on board.

The first indication that all was not well with the weather came with the arrival of a long swell running at an angle to the swell we had been comfortably riding. After some hours of steaming through a rather confused sea state the new swell started to dominate the situation and the ship started to roll uncomfortably. Captain Stewart altered course towards the east so that the ship rolled less. We could see some cloud on the eastern horizon and were struck by the unusual appearance of the sea. The wind we had experienced for some days had died away and the swell had a smooth oily appearance. An air of tension suddenly pervaded the ship and I could see the expressions on the faces of the more experienced crewmen as they assessed the situation.

Captain Stewart turned to the first mate after studying the eastern horizon for the tenth time in as many minutes and said "We are in for a strong blow by the look of it."

"Aye, Sir. It looks very ominous," agreed the first mate.

"Take Mr. Smiley with you and go around the ship with the bosun and some men and make sure that all dead lights are closed, hatches shut and dogged and anything that is not fixed to the ship is shored into place."

"Aye, Sir," said the first mate "Come along Mr. Smiley. Shake a leg!"

There followed an exhausting five or six hours as we took every precaution that experienced sailors could devise to ensure the safety of the ship in the storm that was clearly bearing down on us. As we worked the atmosphere on board changed dramatically and I realized suddenly that there was fear in the air. Most of the men worked stoically away, but there were some whose fear was almost palpable as they spent more time looking at the horizon than at their tasks.

Seeing their fear I realized that I was frightened as well, although I tried not to show it.

The mate, with the bosun and his men, methodically examined the ship from the bows to the stern. I noticed and understood the seriousness of our situation when I saw the mate pulling, pushing and carrying with the bosun and his men, and I joined in where ever I could. Both anchors were securely lashed to the forecastle deck. The doors to the paint locker and stores under the forecastle were dogged closed. The cargo stowage was checked and reinforced where necessary and then the hatch covers were checked and all the fixings tightened. The life boats were securely tied down onto their chocks and the canvas boat covers firmly secured after checking that oars were lashed to the benches and food and water were stowed safely in the lockers inside. We turned our attention to the masts and rigging when we had finished on deck. Some small storm sails were hauled up and rigged in place of the usual canvas and securely tied down onto the yards. The lashings on all the remaining sails were checked and then a second set of ties were fixed to ensure the sails could not accidentally blow free.

In the meantime another small group of men with the second officer in charge worked methodically through the accommodation to secure anything that could slide about on deck and cause injury.

In the engine room the chief engineer was taking similar precautions and in the galley the cook was preparing as much food as possible before the galley fire had to be extinguished and the cooking pots secured.

All the time the motion of the ship was becoming increasingly violent as the wind and sea rose in time with the advance of the storm. Back on the bridge there was nothing left to occupy our minds and hands and we had to wait for nature to do her worst. We had done our best to prepare the ship for the onslaught to come but we couldn't do anything about the natural fear of the unknown forces bearing down on us.

The captain reduced speed and headed more directly into the approaching seas and whilst we were pitching considerably more than I had previously experienced the seas rarely broke over the forecastle. With the enforced idleness my fear increased. I could feel it in my stomach and I had a strong urge to visit the heads even 'though I had been there not many minutes before. My knees felt as if they were trembling and I know my hand was, as I could see the tremors when I reached out for a cup of coffee the cook's mate brought to the bridge.

Although I was trying to hide my apprehension my fearful reaction to the approaching storm must have been visible because the mate said quietly to me "Being afraid of the unknown is quite natural, Mr. Smiley. Even those of us who have experienced severe storms at sea before, are secretly fearful, because we do not know what is going to happen in this particular storm. We have a good captain, a well found ship and we have taken all the precautions we can. Now we must wait and you must learn to master your fear and not let the men see it. You are an officer and they will look to you for clear headed guidance during this crisis."

"Aye, Sir. I will do my best."

It was the only response I could give and the mate gave me a thump of encouragement on the shoulder that almost knocked me over.

Before long Mr. Evans appeared for his watch and I had duties to attend to that took my mind off my fear. It was still there, but I had drawn great comfort from the mate's words. To know that experienced officers like him were also fearful made me feel stronger although in retrospect I suppose it could have made me feel worse.

As the day progressed the storm bore down on us. The sky had become full of black threatening clouds shot through with flickering streaks of lightening. The screaming of the wind and the continuous crashing of thunder was almost unbearable already, but the wind continued to increase in ferocity and the seas to get bigger and bigger. The wind started to blow the tops off the waves and as far as I could see big patches of yellowy white foam tumbled along the waves. The noise of wind and sea was deafening. The ship rose and fell with increasing violence and very soon the bow would fall, fall, fall and bury itself in the face of the next giant wave with a crash that shook every plate and rivet in the hull. The forecastle would disappear for much too long for peace of mind in a welter of foaming water that ran off over the sides in torrents as the bow climbed skywards clear of the water before starting to fall again. It was rather like looking at a rock on the seashore that was being alternately submerged and exposed by each passing wave. I decided to stay on the bridge, when my watch with Mr. Evans was finished, as I was sure I would be immediately seasick if I ventured below. But to maintain my position and defy the exaggerated up and down movements of the ship I had developed a grip on the rail that a limpet would have been proud of.

I concentrated very hard on the mate's homily and was desperately trying not to show my abject fear, when I happened to see the helmsman. He was standing calmly with his legs astride and could not have been more perfectly balanced in front of the wheel if the deck had been completely stable. As I watched him I noticed that he would turn the wheel a few spokes one way and then a few more the same or the other way and the ship always managed to meet the worst of the approaching seas with her bows. Looking out over the helmsman's shoulders at the approaching storm driven waves, I could see no reason for his actions, but knew that he was successfully easing our passage through the storm. Captain Stewart returned to the bridge, looked around the horizon and tapped the barometer. I think the elevation of his eyebrows must have mimicked the depression of the mercury, as he looked even grimmer than he had a few minutes before.

He saw me observing the helmsman and said calmly "When there is time you should watch him carefully, Mr. Smiley. There are few helmsmen better at reading the sea"

He looked around what was visible of the horizon and ordered, "Mr. Smiley, this storm will go on for at least another day and you cannot stand there without food all that time. I need you strong and full of energy if there is a crisis. Go below and get some food and as much rest as possible and come back on watch with Mr. Evans."

"Aye, Sir," was all I could say and I turned and left the bridge.

In our cabin I found Mr. Evans already wedged in his bunk reading a book and looking as calm as any one could with the ship rising, falling and rolling as it was. I followed his example and realized that my fear of instant seasickness was unfounded and I followed Mr. Evans example and wedged myself in my bunk with a book about navigation that the captain had loaned to me.

After an unsatisfactory cold lunch, as the ship's gyrations prohibited cooking, Evans and I made our way to the bridge to start our watch. It was only early afternoon and already nearly dark.

The wind was screeching and howling like a wild animal and the clouds seemed to be brushing the tops of the masts. I couldn't tell if it was rain or spray but water was being driven horizontally by the strength of the wind.

But it was the sight of the sea that made me fear for my life. I had never seen such an appalling sight. As Evans and I arrived on the bridge we could only grab hold of the rail as the bows started to fall into the trough between two enormous waves. We were going down the back of the previous wave towards the base of a wall of water that appeared to be higher than the foremast. The whole structure of the ship seemed to vibrate as the propeller came out of the water and raced until the engineer could cut back the steam supply. He then had to re-open the steam supply as soon as the propeller re-entered the water so that we maintained steerage way as we ploughed into the next wave. Without the ability to steer we would broach to and once that happened we would soon be broadside and a full capsize was inevitable the seas were so big. Our lives for those minutes depended on the skill of the engineer to start and stop the engine without any external guidance.

With that realization, the fear that I had managed to hold in check for some hours struck again. My bowels turned to water and my legs felt so weak I was sure I would fall to the deck but for the tight grip I had on the rail.

The bows disappeared into another approaching mountain of water and we kept on going downward. The buoyancy that normally started to force the bows up appeared to be absent and it seemed as if even the bridge was going to feel the full force of the approaching wave. At the last moment the bows started to rise and the top of the wave passed just below the bridge deck with an indescribable cacophony of noise. All we could see forward of the bridge were the masts protruding from the maelstrom and as the wave passed astern we could see that it had taken the smashed remnants of our life boats together with some of the davits with it.

Captain Stewart turned to me after examining the damage on the boat deck and ordered, "Mr. Smiley, go below and aft. Examine the deck where the davits were fixed. If there are any holes in the deck plate get some men from the bosun. Use timber and canvas to block the holes to stop water coming in."

For some seconds my fear was so intense that I could neither move nor speak and I could sense the Captain's anger at my insubordination starting to rise. The Mate and Mr. Evans were both staring at me and I knew I had to move and respond or be branded a coward for the rest of my days.

I took a deep breath, gritted my teeth, straightened my back and said, "Aye, sir."

I turned and left the bridge as quickly as the violent motion permitted with the first mate's, "Don't forget what I told you, Mr. Smiley" echoing in my ears.

I was so frightened that my legs could barely support me and I almost fell down the ladder to the next deck. I wanted desperately to find a dark corner to curl up in and then put my hands over my ears to blot out noise of the storm and the ship being twisted and shaken. I just wanted to hide from the worst experience of my life and it was only the greater fear of Captain Stewart's anger and disgust that prevented a public demonstration of cowardice.

I took an oil lamp from a hook in the companionway and hurried aft to the area below the lifeboat station. I knew from the sounds of cascading water that there were some big holes in the deck plates long before I reached there. I examined the port side first and then went over to the starboard side. On both sides of the ship where the davit base bolts had been pulled out of the deck plate there were a series of small holes to plug. The serious problem was on the port side where the davit bolts had held and a piece of the deck plate had been torn from its rivets on three sides and bent upwards to form a wedge shaped opening about three feet square and two feet deep at the top. Water came sluicing in through this opening as each mountainous wave passed.

As quickly as I could, I staggered back along the companionway to find the bosun. I described the damage to him, ordered him to send a messenger to the bridge to inform the captain about it and then set off back to the damaged area with the ship's carpenter and a group of seamen carrying dunnage, wedges, and canvas.

We had nothing big enough to cover the opening in one piece so after a few moments of thought and a brief discussion with the carpenter I ordered him to start on one side of the hole and build frames consisting of a horizontal and two uprights held rigidly between the upper and lower deck plates with folding wedges. We sandwiched a thick piece of canvas bigger than the hole between the horizontal and the upper deck to seal the gaps between the timbers as best we could. It was like working under a waterfall and we were all soaked and gasping for air before many minutes of frantic activity had passed but progressively we closed the opening and the cascades of water steadily diminished to a trickle. As soon as we had finished I instructed the carpenter to split the group into two gangs and seal up all the other holes where the davits had been torn out.

The messenger I had instructed the bosun to send to the bridge came back and said the captain wanted to know how long it would take to seal the major damage as one of the bilge pumps had blocked. I could feel some sympathy for the messenger as his paleness and shaking limbs showed clearly how frightened he was and I could only marvel at how confident I now felt having forced myself to overcome my fear. I put the messenger to work with the other men and went back to the bridge to report progress.

Conditions had deteriorated whilst I had been below. It was now completely dark and the helmsman had to steer a compass course and could not see enough to ease our passage through the mountainous seas. As a result the ship was being assailed by huge walls of water that seemed to come at us from all directions, except directly on the bow.

The ship pitched and rolled and staggered from crest to trough to crest in a mind destroying cacophony of noise and in the middle of the bridge, Captain Stewart stood swaying to the motion and looking as if he was enjoying his fight with the elements.

He saw me arrive on the bridge and beckoned to me. "What is the situation under the lifeboat station now, Mr. Smiley?"

"The big hole on the port side has been sealed with canvas and dunnage, Captain and the leak there has been reduced to a trickle. The carpenter has four men with him to seal up the remaining small holes."

"Thank you, Mr. Smiley. Return below and when the men have finished send them back to the bosun. Report back to the bridge and complete your watch when you have finished below."

"Aye, sir."

About thirty minutes later I staggered back along the companionway, bouncing from wall to wall as the ship lurched and rolled savagely in what was becoming more of a beam sea and climbed up to the bridge. Captain Stewart had just joined the Mate and Mr. Evans and he beckoned me to join them when he saw me.

He said, "The Engineer cannot repair the broken bilge pump. He needs a blacksmith to straighten and temper the bent shaft. The other pump cannot deal with the amount of water that is entering the hull. Fortunately you managed to seal the major leak quickly, Mr. Smiley, or our situation would be much worse. We are slowly making water and whilst not dangerous it is undesirable to lose any of our buoyancy. If the second pump also fails then our situation will deteriorate very rapidly."

I said quickly, "Captain, I can repair the shaft if you give permission."

With much more patience than I deserved, Captain Stewart took time in the middle of the storm to say, "I know you have the skill, Mr. Smiley, but you are an officer and must think about the implications of what you are suggesting. We can barely stand, the deck is heaving so much and you wish me to give permission for you to light the forge. I doubt if the coal will stay in the forge long enough to catch fire and if it does I have no wish to see red hot coals rolling about the deck. A fire on board is not desirable at any time and in a storm like this we have enough to think about already. In any case, assuming the coal stays in place and the shaft is heated satisfactorily so that you could work on it how do you propose to stand still to use your tools. Clearly it is not possible in these conditions."

He was right and I felt a fool for not thinking it through before eagerness opened my mouth.

I uttered the only appropriate response, "Aye, sir."

Captain Stewart turned to the first mate and ordered "Rig the hand pumps, Mr. Mate and organize a team of off duty men to start pumping. Mr. Evans will remain on watch with me. Mr. Smiley, I want you to go around the interior of the ship and stop up any leaks you find."

"Aye, Sir," we said almost in unison and the first mate and I left the bridge to carry out our instructions.

I went to the bosun, explained my orders and left with two men to start my inspection. If I found a leak I would send one man back to get men and materials to affect the repair. Both men were clearly very nervous and were bleeding from cuts to their heads sustained when they had been thrown against an unyielding piece of the hull.

One said in a voice that cracked and quavered from fear, "Are we going to sink, Sir?"

"Not with me on board," I replied with counterfeited confidence as I remembered once again the mate's homily.

We went forward along the lower deck and unbolted the hatch cover leading into the upper tier of the forward hold. We climbed through into the hold and stood for a moment to listen to the creaking and groaning of the cargo as it moved against its props and lashings. I was thankful we had no heavy machinery on board that could break free and threaten the life of the ship by crashing about the inside of the hold as the ship pitched and rolled. We crawled forward over the cargo and started to open the hatch that led into the space just below the forecastle. Fortunately we were cautious and had progressively loosened each bolt only a little at a time, so when the blanking plate suddenly freed itself from its seal it could only move a small amount. Even so the pressure of water spurting around the edge of the plates was very great and soon there was a large puddle on the deck and sea water started draining down into the cargo below us in the hold. I set one sailor to retighten all the bolts and sent the other to the bridge to inform the captain what we had found.

I crawled back across the cargo with the intention of continuing the search for leaks. I hung my oil lamp on a hook beside the hatch. As I started to enter the hatch the ship lurched violently and the side of my head slammed into the edge of the steel bulkhead. My eyes registered a shower of sparks then nothing until I felt myself being moved and tried to open my eyes. One did and I saw the first mate's anxious face staring down at me, but the other stayed closed and I had the worst headache I had ever experienced. After a few minutes water was splashed on my face and my second eye opened.

The mate said, "Lie still for a moment Mr. Smiley, you have a bad cut on the side of your forehead. I'll wash it and bind it up then you can try to stand."

"Aye, sir."

A little later, after the first mate had finished bandaging my head, he helped me to my feet. I stood upright, but had to be held up and balanced against the extravagant movements of the ship, for some minutes. Then I shook off the supporting hands and stood on my own.

"Very well, Mr. Smiley, please carry on with your inspection, and I will go up to the bow. When you finish report to the captain on the bridge."

"Aye, sir."

With a sailor following me I searched through the rest of the ship but could find no more places where water was entering the ship. I sent the sailor to the bosun and then went to the bridge to report. Captain Stewart looked at me with concern on his face but listened to my report and then sent me below to get the bandage changed. When I looked in a mirror and saw the blood soaked rag wrapped around my head I was surprised at how bad I looked. The cook unwrapped the old bandage, cleaned the wound and made sure there was a good thick pad of clean cotton over it before he bound it up again.

He said in a matter of fact way "I see you hit your head on the edge of a hatchway, Mr. Smiley. It's a clean cut and the bleeding has nearly stopped. You'll have a good scar to brag to the girls about when it heals."

He was correct and the scar that you can still see on the side of my forehead is the result of an unfortunate collision between my head and the steel plate at the edge of a hatch. I see it every time I comb my hair and it has been at least a daily reminder of the day that I was nearly branded a coward. The sight and feel of it, has served to stiffen my backbone whenever my life appeared to be in danger.

The ship had been through two days of torture, but when I went back on the bridge after having my head bandaged by the cook, I found that the wind had eased a little. It appeared that we would survive after all. After this experience I didn't think I would ever be so frightened of a storm again. I would have a healthy respect for the strength of Mother Nature of course, but not near paralysis from fear.

As the day progressed the wind started to ease and when the skies cleared Captain Stewart was able to fix his position at noon for the first time in two days. We had been steaming steadily into the wind and sea for the whole of that time, but when the position was plotted, we found that we had drifted back almost to Madagascar. If the storm had persisted for another night we could have run aground on the island. We were lucky.

As soon wind and sea permitted the manoeuvre, Captain Stewart resumed his course for Bombay and we started to take stock of the damage the ship had incurred.

When we reached Bombay and found out over the next days and weeks how many ships were believed to have sunk during the storm we could count ourselves very lucky indeed.

Although we never carried cargo that was likely to attract pirates, there was always a possibility that we could be boarded. To ensure that we could at the least defend ourselves if attacked, Captain Stewart insisted that we all practiced with daggers, cutlasses and swords and we also had target practice with pistol and rifle. Shooting at an inanimate object was quite easy and I became a reasonable marksman, but when it came to fighting with sharp blades against another member of the crew this was a very different proposition. Even in practise mistakes happen and the thought of accidentally maiming or killing someone gave me nightmares. I wasn't too keen about being maimed or killed myself, so practicing with a dagger or cutlass was not an enjoyable experience. I had to obey my orders of course and like everyone else on board, I developed sufficient mastery of the weapons to give a good account of myself if the need arose.

Captain Stewart kept all the weapons under lock and key in the armoury behind his cabin. He did this on the assumption that he would have sufficient notice of an attack by pirates when we were at sea, to be able to arm all the officers and men in his crew before the boarders could get on board.

What Captain Stewart had never anticipated was an attack whilst we were moored in a safe harbour with only an anchor watch on duty. Only a small number of the crew were asleep in their bunks and the rest of them were on shore enjoying the local drink and probably the women as well.

But it happened.

I must have been about eighteen or nineteen at the time. I hadn't gone ashore with the others as I had no money to spend on wine and women and had gone to bed feeling a little disgruntled as a result.

I awoke that night knowing something was very wrong.

There was an unusual and pungent smell of long unwashed body and soiled clothing filling my nostrils. As I started to sit up a filthy hand clamped down over my mouth. I saw the light from the porthole reflecting on a long knife blade that appeared to be about to plunge into my throat, so I lay still again and the hand moved to my shoulder and urged me out of the bunk. I was taken up onto the foredeck where I joined the other members of the crew that had been captured.

There were only four of us and as I was certain that the captain and first mate had been on board when I went to my bunk, I was fearful that they had been killed or injured resisting capture. Only one man out of the three captured with me had any real experience that could be counted on in an emergency, and he was the helmsman, Stubbins. The other two were still wet behind the ears.

I knew that the second and third officers had gone ashore with the intention of staying the night if they could find "suitable accommodation." I had no doubt they would be well looked after and would not reappear until late the following day and certainly much too late to help in this situation.

The pirate who had captured me was joined by two others. I looked at these three ill favoured and dirty members of humanity and wondered what they wanted with us and a ship with no cargo worth stealing.

We found out after they jabbered amongst themselves for a time. They had no use for us. They wanted the ship and we were forced at knife point down into a boat moored alongside. The mooring line was cut and we started to drift away towards the open sea. In the pale moonlight I realized that the current was taking us against the wind and noticed that we didn't drift very far from the ship. When the tide started to turn the current slackened, the wind had more affect and we soon found ourselves close to the ship again. I told everyone to be quiet and by paddling carefully with our hands we managed to guide the boat back to the gangway where we tied up again as quietly as possible.

We sat in the boat for a little time as quiet as novices in church and listened. We could hear faintly but clearly, drunken singing. There was some shouting but after a time silence. Leaving the two inexperienced hands to guard the boat Stubbins and I climbed quietly up the gangway and looked along the deck. We could see two of the pirates stretched out on the forward hatch cover and each had a bottle of brandy beside him. The third man was not visible and we didn't know if there were any others in the party who had attacked us that we hadn't seen. I hoped not.

Stubbins slipped along the deck like a ghost, picked up a coil of rope, cut off a length and had tied up the first man before I had recovered from my surprise at his movement. I started to follow him and he cut off another length of rope which he pushed into my hands with a gesture towards the second man. I grabbed the rope, ran to the second man as quietly as possible, grabbed his head, lifted it and then bashed it as hard as I could against the hatch cover. It made a very satisfactory thud and he went limp. I turned him onto his face tied his hands tightly behind his back and then tied his feet and trussed them tightly towards his hands. I stuffed the dirty greasy end of his head scarf into his mouth to gag him.

Stubbins, I noticed was doing the same.

I looked around for the third man and felt my heart lurch as I saw him bearing down on me with his knife high in the air. He clearly had not been drinking and rather stupidly I wondered if he had signed Evans pledge. At the last possible moment I threw myself sideways and simultaneously a shot rang out and my assailant collapsed on top of me. He was dead I realized when I managed to extract myself from under his dirty smelly carcass.

I looked up to where the shot had come from and saw Captain Stewart on the roof of the bridge and realized how he had escaped capture. Moments later the first mate appeared behind the Captain's shoulder

The guards from the local prison were very quickly on board. They put the two live prisoners into manacles and leg irons and took them away together with the body. The two we had captured had been sentenced to death for some brutal murders and we were assured by the commandant of the prison that they would be very carefully guarded until their sentences could be carried out. In the circumstances we were lucky to have been cast adrift. Another murder or four could have made little difference to such hardened criminals.

For my part I had learnt a valuable lesson about planning for every conceivable eventuality. I know Captain Stewart had learnt the same lesson because the next day he established small caches of weapons in well constructed and locked cupboards in different parts of the ship and gave keys to senior members of the crew.

The last experience I will describe from this learning and maturing period of my life is one of which I am not proud, but like most life experiences I was a better person at the end.

At least I like to think so.

You will realize, of course, that when I was off watch and in port I did what my shipmates did. We went ashore and enjoyed whatever was on offer. My fellow officers were as quick to instruct me about how to drink and buy the services of a local woman as they were to teach me seamanship. There was no reason for me to reject their example and I can only marvel at the good fortune that prevented me from catching the pox. So many other sailors had caught it and died.

Perhaps the officers procured a better class of woman. They

were certainly very expensive I remember.

The particular incident I have in mind started when the second officer and I went ashore in a very attractive tropical port that had better remain anonymous.

We had found a small hut on the water front that was thatched with palm fronds and looked quite attractive. It had large woven shutters in place of windows and these had been raised to allow the sea breeze to flow through the room. To provide some light there were a few oil lamps scattered about and they flickered and smoked in the draft. At the end of the room opposite the door and covering half the length of the back wall was a bar and to the right of the bar a few locally made rough tables and benches. The second officer and I chose one of the tables, and I sat with my back to the wall. We were sampling a drink that was called Island Whisky by the barman. Clearly it had no connection with Scotland, apart from its name, but it had the fire to warm the stomach appropriately. Equally important it was cheap. Standing by or leaning on the bar was a small group of dark skinned women with black curly hair who ranged from the juvenile to the ancient in age and from attractive to ugly in appearance.

Regardless of their ages and appearance, my red hair seemed to be attracting a great deal of attention and discussion amongst the assembled women. One of the younger women, after some backchat and pushing from her companions, came over to our table and sat down.

She was a very attractive young woman with sparkling deep brown eyes and just enough clothing to maintain her modesty. She said something, but in a language we could not understand. The three of us sat and looked at each other in frustration for a long moment. Then, when the chorus of encouragement from her cohorts reach a crescendo, she reached out her hands and pulled the bottom of my shirt out of my trousers. Before the Island Whisky would let me stop her, she had pushed my shirt up and started examining the hairs on my chest with great interest. She turned back to the other women, nodded, pointed at my chest, looked down, and said something that had them all "ooing" in anticipation.

Where this could have ended is a matter of conjecture as suddenly everyone went quiet, and the girl went as white as a black-skinned person can.

A very big man had come into the room and was striding towards the bar. He noticed the girl sitting beside me and then saw her hand on my chest. His eyes widened for a moment then he shouted something as his hand slid behind his back and reappeared with a wicked looking knife clutched in his fist.

He gestured at the girl and she disappeared back into the crowd of women who then closed ranks with their backs to us. He gestured with his knife that I should stand up and I pulled my shirt down as I did so. As he sliced at me with his knife I stepped back, but not quickly enough and the point sliced through the front of my shirt and cut across my ribs. I looked down as the pain cut through the alcoholic haze and again failed to move far enough and the next cut burnt across my chest. I could feel my temper rising and I threw the contents of my glass in his face. He stepped back to wipe his hand over his eyes and before he could renew his attack someone pushed the hilt of a knife into my hand.

Suddenly the anxious hours of training with a knife paid an unexpected dividend. My anger evaporated and I was full of confidence. I pushed past the restraining hand of the second officer and started to go after my assailant. I was shocked but exhilarated by the realization that I wasn't interested in just retaliating and cutting him, I was intent on teaching him a lesson, killing him if necessary. I didn't realize that I was capable of such violent thoughts. He must have seen the look in my eyes and known what I intended because he started to back away. He was a coward as well as a bully, and I went after him and cut him as he had cut me, then I sliced him across the chest again. I stepped back for a second and then went forward to attack him again but he threw down his knife and ran from the bar.

The second officer looked at me as if he had never seen me before and said "Good God, Jason, I thought you were going to kill him."

"I intended to," I replied calmly, "but he ran away before I could."

"You will have to be careful Jason," he said.

The bar was in turmoil and not a place for us to linger and in any case I needed to get my cut and bleeding ribs cleaned and bandaged. We walked to the landing point and went back to the ship. The cook was not well pleased to be dragged from his bunk to deal with the result of a fight but treated me without too much fuss when the second mate had related what had happened.

So I acquired some more scars to brag to the girls about, but at the same time I was ashamed of my lack of restraint and worried that I might really hurt someone one day if something similar should happen again. The scars on my ribs do serve as a reminder that I have to restrain my temper and keep control of a vicious streak I did not know I possessed.

When I was approaching my twenty second or twenty third birthday, we made our customary landfall on the west coast of India and anchored in Bombay harbour after another long and uneventful voyage. I had now been a cadet for some years and was starting to feel as if I was overdue for promotion to third officer. Unfortunately this was not likely to happen in the near future as there seemed to be no prospect of one of my superior officers being promoted out of the "Earl Canning."

As soon as practical after our arrival we started discharging our cargo and had unloaded about half when Captain Stewart had a visitor.

Fat, florid of complexion, sweating profusely in the not very hot midday sun, Sir Algernon Cuthbert Cummings, the Bombay Representative of the Anglo Indian Telegraph Company, heaved his not inconsiderable bulk up the steeply sloping gangway having ponderously transshipped from a local ferryboat.

He climbed awkwardly down to the deck and demanded, to all within earshot, "Take me to your Captain," and moments later "Immediately do you hear."

As the only officer on deck at that moment I introduced myself, "Good afternoon, sir. I am Cadet Smiley, sir. The captain's cabin is this way if you will follow me."

I lead our imposing visitor to the captain's cabin, knocked on the door and when Donovan answered said, "This is Sir Algernon Cummings to visit the captain."

As I went to resume my duties I heard Donovan say, "If you will just wait a moment, sir, I will inform my captain that you are here."

In a hot climate the portholes are kept open and Captain Stewart's was no exception. We heard nothing of the captain's utterances, but his visitor would occasionally let his enthusiasm overcome good sense and decorum, and pompous phrases delivered in an upper crust and fruity voice, like "For Queen and Country" and "Doing one's duty" and "Assisting in this great enterprise" escaped from the captain's cabin through the porthole.

After about an hour the captain escorted his visitor to the head of the gangway and watched the ponderous bulk waddle down to the ferryboat, which nearly capsized as he stood on the gunwale to get in. He watched calmly as his erstwhile visitor lumbered to his waiting carriage and even across half the width of the harbour he heard, as we all did, the carriage springs screech in protest as he climbed aboard and plumped him self down.

Sir Algernon Cuthbert Cummings was driven away and not seen again, as far as I am aware.

Captain Stewart returned to his cabin, sent for the mate and for another hour comparative peace returned to the ship as loading and unloading continued without incident.

SEVEN

Dead Man's Shoes

Following his usual practice of keeping us informed of changing circumstances the captain called a meeting of all the officers in the late afternoon, some hours after his surprise visitor had left.

Captain Stewart said, "As you are all aware by now, Sir Algernon Cuthbert Cummings visited me this afternoon. You are probably not aware that he is the Bombay Representative of the Anglo Indian Telegraph Company.

Captain Stewart paused to drink some water and then went on, "The Telegraph Company needs to send a party of surveyors to the Oman in connection with the construction of the electric telegraph between Britain and India. The information the surveyors have to obtain is required urgently as work to lay the submarine cable from Gwadur is reported to have already started. I understand from Sir Algernon that the originally proposed location of the telegraph repeater station on the narrow neck of land between Malcolm's Inlet and Elphinstone Inlet on the Mussandam Peninsula is being abandoned due to the animosity of the local tribesmen."

Captain Stewart stopped and looked at us for a moment before saying, "As the first mate already knows I have been requested to take the surveyors to a small isolated island in Elphinstone Inlet where the Telegraph Company now plans to establish the repeater station. We will have to wait about three days whilst they do the survey work and then return to Bombay with all possible speed. Our schedule will be delayed by about ten days but I do not believe this will be of any significance."

Captain Stewart indicated on a chart he had open on his desk the location of Elphinstone Inlet in relation to Bombay and went on, "The Telegraph Company doesn't wish to rely on a sailing ship and the vagaries of the wind. They are convinced that they can only carry out the task with the required degree of urgency if they hire a steam driven ship. The

Earl Canning is the only steam driven ship in Bombay at present and that is why we have been requested to stop discharging cargo and sail as soon as possible."

Captain Stewart turned to the Chief Engineer, "We will be steaming for about six days, Chief, do we need to bunker before we leave?"

"Aye, sir. It would be prudent to fill the bunkers. If you order the coal barges immediately we can finish loading before tomorrow night."

"Very good," said Captain Stewart. "I'll issue the necessary order. If you wish to start making preparations Chief, you have my permission to leave this meeting."

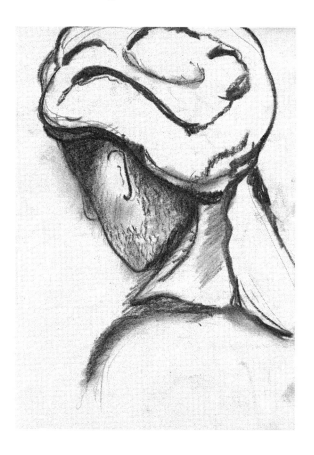

"Thank you, Captain," said the Chief Engineer as he got up and walked to the cabin door. "I'll start getting up steam."

Captain Stewart resumed his narrative as the chief closed the cabin door. "I have the company's authority to accept casual charters, provided regular customers are not inconvenienced so I have contacted the owners of the various consignments of cargo remaining on board. They have all advised me that it will not cause difficulty if discharge is delayed for one or two weeks. Consequently, I have decided to accept the charter."

Not that I could refuse," he added thoughtfully, "Two of the Gold Star Line directors are also directors of Anglo Indian, and they would not have supported me if I had refused to take the charter."

"Shore leave is cancelled. After a long voyage I know all the crew have been waiting for unloading to finish so that they could have a run ashore, but circumstances have changed. They will have a run ashore in ten days time. Leave for you officers is also cancelled. So Mr. Smiley will have to wait a little longer before he renews his acquaintance with the delights of Bombay," he added with a wink in my direction. The other officers chuckled at that, as I had been talking about what I should see and where I should go with some enthusiasm.

The captain concluded by saying, "We need to secure the remaining cargo, close the hatches and make all ready for sea. I wish to sail as soon as we finish coaling and our passengers are on board with their equipment."

"Any questions?" Captain Stewart asked and when no one responded he said "Very well gentlemen, please carry on," and to the first mate, "Mr. Richards, please remain."

We started putting Captain Stewart's orders into affect whilst the captain and mate studied the little navigational information they had available and planned the route to be taken.

The prospect of new faces on board and a change of schedule were very welcome to the officers and the news soon spread amongst the rest of the crew who accepted the delay to their shore leave stoically.

Next day during the late afternoon whilst Evans and I were on watch, we saw a barouche and a wagon arrive on the shore opposite where we were anchored. Five men climbed down from the barouche and all went to the wagon except one individual, who strode to the water's edge and waved his helmet as he hailed a small passing Shu'ai. I noticed his hair was white and assumed he was quite old but he moved with the spring of a young man in his step. After some arm waving and shouting, that we could hear but not understand because of the distance, some money changed hands and the men at the wagon started to carry boxes and bags down to the water's edge. They passed them up over the bows of the Shu'ai to the crew of the boat who stowed them on deck, then climbed on board themselves. The Shu'ai was poled off the bank and the Indian crew commenced rowing it out to us and tied up alongside the gangway. The leader of the group climbed over the side of the boat onto the gangway and as he walked up the steeply sloping steps as if he was out for an afternoon stroll in the park, I clattered down from the bridge to meet him.

At the top of the gangway he saw me and said in a gentle, but arresting voice, "I am James McFadden, Chief Surveyor of the Anglo Indian Telegraph Company. Please take me to your captain."

And of course, I did as I was requested immediately.

On closer inspection I found that McFadden was of medium height and slim build. I thought he was probably about fifty years old. He wore a neatly trimmed white beard and his white hair was cut short as well. The little I could see of his face was tanned to the colour of teak and wrinkled like a prune. His eyes were very pale blue and so intense it felt as if he was looking at something behind me when he looked in my direction. Every movement he made was quick as if he was in a perpetual hurry. He wore a jacket and trousers of a tough looking material that had clearly been used in rough country. He had the air of a man who knew exactly what was needed, why it was needed and the best way to get it.

Remarkably, for a man with a surname like McFadden, he had no trace of a Scottish or Irish accent. In fact I could detect no accent at all.

When I compared our recent visitor with Mr. McFadden I could only marvel at the differences between the political leaders like Sir Algernon and the skilled personnel who made reality of their ideas.

I was surprised to find that Donovan was not present when I knocked on the captain's door so I introduced McFadden to Captain Stewart myself and then went back on deck to my resume my watch with Mr. Evans.

When I returned to the bridge, I found that the rest of the survey party had climbed off the boat and stationed themselves at intervals on the gangway. The Indians on the Shu'ai were passing the bags and boxes one by one over the gunwale of the boat to the man standing at the bottom of the gangway. He turned and passed the item to the next man up. It progressed from man to man until it reached the top of the gangway where one of the seamen took it from the man at the top and piled it all on deck beside the head of the gangway. The men came on board themselves as soon as all the items had been stacked on deck. One by one, as they reached the top of the gangway, they jumped down on to the deck, picked up a bag or box and turned to walk forward. In a few minutes they were sorting out the equipment on the hatch cover over the forward hold and checking that everything was there and in working order.

When this was finished they laid out palliasses and personal items and then stood around talking. It was very noticeable that the four men divided themselves into two distinct groups once the work of unpacking and sorting had been done.

Although I had no idea what their individual assignments could be, it was clear that two of the men were better dressed and seemed more articulate than the others.

Before many more minutes had passed, Captain Stewart and James McFadden came down the bridge ladder and walked along the deck to the forward hatch. The latter who was obviously very pleased by the way his team had settled in said, "Is every thing here and in working order?"

"Yes," replied one of the better-dressed men.

"There will be food along soon," said McFadden. "I see you are going to sleep under the stars tonight. I know you're used to that, but not so used to being rocked in the cradle of the deep, I imagine."

This last remark raised a few chuckles from those who overheard it but clearly raised a bad memory in McFadden's mind as he turned to the captain and said with a trace of concern audible in his voice, "I hope the sea will be calm for the next few days. I don't enjoy being on a ship."

Captain Stewart predicted confidently, "I'm certain it will be a calm crossing as the barometer has held steady for some days. I cannot be so sure about the return voyage yet but the weather is usually relatively calm at this time of year."

McFadden seemed to be quite relieved and said cheerfully, "Thank you for your encouragement Captain Stewart. Now, Captain, if you will excuse me I'll join my people."

"Of course," responded the captain. "I'll have an awning rigged in the morning to give you some protection from the sun."

"That's very good of you, Captain. Thank you."

McFadden then climbed up onto the hatch cover to sort out his own equipment and lay out his palliasse. The ship's cook brought a steaming cauldron of meat stew with vegetables, together with bowls, spoons and hard ship's biscuit for the surveyors' dinner. They tucked in with a will and then settled down for a night under the stars.

We sailed from Bombay in the last of the evening light and held a westerly course for the first part of the night. We then turned to west-northwest towards Muscat and the Mussandam. Our departure from Bombay, the journey across the Indian Ocean to the Oman coast and the subsequent voyage along the coast to the Mussandam were totally without incident.

With a calm sea and no other ships in sight for most of the voyage the crew were able to take advantage of the calm conditions and mend damaged clothing, carve little ornaments out of wood, ivory or bone or just laze under the awnings during their off duty hours.

The light hearted atmosphere on board started to change as soon as we came into sight of the Oman Coast. This is a coast to be very, very careful of. Precipitous cliffs of brown rock falling sheer in to the sea, with a few beaches along the way where a landing could be made and local fishermen eke out a living. The foot of the cliffs were bearded with white foam where the waves crashed into the sheer rock faces and the sea boiled where the incoming waves smashed into the breakers that had been reflected from the cliff. A good boat would not last five minutes in these conditions, even on a calm day and a fragile human body would be pulped in no time.

We were just off the entrance to the Elphinstone Inlet in the late afternoon and Captain Stewart decided to proceed with caution. He had never been into the Elphinstone Inlet before and had only very scanty information with which to safely navigate his ship. Even our destination was only sketched on a piece of paper that McFadden had brought on board. As a result Captain Stewart decided to sail slowly out to sea until midnight and then turn onto the reciprocal bearing in order to close the coast in the early morning at about four bells in the morning watch. This would give the maximum amount of daylight in which to enter the inlet and find somewhere to anchor near to our objective.

Early next morning at the entrance to the Khawr As Sham, as the Elphinstone Inlet is known in Arabic, the captain reduced speed until we had only a little more than steerage way. As a precaution he stationed two seamen with a twenty-fathom sounding line in the bow. The water appeared to be consistently deep with no trace of shallows along the centre of the inlet but the regular reports of, "No bottom with this line, sir," as the lead was cast at regular intervals allowed the captain to maintain his course with greater confidence.

I was off watch but returned to the bridge to have my first sight of this unknown country called Oman in Arabia. The inlet was an awe-inspiring sight and totally outside my experience. If the slopes had been green it would have been like sailing along a huge lake in a mountain valley. The reality was very different. Rock slopes, completely devoid of vegetation, descended steeply, almost vertically in some places and disappeared into the blue green sea. The colour of the rocks shaded from medium to pale brown and appeared white where it was directly in the sun and reflecting the light. The sky was cloudless and a deep blue. In some places the rocks were deeply marked with sloping lines and in others the rocks were contorted into strange arched shapes.

There seemed to be nothing for anyone to hold on to if they were unfortunate enough to fall into the sea and then fortunate enough to swim to the foot of the cliffs. I saw nowhere where someone could climb from the water even if they were able to find a handhold on the rocks at the water's edge. In many places the sea had undercut the rock face and in others huge, jagged blocks of rock had fallen into the sea and were visible at the surface. In a few places, where a side valley came down to the sea, there was a small sandy beach but the cliffs behind the beach were so precipitous it appeared that it could only be reached by boat. We saw no sign of boats or local people that morning.

There was a strange brooding atmosphere and everyone on board was unnaturally quiet. It was as if no one wanted to wake up whatever danger lurked in the unknown waters we sailed over. We felt insignificant surrounded by these high, steep, barren rock faces. It was a lonely, uninhabited, poor and cheerless place even in the bright hot sunshine.

We crept cautiously along the inlet, and when we arrived in the vicinity of the island shown on McFadden's sketch, the captain called the bosun, ordered the engine stopped and we hove to.

When the bosun arrived on the bridge Captain Stewart said, "I plan to anchor here, Bosun, and I need to be certain there are no hidden shallows where we will swing on the anchor. Use one of the boats and take soundings of the seabed all around the ship and then report to me when you have finished."

"Aye, sir," said the bosun as he left the bridge, calling for a boat crew as he went.

Captain Stewart kept the ship on station by using the engine when we drifted away from the position he had chosen as an anchorage. The bosun completed a pattern of soundings around the ship and returned on board as he had been ordered.

He came to the bridge and said, "Soundings complete, Captain. There is at least twenty fathoms over the whole area."

"Thank you, Bosun. Then we'll anchor here."

By the time we had anchored, lowered the gangplank and put a boat in the water, it was really too late in the day for the surveyors to go ashore to establish their base camp. McFadden and Captain Stewart agreed that the surveyors would go to the island early in the morning of the next day. This would give them time during the evening for any last minute planning and so on before they left. We reattached the falls from the davits and lifted the boat clear of the water for the night.

The island we had been sent to survey was close enough to our anchorage for us to see that it was simply an uninhabited, barren piece of rock sticking out of the sea. It was quite small in area and one half was about twice the height of the other. It was probably the top of a mountain that was a little lower than those surrounding us. It was the most uninviting piece of land I had ever seen.

I didn't like to imagine what would have happened to us if there had been another mountain top on our route from the entrance to our anchorage, but low enough to be submerged and invisible just below the surface. A trap for the unwary and Captain Stewart's use of a leadsman to warn him about shoaling water during our approach was now more easily understood.

During the night Captain Stewart set extra lookouts. We hadn't seen anyone, but he felt it was better to be prudent as no one had any clear idea how friendly the local people would be. In Bombay we had been told about the ferocity of the Omani tribesmen in the mountains in this area. Shooting at anyone who appeared to be approaching one of their settlements we had been told, but couldn't judge whether this was fact or only a rumour. However, Sir Algernon's statement that the location of the repeater station was being changed because of the animosity of local tribesmen seemed to support the story we had heard and dictated caution. Even the crew members who were not on watch had a disturbed night because of the uncertainty of the situation and our close proximity to a potentially hostile land.

The next morning after a substantial breakfast the surveyors started to check over the equipment again and pack their personal kits ready to camp out on the island.

The first mate and McFadden compiled a list of foodstuff that would last at least three days and enough water in casks to last at least twice as long. The cook and the bosun were ordered to prepare everything and stack it adjacent to the head of the gangway ready to be loaded.

I was a very interested onlooker when they were checking their survey equipment and I was pleased to see that all of it was familiar from the days when I had helped the Ordnance Survey surveyors.

McFadden noticed my interest. In particular he perceived the interest with which I looked over the optical instruments they had unpacked and was sufficiently intrigued by my knowledge to say, "You obviously know what these instruments are but I do not see why you should. Why do you, an officer in the merchant navy, have such knowledge? Do you know how to use any of them?"

"To answer your last question first, Mr. McFadden, I do know how to use them. Some years ago an Ordnance Survey team was working near my village and the chief surveyor was prepared to teach me, a country boy, as much as I could learn whilst they were in the area."

"Amazing" said McFadden to me and then to his team he said, "Gather around everybody. Please stay and listen if you wish, Mr. Smiley."

The survey team grouped themselves in a rough semi circle in front of McFadden and I stood beside him. McFadden gestured to me and said, "I have invited Mr. Smiley to listen to my briefing as he has worked with the Ordnance Survey. I think it might be useful to have someone on the ship that is familiar with surveying and what we plan to do."

He paused for a moment to look at the barren lump of rock and the cliff behind that he was to survey, then said, "I will review the tasks we have to complete in the next three days and I want to emphasise that the information we are instructed to obtain is required urgently. There will be no time for us to return here to correct any mistakes, so your work must be checked and proved accurate as the surveying proceeds. There are three separate pieces of work to be performed. First we need a complete topographic survey of the island down to the water line. I will carry out this work with Tomlinson as my Chainman. The second task is on the main land where a survey is required from the beach closest to the island, up the cliff to the ridge, across the top and down to the sea the other side. Surveyor Carmichael with Davidson as chainman will do this. The third part of the work requires a seabed survey from the island to the beach. Captain Stewart will provide the boat and crew for the sounding work which will be supervised by Surveyor Ellis."

As each man was given his task he raised his hand in acknowledgment and I was amused to find that the surveyors Carmichael and Ellis were the two better dressed gentlemen I had identified the evening they came aboard in Bombay. Education and dress did go hand in hand it seemed.

McFadden continued, "After a brief discussion with Captain Stewart about the amount of equipment we have to take to the island we have decided that two trips are essential. Consequently, I shall go to the island with Carmichael and Ellis for a reconnaissance. You Tomlinson, with Davidson to help, will supervise the loading and then bring all our equipment and personal kit on the second trip. We don't expect to make a third trip. Very well gentlemen, please get everything ready to load and I will inform Captain Stewart that we are ready to leave as soon as the boat is available," and he walked away to climb the ladder to the bridge.

The ship's jolly boat was lowered back into the water and the mast stepped and rigged. Evans was put in charge with two able seamen as crew. He was absolutely overjoyed to be freed from the confines of the ship and the prospect of being on land, even a very hot and barren land, made him almost dance with delight.

I was envious and very disappointed to be excluded from the group, but there was no need for us both to go and he was a much more experienced small boat sailor than I was. Consequently, when he went down to organize the boat, I took over his watch on the bridge with the best grace I could muster. The ship was lying with the bows into a gentle southerly breeze and the island was almost due north of us beyond the stern.

The jolly boat was cast off, and Evans ordered his crew to hoist the small lugsail to take advantage of the breeze that was blowing. Evans waved cheerfully and sailed away towards the island on the long run that would take him to the western and lower end of the island. The captain took a last look around the horizon and went below to his cabin. I watched the jolly boat for a few moments and clearly the whole party were enjoying themselves. Like a Sunday School outing I thought as I resumed my duties as officer of the watch and checked that the ship had not drifted off position.

Fifteen minutes later, when the boat with Evan's party in it were about half way to the island, the captain came hurrying back to the bridge. Nothing had changed that I could detect. The sky remained a cloudless blue and the breeze was slightly lighter if anything, but that was all. But clearly Captain Stewart was worried. He had seen or felt something while he was in his cabin, that I hadn't detected and from the expression on his face, the instincts of a very experienced sailor were giving him considerable concern.

He picked up a telescope and started to scan the horizon. He looked seaward and then slowly but progressively examined the visible horizon, carefully studying the shore line and the tops of the surrounding hills. He said nothing and may not have known what he was looking for, but he suddenly stopped moving and studied a particular area almost directly in line with the island for several moments.

He suddenly snapped the telescope shut, reached above his head for the lanyard controlling the ship's whistle and blew five short blasts, the danger warning, followed quickly by another five blasts and then another five. He rang the engine room telegraph to standby and ordered me to signal the boat.

"Jason! Quickly! Hoist flags 'U' over 'K' over 'X'."

Even as I rushed to the flag locker, a tiny part of my mind registered the fact that the captain had addressed me as Jason instead of his customary Mr. Smiley. I was thankful that my many hours of practice under the bosun's watchful gaze were being rewarded, as I had all three flags, bent on, hoisted and flying within a few moments of receiving Captain Stewart's terse order.

As I carried out the instruction, I remembered that 'U' means 'you are standing into danger', 'K' means 'you should stop your vessel instantly' and 'X' means 'you should stop carrying out your intentions and watch for my signals'. The captain had sent a very comprehensive message with the minimum of wasted effort but the wind was now very light and, as it was blowing almost directly from the ship towards Evans, I did not think he would be able to see them. Captain Stewart called the engine room on the voice pipe in the corner of the bridge near the telegraph and the half of the conversation I heard was,

"Chief?"

"Call the Chief Engineer immediately."

"Chief?" captain here. There is a storm approaching. Raise steam as quickly as you can. How long before I can use the engine?"

"I see. That may not be soon enough. You will have to do better!"

There was a significant pause as the captain listened to the chief and he then said, "I see. If the storm that's coming causes the anchor to drag, you may not have an engine to worry about this afternoon."

The captain obviously thought the wind direction was preventing Evans from seeing the flag signal as he blew another series of danger warnings on the steam whistle just as the first mate arrived on the bridge followed closely by the second officer.

Captain Stewart gestured towards the north and said, "There's a bad storm coming and Evans is right in its path."

Captain Stewart turned to the second mate and ordered, "Go round the ship and make sure all portholes and hatches are closed. Tell the crew there is a severe dust storm coming and all off watch crew are to go to their mess rooms to wait further orders."

In company with the captain and Mr. Richards, the first mate, I used a telescope and looked in the direction the captain had pointed and could see low, dark, rolling clouds rushing out of the mountains towards us. It came even closer as we watched and the sea between the mainland and the island began to smoke and boil from the fury of the approaching wind. Suddenly the main land behind the island became a blur and then disappeared. Between the island and the "Earl Canning," our boat with Evans and the surveyors on board sailed serenely on. They were clearly unaware of the approaching danger, possibly because they were close enough to the island for its bulk to block out most of the mainland and the approaching storm beyond. They had obviously heard the siren and knew something was amiss, as we saw in our telescopes Evans pass the tiller to one of his crew and stand in the stern of the jolly boat looking back at us with the small telescope that he always carried with him. We could see the dust being blown like smoke horizontally from the top of the island as the storm approached it, but we were incapable of indicating where the danger to Evans and his party was coming from. Apart from the helmsman, everyone was looking back towards us.

The bosun arrived on the bridge. He had also heard the steam whistle blowing and knew from experience that he would be required in an emergency.

He reported directly to the captain who said, "Ah Bosun, just the man. There is a storm coming. Set an anchor watch. Two of your most experienced hands. I need to know immediately if the anchor starts to drag. Put some men at intervals along the deck so that there is no delay passing information to me from your men on the forecastle."

The captain again blew on the whistle to attract attention to the storm and as he did so a freak gust of wind blew our signal flags out to port. Evans saw the hoist, spun round and saw the approaching danger himself, and the lugsail started to drop. But his action was far too late, as the sail was not half down before the boat listed steeply in a sudden violent blast of wind. Both boat and occupants disappeared from our horrified view into an impenetrable blanket of dust.

We watched with fascinated horror as a thick brown cloud of dust, only rising a few hundred feet into the air, roiled and boiled rapidly across the sea towards us. Amazingly there was a serene blue sky above it and turbulent white capped sea at its base. The noise from the wind was deafening and seemed louder than the hurricane winds I had experienced a few years before.

My thoughts and prayers were with my friend Evans who was fighting three enemies at once—the sea, the wind, and the dust.

Seconds later, with the sun blotted out by a swirling cloud of fine brown dust, the wind from the storm hit us as well and the ship listed to port from the strength of it before starting to drift down wind. We could see only a few feet due to the thickness of the dust and breathing became extremely difficult. Captain Stewart put a cloth over his nose and mouth and shouted over the wind for us to do the same.

A report from the anchor watch relayed along the deck said simply, "Drifting, Sir," which was to be expected as the wind had reversed direction and we had to drift down wind to twice the length of the cable before the anchor would start to take hold on the seabed. The next report, "Dragging, Sir," meant we had drifted far enough for the anchor to start dragging across the top of the seabed without digging in.

Captain Stewart had prudently moored in the centre of the inlet but we could not drift too far down wind without running aground on the cliffs. Captain Stewart felt his way to the engine room voice tube and called the chief. "Anchor's dragging, Chief. Give me slow ahead as soon as you are able," and listened to the reply.

He beckoned to the first mate. Over the wind he shouted, "Mr. Richards, call all hands and prepare to make sail. I cannot wait much longer for the engine. Do not set the sails without my order as we will drift even faster down wind until we can get the sails to draw and get steerage way. Instruct the anchor watch to prepare to slip the anchor if we cannot recover it quickly enough."

Mr. Richards left the bridge at the run and clattered down the bridge ladder. Shortly afterwards I heard his voice booming around the ship followed by the sound of many footsteps on the iron decks.

For the moment I had no specific duty to perform and could only hold on to the rail and hope the storm passed as quickly as it had come. The blinding thick dust and the swirling wind disorientated me, and I had no idea which way we were drifting. After a short wait that must have seemed like hours in duration to the captain, a message was relayed from the anchor watch along the men lined up along the deck.

"Anchor holding, Captain."

And after a few more minutes the message was repeated and to the intense relief of everyone on board the engine room reported almost simultaneously that the engine could now be used.

The captain acknowledged the message from the engine room but did not immediately start the engine. With the anchor holding there was no need to move the ship as we could have been sailing into, as easily as away, from danger as we did not know where we were. The watch made fast all the sails and were dismissed below. For the rest of the storm the positive reports from the anchor watch were repeated every few minutes.

After about twenty minutes, although it seemed infinitely longer, the wind started to abate. With the slackening wind the density of the dust in the air reduced and soon we could see the outline of the island and the sea between. There was no sign of our boat or her crew and passengers on the bearing where we had last seen them.

The crew stood at the rail all around the deck of the ship to look for their mates and we officers used our telescopes to scour the sea and coastline in the vicinity of the island for a sign of our boat and the men who had been on board.

Suddenly one of the seamen shouted, "There!" and pointed out over the port side and away from the island. As one man we turned and ran to the port rail of the bridge and there, without benefit of telescopes, we could clearly see the upturned hull of our boat but, tragically, no sign of the occupants. It appeared from its position relative to the island that the wind had capsized the boat and it had then drifted past us in the storm when our anchor took hold again.

Captain Stewart stood like a statue for a long moment, looking at the upturned hull of our boat and gripping the rail so tightly that his knuckles and fingers grew white. He turned and looked towards the island, then at the wind vane and then studied the shore to the east of us. He said quietly, and more to himself than his officers, "If there are any survivors, they will be near that promontory."

Then in his commanding voice he said, "Mr. Richards, if you please. Lower the two lifeboats and make sure there is plenty of water in each. Mr. Judd will take charge of N0.2 lifeboat, and he will search seaward along the shore line from there," and he pointed to a small promontory of rock jutting into the sea off our starboard beam, "until dark then he will return to the ship."

He paused momentarily then turned to the first mate "You will take charge of N0.1 lifeboat. Take the bosun, additional men and some oars with you. First search under the jolly boat and then right it. Use the extra men to bale it out and row it back to the ship. After dealing with the jolly boat search the eastern coast line from that promontory landward until dark."

The boat crews were assembled and set off on their miserable task with very sombre faces. The bigger No 1 boat was rowed out to the upturned jollyboat and one of the crew dived underneath to look for survivors. The shake of his head when he resurfaced was enough to lower our already low spirits another notch. He dived under again and surfaced with the lug sail billowing out behind. It was pulled into the life boat. The jollyboat was righted and three men started bailing it out in preparation for rowing back to the ship.

The first mate then took his boat to search for survivors along the southern shore. With the mountains falling almost sheer into the sea and in some places being undercut by the action of the waves there was little hope that someone would have been able to get ashore but the search for survivors had to be made.

After the boats had started to search the coastline, the captain watched each boat alternately with his big telescope in the hope that he would see some sign of excitement but there was nothing. There was a short period of quiet inactivity as everyone tried to come to terms with the tragedy we had witnessed, but that was suddenly interrupted by the noise of something banging on an iron door.

The captain sent me to investigate. The noise came from somewhere near the bows and I traced it to the door of the paint locker. I opened the door and Tomlinson and Davidson the two Telegraph Company Chainmen stumbled out, blinking in the light. They were extremely agitated and not a little annoyed. Why had we locked them in this little dark room, was the first coherent question they posed after a good deal of shouting and cursing. My inability to provide an answer, since I had no idea what they were talking about, simply served to increase the level of indignation they felt.

They demanded to see the captain, so I led them to the bridge.

"Why did you go into the paint store?" shouted Captain Stewart in a voice that overcame the litany of complaints by virtue of superior volume.

Tomlinson, in a surprisingly calm tone considering what he had been uttering with his previous breath said, "When we heard that there was a storm coming, we moved all our equipment into the nearest store room. We had just carried the last pieces inside when the door slammed shut and in the dark we couldn't find a door handle so we could not get out. We banged and banged but no one came."

Captain Stewart explained the events of the past hour and told them, "I have sent both the lifeboats to search along the coast for survivors, but I do not think they will be successful. I'm extremely sorry but I think that all your colleagues have been drowned."

And so it was. The boats crews searched diligently and returned to the ship some hours after dark exhausted and blistered from rowing hard. Both the First and Second officers reported that they had seen nothing of our colleagues. They had found no trace of the food and other items that had been carried in the boat. Everything had vanished.

Suddenly the stark reality that we had tried to ignore had to be faced. The men we had eaten and talked with only a few hours ago were dead. Some of the men wanted to continue searching, as they did not wish to believe what had happened, but it only put off the inevitable acceptance of grief and mourning. Tomlinson and Davidson took consolation in each other's company and late in the evening I came across them standing by the rail, each with an arm about the other, and silently weeping for the memory of their lost colleagues.

A happy and competent group of surveyors had been torn apart by the savagery of nature.

Captain Stewart maintained a calm, unemotional demeanour throughout the harrowing experiences of the day and it was only in the evening when every thing that could be done, had been done, that his iron grip on his emotions cracked and he went to his cabin to weep silently for the men he had inadvertently sent to their deaths.

I sensed that the question of what he should have done differently and by so doing prevented a tragedy, would haunt his sleep for many years but in reality there was nothing that could have allowed him to predict the storm.

For my part I went back to the cabin where I had lived with John Evans. I realized that he had been the first and only real friend in my life and I missed his company and cheerful confidence immensely already. I packed his books, uniforms and a few personal belongings and the pamphlets he had brought on board about the evils of alcohol, into a box. I stared at the portrait of the lovely sister he had been so proud of and wondered who would have the task of breaking the news, and the hearts, of this family, before I carefully placed it in the box with the other items. And as I picked up this small box of relics, to take to the bosun for safekeeping, I realized how meagre the physical remains of a good man could be. I wept copiously for John Evans that night.

The next morning, a more than usually miserable looking Donovan came to summon me to the captain's cabin and when I stood in front of Captain Stewart's desk I could see that the captain had been deeply affected by the tragedy. John Evans and the other two members of the crew, who had died, had sailed with the captain for long time and he was full of self-reproach. Mr. Richards was with the captain when I arrived.

I heard the first mate say, "Captain, there is really nothing that you could have done differently yesterday. The storm could not have been foreseen, but you sensed something was wrong long before anyone else and did everything possible to save the men in the few minutes that were available. If Evans had been able to see our signals and act more quickly the outcome might have been different, but with the wind and sea that developed yesterday the survival of our jolly boat was very unlikely as you know."

"Thank you for your support, Mr. Richards. Please continue with your duties," responded my very unhappy captain.

After the first mate had left the cabin he turned to me and said, "We have suffered a great loss, not only individually, but as a ship's company because we rely on each other all the time.

"The life of a seaman is always dangerous and no matter how hard we try to safeguard each other, tragedies like yesterdays accident, will unfortunately occur. You have suffered a particular loss Mr. Smiley, because you have been constantly in Mr. Evans company both on and off duty for some years. His weekly reports have always considered your progress to be excellent. I too have been satisfied with your progress and both the first mate and the have commended you.

"The life of the ship must go on and as a result of the accident I am short of one watch-keeping officer. I have decided to promote you to the position of third officer with effect from today. I wish it could have been in happier circumstances.

"Thank you, Mr. Smiley. Report to the First Mate and he will assign your watch keeping duties."

"Aye, Sir," I said and left the cabin. I was pleased that I was considered worthy of the promotion but would have wished I had achieved this honour by other means than dead man's shoes.

Later in the day the captain called us to his cabin. When we were all present he said, "Gentlemen, I have decided to sail for Bombay at dawn tomorrow morning. Without the surveyors we cannot accomplish the work which we were sent here to do and I need to report the tragedy to the relevant authorities as soon as possible. There may be some way for the Anglo British Telegraph Company to organise another expedition in the time they have available. Before we sail I will hold a short service of remembrance. That will be all, gentlemen."

As we all stood up to leave the cabin, I said, "Captain, sir, may I have permission to speak?"

He looked at me and I could see the refusal forming in his eyes but he relented and said, "You don't usually waste my time Mr. Smiley, so what do you want to say?" and he motioned to the other officers to resume their seats.

I rapidly assembled my thoughts and said, "Captain, before I joined the ship I was able to spend some time with a team from the

Ordnance Survey. The chief surveyor taught me how to use a level and a transit and I also learnt how to make surveys in the field and book the results. He offered me a job as an assistant surveyor, but Mr. Smiley refused permission for me to take it. I was present when Mr. McFadden briefed his team so I know what they were required to do. The instruments and other equipment are still on board together with the two chainmen Tomlinson and Davison. Sir," I concluded, "I know how to use the instruments and I am confident that I can obtain sufficient information in two or three days to ensure that the voyage will not be a waste of time and more particularly that Mr. Evans and all the others have not died uselessly."

"It's a very good idea, Mr. Smiley, but I would have to be convinced that you know enough about surveying to get the information required by the Telegraph Company before I will change my decision about leaving."

"Sir," I suggested, "If we go on deck I can easily demonstrate that I know how the instruments should be assembled and used."

"Very well," he said and led the way out on deck.

After demonstrating how the instruments were assembled and then describing how the instruments were used the captain warmed to the idea. The chainmen who had at first been dismissive also saw merit in it.

After considering what he had seen and heard for a moment or two, Captain Stewart said, "Very well, Mr. Smiley, present a written plan by the end of the first watch in the morning, and if I'm satisfied with it I will provide whatever facilities you require to complete the survey."

"Thank you Captain," was all I could say as my brain started to grapple with the problem I had set myself.

It was an enormous task and the more I thought about it the more enormous it appeared. Here I am I thought, Jason Smiley, third officer with about one hour's seniority, about to undertake on my own, a task that three experienced surveyors hoped to accomplish but had openly questioned their chances of completing in the few days they had available. I had only about a week of casually acquired surveying experience and wondered if I had been just a little too impetuous when I made my suggestion. No, I decided. I owe it to John Evans and the rest of our dead colleagues and friends to produce a workable plan by morning, so

I settled down to think it out.

Clearly I could not obtain as much detail as the original survey party had intended, but I could survey the main features of the island and the ridge between Elphinstone Inlet and Malcolm's Inlet on the other side. The seabed contours between the island and the mainland could be obtained by the ship's crew very easily, as they were accustomed to taking soundings. As I thought about it, the details of the work were fitted to my expertise, and when the morning came, I was able to present a workable plan to Captain Stewart.

With his agreement and wishes of good luck still in my ears, I sat on the forward hatch cover with the two chainmen and told them how I intended to proceed. Then whilst they loaded the boat with the survey equipment, food and water, I told the bosun how and where to set up a tide board and to start a seaman reading it every quarter of an hour until the work was complete. Miraculously, the bosun produced an hour glass that had been graduated in fifteen minute intervals so all the seaman had to do was stay awake. The bosun needed no instruction about taking soundings and soon had a second crew organized in another boat.

Captain Stewart had the boat rowed to the island. After the tragedy of the day before he was unwilling to let us use the sail and the seamen who rowed us were soon soaked in sweat even although it was still early in the day. The helmsman grounded the bows of the boat on the only piece of sand he could see. It turned out to be the only reasonable beach on the island.

Whilst the boat was being unloaded I climbed to the top of the island. There was a little sun-dried scrub, but essentially the island was a barren, roughly oval, lump of brown rock protruding from the sea. At one end it was raised slightly above the general level and all round the perimeter of the island, the rock dropped steeply into the sea with very few landing places beyond the one we had used. There was no sign of life, not even the ashes from an old fire.

I had decided that the quickest way to survey the island was to use the transit and a system known as tachometry and immediately set out a base line on the top of the island along its longer axis. I set up the transit at one end of the base line. The chainmen, each holding a surveyors staff, started to walk in a methodical way, around and across the island. At each salient feature they would stop and I would read and record the three stadia readings and the vertical and horizontal angles that defined the position. Whilst I was reading and recording the information at one position the other chainman was walking to the next point and this speeded up the work considerably. When necessary I relocated the transit to another position on the base line.

We worked for some hours and the sun rose higher and higher in the brilliant blue sky and the temperature rose steadily in unison. Although early in the Arabian summer season it soon felt as if we were working in the mouth of a furnace. The heat radiated from the rocks and we all started to develop raging thirsts. We soon had to stop and retreat to the boat where the sailors had hung a sheet of canvas over oars they had lashed together to make an awning. To be able to escape the merciless attack from the sun was a blessing and we drank copiously and later ate some of the food we had brought.

Later in the day, when the temperature had started to abate, I resumed the survey on the top of the island. When this was completed I needed to survey the shoreline and to accomplish this I put a chainman with a staff in the boat. The boat's crew rowed slowly around the island and at intervals grounded the bows against the shore so that I could survey the water line. I moved the transit around the perimeter of the island so that I was able to see the staff. Where there was space the chainman landed on the island so that I could survey any beaches we found. At sunset we returned to the ship exhausted from the heat and slept until dawn.

Next morning the task was very different. No instrument work except to establish a starting point on the mainland from the baseline on the island. Then it was just unremitting, painstaking, hard work under a blazing sun climbing up the steep slope to the ridge over loose fragments of rock, measuring vertical and horizontal distances as we went along. The chainmen worked with the chain and plumb line and I recorded the readings. The sun beat down on us. The sweat dripped off us, and I had the greatest difficulty keeping my hands dry so that my field book did not dissolve into a soggy, illegible mess.

At the ridge, as I straightened up and my head rose above the level of the rock, I found myself looking into the barrel of a rifle a few scant inches from my nose and nearly fell back down the rocky slope from the shock. I have never experienced such a feeling of fear.

My heart started to pound. For some reason I held my breath and it was only by the application of great muscular control that I prevented the suddenly liquid content of my bowels from discharging itself into my breeches. I have never looked death straight in the face before and pray I will never do so again. I steadied myself, with a supreme effort of mind over muscle and managed to ignore the hole in the rifle barrel that looked the size of a drainpipe. I expected it to belch fire and lead at any second but forced myself to look along the rifle at the figure holding the butt. Dark, unblinking eyes stared from a swarthy, tanned face surmounted by a turban; nothing else was visible. I raised both hands slowly and showed the recumbent figure behind the rifle that they were empty and then equally slowly I reached over and with the back of one hand started to push the rifle barrel to one side so that it pointed over my shoulder and not between my eyes.

At first there was a lot of resistance but suddenly the rifle moved and fell to one side with a clatter, followed by an explosion and the whistle of a departing ball. I vaulted over the edge of the ridge ready to join battle with the gunman although I had no weapon, but the Arab had not moved and I realized as I knelt beside him that he was dead, although the reason for his death was not apparent.

Two ashen-faced chainmen followed me over the edge of the ridge and collapsed beside me on the sun-baked rock. I had no time to explain what had happened before I heard a blast on the ship's whistle. They had obviously heard the rifle shot and I could see the light reflecting off the object glasses of several telescopes as my shipmates examined the scene. I stood up and urged my two companions to their feet and waved to the ship to let them know we were not injured.

A few seconds later there was a thud as a jet of sand jumped into the air and then came the crack of a rifle. We looked along the ridge in the direction the sound had come from and saw three local men with rifles walking towards us. It was one of them who had fired and another of them stopped, took aim and fired at us and fortunately missed. Clearly someone else had heard the shot and had come to investigate.

I stepped in front of my companions, said, "Keep down!" and with my hands stretched out to show they were empty, started to walk along the ridge to meet the three natives.

To the impotent observers on the ship it must have seemed a suicidal thing to do, but if we had tried to climb down the ridge to the poor safety of the boat, they could have used us for target practice if they had wished to and picked us off at their leisure. I felt instinctively that it was better to show confidence and lack of fear rather than run away, which was what I wanted to do.

The third man, who had walked a few more paces, stopped to aim then lowered his rifle as I walked up to them. We stood looking at each other not knowing what to do next and then one of the three pointed at my hair and said something to his companions. The next thing I knew was that all three of them were walking around me to look at and touch my hair. Obviously they had never seen hair this colour before and they started to rub bits of it between their fingers to see if the colour would come off. One of them whipped out a knife and cut a hank of hair from above my forehead. It was as well that he was very quick and I had no idea what to expect, because he could have taken some of my nose or ear as well if I had flinched.

They examined the hank of hair closely. They spat on it and rubbed it between their palms but there was no sign of colour and clearly they were mightily impressed with my crowning glory.

After a while I turned, beckoned them to follow me and lead them back to where the dead Arab was lying. There was a lot of wailing when they saw the body. Two of the Arabs immediately pointed their rifles at me, with the clear intent of extracting an eye for an eye, but the leader of the trio who was examining the body said something in Arabic that pacified his two companions. He pointed to a burn mark on the man's back and I wondered if he had been struck by lightening in the storm.

They slung their rifles over their shoulders and two of them picked up the body. They said something to us and turned and walked away. We watched them go with such a feeling of relief that my knees turned to water and I had to sit down.

Surveying down the ridge on the Malcolm's Inlet side was something of an anticlimax after the events of the morning and we carried on with the remaining work regardless of the heat. We wanted to be finished and get away from this place as soon as possible. In the early evening after we had climbed back over the ridge we returned to the boat hot, thirsty and tired. I was very pleased we had been able to achieve so much in such a short time and in no small measure this was due to the untiring efforts of the two chainmen.

When we came back to the ship it seemed that everyone on board had come on deck to greet us including Captain Stewart. The congratulations and pats on the back and cries of "Very well done, Mr. Smiley, Sir" seemed to go on forever and I developed a sore back to go with the tired one.

I went with Captain Stewart to his cabin and explained what had happened during the day. He instructed me to prepare a detailed written report and said he would send it to the Telegraph Company and to the owners.

He went on to say, "I am very proud of the way you have performed an extremely arduous task and particularly proud of the bravery you showed when you faced armed natives when completely unarmed yourself. If you had taken any other action all three of you would probably now be dead together with the boat's crew. Well done. That will be all Mr. Smiley."

"Aye, sir" I said and went to the mess for a meal and then on watch.

I took up my duties as the third officer. As I did so, I had time to recall the way in which I had coveted promotion from cadet to third officer not so many days before and realized that I would have gladly remained a cadet if it had meant keeping Evans alive.

All members of the crew attended a brief memorial service held by the captain on the fore deck, then we pulled up the anchor and set sail for Bombay, as we had achieved as much as we could achieve. Using the engine we steamed along the Elphinstone Inlet and away from the island with a sense of release. I think we all heaved a silent sigh of relief as we felt the bow lift to the first wave coming in from the open sea. The weather was good and Captain Stewart made use of the favourable wind by setting some sail whilst continuing to run the engine and thereby reduced our journey time considerably.

I think he felt speed was more important than economy in the circumstances.

EIGHT

Bombay

We arrived back in Bombay and anchored in the early morning light, with the city framed to the east by the towering Western Ghats mountain range on the mainland. Just another ship arriving. I suppose it was routine event for a port that saw so many arrivals.

Routine, that is, until Captain Stewart went ashore in his best uniform to report the tragedy. He intended to go first to the governor, then to the manager of the Anglo Indian Telegraph Company and finally to the harbour master.

When he came back on board he came directly to the bridge where I was on watch and Mr. Richards the first mate was checking a chart. It was clear from the expression on his face that he had experienced a harrowing few hours.

The mate asked, "Was it very bad, Sir?"

"Yes," he responded, "Very." After a moment of silence as he reviewed the morning's events, he said, "It would have been difficult enough if I had only needed to explain about the tragedy once. But they couldn't grasp what I was saying to them initially and I had to go through it all again. I went to the governor first. He had just arrived in his office and greeted me like a long lost son when I was shown into his office. Then he went into raptures about some scheme he was developing to improve drains or some such thing in Bombay. I started badly by interrupting his joyous monologue when he was in full flow and made matters worse by saying, 'I have tragic news Sir David'."

He said rather crossly, "What is it Captain Stewart? Are you going to spoil the start of my day?"

"Yes, Sir David," I said solemnly. "The three surveyors, Third Officer Evans and two of my crewmen have been drowned. Their boat capsized in a sudden, violent storm as they sailed from Earl Canning to the island."

"Did you not see the storm approaching, Captain?"

"Not in time, Sir David. It came boiling down out of the mountains and changed calm weather into a violent, blinding sand storm in a few minutes. We tried to warn Mr. Evans, but he didn't see our signals in time. We searched the coast as soon as the storm cleared but there was no sign of anything but the upturned boat. It's all detailed in my report Sir David."

Captain Stewart went on, "I handed him the report and he sat down with a very serious expression on his face and read through it. After he had finished, he put the report down on his desk and said, 'This is dreadful news, Captain. Does anyone else know yet?'"

"No Sir David. I must go to the Telegraph Company and then to the Harbour Master."

"No," he instructed. "I'll send messengers to bring them here," and he rang for his secretary and said, "Send a messenger to Captain Denison at the Harbour Office and Mr. Peterson at the Telegraph Company Office asking both gentlemen to come to my office as soon as possible."

"Captain Stewart," the governor suggested, "Perhaps you would like to wait in the ante room until they arrive."

"So I did as the Governor suggested. I went out side and sat in a silence broken only by the ticking of a big, brass faced, grandfather clock in the corner of the office until the Harbour Master arrived. We were shown into the governor's office immediately."

Captain Stewart went on, "I told the Harbour Master what had happened and while he was reading my report, Hugo Peterson, the manager of the Anglo Indian Telegraph Company arrived. Of course I had to go through the whole painful story again but the manager greeted the news with incredulity and I had to repeat it. Peterson then turned to Sir David and said 'I assume from what I have heard this morning that Captain Stewart was negligent and is responsible for these untimely deaths'."

The first mate broke in to say, "But that's ridiculous, Captain, you could have done no more. What did Sir David say?"

"Actually it was Captain Denison who spoke first and he said quite bluntly, 'When you read Captain Stewart's report, as I have done, you will realize that Captain Stewart is completely blameless'."

"Then Sir David said sharply, 'You jump to conclusions, Peterson. You have spoken without knowing the facts and you should apologise for impugning Captain Stewart's reputation'. 'I'm sorry Sir David' Peterson responded 'and I apologise for my ill considered remark, Captain Stewart'."

Captain Stewart stood quietly on the bridge in thought for a moment then said "I don't think his apology was genuine. I'm afraid there are many arm chair sailors here who will think the worst just like Peterson. I can only hope that Sir David and Captain Denison will continue to support me."

"Sir David then dismissed us," the captain continued, "and told us to deal with the consequences of the tragedy as it affected our individual responsibilities and sphere of influence in Bombay. For my part I can do no more than notify the company and then write to John Evans parents and the families of our two dead sailors."

The bad news soon escaped from the official offices and spread through Bombay like wild fire.

In its wake came the exaggerated and conflicting accounts of what had happened to whom and as Captain Stewart had feared, the accusations that he had caused the deaths of all six men by his negligence soon followed. Fortunately enough people in senior positions knew exactly what had happened and they had Captain Stewart's written report to verify his verbal testimony. They were in the best position to scotch the rumours quickly, otherwise it could have been quite damaging for Captain Stewart's reputation as a senior and competent captain.

The deaths of McFadden, the Chief Surveyor, and Carmichael and Evans, the two assistant surveyors, were greeted with shock and stunned silence as they were all well known in the local community.

The Surveyors had no family in Bombay, but the members of the British community mourned for them. I should record also that they performed the same loving duty for our three lost crewmen although none of them were known in Bombay.

A service of remembrance was held for all six men at the Church of the Holy Name in Bombay.

On the day of the service the church was full of soberly dressed men and women who had come to pay their last respects. Also present were the governor with his wife and aides, a director and the manager of the Anglo Indian Telegraph Company and of course, the captain, officers and all the crew from the Earl Canning in uniform. During the progress of a sombre service the captain read a eulogy for our lost shipmates and the manager of the Anglo Indian Telegraph Company performed the same service for his surveyors. Many of the congregation who had known one or other of the surveyors personally felt the emotion of the situation and handkerchiefs were used, openly by the ladies and more discreetly by the men.

I noticed Tomlinson and Davison sitting in one of the front pews dressed in black and still supporting each other as they had done continuously since the tragedy.

For me and maybe for others, the lack of a focus for our grief was a burden. If there is a coffin and it is carried ceremoniously to the graveyard and buried with due service, it brings the first phase of the tragedy to a close. The healing process can then begin. Because we could not find the bodies of our dead colleagues, the service lacked the finality of a burial and after the service I found it very difficult in the first days to ignore what had occurred and resume the daily routine as if nothing had happened. But life has to go on.

Some days after the service of remembrance short, fat, balding, Hugo Peterson came on board and was taken to the captain's cabin. Shortly afterwards I was called to the cabin, and when I went in I was introduced to Mr. Peterson. Captain Stewart then said quietly, "Mr. Smiley, I have given Mr. Peterson the report you prepared together with your field books, but Mr. Peterson would like you to describe how you performed the survey."

"Aye, sir," I said then politely to Mr. Peterson "Are you a surveyor, sir?" because I had learnt that it does help to know the level of knowledge of the person I am talking to. Some of the basic detail can be omitted from the account if there is already a level of understanding of the subject.

Peterson mopped his streaming face with a large handkerchief and said, "I am an accountant," and then added in a very condescending tone "If a lad like you can make a survey I'm sure I will have no difficulty understanding you."

I looked at Captain Stewart for guidance but he was too surprised by Peterson's answer to provide any words of wisdom.

I think I was a little piqued by the way Peterson had belittled people like McFadden, Carmichael and Evans and quite deliberately, I larded the accurate description of the work I had done with as many technical terms as I could articulate. It was not long before a puzzled frown appeared and strengthened on Peterson's face and when I mentioned tacheometry, he said, "Tachy what?" and reached rapidly into his pocket.

He pulled out a watch which he stared at momentarily before saying, "I am late for another appointment." He jumped up grabbed the report and field books and started toward the cabin door. "Good afternoon Captain, Mr. Smiley. Very interesting I'm sure. If I have any questions I will call on you, Captain."

He rushed out of the cabin closing the door quickly behind him. Captain Stewart and I stared at each other in silence for a moment. "Deuced complicated business this surveying. That will be all Mr. Smiley."

"Aye, sir," I said and as I closed the cabin door I heard the captain give a great bellow of laughter. I couldn't help giving vent to a little chuckle myself as I thought of the way Peterson's pompousness had so suddenly deflated.

Some time later I received a very nice letter of commendation from the new chief surveyor. He had been impressed with the accuracy of the work we had done in such a short time, particularly in the tragic circumstances that had prevailed and sent with his letter a copy of the drawing they had made from the survey data. I was surprised to find that I was named on the drawing as the Surveyor.

It was an unexpected honour.

Some months later I discovered that Captain Stewart had written a report to the Telegraph Company about my potentially dangerous meeting with the tribesmen at Mussandam. He had also sent a copy to The Managing Director of Gold Star Line at the head office in Liverpool. Captain Stewart permitted me read a copy of the report and I came to the conclusion that the whole incident had been much exaggerated. There was nothing I could do about it but accept as modestly as possible the praise I received and hope the whole business would be soon forgotten.

It was with sadness and a great deal of anger that we received some very bad news a week later.

Peterson, the Telegraph Company's manager came on board to see the captain about various matters relating to a consignment of cargo we were discharging. After the meeting and as Captain Stewart was escorting Peterson to the head of the gangway, Peterson said quite casually in the hearing of myself and several of the officers and men, "Did you know, Captain, that the survey young Smiley made for us wasn't urgent after all? Sir Algernon had misunderstood the message. Actually, there was no urgency at all as the cable will not be laid for some time. Good afternoon, Captain." Then he walked down the gangway apparently without a care in the world.

He said no word about the unnecessary waste of life, and we could only stare open mouthed after him because we certainly cared. Six good men had died because of the pompous incompetence of a man who occupied a position of authority due to his parentage and not merit.

We finished discharging our cargo and then loaded a cargo of cotton for Liverpool.

I soon settled into the routine of the third officer's duties and the daily poignant reminders of Evans presence faded in intensity with the passing days and many tiring duty hours.

Two days before we were due to sail, Captain Stewart called his three officers to his cabin. When we were all assembled he said, "I have received an invitation to attend a ball and reception at the governor's official residence tomorrow night. The function is intended to honour the captains of the three Royal Navy frigates that have just arrived and is due to commence at eight in the evening. I have been invited to bring you three gentlemen with me if duty permits. I am sure I can make sure that duty will not be an impediment, and if none of my officers has an objection, I will send an acceptance immediately."

Of course we all said how delighted we were to be invited, and then we were dismissed by the captain with his, "Very well, I'll accept the invitation immediately. We will meet on deck and leave promptly at seven bells in the dog watch tomorrow."

Not that there was any possibility of refusing the invitation.

Even if the governor had been the worst rogue in the country, it would have been necessary to remain on the right side of authority if one wished to continue trading successfully in this part of the world.

In actual fact, we were blessed with an intelligent and honest man, who dealt fairly with every one he met in the course of his duties and it was a pleasure for us to accept.

Just before seven bells, when I came on deck, the number one boat was already in the water and moored to the foot of the gangway. The bosun with six of our sailors to man the oars, were all at their places in the boat, and I noticed that they were all very smartly turned out in clean, pressed company uniforms. At seven bells, on this sultry Indian evening, the captain, first mate, second mate and myself climbed down the gangway one behind the other and boarded the boat trying not to touch anything wet or dirty. At a nod from the captain the bosun gave the order to cast off, and we were then rowed smartly across to the shore.

We disembarked at the boat steps and walked the few yards to the carriage that Captain Stewart had arranged. In our clean, carefully pressed uniforms, white caps and highly polished buttons and boots, we looked quite smart, and I believe we brought credit on our ship.

Before entering the carriage, Captain Stewart turned to the bosun and said, "you can return to the ship. Return here at midnight to transport us back on board."

"Aye, sir," said the bosun and saluted.

He went back down the steps, climbed into the boat and called out to the bow man, "Push off there," then, "All together. Lively now," and they rowed back to the ship.

The captain climbed into the carriage, and we climbed in after him in descending order of rank. When we were all seated, we set off at a brisk trot towards the governor's residence. It was not a great distance from the quayside so after a relatively short ride, the carriage turned in through a pair of wrought iron gates set in the massive boundary wall and crunched along a gravel drive lined with flickering oil lamps to the main entrance to the mansion.

The governor's residence was a massive stone building in the Portuguese style much favoured by local architects. In front of the building and illuminated by many oil lamps we joined the queue of coaches bringing other guests to the ball.

As each carriage drew up under the porte-cochere, a uniformed attendant opened the carriage door and placed wooden steps below the opening, to enable any ladies in the coach to make an elegant descent. As we waited our turn to disembark we had a spectacular view of all the ladies and gentlemen who were arriving before us. The men wore sombre black evening wear or the colourful dress uniforms of the various field regiments stationed in the area. From the Royal Navy an Admiral, attended by a bevy of captains and first lieutenants had just descended from three carriages. They were all resplendent in their dress uniforms and walked into the reception with their swords clinking and medals flashing with reflected light from the chandeliers.

I sat entranced by the sight and the perfumes, of a procession of ladies in long ball gowns in white or pale hues or sometimes a strong red or blue. From the waist down all the ladies seemed to wear the same design of dress, apart from the applied decoration of pleats and ribbons and so on. Waists were narrow and the skirt flared out over the hips and then swept to the ground. Above the waist the bodices varied considerably, especially, it seemed, with age. The more matronly ladies were either completely covered or had a small demure opening at the base of the throat. The younger women wore gowns that had much more revealing bodices and displayed a generous amount of bosom. Some even had bare shoulders, a sight I had never seen in my life before. And never had I seen such beautiful women. I had been in an all male society so long that the sight of all this beauty made my palms hot and sweaty and my breeches feel far too tight.

The captain suddenly leant towards me and said in a stern voice, "Third Officer Smiley. Close your mouth. You're gawping at them like an idiot."

"Aye, sir," I said and hastily closed my mouth, embarrassed to realize that I had been staring open mouthed at these lovely ladies and tried to concentrate on more prosaic and less exciting happenings about me.

When we reached the Porte Cochere in our turn, we alighted from the carriage, walked up the steps into the reception area and joined the line of guests waiting to meet our host and hostess. Captain Stewart was in the lead and I brought up the rear.

It is always something of a surprise that people are often the exact opposite of what one would expect from the surname and the governor was no exception.

Sir David Tallboy was a short man who made up in girth what he lacked in stature. His face was round and pink, almost cherubic, but his eyes were pale blue and shrewd looking, and one felt instantly that here was a man of power who knew exactly what he was doing and why. He was dressed conventionally in black.

His wife, Lady Megan, was a little taller than her husband but was elegance personified. An attractive woman and at fifty something years old, still capable of turning male heads. In her twenties she must have been a real beauty I thought. She was courted and won by Sir David when he made regular business visits to her father at his mansion in the lake district of northwest England. She was wearing a dress made from a material coloured a delicate shade of mauve and a broad brimmed black hat trimmed with a broad mauve ribbon tied into a bow at the front. The skirt of the dress was long and pleated and reached almost to the floor. The bodice was demurely cut with a high square neckline, but the bust was emphasised with a vee of black lace from the shoulders to the waist. The long narrow sleeves were finished with black lace and she carried a black, drawstring necked, evening bag. She looked lovely, and once again I was guilty of staring open mouthed at her until the mate noticed and gave me a nudge in the ribs that brought me down to earth.

I stepped up to Sir David when my turn came but before I could draw breath to say, "Good evening," he said unexpectedly, "I am very pleased to meet you Mr. Smiley. I have read some reports describing your recent adventures, and am I am proud of the fact that that you are fellow countryman. The Empire needs more people of your calibre."

I stammered an embarrassed, "Thank you, sir," and was about to move on when I realized that Captain Stewart had returned to stand beside me and had overheard Sir David's comments.

He said quietly, "Mr. Smiley is a credit to my ship, Sir David."

Before the governor could respond, Lady Megan turned to the captain and said, "I am sure he is a credit to you as well as to your ship, Captain," and to me, "Like my husband, Mr. Smiley, may I say how pleased I am to meet you and say that you are very welcome here tonight."

As she turned away from me to greet the next guest she said, "When all the governor's guests have arrived you must attend on me. I want to hear all about your adventure at first hand and not from someone who was not present."

"Yes, of course, Lady Megan," I said with some surprise, as I didn't think that my recent activities would be of the slightest interest to anyone and particularly at a function as important as this one.

Just before the time we expected dinner to be served, I made a point of placing myself close to where Lady Megan was engaged in discussion with the wife of the harbour master. The lady in question was large and clad in a voluminous red satin dress with "leg o' mutton" sleeves trimmed with black lace. There was a decoration made of black lace across her breast and around the shoulders. The ensemble was crowned with a small round black felt hat.

When Lady Megan looked up and saw me, she excused herself from the harbour master's wife, and with her hand on my arm she led me to a chaise longue in a quiet part of the main salon, where we could sit down side by side.

"Odious woman," said Lady Megan undiplomatically, but quietly, as she indicated the back of the departing lady, then added, "She is always complaining and always about something that is unimportant or insignificant to everyone, except herself."

Lady Megan settled herself more comfortably and said, "Now Mr. Smiley, I am so much older than you are that I hope you will not be offended if I call you Jason."

"No, of course not," I responded wondering how she could possibly have known my Christian name.

"I want to hear all about your adventure, but first I would like to ask you a personal question." She was silent for a moment and then asked, "May I?"

"Of course, Lady Megan," I replied knowing instinctively that a refusal wasn't really possible.

"I noticed, as I'm sure others have done, that you bear a strong resemblance to Captain Stewart, but you have very different family names. That makes me curious, and I wondered if you are related to the captain. I hope you will excuse me for being inquisitive."

"Of course," I said, answering the last question first, as I wondered what to do about the first.

Then I said, "Yes we are related," as I hoped forlornly that such a bare statement would be sufficient, but it wasn't.

"Your answer suggests that you are ashamed of the relationship. I would have expected you to be proud to have a blood relationship with a respected man like Captain Stewart and be eager to talk about him," she said.

When I didn't respond she said, "I find it very surprising that you don't want to talk about your relationship with the captain. Did Captain Stewart do something shameful?"

"I don't know, Lady Megan."

"That is very strange, Jason. Here you are, working under the direction of a man who might have done something ungentlemanly, but you do not know what it is and do not want to discuss it."

She looked quizzically at me for a long moment and then said, "I think it will help you overcome your confusion if you talk about your relationship. Will you tell me?"

"Yes," I said and told her everything I knew.

At the end of my explanation she asked, "Is Captain Stewart married?"

"No," I said, "not as far as I know. I have never seen him with a lady nor heard him talk of one."

"It appears to me that Captain Stewart has behaved quite admirably. He honoured your mother's wishes and stayed away from Pickworth for seventeen years or so. He didn't admit the truth until there was no one alive who could be hurt by it, and he has helped his son make a good start in life. He didn't have to do either as only he was aware of the truth. I think I understand why you retained the Smiley surname, but I believe your decision was wrong."

"Now, Mr. Jason Smiley Stewart, I would like to hear a complete account of your escapade in Mussandam."

For a moment I was at a loss to know where to start, but after a moment's reflection I said, "I am sure, Lady Megan that you will not wish me to speak about the tragedy we suffered shortly after we arrived in the Elphinstone Inlet," and she nodded her head in agreement.

"Well Lady Megan, it happened like this. After the tragedy, Captain Stewart called all the officers to his cabin and informed us that he had decided to return to Bombay immediately. In his opinion the survey could not be completed because the surveyors were dead. He told us that he thought it was imperative to advise the authorities of the accident as soon as possible and if the survey was as important as we had been told, there might be time to send another expedition."

I paused for a moment wondering how much of the detail Lady Megan would wish to hear, but she said, "Tell me every thing," as if she had read my thoughts.

I went on, "Captain Stewart did not know that I had gained some experience of land survey before I joined the Earl Canning, and he was rather sceptical about my claim to be able to do something worthwhile before we sailed. However, he allowed me time to make a practical demonstration of my knowledge. After I had persuaded both the captain and the two chainmen from the Telegraph Company that I did know what I was doing, I was allowed to proceed. On the first day we surveyed the island using a technique called tacheometry, and on the morning of the second day we started to survey up the cliff to the ridge between Elphinstone and Malcolm Inlets just using chains and plumb lines."

I paused for a sip of water then said, "Climbing the steep slope was extremely hard work, and all three of us were looking forward to stopping on the ridge for a rest and a long drink of water. I was in the lead and found that the top four or five feet of the cliff face were almost vertical. I straightened up and as my eyes popped over the top edge of the rock I found to my absolute surprise and considerable terror that I was looking into the barrel of a gun. The end was only inches from my face and looked as big as a drainpipe. Beyond the black round mouth of the barrel, I could see two brown eyes glaring out of a face that was as old and as brown and lined as a piece of well used leather. My instinct was to duck back down into the shelter of the cliff, but I didn't dare to. I thought the tribesman might fire if I moved suddenly. At the same time I realized that I might have bumped into one of the chainmen and that could have sent him tumbling back down the slope to the beach.

So I reached up slowly with both hands exposed to show I didn't have a weapon and very, very slowly I started to push the gun barrel gently to one side. It seemed to be held very firmly, and I had to push quite hard before the barrel moved. Then, it suddenly seemed to jump sideways, there was a deafening bang, a jet of powder smoke and I'm sure I heard the whistle of the ball as it sped so closely past my left ear that I felt the wind of its passage. Then the echoes of the bang rattled back from the surrounding cliffs."

I paused again reliving the fear of that moment, then went on, "I dragged myself over the edge of the cliff and onto the ridge as quickly as I could. I expected to have to fight the man although I had no weapons, not even a good sized lump of rock. But I found him lying unmoving face down on the cliff top. I was vaguely aware of the chainmen climbing onto the ridge chattering excitedly and the ship's siren blowing. I realized that he must be dead and consequently no longer a danger to us. I straightened up from my examination of the dead tribesman and moved to the edge of the cliff so that I could wave to the ship to let them know we were unharmed. I knew the captain would be looking at us with a telescope. At the foot of the cliff I noticed the white faces of the boat crew staring up at me and gestured to them to stay with the boat."

After a sip of wine I continued, "I was just about to make a close examination of the Arab who had given me such a fright, when there was a thud and spurt of sand near our feet and a distant bang. I looked towards the sound and saw three men hurrying towards us. One, clearly the man who had fired at us, was trying to reload as he hurried towards us and another was just starting to kneel down in preparation for firing at us. The third man continued to hurry towards us. They all wore the dish dash and turban of the local Oman people and clearly the soles of their bare feet must have been like leather as they came across the red-hot rocks with some speed and agility. The second man fired but fortunately missed us but the ball passed closely enough for us to hear it whistle past.

I realized we were standing on open ground and defenceless. If we retreated back down the cliff the tribesmen would be able to stand at the top and fire at us at their leisure if they wished. If we could not defend ourselves or retreat, our only chance was to hope that they would not attack an unarmed man. I ordered the chainmen to lie down and then started to walk towards our attackers with my open hands displayed and all the confidence and bravado I could muster."

"Were you afraid, Mr. Smiley?" Lady Megan interjected.

"Yes of course, and I remember the strange thought that flashed through my mind as I was walking towards them, as calmly as I could manage. It was 'If you hit me, please kill me, don't leave me a cripple'. I think I was more fearful of pain than death at that moment."

I stopped for a moment and Lady Megan was completely still and silent, waiting for me to resume my tale.

I went on in a quiet voice "The Arabs saw me walking towards them and stopped firing. We walked slowly and carefully towards each other. When we met I realized that apart from the guns they carried, each man had a large Kanjar fastened to the belt around their waists. Their clothes were rather old, stained and smelled strongly of fish amongst other odours but the guns they carried were clean and decorated with some engraving on the breech and what looked like a silver inlay on the wooden butt. They were fascinated by the colour of my hair and obviously thought it was dyed. They poked it, twisted it and disputed over it.

"The leader of the group growled something to his men, whipped out his Kanjar and cut off part of my forelock" and I indicated casually where the piece of hair had not yet grown back, leaving me with a slightly lopsided look.

"He was so quick and the dagger so sharp that I didn't have time to even move, which was just as well, as he looked evil enough to have removed my ear or nose without a qualm if I had. Strangely, I noticed the beautiful decoration on the silver scabbard he sheathed his knife in. They tried rubbing the piece of hair in spittle but the colour still did not come off and they just looked perplexed. As the leader put the lock of hair into a small silver box I pointed to the Arab who was lying on the ground behind me.

They all ran to the body and immediately assumed that I was responsible for the man's death. From the way two of the Arabs turned their guns towards me, I was quite certain that my last moments had come as they could not possible miss from a distance of three or four feet. From the look on the faces of Tomlinson and Davison, who were just scrambling to their feet, they thought the same. Fortunately, the leader examined the body, decided that I was not responsible and said something in Arabic that caused the guns to be lowered."

I turned to Lady Megan and said in conclusion, "The Arabs picked up their comrade and carried him away. We had a drink of water, completed the survey and returned to the ship."

A deep voice from behind us said, "That lady Megan is what I call courage."

As we turned and found the admiral and two of his captains standing behind us, the admiral said, "If you were one of my officers Mr. Smiley, my next report to the Admiralty would include a very favourable report on your conduct. Very well done! sir"

"Thank you Admiral," I said as I jumped to my feet and stood to attention. The captains also offered their congratulations and then moved away to follow their admiral. I sat down again feeling more than a little pleased with myself at receiving praise from an admiral of the Royal Navy.

Lady Megan turned to me and said quietly, "Is your mother still alive Mr. Smiley?"

"No Lady Megan she died some years ago."

"That is a great pity, Mr. Smiley, as she would have been so proud of her son's courage." She stood up and said, "Please come with me, Mr. Smiley, I wish to introduce you to my niece, Miss Mary Thomas. She is here on holiday."

We walked across the room to where a group of army officers in their brightly coloured, gold braided dress uniforms were competing with each other for the attention of a very attractive young woman seated on a chaise longue.

Lady Megan walked into the group and said, "Excuse me, gentlemen, I wish to speak to my niece."

They went away, reluctantly and not very far, as Lady Megan's niece was not only unaccompanied, but was by far the most attractive as well as eligible young woman at the ball.

Lady Megan stood holding my arm and said with a smile, "Mary, my dear, I would like to introduce you to Mr. Jason Smiley. He has just been telling me about his recent dangerous brush with the Oman Arabs. Mr. Smiley, I would like you to meet my niece. She is here on holiday from South Wales and must shortly set off on her voyage home. If you are not already engaged for dinner Mr. Smiley, perhaps you would be kind enough to escort my niece."

"I am not engaged for dinner and should be honoured to escort, Miss Thomas," I managed to answer politely.

Miss Mary Thomas was slightly shorter than me and was wearing a pale lilac, full skirted, pleated dress with a much more modest bodice than many of the ladies were dressed in that evening. However, it didn't completely disguise the fact that she was a very shapely young woman.

Her hair was long, dark and had been brushed until it shone in the candle-light. She had brown eyes, freckles on her small turned up nose and the most perfect oxbow lips I had ever seen. She was a delight to behold, and it was an honour to be her escort if only for a few minutes.

I was so close to this vision of loveliness that I felt my heart beat accelerate. I managed to control my breathing and with as much calmness as I could summon, I said formally "Good Evening, Miss Thomas. May I have the honour to escort you in to dinner?"

She acknowledged my greeting with a smile and said, in lilting accent that I later learned was typical of the Welsh from the south of the country, "My Hero!" and pretended to swoon. Her slightly humorous acknowledgement of my recent exploits was made so sweetly and unex-pectedly, that all who heard joined in my laughter.

A few minutes later, we joined the dinner procession led by Lady Megan and Sir David Tallboy and walked into the dining room in a com-panionable silence, as if we had known each other for years not seconds. It was a big room and alive with liveried servants bustling about with soup tureens and plates and bowls of food. The tables were spread with damask clothes and the silver cutlery sparkled in the light from the many, multi-branched candelabra that had been set around the room. Miss Thomas and I sat side by side towards the end of the top table, and I marvelled at the stroke of good fortune that had brought me to such a position. I expected to be on one of the other tables in accordance with my lowly rank.

As there were many more men at the reception than women, we had a number of army and navy officers seated around us. I was very glad to see that none of the young officers who had been vying for Miss Tho-mas's attention earlier were seated anywhere near us. It was an unreason-able feeling I suppose, since I was in my best uniform, but the military air and smart bright uniforms of the army made me feel slightly insignificant even if Miss Thomas had called me her hero.

It was very hot because of the candles and the press of people. It was also very humid. Not comfortable conditions in which to eat hot food, but we took a mouthful or two of most of the dishes presented to us and drank sparingly of the wine that passed rapidly around the table in the hands of several wine waiters.

I had never sat beside such an attractive young woman in all of my life before and my capacity for social conversation deserted me utterly, not that it was good at the best of times. I sat there drinking in Miss Thomas's fragrance and enjoying her beauty, absolutely dumb from the pleasurable sensations invading my body. I must have been an exceedingly dull dinner companion and I have no knowledge what we said to each other if anything at all. Fortunately for me she did not construe my silence as indifference.

At the end of the meal and after the toasts to The Queen and the Royal Navy had been proposed, seconded and drunk, the ladies left the table so that the gentlemen could partake of port, brandy and cigars.

After about half an hour we returned to the ballroom and I was very gratified when Miss Thomas came directly to me when the ladies returned. The musicians tuned up and as the first chords of music rang out a young army officer, a major, appeared in front of us.

He said, "May I have the pleasure of your company for the first dance, Miss Thomas?"

"I'm very sorry" she said "but this dance is already promised to Mr. Smiley."

"Perhaps you will honour me with the next dance then?"

"No that is also promised. Now if you will excuse us," and we left him standing staring open mouthed and clearly wondering what attributes this merchant navy officer possessed that Miss Thomas preferred him to a major in the dragoons. I wondered as well, and my wonderment grew as the evening passed and I found that every dance except for some duty dances had been promised to me. Even more wondrous was the fact that it had never occurred to me to ask for a dance in the first place, as dancing is not one of my social graces. I silently blessed the captain's sister for instructing me in the little I knew.

The evening passed in a mixture of dancing and sitting and talking. Now that we were together, I found my tongue and started asking Miss Thomas about her home and her family. She lived in a big house built so close to the sea one could hear the waves breaking on the beach. She described her mother as a loving and caring person and her father as intelligent and hard working. She didn't say so, but I had the impression that he was a rather strict man. In turn I described my life at sea and some of the places the ship had called at. Time flew by and suddenly it was time to return to the ship. I do not know if she had eyes for anyone else, but I certainly had eyes for no one but Miss Mary Thomas. My life had changed irrevocably. For the first time in my life I knew what it was like to fall helplessly in love.

She came with me to the top of the steps when it was time to leave and returned my bow with a curtsy. She said very quietly and privately to me, "Mr. Smiley, it would be a pleasure to meet you again."

Then she turned back before I could reply, and I could only stand staring after her as she walked away into the grand house and was lost from view.

From behind me I heard Mr. Richards, the mate say to someone, "I'll wager that young Smiley will be off to Cardiff five minutes after we dock in Liverpool," and then a gust of gentle laughter.

We went back to the ship and in the middle of the next day we closed the hatches and sailed for Liverpool.

NINE

Homecoming

Our voyage back to Liverpool was uneventful.

In one respect this was a great pity as it gave me much too much time to daydream about Miss Mary Thomas.

She had made a much deeper impression on me than I realized, and my thoughts soon turned to the prospect of meeting her again. No sooner did the anticipation of a meeting take root in my mind than I realized I did not know where she lived, except that it was in South Wales, on the coast somewhere near Cardiff.

Equally problematic was the fact that there was no way to make contact with her. Writing to her at the governor's residence would not help as she would have left there long before a letter could possibly arrive.

The hopelessness of my situation became a bigger burden as each day passed. I only knew her name and not her address. How could I hope to find her without having the slightest information about where she lived? Wild thoughts of leaving the ship in Liverpool and tramping the coast near Cardiff buzzed in my brain, although what I would do for money whilst I searched wasn't even considered. She had said she would like to meet me again, but was that simply politeness? It hadn't sounded like it at the time, but how could I know without seeing her and how could I see her when I did not know where she lived.

And so my thoughts went round and round, and my shipmates became increasingly irritated by my preoccupation. But I didn't notice and failed to heed the less and less polite hints they gave me.

Then Donovan came to my cabin one afternoon and told me to report to Captain Stewart in his cabin immediately. I did as I was instructed and whilst the captain sat as his desk as usual, his normally relaxed and cheerful countenance had been replaced with a much sterner countenance. With a tone of voice I had never heard before, and hope

I will never hear again, he said bluntly, "Mr. Smiley, you are behaving like a love sick child, and you are not performing your duties to my satisfaction. The first mate and second officer have to be extra vigilant when you are on duty because they have to prevent the mistakes you make due to inattention, growing into disasters. You are not doing your duty as you should, Mr. Smiley, and this has to stop and stop now. Your performance since we left Bombay has been so bad that I will have to review my decision to appoint you as third officer if it does not improve immediately. You must put Miss Mary Thomas in the appropriate compartment in your life and concentrate on your duties before your negligence causes an accident."

For a moment I did not completely take in what had been said. Then some of the pointed comments such as, "Asleep again Mr. Smiley?" or "Forgotten what I taught you?" made by my fellow officers as they had to countermand my orders, came back to me. I knew I was being given a final chance to make a success of my career as a deck officer.

I could only make one response. I said, "Captain Stewart, sir, I have behaved very badly, and I apologise for the trouble I have caused by my stupid selfishness. It will not happen again."

Captain Stewart said bluntly, "It must not happen again, Mr. Smiley. Dismiss."

I left his cabin a very chastened individual. After being in everyone's good books for so long, the Captain's anger was a chastening experience, and I put away my dreams when I was on duty. But they came back in full force when I went to my cabin, and they succeeded in disturbing my sleep night after night.

After we had docked at our usual berth in Liverpool docks, the captain sent Donovan to call me to his cabin.

I said jokingly to Donovan, "I hope I'm not in trouble again."

Donovan's terse, "Not this morning as far as I know, Mr. Smiley," was hardly reassuring.

However, as I was sure my conduct had been exemplary since I had received the captain's warning, I went to his cabin with reasonable confidence and knocked on the door. Captain Stewart was sitting in his customary place at his desk, but the desk was uncharacteristically covered with ledgers and other papers.

He said, "Good morning, Mr. Smiley, someone from the ship has to go to see Mr. Evans family and deliver his personal affects. A company director visited them so they already know the circumstances of John's tragic death, but even so it will not be easy to meet them."

He gestured at the papers strewn on his desk and went on, "I am preparing the end of voyage report for the owners and that will take some days to complete. You are the only officer I can spare at present. Even though it will mean some extra duty for Mr. Richards and the Second Officer, I have decided to send you to Caernarfon as my representative. In any case it's appropriate that you go, as you lived and worked with John Evans for a long time and knew him better than anyone else on board. I wish you to express my heartfelt condolences to the family and tell them that I will visit them in Caernarfon as soon as the urgent business of the ship allows. You will find Mr. Evans home just outside Caernarfon on the Llandeilo Road near to St. Peblig's Church Vicarage."

Captain Stewart opened a drawer in his desk and took out a purse and a sheet of paper. The purse clinked when he set it down on his desk. He opened the purse and set out in front of himself three gold sovereigns and some other miscellaneous coins. I noticed there were a few half sovereigns amongst the crowns, shillings and sixpences.

He put the money back into the purse and said, as he handed it to me, "Please count the money and sign for it on this receipt," and he handed me the piece of paper.

"The money is for your expenses during the journey to Third Officer Evans home and return. I shall expect a detailed accounting of your expenditure when you are back on board."

"Aye, sir" I said.

I duly counted the coins and signed the receipt for five gold sovereigns that the captain had prepared. The coins went back into the purse and then into the safety of my pocket.

"Collect Mr. Evans personal affects from the bosun and leave tomorrow at six bells in the morning watch," Captain Stewart instructed.

"Aye, sir" I said and left the captain's cabin to find the bosun.

Next morning I left the ship as instructed. I was wearing an old uniform and carried my best one in a duffel bag so that I would look as presentable as possible when I reached the home of Mr. Evans' family.

My journey was achieved by rail and horse drawn carriage, at a pedestrian pace and with a level of tedium too boring to recount. I progressed by stages first to Chester, then along the north coast of Wales through Abergele, Conway and Bangor. In Caernarfon, which I reached part way through the morning of the second day, I went to a small inn just inside the town walls called "Tafern Bachgen Du" and hired a room for the night. It was a small room under the eaves with a dormer window looking out on to North Gate Street.

I climbed up the stairs to the room in order to change into my best uniform and then, carrying the small parcel containing John Evans personal affects, decided to go out to hire some sort of conveyance to take me to the Evans home.

After asking the landlord for information, I walked to a nearby stable where I was able to hire a horse drawn trap and a driver to take me to the home of the Evans family.

I was extremely fortunate to hire a pony and trap with a driver as it was Market Day—and even more fortunate that the driver, pony and trap were so excellently prepared. The paintwork on the trap gleamed from the polishing it had received, and the pony had been groomed until its russet coat shimmered in the sunshine. The driver looked magnificent. His well-brushed black bowler hat surmounted a neatly trimmed, black beard framed, ruddy face. His eyes were a piercing blue. He wore a coat of a thick dark green material that had two vertical rows of highly buffed brass buttons, tan coloured breeches and a pair of black polished boots a Grenadier Guardsman would die for. He spoke Welsh as a matter of course, but he had a sufficient grasp of English to enable us to communicate with ease. I described to him where I had to go and why.

I said, "I want you to take me to the Evans house and wait for me while I am talking with them and then I want you to bring me back into Caernarfon because I'll stay the night at the 'Tafern Bachgen Du'. How much is your fee for the duty I have described?"

He scratched the side of his head with the end of his whip shaft and after a little thought named a figure that was about half what I would have expected based on experience in Liverpool. I accepted his offer with a haste that made him review it mentally, but he didn't seek to change it. I climbed up onto the trap and we set off to find the Evan's home in brilliant sunshine under a blue sky studded with lumps of fluffy white cloud.

We found the house without difficulty, and the driver stopped the trap under the shade of a convenient overhanging tree.

So in the sunshine of a lovely day, I walked the last few yards to the front gate of the house where my friend and mentor John Evans had lived for so many of his formative years.

The house he had come back to for a holiday at the end of every voyage except this one.

As I stepped inside the gate, a feeling of sadness seemed to reach out and envelope me. It was an illusion, of course, but the sun seemed to shine less brightly and the sky became less blue as I walked to the front door. The curtains were tightly drawn and the front door was framed with some flowing black material. The knocker had been muffled with padding that was covered in black material tied into a bow. I noticed that the ends of the bow ribbons hung down nearly to the threshold in the doorway.

I took hold of the knocker and used it, but it gave off a sullen thud, due to the padding. I imagine that the Evans thought the rat-a-tat of a doorknocker would have been an inappropriately cheerful noise for a house in deep mourning as this house clearly was.

The door opened and a small woman in the black dress and mob-cap of a servant stood in the doorway and looked at me.

I waited a moment, and as she said nothing, I introduced myself. "I am Jason Smiley from the 'Earl Canning'. I would like to see Captain and Mrs. Evans, if possible. I have Mr. John Evans personal affects to give them," and I held the package out so that she could see it.

The maid turned away from me with a sob and disappeared back into the house without another sound. The door swung shut, and I waited on the step feeling like an unwanted tinker.

A few minutes later the door opened again and the same maid stood in the hall and said, "Please come in, Mr. Smiley. Captain Evans will see you."

She stood back to let me enter, then closed the door, before noise-lessly preceding me along the hall. In comparison with her silent steps, my boots made an unseemly noise on the tiled floor and my footsteps seemed to echo through the whole building. She opened a door and led me into a room made gloomy by the drawn curtains. Captain Evans dressed in funereal black, stood tall and erect in front of the unlit fire.

He held out his hand for the package I was carrying, "My wife and daughter are indisposed," he said. "John's death has been a devastating shock for them both. Are these my son's belongings?"

I nodded and handed him the small package that contained the meagre remnants of John Evans' life on board the Earl Canning.

I said, "Captain Evans, as Captain Stewart is unable to see you personally for a few days, he has instructed me to extend his deepest sympathy to you, your wife and . . ." but I could not finish as he interrupted angrily.

"I'm not interested in your Captain's sympathy, particularly when it is delivered by a junior officer. If Captain Stewart had performed his duty competently my son would still be alive. I have received letters from Bombay telling me what happened. You are not welcome here, Mr. Smiley, please leave this house immediately."

I said, "I do not know what you have been told by people in Bombay but I know that Captain Stewart did all he could to prevent the accident." I would have gone on in the same vein but decided it was better to leave as Captain Evans was growing angrier by the second and clearly had no intention of listening to an opinion other than his own.

He had made his mind up about culpability and nothing was going to change that.

As I walked along the hallway I heard a footstep, turned back and came face to face with John Evans' sister. She was no longer the beautiful young woman in the portrait John Evans had been so proud of.

Her face was distorted with grief and she hissed at me with all the spite and venom of an angry snake "Why are you alive, Mr. Smiley? You should have been in that boat not my brother. You should have died, not our John. I hate you for standing there so healthy and full of life. I never want to see you again." She whirled around and away from me and disappeared through a curtained opening at the end of the hall.

I stumbled along the gloomy passageway, opened the door and thankfully returned to the sane world in the sun outside. In the road, beyond the gate to the house, I stood in the sunshine and heard the birds chirruping. I thought back to the day when John Evans had so proudly shown me the portrait of his sister, and I remembered my lustful thoughts of visiting with disgust, as I contemplated the vision of the harridan I had just left and hoped I would never have the misfortune of seeing her again.

I walked back to the horse and trap and was driven back into Caernarfon although I was too wrapped in my thoughts to notice which way we went. I paid off the driver and walked the short distance to the inn where I had a meal but cannot recollect what I ate and then went to bed. My sleep was disturbed by the animosity of Miss Evans' words and the violence of her posture, and I was glad to be called in the dawn to get on the coach and start the trip back to the ship. The journey back was no quicker than the journey out, and I reported to Captain Stewart as soon as I returned on board. He listened to my account of my meeting with Captain Evans and his expression became very grave, but he didn't comment.

He was shocked by the way I had been treated by Miss Evans and said, "Grief can cause people to act in strange and unworthy ways, and I am quite sure that Miss Evans will live to regret the comments she made to you. You had no involvement in the tragedy that caused her brother's death, and you are not mentioned in the reports for that reason. You were simply the watch officer that disastrous morning."

He looked as if he were about to say more but contented himself with, "That will be all Mr. Smiley. Report to the mate."

"Aye, sir," I said as I left the cabin.

After the mate had given me my orders for the next days, he gave me a letter and I took it below to my cabin to read in private as my first watch would not start until eight bells in the afternoon.

I could not imagine who could have sent me a letter, and then noticed it came from Bombay which made the mystery even more impenetrable.

It was a shock to realize that the events of the past few days had driven thoughts of Mary Thomas from my mind when she had been a constant companion for all those weeks since the ball. I felt very guilty, and when I opened the letter I couldn't believe my eyes when I saw that it was signed Mary. I was so eager to read it that I almost tore it in half trying to unfold it too quickly.

Residence of the Governor of Bombay
Century House
Bombay

3rd Officer Jason Smiley
SS Earl Canning
C/o Gold Star Line
Liverpool

Dear Mr. Smiley

I was surprised that you did not call to pay your respects after the ball, but Aunt Megan told me that you would have been unable to leave the ship so soon before sailing; so I forgive you. I said that I hoped we would meet again but your departure from Bombay meant that this happy event would be impossible as you do not know where I live in Wales.

Aunt Megan has assured me that I am not behaving in an unladylike way by writing to you like this because as she said, "sometimes luck needs a little help." I think my Aunt Megan quite liked you and I'm sure my Mother will as well when she has met you.

I live with my Mother and Father at Porthkerry House, which is situated on the coast eleven miles west of Cardiff.

I hope you are in good health and look forward to a reply.

Your Forgiving Friend,
Mary.

I sat in a stunned silence for many moments. My fears of being unable to see Mary again, dispersed because Aunt Megan wanted to give luck a little push.

I went on shore and bought writing paper and envelopes then rushed back on board ship. I sat down to write a suitable reply in a fever of anticipation and neither did I know where to start, nor what to say after I had succeeded in starting.

My indecision would have been terrible to see but fortunately there was no one to witness it. I started and blotted the page so it was screwed up and thrown into the corner of the cabin. I wrote a few lines and didn't like them. This page was screwed up and thrown into the corner. There were soon more screwed up sheets of paper than fresh clean ones. I went on deck to try to think, but I could not make more order of my thoughts in the fresh air than I had in my stuffy cabin.

When the mate came on deck for a breath of fresh air I took a great liberty with his good nature and asked for his advice. I told him what Mary had said and his counsel was so simple and straight forward that I could have kicked myself for not thinking of it.

He said, "Write respectfully to Miss Thomas's father but do not mention her letter. Say you had the honour to meet Miss Thomas at the Governor's Ball in Bombay and should be grateful if he would grant you permission to pay your respects when you are next at home on leave."

I did as the mate suggested. I wrote a letter, posted it and settled down to wait as patiently as I could for a reply, hoping all the time something would delay the date of our departure.

Captain Stewart returned a few days later and we started final preparations for our voyage. Late in the morning of the day before we were due to sail, two letters arrived. One for the captain and one for me from Wales, but it hadn't been written by Mary. I had studied her writing until I was familiar with every curl and twist of her letters. I had so looked forward to seeing a letter from her that this unfamiliar hand was a bad shock. I expected the worst, but was on watch and would have to wait another three hours before I could go to my cabin and read it. Meantime it felt as if it was burning a hole in my pocket and I checked compulsively to make sure it had not dropped out.

Three hours later just as I was handing over the watch to the second officer, the mate came to the bridge closely followed by the captain. Captain Stewart told the mate that he had just received orders from Captain Downing that the ship would remain in port for a further week to take on a special cargo for Bombay. He turned to me and said there would be a passenger on board and I would have to share my cabin.

Then he added with a grin, "As you are the only member of my crew to have recent experience of seasickness, Mr. Smiley, you will be the best person to help our passenger, will you not?"

"Aye, sir," was all I could say as it was many years since I had been so inflicted.

Captain Stewart then went back to his cabin and I was free to go to mine. In my cabin I sat on my bunk and turned the envelope over in my hands, more than half afraid to open it now that I could, in case it contained bad news. Curiosity soon overcame fear and this time I summoned the patience to slit the envelope with the knife I carried on my belt.

Porthkerry House
Barry
Glamorganshire
South Wales

Dear Mr. Smiley,

Thank you for your letter, which I am answering on my husband's behalf as he is away on business for the next half a year.

My daughter has told me of your meeting at the Governor's ball and I have also received a note from my cousin, Lady Megan, who was much impressed with your modesty and bravery.

My daughter and I would be pleased to receive you at Porthkerry House when you are able to take leave from your duties. We shall be in residence for the next six months and look forward to learning when you can visit. I will send the carriage to Cardiff to meet you when I know what time you will arrive.

Yours sincerely
Mrs. Agnes Thomas

I bounced from my bunk and was out of my cabin and knocking on the captain's door almost before I had read the last sentence.

He shouted, "Enter," and I did and closed the behind me.

I said, "Captain, sir," and stopped in total confusion, as I had not considered for one second what I would say. Captain Stewart noted my hesitation and also the letter still open and clutched in my hand.

He reached out and took it from my fingers and said, "With your permission, Mr. Smiley, perhaps I should read this."

I nodded and said, "Yes, Sir."

He read it and said, "This concerns the young lady you were daydreaming about when we were coming back from Bombay, I presume?"

"Yes, sir," I said.

"And this is a reply to the letter you sent to the young lady's Father?"

"Yes, sir," I said assuming that the first mate had told him.

"And I suppose you want permission to go and visit Miss Thomas now that our sailing date has been postponed?"

I gulped with suppressed excitement and surprise but managed to say, "Yes, sir," once again.

"You realize, Mr. Smiley, that if I let you go your duties will have to be done by the remaining officers?"

"Yes, sir," I responded.

"And you understand that at sometime in future you will have to repay the debt?" he went on making quite sure I understood that it was a favour I was asking for, not a right.

Again I responded with the only possible answer, "Yes, sir."

There was a pause, probably only a few seconds long but it seemed like years, then Captain Stewart said, "First of all find out how you can travel from Liverpool to Cardiff and back and how long the journeys will take. If there is time to go and return within the extra week we will be in port I will give you permission to leave the ship, but you will have to write to Mrs. Thomas and tell her when you will arrive in Cardiff before I permit you to set off."

I said a heartfelt, "Thank you Captain."

"That will be all, Mr. Smiley."

"Aye, sir," I said as I left the cabin as quickly as decorum allowed.

Fortunately I was not on watch so I was able to obtain permission to leave the ship from the watch officer without difficulty. After signing out I left the ship and hurried along the quay. As I came out of the dock gate, a horse drawn cab was passing. I flagged it down and hired it so that I would get to Lime Street Station more quickly. At the station I found that I could easily travel to Cardiff in a day and the return journey was also possible in a day. I rushed back to the ship gave Captain Stewart the train times for both journeys and with his agreement composed and posted a letter to Mrs. Thomas telling her when I would arrive.

The captain would not let me leave the next day as I wished. "It's no good arriving before your letter," was his sage advice, but he let me go the day after that.

"One day there and one day back. If you cannot make a good impression in the three days you are there," he said but didn't continue. He gave me the good advice a father would give a son at such a time, and I was sent on my way with his blessing.

TEN

Porthkerry House

At three bells I was roused by one of the watch keepers. Probably because I was so excited by the thought of seeing Miss Thomas again, I had slept badly until it was nearly time to get up and had then fallen into the deepest of sleeps. Erect but still more than half asleep, I shaved and washed in cold water. I was then alert enough to put on a good working uniform and pack a small duffle bag with clean clothes and a carefully folded best uniform. It was too early for breakfast on board so I made my way to the head of the gangway to sign out at four bells.

Brian Davis the second officer said, "Good morning, Mr. Smiley. Off on another journey? I hope this one is happier for you than the last one."

"I hope so too, Mr. Davis," was all I was prepared to say, but my fingers were firmly crossed in the hope that nothing would happen to prevent my safe arrival at Porthkerry House in Barry.

I walked down the gangway, along the deserted quayside and opened the wicket set in the middle of one of the main gates. As I stepped out into Waterloo Road, the gatekeeper roused himself enough to grumble, "Shut it after you," in almost incomprehensible Scouse and then he settled back to sleep the remaining night away.

As I walked along Waterloo Road, the sound of my boots striking the granite sets echoed back from the dock wall. The closed and shuttered warehouses opposite sent another echo back that made it sound like two people walking not quite in step in the otherwise quiet, before dawn hours. As I walked, I looked in vain for a cab to speed me to the station and I pondered upon the wisdom of employing a watchman whose ability to provide security was in inverse proportion to his ability to sleep. I could find no wisdom in the proposition or a good reason to support it. But as my brain and body responded to the rhythm of my march, my thoughts turned back to the journey I was to make and the lovely young woman who had made it possible for me to make it. The anticipation of our meeting caused both my pulse and my stride to speed up so that I was in danger of arriving in the station at an undignified trot holding my uniform cap on my head.

It would have been a sight that would surely have brought the displeasure of Captain Downing down upon my head like a thunderbolt if he had chanced to witness it.

So I controlled my feelings and arrived amongst the assembled early, or possibly very late travellers at Liverpool Lime Street Station at a dignified pace more suited to my uniform.

I made the journey to Cardiff by train. It was a long, slow, rattling, smutty progress on several different railway lines, but the chocolate and cream liveried, Great Western Railway, carried me over the last stage.

As my destination drew closer, I began to worry if there had been time for my letter to arrive and how I would recognize the Thomas's carriage if it was there and what I would do if it was not. I calmed myself to some extent with the thought that at least I now had an address, and I supposed it would be possible to hire a horse or a trap somewhere in the city and get directions to Barry.

The train ground to a halt in Cardiff, and I climbed stiffly down and walked out into the busy area in front of the station mentally preparing myself for a bitter disappointment. But my concerns were unfounded as Miss Thomas had come in her father's coach to meet me. Sensibly, she had stayed in the coach and taken advantage of the height it afforded to have the best view of the exit. I think she must have seen me long before I had any indication that she was even at the station. As I pushed my way through the crowds, frantically looking around me, I suddenly found Miss Thomas standing in front of me. She was even more breathtakingly beautiful than I remembered, and I was momentarily speechless from relief that she was really there and pleasure at the stunning picture before me. We greeted each other with the formality demanded by convention although it was only with the exercise of considerable restraint that I stopped myself from embracing her immediately.

"Good afternoon, Miss Thomas," I said gravely.

She responded with an equally reserved, "Good afternoon, Mr. Smiley."

"I am so pleased to see you again," I said as calmly as my thundering heart would allow.

She responded calmly in her delightful Welsh lilt, "As I am to see you, Mr. Smiley," Her smile of welcome seemed to light the streets, and I started to dare to hope that she might have eyes for me alone, as I had dreamed she might.

Through my euphoria I heard her say, "I am very pleased to welcome you to Wales and also to welcome you on behalf of my mother and father, Mr. Smiley. Please give your bag to James." She indicated the coachman with a gesture and added, "Please get in the coach and we will start the journey home. It's about fifteen miles and will take us at least two hours."

I did as I was asked and found myself sitting opposite the lady of my dreams, but I was sadly disappointed to find that there was a servant girl sitting in the coach with us. My eager thoughts about starting my courtship of Miss Mary Thomas died with my first sight of a bob cap and starched apron. I should have anticipated a chaperone, but it was an unwelcome surprise to find that I could not speak as I wished.

But in retrospect it was probably as well.

When we were all on board the coachman clicked the horses into action, and we drove away from the station along St. Mary Street past a long row of shops. We turned left in front of Cardiff Castle and crossed the bridge over the River Taff. As we progressed, Miss Thomas started to point out various interesting landmarks. We passed Llandaff Cathedral and soon travelled beyond the boundary of Cardiff, heading in a westerly direction along the Cowbridge Road. At the cross roads just to the south of St. Fagans, we took the road that led towards the south west.

Once out of the city, the coach started to travel quite quickly, as the coachman tried to get us to Porthkerry House before dark. Over the years I have been driven in a variety of horse drawn wagons without any adverse affect, but I found that the lurching and swaying of the coach as it negotiated the lumps and bumps in the unpaved track, was producing the same feelings of discomfort and distress that I had experienced when I was so badly seasick on my first voyage. I had a sudden fear that I was going to disgrace myself in front of the lady of my dreams, but could think of no way in which I could bring the journey to at least a temporary halt, without admitting my weakness.

My feelings of nausea increased and my conversation with Miss Thomas became less and less enthusiastic as the minutes ticked by. I noticed that Miss Thomas had become a little paler and quieter since we started our journey, and I wondered if she was also affected.

I was on the point of articulating my weakness and request a few minutes of calm when the maid servant saved my bacon. She had become exceedingly pale and suddenly stood up. She shouted something to the driver, which I presume, was the Welsh for Stop! The coach slowed in response to the driver's pulls on the reins and shouts of "Whoa, there!" as she rushed to the carriage door and threw it open. She stepped quickly through the doorway, jumped down, tripped and fell into the long grass and weeds beside the road. I jumped down and had just enough time to help her stand up, when she doubled over and vomited copiously. I could do nothing but stand and support her until the first waves of sickness past. Over the servant's bowed head, I could see Miss Thomas saying something forceful to the coachman and the alternate nods and shakes of his head as he listened to his mistress's instructions. I realized that my own feelings of nausea had completely disappeared in my attempt to ease the servant girl's suffering.

She wasn't sick again, and after a brief rest we resumed our journey at a more comfortable pace.

Miss Thomas's colour had recovered to her normal peaches and cream and shortly after we started our journey again she said, "Thank you for helping Elsie, Mr. Smiley."

"That's alright, Miss Thomas. I know how very unpleasant it is to be seasick and did what I could to help her," was all I could say.

The maid mumbled an embarrassed, "Diolch Yn Fawr," and relapsed into a pallid silence.

The road rambled through the countryside generally following the boundaries of the farms that patterned the area. The land here is relatively high I noticed, about 300 feet above sea level, and is a mixture of woods, open grazing and small farms. Mary named some of the parishes we passed and greatly enjoyed my clumsy rendition of names like Pen Coedtre or Merthyr Dyfan or Cwm Cidy which she pronounced so fluently in her delightful Welsh accent. I was much more at home with Nightingale Cottages and Knock-man-down Wood. At the end of

Knock-man-down Wood we drove down into a valley and after crossing a brook followed the well-maintained track up into the woods on the other side. The track ended at Porthkerry House which was in sight, sound and scent of the sea.

The house is set on a small plateau cut into the side of the hillside, the cliff really, below St. Curig's church. I found later that a wrought iron fence borders the garden in front of the house. Beyond the fence there is a narrow strip of springy, dark green grass, sprinkled with clumps of flowers known as sea pinks.

In the rosy glow projected by the setting sun, the coachman brought the carriage to a halt in front of the house and we climbed down rather stiffly. The coachman handed my bag to a male servant who had appeared as we stopped and then drove the horses away towards the stable.

Mary, with Elsie a forlorn and pale shadow beside her, led me into the house to meet her Mother. Mrs. Thomas was seated in a well-lit room reading a book in a green leather binding. There was a colourful tapestry mounted on a frame on a stand in the corner where she sat. Scatter rugs covered the polished hardwood floor and there were some nice oil paintings on the walls. Some of the pictures depicted floral arrangements and others country scenery. There was some embroidery on a side table and I felt that this was Mrs. Thomas's workroom.

She put her book down when we came into the room and stood up to greet me in a gentle, husky sounding voice, "Good evening, Mr. Smiley. I am so pleased you were able to come to visit us for a few days. I'm sorry my husband will not be here during your visit, but as you know he is away on business."

"Good evening, Mrs. Thomas, it is an honour and a pleasure to be here. Please let me thank you for your invitation and for sending the carriage with such a lovely guide to meet me."

Mary smiled happily, but said nothing.

I was amazed by the strong resemblance between Mrs. Thomas and Mary. She could have been Mary Thomas's elder sister, and I said impulsively, "If I had not known that you and Miss Mary are mother and daughter, I would have imagined you were sisters."

Mrs. Thomas seemed pleased with my unintended compliment and said "That's very kind of you. What a nice thing to say and quite a complement to an old lady."

"But you are not old, Mother!" and I echoed Miss Thomas's quick comment,

Mrs. Thomas smiled happily at her daughter and then said to me, "Porthkerry House is quite a long way from the nearest village, and as a result, we make our own entertainment. Over the next few days, I am sure my daughter will show you some of the local countryside—plenty of exercise and good Welsh air before you go back to sea—and I have invited some neighbours to a small dinner party on the evening before you leave.

In the evenings we generally sew or read and you are welcome to use the library as often as you like and read whatever is there that appeals to you."

After completing her small speech of welcome, Mrs. Thomas tugged gently on a bell pull and after a short wait whilst Miss Thomas described Elsie's illness on the journey another maid appeared.

"Please take Mr. Smiley to his room," Mrs. Thomas instructed the maid and then to me she said, "Please join us for a sherry at seven thirty and we will have dinner at eight, if that is convenient?"

Of course it was and I said, "Seven-thirty will be perfectly convenient." Then I followed the maid upstairs to find my room and dress for dinner.

Punctually at seven-thirty I came downstairs in my best uniform and was met in the hall by the male servant who had taken my bag earlier. He said his name was George. He asked how I was and ushered me into a small, comfortably furnished room where he presented me with a sherry in a small glass with a shield etched into it. I waited patiently, and Mrs. Thomas arrived at about a quarter to eight looking slightly flustered. She was full of questions and trying her best to conceal her agitation.

"Good evening again, Mr. Smiley. I'm sorry I'm a little late. I hope the sherry is to your taste. Do you have everything in your room that you need? Please tell me if you need anything or inform one of the servants."

She accepted a glass of sherry from George, and as she took the first sip, I said "No apology is necessary, Mrs. Thomas. I have everything I need in my room, thank you, and the sherry is delicious."

We sat in silence for a few minutes, and then I asked, "I wonder if you know how Lady Megan is. I met her in Bombay at the governor's reception, and she introduced me to your daughter."

"I had a letter from Lady Megan just yesterday, and she wrote that she is very well," Mrs. Thomas answered, but any further comment she had contemplated was prevented by the arrival of Miss Thomas, just as the gong for dinner sounded in the hall.

"So you actually decided what to wear," said Mrs. Thomas with a little edge to her voice, and in a sotto voce comment I'm sure I was not supposed to overhear, she added, "More than once I expected you to appear in your shift."

"Oh! Mother!" said Miss Thomas, and then to me, "Good evening, Mr. Smiley, I'm sorry to have kept you waiting."

And once again I said, "No apology is necessary, Miss Thomas," and then added with enthusiasm, "And may I say that you look beautiful this evening."

"Thank you, Mr. Smiley," she responded with a smile of pleasure and a slight blush.

George opened the door dividing the reception and dining rooms. We walked into the dining room, and Mrs. Thomas ushered me to the head of the table. She said by way of explanation, "My husband is away so you must take his place if you don't mind."

"I should be honoured," I responded and took my place at the head of a very fine dinner table. It was laid with a freshly ironed cotton cloth and the silver cutlery glinted in the candlelight. On my right sat a radiant Miss Thomas, and on my left her equally attractive, but slightly older mother. I could not believe my good fortune, and pinched myself to ensure that I wasn't dreaming.

Elsie, who had recovered from her sickness and George, officiated at our dinner, and they ensured that everything progressed smoothly.

At Porthkerry House dinner was a mouth watering meal.

I had become accustomed over the months, to the food presented by the ship's cook on board Earl Canning. It is wholesome, but unexciting in variety and presentation.

This dinner was a revelation. It showed what could be achieved with normally available ingredients when the cook had skill and knowledge. We had a bowl of thick vegetable soup as a first course.

"This soup is delicious," I commented as I accepted a second helping.

"It is, isn't it," agreed Mrs. Thomas. "The base for the soup," she explained, "is a thickened chicken stock that has been given a slightly peppery tang. Cook cuts the vegetables into uniform cubes and adds them to the hot stock, so that they are cooked to perfection when the soup is to be served. We often have soup like this for lunch on a winter's day and serve it with freshly baked crusty bread."

As Elsie cleared the soup plates and tureen from the table, George ceremoniously carried in a big silver platter, placed it in front of me, and lifted off the silver cover with a flourish. There in front of me lay a steaming roast, flanked by a carving knife and carving fork.

I suddenly realized why I had been placed in the seat of honour. *Dear Heaven!* I thought, *I have to carve the joint.*

The intense joy I had felt up to a moment before, evaporated as I realized that I had to perform a commonplace task that I had seen a lot of people perform many, many times, but had never before attempted. And to make matters worse, my initiation had to be performed in front of the two most important people in my life.

I sat there motionless with shock for a moment but realized that I had to act. With the composure of an out and out confidence trickster I stood up and grasped the carvers. I assumed it was a piece of roast pork because the skin had been scored in lines. I noticed also that the lines were regular and realized that if I used them as a guide, the slices would be about the right thickness. I had the dexterity that comes from a lifetime of handling different implements, and the knife was as sharp as a razor. So in no time at all, I had reduced the joint to slices of equal thickness as if I did the task every day of the week.

I put down the carvers and George took away the carving plate and started to serve the slices onto hot plates. With heartfelt relief that the ordeal had passed without a catastrophe, I collapsed into my seat as if someone had cut off my legs, but no one seemed to notice.

Elsie placed the plates in front of us and George followed her around the table with the vegetables in a big divided bowl from which he served each of us in turn. As the plate filled up in front of me, I started to take a more active interest in the food that was being served. The roast was a boned shoulder of pork that had been filled with an apple and nut stuffing and rolled. It was accompanied by roast potatoes and buttered cabbage. The sauce was hot, dark and complemented the pork perfectly. There was white wine available, but none of us drank more than a glass. Yet we all managed a small second helping of the pork.

For our desert the cook had prepared a blackberry and lemon pudding. It was delicious.

When we had finished eating, Mrs. Thomas asked if I would like to have brandy and coffee. When I declined the offer of brandy, we all adjourned to the small reception room where we had met before dinner. Mrs. Thomas ordered the maid to serve our coffee there, and we sat around a very nice circular oak table on comfortably padded chairs in the mellow light cast by a large candelabrum whilst we waited for it.

After the maid had served us coffee and left the room, Miss Thomas said, "If the weather is good tomorrow, Mr. Smiley, perhaps you would like to go for a walk and see something of the local country side? It's well worth seeing," she added with enthusiasm.

"I would like that very much, Miss Thomas," I responded, hoping that I would have Miss Thomas's company without a chaperone, but without really believing that such an event would be allowed to take place.

"We can decide where to go in the morning if the weather is good and leave after breakfast if that is agreeable to you, Mr. Smiley?"

"I should be delighted to fall in with any plans you make, Miss Thomas," I said.

Mrs. and Miss Thomas talked briefly about where we could go and discussed the advantages and disadvantages of several places without coming to a final conclusion. All the time they talked quietly together, I could feel the gathering affects of an early morning, long journey and a good dinner. Concentrating on their conversation became more and more difficult and inevitably Mrs. Thomas noticed my drooping eyelids.

She said, "You must be very tired after your long journey, Mr. Smiley. Miss Thomas and I will not be offended if you wish to withdraw."

"Thank you for your consideration, Mrs. Thomas. I do think it would be sensible if I retired for the night as I am becoming very poor company for you and Miss Mary."

And so it came to pass, that after pining for Miss Thomas's company for more months than I cared to remember, I was too tired to enjoy it when the opportunity arrived and had to say goodnight and go to bed where I slept like the proverbial log. How I regretted those lost minutes when I was next at sea.

Next morning George knocked on the bedroom door and woke me up as he pulled the curtains and let the early morning sun flood into the room.

"It's a lovely morning, Mr. Smiley. I hope you slept well, Sir?"

"Like the dead, George," I answered as I swung my legs out from under the covers and headed for the wash stand to wash and shave.

"There's hot water there, sir" he said, as he indicated a small, highly polished copper kettle. "Is there anything else I can get for you, sir."

"No thank you," I responded.

"Very well, sir. Breakfast will be served in the morning room at eight." Having imparted that vital piece of intelligence, he left me to get ready for my first day with Miss Thomas. I couldn't believe how lucky I was and was barely able to refrain from bursting into loud songs of joy.

When I had washed and dressed in a clean, tidy working uniform, I skipped down the stairs like a ten year old, scarcely able to control my high spirits as I anticipated a day in the company of the beautiful Miss Mary Thomas with or without chaperone.

Mrs. Thomas was already in the morning room when I arrived, and when she saw me she stopped serving herself kedgeree long enough to say, "Good morning Mr. Smiley. I only have to look at your face to know that you have slept well and feel ready to face the world. Please help yourself to breakfast."

"Thank you Mrs. Thomas. I feel fine today and certainly slept well. I hope you slept well also?"

"Yes! Thank you. My daughter will be down for breakfast shortly, but there is no need for you to wait for her."

I was very hungry and decided to take Mrs. Thomas at her word and had consumed a substantial breakfast before Miss Mary came into the room. We exchanged the customary morning greetings, and then, as she ate, she restarted the discussion with her mother about where we should go. Actually there was more than one route that we could take, but in the end they agreed an itinerary that would suit the tide. As I listened to their discussion, I decided that it didn't sound too onerous, but I had forgotten of course that Wales is not as flat as Lincolnshire.

We left Porthkerry House about mid morning with Elsie maintaining a discrete distance behind us. It was a brisk start to the day, and the sun shone intermittently as the clouds drifted past on a stiff westerly breeze. We walked down the path through the garden and left the grounds of the house through a gate in the railings at the foot of the slope. We walked across the dark green springy grass towards the sea and I noticed on the seaward edge of the grass that there was a bank of bluish-grey limestone pebbles. We climbed up onto the top of the bank and were confronted by a vista of blue, grey waves with occasional small white horses extending to the horizon. Here and there the surface of the sea was speckled with the little white dots of groups of seagulls. Below us, at the edge of the sea, there was a border of white foam where the waves broke against the pebbles in a rhythmic "shurshing" sound as the pebbles rattled and ground against each other in the turbulent up rush and back wash of each wave.

Miss Thomas adopted the role of guide with great enthusiasm. With elegant waves of her hand to indicate direction she said, "This is the Bristol Channel and over there is Somerset. That way," and she pointed to the east, "is Cardiff and Bristol. That way," and she pointed to the west, "is Ireland and America. Except for a small area near the Bull Nose Cliff," and she pointed at a rocky promontory about half way around the bay "The whole of the bay from Cold Knap Point at the far end along to Porthkerry is covered with these limestone pebbles. The pebbles are quite big at the top of the beach but they are worn down by the action of the waves into quite small pieces. At Bull's Nose at low tide there is a sandy bay with rocks either side. When I was a child, it was one of my favourite places on a sunny afternoon as there are so many rock pools to explore."

We stood and watched a schooner beating down channel against the wind and listened to the rhythmic sound of the sea grinding the pebbles together on the shore.

Mary said, "On a day like today when the waves are small, the sea can make a very soothing noise. But when there is a gale and the waves are big, the noise is frightening and can be heard in the house even with the doors and windows shut. Sometimes the spindrift from the breaking waves is blown over the top of the pebbles and across the grass into our garden."

Mary pointed to where the waves were breaking against the small rocky promontory she had called Bull Cliff and said, "The tide is too high to go along the beach this morning, so we will go that way." She then started walking towards a tree-covered hill. "We will come back along the beach past Cold Knap Point," she added.

She pointed at the diminutive headland that was just visible on the horizon. It looked a very long way away and that was only half the walk.

I realized that Miss Mary Thomas may live in a big house and have wealthy parents, but she was dressed sensibly for walking in the country and clearly walked extensively in the area. I very soon began to wonder if her short walk might prove to be very long for my seaman's legs as there are not many hills at sea.

We climbed back down the pebbles and set off across the grass and joined a path that skirted along the landward edge of Cliff Woods.

Miss Thomas said, "I would like to thank you again for looking after Elsie. That was very kind and thoughtful of you."

"It was nothing really, and I was pleased I could help her."

"Elsie doesn't think it was 'nothing" returned Miss Thomas, and went on "You have made a friend for life in Elsie. She tells anyone who will listen to her what a kind and considerate man you are. I have never been sick like that, even when I went on a ship to Bombay."

"I envy you!" I answered with feeling.

"Have you suffered like that, Mr. Smiley?" she enquired.

"Yes! I was very badly seasick on my first voyage. It lasted for several days because the ship never stopped moving, and I felt so wretched that I wished I could die before I started to recover. I knew how Elsie must have felt and helped her without thinking about it. Fortunately, it is possible to stop a coach and that allows a quicker recovery."

It was a gentle slope and we had the time and breath, to talk about inconsequential things, such as the weather and the colour of the leaves, as we came to know each other better.

In the distance we heard the sound of a hunting horn and Miss Thomas said with a note of disgust in her voice, "Did you hear that! Mr. Smiley? The hunters are out again."

I was a little puzzled by her comment as the hunt is such an every day feature of country life. I said carefully, "Yes I recognize the sound. We have several hunts near where I live. The farmers enjoy the sport."

She said with some feeling, "The farmers may, but I do not imagine that the fox does."

This was a strange attitude for someone born to the country life, and I said, "I have never been a farmer but I know that the farmers consider the fox to be a pest that has to be controlled. When a fox kills far more chickens than it can eat and leaves the carcasses on the floor of the hencoop, I can understand the farmers' anger. The hunt is the traditional way of dealing with foxes, and I have never thought of it as anything other than the farmers remedy for a problem."

"When I was a little girl I was given a week-old fox cub by a local farmer." Miss Thomas looked quite sad and then after a short pause said, "I fed it and played with, it and it grew and became quite tame. It was like having a small red dog nipping playfully at my heels. It was my only companion in the lonely hours of growing up without any siblings or friends of my own age to play with. It was something warm and alive I could love. One day I was playing with Rufus on the grass outside the house when the maid came running to me, grabbed me by the hand and dragged me into the house screaming 'The hunt's coming'."

Miss Thomas paused to allow us to pass decorously through a kissing gate and resumed her story, "I could hear the noise of hounds yelping and the Huntsman's horn blowing, and as we stood in the doorway, a big old male fox ran panting past. Seconds later, the hounds appeared, saw Rufus, and tore him to pieces in front of my eyes."

Miss Thomas stopped talking with a loud sob and stood stock still with tears of remembrance in her eyes. Elsie pushed past me on the narrow path in order to comfort her mistress, and I stood wondering what I could or should do. In the end neither Elsie nor I needed to do anything as Miss Thomas rapidly regained her composure.

After a sniff or two and a dab at her eyes Miss Thomas said simply, "Whenever I hear the horn, I remember that time and wonder how the hunted fox feels."

Then she added with feeling, "It would be so much better if a huntsman took the place of the fox. At least he would know why he was being chased by a pack of hounds and farmers on big horses. The fox only does what is natural for him and doesn't know any better."

The path soon disappeared into the wood, and we climbed up the side of the valley and passed a small group of cottages. Cliff Wood Cottages, Mary called them, and as we passed she exchanged greetings with a woman working on her vegetable plot.

"Good morning Mrs. Morgan, that's a lovely crop of potatoes you have there."

"Good morning Miss Mary, it's a lovely morning isn't it. Thank you, but I hope the spuds will look as good when we dig them. Last year they looked just as good before we dug them out, but they had some scabby growths and rotted away. Please give my greetings to your Mother, Miss Mary."

"Of course I will," responded Miss Thomas as we continued on our way.

"Did you see the hollyhocks?" she asked me.

"Yes, I did; they were a lovely colour. She also had some lupines, and I thought I saw some delphinium as well."

"I saw the delphinium but didn't notice any thing else. Do you enjoy gardening Mr. Smiley?"

"I enjoy looking at a well kept garden but have done very lit-tle gardening on my own. My mother was very skilful in the garden and mainly grew vegetables. But she also grew flowers as she said it made the garden look more cheerful. I helped with the heavy work, and she always told me what she was doing and why and made sure I learnt something about the flowers and vegetables she produced. She bottled, pickled or preserved the fruit and vegetables she produced. I think she knew a lot about the medicinal properties of the plants because she always had a salve or drink if I was unwell."

"Do you remember which plants she used?" asked Miss Thomas with interest, but I had to admit that I did not recollect much about this aspect of my Mother's industry.

"She started to teach me but died before I had learnt anything of value" and I paused, saddened by the sudden memory of my Mother.

Miss Thomas must have sensed my feelings, as she said gently "When you are young and your Mother dies it must seem like the end of the world."

"Yes," I said not knowing what else I could say.

We came out of the woods on the seaward side and had a magnificent view out over the Bristol Channel. Opposite and about thirty miles away across the sea, a high promontory on the coast of Somerset could just be seen through the haze.

Miss Thomas said, "That's Brean Down," then added with a little laugh, "We have a local saying about the weather. If you can see Brean Down, it's going to rain, and if you can't, it is!"

We stopped to look at the view and for me to recover my breath. I was thrilled that Miss Thomas was comfortable to stand quite close to me. We did not touch of course, but we were no longer keeping the sort of distance that strangers are comfortable with.

We walked along relatively flat open ground and passed the ruins of Barry Castle. Below the castle was a small group of thatched cottages and a well where we were very glad to have a cup of cold clear water. From here we walked to St. Nicholas's Church and stood for a while by the flagpole looking out over the sea. Mary pointed out Barry Harbour with Little Island and the Marine Hotel beyond. We stood in companionable silence for a while sharing the view and then started to walk down towards Watch House Bay and Cold Knap. When we reached the beach, the tide had dropped, and I could not believe my eyes. When we started our walk, the sea had been close to the top of the pebbles, and now it was about twenty feet lower and sand was exposed at the edge. As a sailor I knew about tides, but this was the first time I had seen for my self how much the water level could change in a few hours in an estuary like the Bristol Channel. We slid and clattered down the pebbles to the sand and walked around the bay passed Bull's Nose and towards Porthkerry House.

Just below the house we had to climb back up the pebbles, and for my tired and aching sailor's legs, it was a frustrating activity particularly on the steep banks of small pebbles on the high water mark. One step up was accompanied by a sliding half a step back as the pebbles moved under my weight, and I felt as if I would never reach the top. We walked back across the grass and into the house where we parted to go to our rooms before meeting again for lunch.

Mrs. Thomas joined us in the dining room and as we ate ham, cheese and pickles she asked Miss Mary and me where we had been. Mrs. Thomas then asked me what I thought of the countryside, and I think both my companions were pleased that I had been so impressed with what I had seen.

After a light lunch we went into the library, and with Elsie maintaining a discrete distance as Miss Thomas's chaperone, we settled down to read and to talk of subjects that interested us.

"I hope you will not think me inquisitive, Miss Thomas, but may I ask what your father's profession is? He must be very successful whatever it is, because I have never seen such a lovely house before."

"I don't mind you asking, Mr. Smiley, but I cannot give you a complete answer as I do not know. My father never discusses his work with my mother and me. He is a businessman and is very active with this new electric telegraph, but I know no more. There are some books and papers about the telegraph on the side table that you could look at if you wish."

"Thank you, Miss Thomas I will look at them whilst I'm here."

Miss Thomas laid her book down, looked at me and said, "I was reminded of the ball in Bombay by something written in my book. What do you remember, Mr. Smiley?"

"My very first memory," I said with a smile of remembrance, "is how beautiful you looked when I saw you for the first time. That was when Lady Megan brought me to where you were sitting in order to introduce me to you."

Miss Thomas blushed becomingly and said, "Thank you, Mr. Smiley."

I added, "My second memory is the look of extreme disappointment on the faces of all those army officers who were competing for your attention when Lady Megan shooed them away from us."

We laughed together over a shared experience.

I said with some seriousness, "I could not believe how favoured I was to be introduced to the belle of the ball in Bombay, and now I am in your company again. God is really smiling on me at the moment, and I could not be happier than I am now."

"I'm pleased you feel like that, Mr. Smiley," said a demure Miss

Thomas, without a hint of how she felt about the subject.

I little later when I went to my room to dress for dinner, I was pleased to find a shirt had been washed and ironed and that my best uniform had been pressed. I didn't expect it, being unused to country house living. I thanked George when he came to see if I needed anything. He explained that it was a normal part of his duties and thanks was unnecessary.

He stopped just as he was about to leave the room and said, "Sir, I hope you will not think me presumptuous, but may I ask you a question, Sir?"

"Of course you may," I responded.

"Is it true you are going to receive a medal from the Queen for bravery, Sir?"

"Not as far as I know," I replied. "Why do you ask?"

"Well, Sir, before you came here, I overheard heard Miss Mary start telling her Mother about your brush with the natives. And then later she said that the Queen should give you a medal as an example to other young men. I should be very pleased if you could take the time to tell me the story yourself."

I looked at him and realized that he was about my age and had never been away from the Barry area. Probably he would never leave this area, and the look of hero worship on his face made me realize that he ought to know the truth and not be misled by other people's exaggerated accounts. There was time before dinner, so I told him what had happened as I had related it to Lady Megan, without bravado or false modesty. At the end of my account, the look of hero worship had not gone, but there was genuine respect in his demeanour that I liked better. I felt that George had become a supporter, even if his position didn't allow him to be a friend.

Dinner followed the pattern set the previous day, but the roast was a sirloin of beef. My carving skills were honed a little further, and I achieved the objective of neatly sliced meat without a disaster. Again we eschewed the coffee and brandy and retired to the reception room to entertain each other as best we could. I talked a little about life on board ship and my duties initially as a Cadet, and more recently as a watch-keeping officer, following the untimely death of John Evans. They were shocked at the way I had been treated by his family, but I think Mrs. Thomas could identify with their grief, if not the way it had been expressed. She thought Captain Evans sounded a little deranged.

Later Miss Thomas sang to her own accompaniment on the piano. I cannot remember what the pieces were called, but two were in her native language and one in French. She had a delightful voice, and I was persuaded to join her to sing as a duet, a hymn that we both knew. I have a reasonable voice and sing with enjoyment in church, but even so it must have sounded like a bittern with a nightingale, her voice was so true and sweet.

The next day Miss Thomas's old wives tale about the weather came true and it rained and rained. It was a grey, dismal dawn, and I had a quiet, solitary candle lit breakfast as neither of the ladies seemed to be encouraged by the weather to arise as early as I had.

After breakfast I went to the library and sat at the end of the long reading table and started to read the documents that Miss Thomas had pointed out the day before. As the hours passed, the day became progressively more dismal. The gale driven rain clattered against sash windows that rattled in their frames from the onslaught. The fire smoked as the wind blustered around the chimney pots and sputtered as big drops of sooty rain fell into the hearth. Before midday candles and oil lamps had been lit and I joined Mrs. and Miss Thomas in the dining room for lunch. Our conversation during lunch was preoccupied with the severity of the weather and was punctuated by sudden silences when blasts of wind shook the house.

After one particularly violent onslaught, I said involuntarily, "May God bless all sailors on a day like this."

"Amen!" said Mrs. Thomas. "This must be a very bad storm for an experienced sailor like you to make such a comment. Have you experienced many bad storms, Mr Smiley?"

"No, Mrs. Thomas, I'm pleased to say that I haven't. Many gales of course, but only one really bad storm and I hope I never have to experience another like it." I thought for a moment that they were going to ask me for details, but mercifully we were interrupted by Elsie who wanted to serve the desert. I would have told them the truth of course but I didn't really wish to relive my close encounter with cowardice, particularly with Miss Thomas as part of the audience.

After lunch Mrs. Thomas excused herself and Miss Thomas

accompanied me back to the library. Elsie came with us of course and occupied her customary unobtrusive position in the corner of the room. Miss Thomas and I sat at opposite ends of the big table and initially engaged ourselves on very different tasks.

Miss Thomas arranged some sheets of writing paper in front of herself and had blotting paper, pen and ink all close to hand. After fiddling with her pen for a few moments she started composing the letters to friends and relations in Bombay that I had promised to deliver as soon as I returned there. For my part, I resumed my perusal of the technical papers that Mr. Thomas had left on the table.

Every so often our concentration was broken by a particularly violent blast of wind driven rain slamming against the library windows and I looked in the direction of the noise half expecting to see one of the windows falling on to the library floor.

I read avidly and understood some of the content, but since they were all technical and required knowledge I didn't possess, a good deal of the text was devoid of meaning. Electricity for example was a subject I knew very little about, and clearly, knowledge of the subject was essential to an understanding of the working of a telegraph. I felt it was important to know more about the electric telegraph but how that was to be accomplished when I spent my life on the sea, I couldn't imagine.

Clearly, Mr. Thomas was very interested in anything to do with the development of the electric telegraph. The documents that were accessible covered the early experiments by Wheatstone and Cooke, which had led to a patent in 1837 and the development of a communication system used extensively by the expanding British railway system.

There were articles about the various submarine cables that had been laid up to that time. Successful cables between England and France in 1845 and between Scotland and Ireland in 1853. Then there was the failed attempt to lay a cable cross the Atlantic in 1857. There was also a small pile of editions of a weekly magazine called *The Telegraphic Journal*. As I had found with the other papers I had perused, I could understand very little of what I read, but this simply sharpened the desire to learn more about the subject. Miss Thomas's father was an object lesson I realized. If a rich man like Mr. Thomas believed the telegraph was important, then I would be foolish not to follow his example and find out more. I felt that the telegraph had to be a development with many opportunities for an energetic young man, and I wanted to be part of its history.

After a time I realized that Miss Thomas's industrious scratching with her pen was slowing down, and it was not very long before she put it down.

When I felt her eyes on me and looked up she said, "As you know, Mr. Smiley, I am writing to a friend about my experiences in Bombay. Amongst other subjects, I have written that Lady Megan introduced us at the governor's ball in Bombay, and since Lady Megan has told my mother what a good impression you made, my mother decided to invite you to Porthkerry House to stay for a few days. I have also told her about your confrontation with the tribesmen in Oman, but I find I am unable to write any more. Although we met for the first time many months ago, we have been in each others company for only a few hours and I know nothing about you, Mr. Smiley, except that you are a person with whom I feel comfortable. I know nothing about your parents or where you live when you are not on your ship. You haven't told me anything about Captain Stewart or about your life at sea. There is so much about Mr. Jason Smiley that I should be pleased to know about if you will only tell me."

She paused for a moment and her cheeks became becomingly pinker as she said "I have to confess that I am intrigued by the physical similarity between you and Captain Stewart and the lack of similarity in your surnames," and her voice trailed off as she left the question unasked.

Her cheeks became pinker in the ensuing silence, but then she added, "Please tell me everything, Mr. Smiley. If you remember I met you in Bombay with Captain Stewart and I remarked the likeness between you as did my aunt."

I didn't know what to say, or more accurately stated I didn't really know where to start. I had always known I would have to tell Miss Thomas about my antecedents, but I would have preferred to choose my own time rather than answer a direct question.

"I have nothing to hide, Miss Thomas, and I will tell you everything you want to know about me, but as I explained to Lady Megan, recent events have turned my life upside down and I do not know what to do for the best."

"That's very enigmatic, Mr. Smiley. Since the weather is so bad and we have all the afternoon, you could start at the beginning."

"Yes I will," I responded, "but first I should explain that much of what I can tell you occurred before I was born. It is based on what I have been told, not on what I can prove."

"I understand," she said.

"I was told that my mother was the daughter of a wealthy farmer who gambled away the family fortune after his wife died. He killed himself when he realized he was ruined, and as a result, my mother was orphaned. Surprisingly, for the daughter of a farmer, my mother had received quite a good education and this helped her obtain a position as a lady's maid in the vicarage in Lenton. The vicar's wife was a good woman who was prepared to take the time and trouble to teach my mother what a gentlewoman was supposed to know about being a good wife and mother. My mother passed on as much of her knowledge as she thought appropriate, but most importantly, she instilled in me the desire to better myself and escape from village drudgery.

I paused to collect my thoughts and Miss Thomas urged me to go on.

I said, "The man you know as Captain Stewart is the brother of the Vicar's wife and was allowed to stay at the vicarage in Lenton when he came home from a voyage."

I went on, "From my earliest recollections, I believed that I was the natural son of Mr. and Mrs. Smiley. I was happy with the idea that I was the only son of the village blacksmith, and at no time did my mother or Mr. Smiley give any hint that this was not so.

Captain Stewart was a chance traveller who came to the Smithy when his horse cast a shoe. He was on his way to see his sister in Lenton and as our Smithy was the only one in the neighbourhood, he stopped for Mr. Smiley to fit a new shoe and then spent the night at the local inn. I met Captain Stewart only because I carried his bags to the inn. For some reason that I couldn't then begin to guess, Captain Stewart offered to teach me about navigation. Later his sister took an interest in me as well and started to teach me some of the social graces I was clearly lacking. I had no idea why they should help me, but I was grateful for any effort that helped me to follow my mother's strictures. When Captain Stewart made it possible for me to become a cadet on his ship and escape from

Pickworth, I was overjoyed. Mr. Smiley was much less so.

When I returned from one of my voyages, I went to Pickworth to see my father and found that he had had an accident and died whilst I was away. Captain Stewart had also heard of the tragedy from his sister. He came to Pickworth and found me in the graveyard where I had gone to pay my last respects to my father."

I stopped, covered in embarrassment at what I was about to say next and said, "Miss Thomas, I am unwilling to go on as what I have to relate next may be offensive to you."

"I cannot believe that a man like you would say something offensive, Mr. Smiley."

"I hope that is so, Miss Thomas, but it is a delicate subject."

I went on, "He had a carriage and we drove to the vicarage in Lenton where, in his sister's presence, he showed me two letters that my mother had written to him. It's clear that Captain Stewart is my natural father, and my mother had married George Smiley to ensure I was not stigmatised as a bastard. Captain Stewart was away at sea and didn't know my mother had conceived until long after I was born. Perhaps the outcome would have been different if he had not been a sailor."

I added, "Lady Megan was probably correct when she said that Captain Stewart had behaved honourably. My mother requested him not to contact me and he honoured that request until both my mother and Mr. Smiley had died and could not be harmed by the truth. He has also honoured his parental obligations to his son, although he could have kept the relationship a secret.

"So you see, Miss Thomas, I have kept the name Smiley in honour of the man who brought me up as well as he could, and I resemble Captain Stewart as he is my natural father.

"Captain Stewart wanted me to change my name to his, but I refused at the time and I'm not sure that I made a sensible decision. I don't know whether I should say untruthfully, that I'm the son of a village blacksmith or admit I'm the illegitimate son of a sea captain. Neither seems very commendable."

"I think you should tell the truth, Mr. Smiley. What your parents did is not correct in the eyes of the Church but that is not really your concern. In their different ways, both did the best they could in the circumstances they found themselves in. In truth, Mr. Jason Smiley hasn't suffered as a result now has he?"

"No," I responded, looking at my circumstances from her very different viewpoint.

When she asked, I told her about my life in the tiny village of Pickworth and how much I had hated being tied to the smithy. Like Captain Downing earlier, I could see that she was not very impressed with my humble upbringing by a village blacksmith; only this time I did not have the advantages of technical knowledge to bridge the gap between my life and hers.

I could only hope that my personality, diligent study in order to improve myself, and the passage of time would demonstrate that I was worthy of her, even with my country village background.

Even then you see I had this half formed hope that one day this attractive and intelligent lady would be my wife.

She made no adverse comment whatever she was thinking about my revelations, but said simply, "Thank you for telling me so much about your early life, Mr. Smiley." Then she picked up her pen again and prepared to resume her letter writing.

I interrupted by saying, "Miss Thomas, before you continue with your letters, I should be pleased to know something about your life, as I expect that it has been very different from mine."

"I should imagine so, Mr. Smiley," she responded dryly, "but it has been no where near as adventurous and interesting as yours has been so far. My life story is quickly related. I am the only child, and as my father is a wealthy man, I have wanted for nothing except the one thing money cannot buy."

"What's that, Miss Thomas?" I asked in a puzzled voice as I could not imagine what she meant.

"It's not possible to buy a brother or a sister!" she said sharply, clearly irritated either by my obtuseness or her memory. "You, Mr. Smiley, see here a mansion exhibiting every sign of wealth and assume the wealth brings happiness. I see a prison, where my childhood years were spent without the companionship of children my own age."

I thought of my childhood and the village children I had played and fought with and said, "I'm sorry to hear that, Miss Thomas. I was also an only child, but I was never lonely. I had all the other village children as companions from as early an age as I can remember."

Miss Thomas continued, "I would have expected it to be so, Mr. Smiley. Until I was past ten years old, there was no one I could confide in nor with whom I could spend time. I had all manner of dolls and other toys, but they cannot speak or move. I lived in a fantasy world my nanny helped me create with her stories. It was better when I had a governess. She was a well educated spinster woman and had travelled all over Europe. She was very well read and not only did she teach me academic subjects every day, but we walked somewhere in this area whenever the weather was reasonable. She taught me so much about the flora and fauna of the countryside and that knowledge continues to be a delight for me. I was very sorry when my father decided that the governess had become a companion rather than a teacher and dismissed her. Most of my life has been spent in this house, and I'm so grateful to Aunt Megan that she made my journey to Bombay possible. It was my first chance to experience something other than Porthkerry House on the outskirts of a small hamlet called Barry, and it may be my only experience," she concluded sadly.

I had very mixed feelings after listening to her. I had asked my question motivated by a tingle of jealousy at her privileged life, as well as by healthy curiosity, and ended up feeling that my childhood had been better than hers even if it had been financially disadvantaged.

Miss Thomas returned to her letter writing, and I tried to forget the inadequacies of my life story and my poor future prospects, in the study of some not too technical articles about the development of the submarine telegraph and particularly the problems associated with the production of a waterproof, strong but light cable that could be laid in deep water. There was also an article about the formation of a government committee to enquire into the subject after some well publicised failures of submarine cable.

There was one slightly ludicrous event that afternoon that I can now smile about, but which seemed all too serious at the time.

Miss Thomas and I had quietly continued with our self appointed tasks with occasional pauses due to the sudden violent noises of the storm. During the late afternoon, I heard Elsie poking the fire and then watched as she shovelled some coal onto the red hot coals in the fireplace. Perhaps the coal was wet or had too much fine material mixed in with the lumps, but the healthy glow disappeared and the fire started to produce thick dark smoke that disappeared rapidly up the chimney due to the strong draft produced by the strength of the wind. I looked down at the magazine I was going through and was aware of a very strong gust of wind hitting the house and then almost immediately heard a cry of alarm from Elsie. I glanced back towards her and saw thick, black smoke billowing out of the fire place under the pressure of a downdraft and enveloping her where she knelt on the hearth trying to coax life back into the fire. Elsie emerged from the smoke coughing and with her eyes streaming from the acrid smoke. As the smoke started to spread out into the library Miss Thomas went to help her maid and we abandoned what we were doing and left the library until the air cleared again.

In the late afternoon we went to our rooms, and in the early evening, with the storm still battering the house, we had dinner to the accompaniment of flickering, smoky candles and the whistling of the wind. It was not an unfriendly meal, but it was a rather subdued and the easy interchange of conversation that had characterised our previous evening meal was completely absent. Several times I tried to start a discussion, but my companions seemed to be too busy with private thoughts to respond enthusiastically to my overtures. I began to wonder if the frank and honest description of my early life had been such a good idea, but I could do nothing to retract what had been said.

After the meal was over, Mrs. and Miss Thomas excused themselves as they were tired after the stormy day and wished to go to bed.

They said their goodnights and I had little option but to return to my room. After a short time I went to bed myself and tried to sleep but couldn't as I worried about the apparent change in the way I was perceived and the poor impression I had made by being honest about my antecedents.

The next day dawned with a clear blue sky and bright sunshine. There was no trace of the previous day's storm and I was relieved to find that I was greeted by both the Thomas's very cordially indeed.

It was a very big load off my mind when I realized that I was still in favour and I would not have to make a premature departure for Liverpool as my worried midnight thinking had predicted. We sat around the table and enjoyed a good breakfast. And as we ate, we discussed the previous day's storm and the improbable tales of shipwrecks and blown down bridges that had percolated up from below stairs. Miss Thomas discussed the route for another walk with her mother and about mid morning we set off with the faithful Elsie, as our ever present, silent shadow.

Outside the garden at the back of the house, we stood for a while and watched yesterday's rainwater as it drained out of the woods behind the house and was channelled into little chuckling rivulets, carrying leafs and twigs down towards the stream and the sea beyond.

Beside one particularly robust little stream Miss Thomas and Elsie started to make little boats out of reeds. Elsie showed me how to pierce the leaf with a thorn and push the stem through the hole to make a curved bow for my little reed boat. We launched them at the upstream end and cheered and laughed as they floated along, first one then the other leading in the main flow and sometimes left behind in an eddy. We watched intently to see whose reed boat would get to the end of the stream first, and there were many congratulations for the winner from the losers and then we did it again.

Looking back, it was a very childish activity for three youngish adults, but we enjoyed it just like children. It really was fun.

We revelled in the sweet, fresh smell left by the rain of the day before and the brilliant colours of rain washed flowers and the many shades of green exhibited by the grass and leaves. Miss Thomas amazed me with her comprehensive knowledge of the local plants and also her enthusiasm for the countryside.

We walked up the path through the woods to St. Curig's Church, as we had heard the bells ringing and Mary believed there was a wedding taking place. It was to be my first experience of the endless fascination other people's weddings have for the distaff side.

As we walked up into the woods, Miss Thomas asked, "You have already been promoted from Cadet to Third Officer, Mr. Smiley, do you expect to make the sea your career?"

It was a very perceptive question, and I thought about my life and prospects for a moment before saying, "Some years ago I believed I would be sentenced to live the life of a craftsman in Pickworth. My father was a blacksmith, and it was more logical to follow his trade, about which I had some knowledge, than attempt something entirely new. Then, out of the blue, Captain Stewart appeared and he started to teach me about an instrument called the sextant and about navigation.

He arranged for me to have an interview with the Gold Star Line, but I was accepted as a cadet on my own merits and not because of patronage. It was an achievement that I am proud of to this day.

"I joined the SS Earl Canning as an ignorant cadet, but I have learnt enough about the sea and matured enough as a man to justify my promotion to Third Officer. Dead man's shoes assuredly and I would have wished it otherwise, but that is the way of the world. I have continued to learn, and I am confident that in time I will become a captain and command my own ship if I stay at sea long enough.

"However, I have this feeling that there should be more to life than sailing to and fro across the oceans carrying other people's cargo, important as that occupation is. The sea is my life at present, but I will explore and exploit every opportunity for betterment that presents itself until I find my true place in life."

After a short silence, Miss Thomas said with feeling "Mr. Smiley, I will pray for your success."

Whilst we talked we had climbed up the hill from the house and were in time to see the bride and groom emerge into the sunshine from the door of the church and listen to the good wishes called out to the newly weds by the boisterous crowd of wedding guests. As she watched the couple enter the bridal coach, Miss Thomas looked intently at the radiant face of the bride and said softly, more to herself than to me, "I hope I look as happy on my wedding day."

As I thought to myself, I hope I'm the lucky groom, I said "Miss Thomas, there can be no doubt about it. You will be a beautiful bride."

"Thank you, kind sir," she said with a big smile and a curtsey.

When the wedding party had dispersed, we walked back towards the sea and joined the path that runs westward along the top of the cliff.

At the beginning of the path Miss Thomas stopped and said, "Mr. Smiley, I think I am correct to say that Lincolnshire is quite a flat county."

"That's correct, Miss Thomas," I replied with puzzlement clear in my voice.

"We are going to walk a little way along the top of the cliff," she said, "so that you can fully appreciate the difference between Lincolnshire and the cliffs of Glamorgan. I would like you to lie down here," she said as she pointed to the grass at the edge of the cliff, "and look over the edge."

In my state of infatuation, I would have tried to fly like a bird if she had asked. So lying down on the damp grass to look over the edge seemed to be no challenge at all. I knelt and put my hands down near to the edge then looked over and wished I hadn't as unreasoning fear flashed through my body. Below my eyes there was nothing but the very, very distant sea and some tiny gulls circling calmly on the wind about half way down. I couldn't even see where the waves were breaking although I could hear them crashing against the shore and feel the impact vibrating through the structure of the cliff. I managed to control the urge to throw myself back from the edge by reasoning that it was only my head that was exposed and the rest of my body was lying on firm ground. At least I hoped it was firm ground. I climbed back to my feet and involuntarily moved several paces further away from the edge.

Miss Thomas said in warning, "As you have seen, Mr. Smiley, the cliff has been undercut by the actions of the waves. When part of the cliff has been weakened enough it collapses into the sea. We must be careful along here. Do not follow the path if it is cracked or if it starts getting very close to the edge of the cliff, as those are signs that the cliff is starting to fall away. It may already be too weak to support your weight so move a few yards inland away from the edge."

She gave me a gentle push on my shoulder, smiled at me, and said, "Now, my intrepid hero, please lead this expedition onwards."

I set off along the path at the cliff edge with Miss Thomas and Elsie in file behind me. Initially I took my responsibilities very seriously and scanned the path for cracks and deviations towards the cliff edge as if our lives really depended on my constant vigilance. I was horror struck at the thought that I could lead my beloved Mary into danger. As time passed I realized that the dangers were not quite as imminent as I feared and whilst I didn't see one crack in the soil, we did come to one place where the path suddenly deviated inland and the still visible route of the old one went straight over the cliff edge at the site of a recent fall.

As we followed the path, we could hear the waves pounding against the base of the cliffs below. I watched in fascination as huge seagulls, with beady, unblinking eyes drifted effortlessly past us at shoulder level on up currents of air, then suddenly turned away to dive precipitously down toward the sea. They would disappear from view only to reappear a few minutes later, drifting along as before. We passed the military camp called the Bulwarks that Miss Thomas said was a relic of the Napoleonic Wars and could see the sea breaking on an offshore rocky reef where Porthkerry Castle was said to have been built. Further on we passed Newton Pool and could see the smoke from some lime-kilns situated a little way inland.

As we walked along a part of the coast path where we could walk side by side Miss Thomas returned to an earlier topic of conversation.

She said, "If Captain Stewart is your natural father, why didn't you change your name to Stewart?" and with an honesty and clarity of vision that was refreshing added, "In this class conscious age, the son of a captain has a much higher social position than the son of a village blacksmith."

"Captain Stewart hoped I would adopt his name, and he was disappointed when I chose not to," I said. "I reasoned that the man I have become has been shaped by the parents who nurtured and cared for me during my formative years. I believed for most of my life that Mr. Smiley was my father and didn't know otherwise until after he was dead. At the time I thought it was correct to maintain the memory of Mr. Smiley by keeping his name. A few years have passed since I made that decision, and now I'm not sure it was the right one. Certainly Lady Megan thought I had chosen wrongly. Perhaps I should publicly acknowledge Captain Stewart as my father, but for the time being I prefer to remain Jason Smiley, as I have always been. In the end, I believe that my status in society will be established by my achievements and not by the occupation of my father."

"I think you will become very important, Mr. Jason Smiley, and I hope I am there to applaud your successes," Miss Thomas responded warmly.

"Miss Thomas, I can only pray that you will."

"I hope you are good at praying, Mr. Smiley," she said with a smile that made my pulses race.

"No," I said, "but I have an incentive to improve."

At Font-y-gary Bay we turned inland to the village of the same name and then we walked home side by side along the country lanes until we came to Rhoose and the path back to Porthkerry.

Suddenly I found that Miss Thomas's hand was nestling in mine and my pulse was thundering in my ears. I have no idea how it occurred as I had made no conscious effort to take her hand. It was as if our hands had an invisible attraction for each other but the joy of this unexpected physical contact was short lived as we suddenly heard an admonitory, "Miss Thomas, you are forgetting yourself!" from forgotten Elsie. Miss Thomas dropped my hand as if it had suddenly grown red hot. Her cheeks became bright red, and she immediately increased the distance between us to several decorous yards.

We had a light lunch when we returned to Porthkerry House and then spent the last hours of daylight sitting together in the library in comfortable easy chairs separated by a wide table. The ever present Elsie was in attendance, but she was a little more watchful after the hand holding we had indulged in earlier in the day. We were both tired from the fresh air and exercise and content to read for most of the time. As usual I was trying to decipher an article in a technical paper and Miss Thomas, who had finished writing her letters, was deep in a book called *Barchester Towers* by an author she named as Antony Trollope. On occasion Miss Thomas would look up from her book and ask a question.

Once it was, "Do you go to church regularly, Mr. Smiley?"

"Not at the moment, Miss Thomas, as we have no facilities on board ship. Before I went to sea, I used to go to our local church at least once on Sunday. Mr. Smiley and I usually attended the morning service as most of the villagers would be there."

"Did you enjoy it?"

"No, not really. I found it very tedious most of the time. Our vicar delighted in long complicated sermons. On many Sundays I lost the trail of his thoughts in a thicket of verbiage before he had finished the introductory remarks." Miss Thomas chuckled. "I was not alone in this, but perhaps I was less skilled at hiding the fact. As he stood in the porch saying goodbye to his parishioners, he would look at me and say, as he had said more times than I care to remember 'I saw that you were not paying attention again, Jason'.

It wasn't really lack of attention; it was a lack of understanding," I remarked.

A little later Mrs. Thomas came into the library to collect a book but didn't stay with us. I think she could see that we were content to be together with the indomitable Elsie as chaperone and did not disturb us. Perhaps she had reached the conclusion that I was an honourable person, but all the same, I wondered if she now knew about my upbringing from Miss Thomas. Nothing was said, and I hoped that Lady Megan's recommendation would be sufficient to overcome my lack of prospects.

We had dinner but I cannot remember what it was. After it, I retired for the night, walking on air with happiness.

The next day was my last full day at Porthkerry House, and after breakfast Miss Thomas and I went for our customary walk with our shadow trailing a discrete distance behind. This time we walked along the lane that led back along the route we had driven in the coach. We crossed Whitlands Brook on the stepping-stones beside the ford with much amusement and some mock screams of terror from Miss Thomas, as she wobbled on a stone above water all of two inches deep. But she took my hand confidently when I offered her the support, although we both knew it wasn't strictly necessary. We walked along the foot of Knock-man-down Wood as far as Nightingale Cottage and then turned back for home. We didn't talk much during the walk. We didn't need to. We were happy to just be together, and we did nothing to offend Elsie's sense of propriety.

We returned to the house in time for a light lunch and then went to the library where we sat in the chairs we had occupied the previous day with the table between us and Elsie watching from a discrete distance.

I didn't dare utter the words I so wanted to use to describe my feelings, as I did not know her very well and couldn't risk offending her by making advances she might find unacceptable. Consequently, I never had the opportunity to hear her expressing similar sentiments of affection and regard for me.

I had to content myself with, "It was very good of your mother to invite me to stay here these past three days, and I have been so very happy here in your company. I will be very sorry to leave you tomorrow morning, knowing that it may be as much as a year before I can enjoy the pleasure of your company again. I would like to write to you if you will permit it."

"If you don't write me a letter at least once a week, I shall be mortally offended and may even think another lady has caught your attention." But her serious expression was soon replaced with a smile so that I knew she wasn't entirely serious, and then she added, "You should remember that my parents may read what you write."

"You can be confident that my letters will be a model of discretion, Miss Thomas, but they will be written with much greater emotion and feeling than the words can convey."

Apart from the fact that this was my last day in Porthkerry House, it was also the day that some of Mr. and Mrs. Thomas's neighbours and business associates had been invited to dinner. The invitations had been sent out some time before Mr. Thomas had known he would be away on business, Miss Thomas explained and said that her father had felt that it would be impolite to cancel at relatively short notice.

Miss Thomas said, "One of our guests tonight will be the Vicar of St. Curig's Church, where we saw that young couple marry, if you remember?"

I nodded in agreement and she went on, "The Reverend Malcolm Blye is a nice old gentleman and very intelligent. I enjoy talking to him because he doesn't reduce everything to 'The Bible says you must do this' whenever I ask him a question. Clearly, his life is ruled by his beliefs, but he can offer help and advise that sounds much more down to earth even though it must be based on his religious thinking." She went on, "Mr. and Mrs. Davies with their daughter, Eileen, are also guests tonight. He is a neighbouring landowner and a close friend of my father's. Mrs. Davies and my mother are intimates and have many interests in common. Their daughter Eileen has been my best friend since I was about ten years old, and we tell each other about everything we do and think. I told her about your fight in Oman, and she is looking forward to meeting such a brave and resourceful man.

She is also very pretty, so I will be very jealous if you look at her too much," Miss Thomas added, but only half in jest, I thought.

"Another guest is Mr. Desmond Wilcox. He is a local landowner and business associate of my father's," she said. The tone and brevity of the description was eloquent of her dislike for the gentleman and suggested she was unhappy that he had been invited, but she volunteered nothing more.

Then she added, "But the guest of honour, at least in my eyes, will be a certain brave, gentleman seafarer named Mr. Jason Smiley," and she stood up, put her hand briefly over mine and was gone from the table and the library before I could draw breath.

I went to my room shortly afterwards as I needed somewhere to go to hide the huge smile of happiness that kept spreading across my face. In fact, it wasn't as private as I had hoped as George was there laying out my newly pressed uniform and ironed shirt. My highly polished boots stood at the foot of the bed. The brass buttons on my jacket shone like gold and the Gold Star badge in my lapel had been burnished to an equal shine.

With a great effort I managed to compose my features and said simply, "Good afternoon, George. How are you this afternoon?"

"Good afternoon, sir. Very well, sir, thank you but busy with the preparations for the dinner party tonight. Is there anything I can get you, sir?"

"No thank you, George. I don't need anything at the moment but you might be able to tell me something about Mr. Desmond Wilcox."

A look that I could only describe as an expression of extreme distaste passed across George's face at the mention of the name, and he paused to search for words to answer my question that were possibly more diplomatic than those that had entered his mind immediately.

He said, "He is a bachelor about ten years older than you, sir and very rich I believe. He has lived in the neighbourhood all his life. The rumour below stairs, sir, is that he has made his interest in Miss Mary known to her parents and has gained the support of Mr. Thomas. He believes he has only to wait until she is of marriageable age and she will fall into his hands like a ripe apple from a tree. Cook believes Miss Mary dislikes Mr. Wilcox and tries to avoid his company. I think he is a rude and conceited individual. He is also extremely jealous of any man that he perceives to be a potential rival for Miss Mary's hand."

He paused for a moment then added with a note of concern in his voice, "Sir, I will lose my position here if you tell anyone I told you this."

I said as calmly as I could, "George, you have my word that I will not speak to anyone about what you have said, and I can only thank you for giving me the information."

George left the bedroom to go about his duties, and I dressed for dinner a very worried young man.

I had no doubt about my feelings for Miss Thomas, and I felt that Miss Thomas liked my company, but an offer of marriage was out of the question in my circumstances. All of a sudden my uncertain situation had become immeasurably worse with the appearance of a rival. And unfortunately, he was a rich rival who was known to the Thomas family. He was also a business associate of Miss Thomas's father and considered to be a suitable husband. The thought of Miss Mary married to another man was bad enough, but to be forced by her father to marry a man she disliked made my blood boil with fury at a situation that was likely to destroy my newly discovered happiness. How I would be able to deal calmly with Wilcox, if he was as rude as George had implied I could not begin to imagine. I had met few rude people during my life and consequently did not know how to deal with them. I felt it might be difficult to keep the peace.

I went downstairs just before seven, which was about half an hour before the time set for dinner to commence. I went in to the drawing room where we were all to gather prior to the meal. I was wearing my best uniform and thought I looked quite smart.

When I entered the room, I realized that someone had already arrived for the dinner. He was standing in front of the fire as if he was the master of the house rather than another guest. He was clean shaven, but his hair was quite long and dark. His face was pale and narrow, and he stared at the world from under thick black brows with little close set eyes. His manservant had turned him out impeccably in a black tail coat, pin stripe trousers, bow tie and brilliantly shiny, patent leather shoes. His white shirt was starched like a board and he had diamond studs in the shirtfront and matching diamond cufflinks.

I said a polite "good evening" to the stranger and was about to introduce myself when he looked me up and down, with an expression that demonstrated total belief in his own superiority and said, "Who are you and what do you want here?"

Realising that this individual could be none other than Desmond Wilcox—with my blood already starting to boil at his insulting behaviour—I said much more calmly than I felt, "My name is Jason Smiley and I have been invited here by Mrs. Thomas."

"Really," he said and added with a sneer, "with that quaint uniform I thought you must be a new servant or part of a cabaret act to entertain us after dinner. What's the uniform for anyway?" he added rudely.

"I am the third officer on the Steam Ship Earl Canning," I answered calmly.

He paused for a moment, clearly puzzled by my calmness in the face of his continued rude questioning. Then he demanded, "Tell me how you are acquainted with Mary."

My blood fizzed with pent up anger at his use of Miss Thomas's Christian name because he had no more right to use it than I, but I said quietly and with more politeness than he was due, "It is really no concern of yours, sir, but Miss Thomas and I met at the ball given by the Governor of Bombay. Lady Megan, the Governor's wife, introduced us to each other. I am honoured to have the friendship of both Miss Thomas and her mother." Then I added politely, "May I know your name, sir?"

He looked at me as if I was something less than a village idiot in intellect for asking, and said, "I am Mr. Desmond Wilcox," and he rudely turned away from me to look at a newspaper.

I had the impression that this man's ability to be rude was rather greater than George had indicated, and as a result I was about to test my ability to keep the peace to an exceptional degree. I had already been close to rewarding his rude behaviour with insults of my own, but I kept hearing my father say in my mind, *He who loses his temper has lost the argument.* I hoped he would prove to be correct.

Any further interchange between Wilcox and myself was prevented by the arrival of Mrs. Thomas, Mary, and very shortly afterwards the other guests. Wilcox greeted Mrs. Thomas and the other guests civilly enough, but his attitude towards Mary was proprietorial and she was clearly embarrassed by it. I started to move towards them intending to interpose myself between them, but Miss Thomas noticed my movement and with a very slight shake of her head made me stop.

Shortly afterwards we went in to dinner with the Vicar escorting Mrs. Thomas and Wilcox escorting Mary, an arrangement that was not at all to my liking, but it was not my place to dispute my hostess's arrangements. If there was an understanding between Wilcox and Miss Thomas's parents, he would expect to escort her and all I could do was accept it, whether I liked it or not. The place at the head of the table was taken by the Reverend Blye with Mrs. Thomas, Mr. Davies and Miss Davies, Miss Thomas's confidant, on his left and Mrs. Davies, Mr. Wilcox and Miss Thomas on his right. I was at the foot of the table opposite the vicar. The ladies were dressed in demurely cut long dresses and all the men, apart from me wore black tailcoats.

The table was covered in a plain white linen cloth and was illuminated by candles in silver candelabra. Polished silver cutlery adorned each place, and it seemed to be alive as the flickering light from the candles played across the surfaces of knives, forks and spoons.

The meal was served on Denbighware dishes and consisted of only three courses as far as I remember. The first course was vegetable soup similar to the one we had enjoyed a few days before. The second course was Welsh lamb which had been roasted to perfection and was served with mint sauce, roast potatoes and vegetables. This was followed by substantial helpings of apple pie and dairy cream. It was delicious and I drank a glass of good burgundy with the roast.

It was one of the best dinners I have ever tasted, but my enjoyment was tempered by the knowledge that the evening could soon be marred for everyone. From what I had been told by George and experienced before dinner, I was sure that Wilcox would make another attack on me because of his jealous disposition. I was certain he would do his utmost to diminish me in the eyes of all the guests including Mrs. Thomas and her daughter. I dreaded the probability of a public confrontation with this rude and conceited man, particularly as there was a risk of losing my already precarious temper and saying things that would have repercussions later. I had to recognize also that my position was not very good. Wilcox was known to and accepted by Mr. Thomas, and so far, I had not even met Miss Thomas's father. I felt diminished and helpless by Wilcox's unending superiority until I remembered the way Miss Thomas had touched my hand and spoken to me. It gave me courage to know she was a supporter, whatever anyone else believed.

Wilcox had a hearty appetite for food and also for alcohol. He must have consumed at least one bottle of burgundy during dinner and had enjoyed several large glasses of sherry whilst waiting for dinner to be served. He dominated the conversation and overrode any attempt I made to participate in it. Without recourse to shouting him down, which in my view would have been unacceptable behaviour on my part, he effectively isolated me at the foot of the table. A symbolic position he clearly thought was appropriate considering his opinion of my inferior status.

When the desert was served, I watched in impotent fury, as he moved his chair closer to Miss Thomas and started a low voiced conversation with her that was clearly not to her liking. She moved pointedly away from his presence, and that annoyed him further. I wanted to intervene, but did not dare to as it would simply provoke the confrontation I wanted to avoid. Worse, I would have been seen to have caused the problem by involving myself where I had no right to be. Everyone and his dog understood that I had no rights where Miss Thomas was concerned.

Whenever I looked at Miss Thomas, which I could not stop myself from doing rather too frequently, I could see him glowering at me over Miss Thomas's head.

As I looked away on one occasion a little voice in my head said, *Understand your opponent!* I wondered inconsequentially who had said it, probably Captain Stewart ex Royal Navy I imagined, but the advice was good. I started to give the problem some serious thought. Here was a man who had ruled the local roost and suddenly another younger cock had appeared. There had been no rivals before and much worse was the fact that the said cock had a bright uniform and had met the lady of his dreams in a foreign land. The stable fabric of his life had been shaken to its very foundation, and the woman he coveted was being wooed by a stranger. I concluded he would try any tactic he thought might be successful in order to regain his position. I almost felt sorry for him until I remembered the material advantages he had.

Clearly he was much more jealous of my presence than George had hinted he might be. I felt it was only a matter of time before he unleashed his rudeness on me again particularly as Miss Thomas had been less than encouraging towards his advances. The frustrations caused by her rebuff coupled with the amount of alcohol he had consumed only meant that he would be incapable of controlling his tongue for very much longer. I hoped that I would be able to keep my temper reined in enough to let it drive my responses without losing control. It was going to be difficult because his behaviour towards the young lady

I adored had already brought my fury close to bursting point.

Elsie was just clearing the desert plates when Wilcox said in a voice thickened by drink, "You don't drink much wine, Smiley. Not good enough for you or are you too young to drink with the men?" Then on a different tack he said, "Sitting there in your fancy merchant navy uniform, I expect you think you are too good for the Royal Navy. Or is it that you are afraid of being hurt defending Queen and country?"

Miss Thomas took a deep breath clearly ready to speak in my defence, but I managed to catch her eye and prevent her intervention whilst Wilcox glanced around the table looking for support. But he found that his rude and unprovoked attack on me had only served to isolate him.

I could see that Mrs. Thomas was outraged by his comments and the other guests were looking embarrassed by his outburst. Clearly everyone had been taken by surprise and didn't know how to react to this unprecedented situation.

I felt my face redden with fury as his charge of cowardice struck me, but I kept control of my temper and didn't respond immediately as I was unsure the best way to deal with his insults.

Wilcox took my reticence as an admission of guilt and said patronisingly "Come, come, Smiley. It takes a man to admit he is afraid."

Miss Thomas again looked as if she would respond, but again I managed to prevent it.

As the vicar drew in a sudden breath with the clear intention of interceding in this unseemly interlude I responded to Wilcox's provocation much more calmly than I thought was possible.

I said, "Mr. Wilcox, our hostess has provided us with an excellent meal and an admirable wine to complement it. I enjoyed the glass of burgundy I had and needed no more." Then, feeling the need to go onto the offensive, rather than burst with suppressed fury I added, "Unlike you, sir, I do not need to drink a bottle at a sitting."

Wilcox was obviously unused to payment in his own coin. He bristled with anger and his eyes screwed up. His chair screeched across the floor as he pushed it back and stood up.

He had lost his temper entirely and shouted, "Are you accusing me of drinking too much? If it wasn't an offence to fight a duel, I would call you out and teach you a lesson, you young jackanapes."

Suddenly I felt better than I had all evening. I leaned back in my chair looked Wilcox in the eyes and said politely, "Mr. Wilcox, it is better for you that duelling is prohibited. You may deride the merchant navy in your ignorance if you wish, but we sail to foreign countries where pirates are still a scourge. My captain insists that we all practice with sword and pistol every second day in order to save our lives and to ensure we can prevent the theft of cargo of value to the owners." I realized that every one's eyes were on me as I paused and said with very heavy emphasis, "You would be dead, sir, before you worked out which end of the pistol to grasp, and if you chose to use swords I would cut you to ribbons with equal facility."

As Wilcox collapsed back onto his chair I said calmly and quietly, "When the time comes, Mr. Wilcox, I will not be afraid to protect my Queen and country. The Royal Navy will find they have a well-trained and experienced officer who will do his duty without thought for his own safety. I doubt that you can say the same, sir."

I went on and my anger had dissipated almost entirely, "You met me for the first time an hour ago and you know nothing about me, Mr. Wilcox, yet you accuse me of cowardice. You have lived in this locality all your life. The only danger you have to face is from a fox or a bird and they don't normally fight back. On the other hand I know what it is like to be captured by pirates, and I know exactly what it is like to be unarmed and face men with rifles intent upon killing me. I can also admit to the fear of death that I felt when I faced down those tribesmen. You, Mr. Wilcox, have had no similar life threatening experience and are in no position to comment on cowardice."

My calm rebuttal of Wilcox's drunken accusations was well received by the other dinner guests who had feared a shouting match if nothing worse. Wilcox stood up again, made a poor attempt of thanking Mrs. Thomas for the dinner he had consumed with such gusto and left in an obvious temper. He knew he had made himself look foolish in front of two people he had hoped to impress.

After Wilcox had left Mrs. Thomas apologised for her guest's rudeness. Then she asked me to relate my recent adventures to her guests as she was sure they would be as interested to hear my account first hand as she was, having only heard an abbreviated story from Lady Megan and her daughter.

After the unpleasant incident with Wilcox, I was more than pleased to have the opportunity to demonstrate that I could be courageous and resourceful when the need arose and felt at the end that I had made a good impression on my fellow guests. Poor Miss Eileen Davies was quite round eyed with hero worship. She was, as Miss Thomas had said, extremely pretty, but I had eyes only for Miss Thomas.

Shortly after I finished relating my story, I thanked my hostess for a lovely dinner and asked her for permission to retire in order to prepare for a very early departure for Cardiff and the journey to Liverpool and my ship.

In the morning both Mary and her Mother arose very early and came to say goodbye and wish me a safe return.

Mrs. Thomas said, "I hope you have a safe voyage, Mr. Smiley, and I look forward to welcoming you to Porthkerry House on your return to Britain."

Then she added seriously, "Desmond Wilcox is an influential man in this area and is a dangerous man when he has been humiliated. You must be very careful, Mr. Smiley."

Miss Thomas said simply, "I am so pleased you were able to visit us. Look after yourself, Mr. Smiley. I shall look forward to reading about your adventures when I receive your letters week by week."

Then they were gone, and I set off for Liverpool.

ELEVEN

Captain Stewart Charged

I had an uneventful journey to Liverpool, and as my mind was full of pleasant memories of Miss Thomas, following my few days at her home, it seemed to pass quite quickly. Of Mr. Desmond Wilcox I spared not a thought, which was to prove a mistake as I later discovered.

When I boarded the ship and went to the bridge to report my return I found the captain and the first mate leaning over the rail and watching the stevedores at work.

I said formally, "Third Officer Smiley reporting for duty as instructed, sir."

Captain Stewart said equally formally, "Welcome aboard, Mr. Smiley, resume your duties at eight bells in the dog watch."

I said simply, "Aye, sir," saluted and turned to go below.

Unexpectedly Captain Stewart said, "Mr. Smiley, did you know that you are a grave disappointment to the first mate. Isn't that so, Mr. Richards?" and the first mate nodded his head vigorously but said nothing.

As I turned back to them Captain Stewart went on seriously, "Yes! You are a grave disappointment. I really have no idea what punishment we can mete out. Upsetting the first mate is a terrible crime."

I was becoming very concerned by the stern tone in Captain Stewart's voice and asked in a very solemn voice, "Can you tell me what it is I have done, Captain? I have no recollection of doing anything to anger Mr. Richards."

"I can Mr. Smiley. You were so eager to go to Miss Thomas that the first mate was convinced you would elope. He expected me to receive a letter from Gretna Green, but here you are reporting for duty as if nothing had happened. He is very disappointed to be proved wrong."

And as I said with great feeling, "I wish I had thought of that," they burst out into bellows of laughter.

After a few minutes of laughter, the captain became serious once more and said, "As you know we will have a passenger joining the ship for the voyage to Bombay, Mr. Smiley. He has something to do with the Anglo Indian Telegraph Company. He will share your cabin for the voyage."

I resumed my duties as one of the watch-keeping officers of the ship and was able to exercise more self-control than previously and keep my thoughts of Miss Mary for off duty hours. My fellow officers, without even the exception of the captain, made some fun of me with comments about keeping out of mischief until the day of my marriage or volunteering to help me on my wedding night if I was too tired and some less than tuneful whistling of the Wedding March. But it was meant in a kindly spirit and accepted in the same fashion. I felt that I had come home again and that was a pleasant feeling.

The last of our cargo arrived two days after my return. Reel after reel of copper wire destined to form part of the overland electric telegraph between Karachi, in India and Gwadur, on the border of Baluchistan.

Our passenger was due to arrive during the evening of the day before we were due to sail. He did and announced his arrival with a clatter of heels sliding down the companion steps followed by a loud thump and a softer thump, thump. I rushed out of the cabin into the companion way and found, in the semi dark of our night lit, little world, a black heap, wheezing noisily on the deck in front of my cabin door. It was not immediately clear which end of the heap was which or whether this shapeless lump even had a top or a bottom end. After a few moments one end did start to emit, in an unmistakably male voice, oaths that even our first mate would have been proud to utter. Soon after, the shape resolved itself into a male figure that was initially able to sit up with some assistance from me, and then stand up. He rubbed his head and various other parts of his anatomy, groaned a few times but did not seem to have come to serious harm.

The male voice said in a masterpiece of calm understatement, "I slipped."

I asked, with considerable concern "Are you hurt?" hoping fervently that he would answer in the negative, as I had no idea how to deal with a serious injury.

He responded, "A little bruised I fear, but otherwise unscathed. I had a bag in each hand and didn't notice in the dark that the companion-way steps were so steep. I missed the second step, could not catch hold of the handrail because of the bags, overbalanced and ended prostrate here," and he pointed theatrically at the deck at my feet.

After a pause, whilst he flexed his arms and legs in order to verify that they were still working correctly, he introduced himself. "My name is Neil Fairweather. I am taking passage to Bombay with you."

"I'm Jason Smiley," I responded. "I'm the third officer and we will be sharing this cabin," and I gestured over my shoulder at the door behind me. I said, "On behalf of Captain Stewart please let me welcome you aboard. For all our sakes I hope your name will be a good omen for calm seas during our voyage."

I stood back to show him into my cabin. Or more accurately, the box with two bunks we would share for some months. He was neither impressed by the size of the cabin nor by the fact that he would have to use the top bunk, but after a moment of reflection said, "I have been in worse," but he didn't elaborate. "Which watch are you on Mr. Smiley? In this tiny space it will be less disrupting for both of us if I eat and sleep at the same times you do."

I was amazed that this civilian stranger should know enough about naval practice to have experienced the disruption of the watch system and also be prepared to live with it when he did not have to. Mr. Neil Fairweather climbed quite a few points in my esteem as a result. With full holds we set sail from Liverpool with the lack of fuss borne of experience, and once again our destination was Bombay. I had posted the first of my promised letters to Miss Thomas the previous afternoon. The composition had not been as easy as the promise to write had been. With my mind full of the charms of the lady and a pen burning with the desire to write sonnets of love, composing a message that would be suitable for Miss Thomas's mother to read was extremely difficult. In the end and after a great deal of head scratching, I managed to compose a credible letter with a few lines each about the state of the weather, my health, the ship and of course, our passenger. I wrote how much I had enjoyed her company and looked forward to our next meeting more than I could put into words. I wanted to write that she would be in my thoughts always, but wasn't sure if Mrs. Thomas would approve, so omitted it to be on the safe side.

It is difficult writing to the woman of your dreams as if she was your younger sister.

True to his word Mr. Neil Fairweather ate when I did and slept when I did. When I was on watch he often came to the bridge, and I soon realized there was much more to this man than appeared on the surface. Never once did he do or say anything out of place, but clearly he was familiar with the duties of a watch-keeping officer. He was also very familiar with the pitching and rolling motion of a ship at sea, and at no time did he give any indication that he was going to live up to the jocular predictions of serious mal de mere suggested by Captain Stewart. I did not know how old he was, but I thought he must be about ten or fifteen years my senior from his general demeanour and obvious, man of the world, knowledge.

One night, when we were lying at anchor waiting to start coaling the next morning, he decided to stay on board rather than sample the delights of the local town. I was grateful for the company as most of the officers and all but a skeleton crew, had gone ashore. The most recent in a chain of letters to Miss Thomas had been given to the second officer of a sister ship on the homebound voyage, and I needed something to take my thoughts away from a pretty, young, lady from Wales. Fairweather and I were leaning on the rail enjoying the breeze, after the heat of the day, when I decided to ask him about his past experiences.

I said, "You are sailing with us to Bombay as a specialist in the electric telegraph. I hope you will not think me impertinent for asking, but I should be pleased to know why you are familiar with the workings of the ship when you are clearly not a sailor."

He turned and leant his back against the rail and said, "I don't mind in the least relating my experiences to you. I was on board HMS Agamemnon when we tried to lay the first submarine cable between America and Britain in '57."

He went on to say that he had been employed by The Atlantic Telegraph Company as an electrician at the time and had been testing the cable as it was laid. It was a joint British, American venture, and the American Navy had allocated the "Niagara" to partner the "Agamemnon." Each ship carried half the cable as there was no one ship available that could carry the whole length.

He went on, "The venture was controlled by the engineers who knew most about cable laying at that time, and they decided to lay the cable from coast to coast. The first ship would sail to a rendezvous in mid Atlantic, laying cable as she progressed. At the rendezvous the cable ends would be spliced together and the second ship would sail to the other coast. We landed the shore end of our cable on the south coast of Ireland from HMS Agamemnon and then sailed for the mid Atlantic rendezvous, submerging cable as we went. We had only submerged about five miles of cable before it caught in the laying machinery and broke. We started again. Ten days and three hundred nautical miles later, an engineer thought the cable was running out too quickly and applied the brake to slow it down. The brake snatched, the cable broke and the end disappeared over the side and was lost at sea and could not be recovered. This first attempt to lay an Atlantic submarine cable was abandoned."

He went on after a pause for thought. "About a year later, the company decided to try again. This time the cable ships met in mid ocean spliced the cable ends together and set sail in opposite directions. The cable parted after only five miles had been laid and the ships returned to start again. They had to try twice more but eventually the cable was laid successfully across the Atlantic. The "Niagara" landed her cable in Newfoundland on 5th August, 1858, and a few days later the "Agamemnon" landed her cable end in Ireland. It was a tremendous triumph for The Atlantic Telegraph Company. Congratulatory messages were sent between the leaders of the Old World and the New in celebration of the achievement, but after about four weeks of operation, the cable went dead."

Fairweather continued, "Those who doubted the wisdom of attempting to connect America and Britain by electric telegraph felt that their opposition to the idea had been vindicated by another failure. I think they are short-sighted. In my opinion each failure simply advances our knowledge of this new science and will lead to more reliable results in future. I am confident that the world needs this rapid means of communication, and I intend to be at the forefront of the development."

I was amazed that he had so clearly put into words the thought that had come to me in Mr. Thomas's library a short time before.

I couldn't believe my good fortune. For the best part of three months I was going to share a cabin and most of my waking hours with a man who was not only enthusiastic about the electric telegraph, but had the knowledge I needed to fulfil at least in part, the ambition I had conceived in Mr. Thomas's study in Porthkerry. While these thoughts had flowed through my brain Fairweather had once again turned to study the shoreline in the evening light.

I turned to him and said, "A few weeks ago I went to visit a friend in South Wales and her father had a number of reports and technical papers on electricity and the electric telegraph amongst other subjects. They were left on a table in his library, and I was allowed to read them, although I failed to understand most of what I read. I am very interested in learning more about the telegraph and how it works. I hope you will not consider me presumptuous if I ask you to teach me as much as you can about the subject."

Mr. Fairweather turned and looked at me, as if he was trying to assess how serious a student I would be. Eventually he responded to my question. "Electricity is not an easy subject to grasp. It is a phenomenon that cannot be seen or smelt and has the potential to kill you if you don't take care. I will be happy to teach you all I know, particularly as it will help pass the time and be a refresher course for me as well."

We soon established the routine necessary to combine eating, sleeping, working, and studying, and Fairweather patiently taught me about a subject that was beyond the comprehension of most people in Britain at that time.

He started his first lesson by saying, "In the first place Mr. Smiley, you must understand the principles of electricity. If you cannot grasp these principles then you will be unable to understand the working of the electric telegraph. A simple analogy is water flowing through a pipe. If you have water stored in a tank, the greater the height of the tower supporting the tank, the greater is the pressure of the water in a pipe at the bottom of the tower. The higher the voltage in a wire, the greater is the electrical pressure. Going back to the water analogy you will understand that as the diameter of a pipe installed at the foot of the tower reduces then the resistance to the flow of water under the same pressure increases. The amount of water flowing through a pipe depends on pressure and resistance.

"With electricity the three concepts you have to understand are voltage, resistance, and current. The higher the voltage, the stronger is the electrical pressure or voltage in a wire. Current is the term used to describe the rate at which electricity flows through a wire. Resistance is simply what the word implies."

He told me about the early experiments with electricity generated by friction devices and then the development of the voltaic cell by the Italian, Alessandro Volta in 1800 which provided a stable, low voltage, high current source of electricity. He taught me all he knew about electrical theory and about newly invented instruments like the mirror galvanometer and the 'Wheatstone Bridge' that he used routinely during cable laying work. He described how cable was made with Gutta Percha insulation around the conductor and then armoured and the way in which it was stored in the cable ships.

He described how the cable was fed from the tanks on the ship and how it was controlled as it was being lowered to the sea bed. He instructed me in the theory of jointing or splicing the cable and I was impressed by the amount of practical detail he had retained He said how important it was to maintain contact with the shore station during cable laying so that any fault in the cable could be discovered quickly.

There was one incident that he described with some relish. The manufacturing order for an Atlantic cable had been divided equally between two competing companies. Only when the cables were to be spliced together was it was discovered that the armour on one cable was left hand lay and the other right hand. It was an incompatible arrangement and one that was overcome only by the ingenuity of the engineers aboard the cable layer.

He taught me the code invented by the American, Samuel Morse, and I was soon able to send and receive messages using a Morse key and sounder he wired up using a lead acid cell and spare parts contained in one of his boxes.

Day by day my lessons continued during off duty hours and so did my lessons in seamanship during my duty hours. As a result time passed very quickly and Fairweather and I established a very comfortable friendship.

All too soon we arrived in Bombay. Neil Fairweather disembarked, and my lessons came to an abrupt end. But I had acquired a working knowledge of electricity and the electric telegraph, and I felt that my mother would have been proud of my diligence. The mate decided that I should prepare the loading plan for our next voyage on my own this time. In the past I had helped him or the second officer, but on this occasion he felt I had sufficient knowledge to do it on my own. I was quite sure that my calculations would be checked by one or other of my fellow officers, but I was very pleased that my progress in seamanship was being recognized and rewarded. There are two basic requirements for a ship carrying cargo between different ports. The first is to ensure that the cargo for an individual port is easily accessible, and in simple terms the first item out of a hold is the last piece loaded in. The second criterion is to distribute the cargo vertically and horizontally in the cargo holds so that the ship's stability is not impaired. There is often a conflict between these two parameters.

Whilst I was working on this problem, a message came from Lady Megan inviting me to call the next day at ten in the morning. This was in response to a message I had sent to the governor's house when we arrived to advise Lady Megan that I had letters for her from Wales.

The next morning, dressed in my best uniform and with my shoes and buttons shining, I arrived just before ten at the entrance to the governor's house. I was greeted by a uniformed Indian servant and led along a corridor and up a flight of stairs to the governor's private apartment. The servant knocked on a large door and then ushered me in to the presence of Lady Megan.

"Good morning, Lady Megan," I said, as I handed over the small bundle of letters I had carried from Wales.

"Thank you," she said as she accepted them from me, "I hope you are in good health Mr. Smiley?"

"I'm very well, thank you, Lady Megan. I hope you and the Governor are as well."

"Yes, thank you. We are in the best of health. Did you enjoy your visit to Wales?"

"Very much, Lady Megan, and I must thank you for writing to Mrs. Thomas as you did. It was very kind and thoughtful of you."

She laughed and said, "You should thank Miss Thomas for that. She persuaded me to write to her mother as you had sailed before she could meet you again. She was very impressed by you, I think. It's a pity that your prospects are not better."

I responded to Lady Megan's politely phrased, "Perhaps your

duties require you to return to your ship," in the only way possible.

"With your permission Lady Megan, I will return to the ship. Please extend my felicitations to the Governor," and I turned to leave as Lady Megan started to slit the envelope of one of the letters I had delivered. The servant was waiting at the door and opened it for me, and I stepped out onto the landing. The governor was passing, and I stopped to allow him to precede me down the stairs.

He greeted me heartily, "Good morning, Smiley, Lady Megan said you were coming to deliver letters from Wales. How were Mrs. Thomas and Miss Thomas when you met them?"

I realized that the governor knew Mr. Thomas had not been at home during my visit and wondered why and how he knew, but responded politely "They were very well, and I enjoyed my visit to Wales very much, thank you."

"Good."

He started to turn away, but then went stopped and said, "I had a meeting with Mr. Fairweather several days ago. He spoke highly of you and was impressed by how quickly you had learned about the telegraph. He was also very impressed when I told him about your escapade in the Mussandam, and he said you hadn't mentioned it. Why was that?"

I answered with complete honesty that I had not thought of it and in any event it would have had no relevance to the subjects we were discussing.

The governor changed the subject completely. "I am an old man, Smiley, and I am accustomed to horses and carriages for transportation and pen and ink for messages. I do not understand the electric telegraph, and at the moment, I do not believe it's a helpful invention. Sometimes it seems to work, but most of the time it has broken down for some reason or other. However, I have to admit that many eminent people are hazarding their fortunes and reputations submerging cables and string-ing wires here, there, and everywhere but with a mixed bag of results. Now that you have learned something about the subject I should be interested to listen to a young man's opinion."

I chose my words with care, "Sir, my mother told me I should never contradict my elders and betters, and so I am reluctant to express a contrary view, particularly to someone like you who holds such an eminent position. I cannot foresee how the telegraph will develop in the future, but I am reminded of something Captain Stewart told me. I think there is a parallel to this situation. He described how some French villagers saw a steam driven vehicle on a street, about one hundred years ago and thought it was the work of the devil. Actually it was the invention of a French military engineer called Cugnot and was the first steam driven cart in the world. This experiment lead to the development of the railways and no one now says that the railways are unnecessary.

"I spent some months studying electricity and the electric telegraph with Mr. Fairweather and I am convinced that it will become at least as important as the railways. Mr. Fairweather has told me that every invention has faults to begin with, and I'm sure that's correct. The railways were no exception to this. Similarly, the mistakes and failures of the telegraph all add to our knowledge and should make the end result better if we are prepared to learn by experience. I have to admit that the development of the telegraph is of great interest to me, and I hope that one day I will be fortunate enough to become involved with it."

The governor patiently listened to my enthusiastic little lecture, looked at me with his shrewd blue eyes, and said, "We shall see, Smiley, we shall see," and stumped off down the stairs. He did not appear to be discomforted by my opposing views for which I was thankful.

I returned to Earl Canning, resumed my duties, and thought no more about my comments to the governor. Involvement with the telegraph appeared to be an unattainable dream and best kept in the background.

The life of a sailor is one of arrivals and departures. Mine was no exception. We finished discharging the cargo we had carried from Liverpool or had loaded for Bombay at intermediate ports during our voyage. As hold space became available, we started to load our return cargo for Britain and this was completed within a very few days.

We sailed without ceremony and had a return voyage that was, thankfully, uneventful. As the days passed and we travelled closer and closer to Liverpool, I began to hope that there would be a letter from Miss Mary Thomas awaiting me when we docked.

In all honesty, I hoped there would be a pile of letters waiting, but realized that I would be very happy to get even one. It would be more than six months since I had been to Porthkerry, and I hoped she would not have forgotten me in the meantime. I thought back to the letters I had written and given into the custody of homeward bound sea officers and hoped that they had remembered their promises to post them as soon as they reached their homeports.

We locked up out of the River Mersey late one blustery afternoon and were shepherded by two tugs towards our usual berth in Victoria Dock. It was my watch and I was on the bridge with the Captain. As we came alongside I noticed Captain Downing and another man striding down the quayside to where our gangway would be positioned as soon as we were tied up.

I turned to Captain Stewart and attracted his attention, "Captain, sir."

"Yes, Mr. Smiley?"

"Captain Downing is on the quayside with another man."

"Thank you, Mr. Smiley."

Captain Stewart glanced over the side of the bridge, gave a brisk salute to Captain Downing who returned the salute with one hand, whilst holding his uniform cap down against the wind with the other. It looked quite comical. The man with Captain Downing was in normal civilian clothing and looked cold and uncomfortable standing in the wind. He gave a half hearted wave.

Captain Stewart returned his full attention to the business of berthing the ship against an adverse and blustery wind that kept trying to blow us to the other side of the dock. Eventually, the tugs pushed the ship close enough to the quay for heaving lines to be thrown from the ship to the berthing men waiting below. Mooring lines were quickly pulled across from the ship and dropped over bollards. We were soon moored fore and aft, complete with springs and Captain Stewart ordered the gangway to be lowered.

He turned to me. "Ring finished with engines, Mr. Smiley."

"Aye, sir," I responded and rang the engine room telegraph and left it set as ordered.

Captain Stewart looked over the bridge rail again, checked that the gangway was being lowered and remarked sotto voce, "I wonder what brings Captain Downing and the Company Secretary away from their nice snug offices to stand on a wet and windy quayside. It must be serious." Then he said to me, "Carry on Mr. Smiley. I will meet my visitors at the head of the gangway." And he turned and left the bridge.

I busied myself on the bridge until the end of my watch, then went to my cabin and sat on the bunk. As always my thoughts immediately turned to Miss Mary Thomas and equally quickly my hopes for a letter in the morning. I went to the mess and ate a solitary meal, as the other officers were on watch or ashore. The meal was soon over and I turned in for the night quite early as there was nothing to stay up for.

In the company of the other two deck officers I was eating breakfast the next morning when Donovan came mournfully into the mess and said in tones of doom "Good morning, gentlemen. Captain Stewart wishes to see all you officers and the bosun in his cabin at eight bells in the morning watch." Having delivered his message, he left without a further word or glance.

We looked at each other in silent enquiry and then sat wondering what had caused the captain to issue this sudden and unexpected summons on our first day in port, particularly when both the first and second mates were due to go on short leaves immediately after breakfast.

"Captain Downing and another man came to see the captain when we berthed last night. I wonder if it has anything to do with them," the first mate speculated out loud, but neither the second mate nor I could offer any insight into the situation.

"Please inform the bosun, Mr. Smiley," ordered the mate.

"Aye, sir," I responded.

As, ordered, we congregated outside the captain's cabin door just before the appointed time, and punctually at eight bells, Donovan opened the door and let us in. We stood in an untidy group in front of Captain Stewart's desk and waited for him to take his place. After a few minutes he came in from his night cabin looking tired, very strained, and a little white around the mouth. He moved to his desk and sat down, with a more than usually miserable looking Donovan, standing just behind and to the captain's left.

"Sit down, gentlemen."

We sat down where we could and waited for Captain Stewart to open the meeting and tell us what was required of us. He moved some papers across his desk then returned them to their original place. He fidgeted and looked uncharacteristically ill at ease.

He cleared his throat, took a deep breath and with a discernable tremor in his usually steady voice, he said, "Before explaining the reason for your presence here this morning, I must warn you that you must not comment by word, or by gesture, on anything you see or hear in this cabin this morning. You must not discuss anything you see or hear with anyone on or off this ship. Is that clear?"

"Aye, sir," we responded in a ragged chorus, and I think we all looked as perplexed as we felt.

"Yesterday, Captain Downing and Mr. Edward Presser, the Company Secretary, visited me when we tied up. They gave me a letter. This is the letter."

He opened a drawer and took out a large brown envelope and extracted from the envelope a single sheet of paper with a very official looking red wax seal affixed to the bottom. From my position it looked very official. The first mate who was sitting closer, gasped audibly as if he had recognized it when he saw it, but said nothing as Captain Stewart glared at him.

Captain Stewart said in a voice shaking with suppressed emotion, "For those of you who have never seen one of these documents, I can only hope that you never have the misfortune to receive one. If you do, it will probably spell the end of your career as a sea-going officer. I have seen one in the past, but never expected to receive one myself. It is a summons, gentlemen. Captain Evans has laid charges of negligence against me, and I have to present myself at a Board of Enquiry into the death of Third Officer Evans."

Totally forgetting the warning Captain Stewart had given us only moments before, I was on my feet with my mouth opening to shout my opposition to the news when I saw him raise his hand to stop me, and he snapped, "My instruction to say nothing applies to you, Third Officer Smiley, just as it does to these other gentlemen. Sit down and be quiet, sir."

"Aye, sir," I said as I subsided into my seat with my blood boiling at the iniquity of the charge laid down by Captain Evans.

Captain Stewart continued, "I have been relieved of my command by the company, pending the result of the Board of Enquiry and the first mate will act as captain in my place until I am reinstated or another captain is appointed in my place. I will leave the ship within an hour, and I expect you to serve the acting captain with the same support you have shown to me. All members of the ship's company who have any knowledge of events on that dreadful day will be required to make a sworn statement and attend the Board of Enquiry in person. I repeat. You must not discuss anything that happened that day with anyone on or off the ship. There must be no hint of collusion or the Board may reject your testimony."

Captain Stewart looked at us one at a time then said, "That is all, gentlemen. You may leave. Mr. Richards please remain seated."

We all filed out in a stunned silence not knowing what to do or to think, but after a few minutes indecision, whilst we waited for the first mate to reappear, the second officer ordered us to carry on with our duties. I went to the bridge, the bosun below and the second officer to his cabin as he was off watch. We had lost our captain and as a result our sense of direction. After living and working together for so many months and voyages, it was like losing a favoured family member.

Following the usual routine, a messenger delivered letters to the ship from Captain Downing's office during the morning of our first full day in port. There were some for the captain and the other two officers but nothing for any of the crew. I sent the bridge messenger to the cabins of the captain and the other officers with their letters. I had received two. Miss Mary Thomas, I was sure, had written one, and my spirits soared, but the handwriting on the other I didn't recognize. In any event both letters would have to be kept until I went off watch, so they were carefully placed in an inside pocket of my jacket.

Just before three bells in the forenoon watch, a carriage clattered down the quay, and the driver pulled the horses around in a big half circle to stop the carriage beside the gangway with the horses pointing towards the entrance. Donovan got out and still looking a picture of abject misery hurried up the gangway and disappeared in the direction of the captain's cabin. A few minutes later, he reappeared at the head of a procession of seamen carrying an assortment of boxes, bags, and packages that they loaded into the carriage. The seamen filed back up the gangway and disappeared. Donovan waited by the coach.

Not many minutes past before Captain Stewart appeared with the mate and they walked down the gangway deep in conversation. They shook hands and the mate stood back as Captain Stewart climbed into the carriage. Donovan climbed up onto the box with the coachman and as that worthy whipped his horses into action, the first mate straightened to attention and saluted. And so our captain was suddenly transported away.

Mr. Richards, in his combined role of first mate and acting captain, climbed heavily up the gangway and disappeared in the direction of the captain's cabin. Thirty minutes later a messenger came around the ship to pass on Mr. Richard's order that the second officer and I should report to the captain's cabin immediately. We arrived within a few minutes of each other and found Mr. Richards sitting in the captain's chair, as he had every right to do. But it still looked strange to us.

The mate stated confidently, "This is a bad business, but I am certain that the Board of Enquiry will find in favour of Captain Stewart. Then the Gold Star Line will reinstate him in this command. However, we have our duty to perform, and when Captain Stewart returns, I want him to be proud of the way his crew has responded to this crisis."

But the second officer was a little less reticent with, "My sentiments entirely, sir."

Mr. Richards, the acting captain, continued, "Until the captain is reinstated, you, Second, will take over my duties as first mate, and you, Mr. Smiley, will act as second officer. As there is no one junior to you Mr. Smiley, you will have to carry out the third's duties as well.

"It will give you less time to think about Miss Thomas, which will be good for you," he added with the ghost of a grin.

We smiled slightly, relieved that a little humour could still be generated in this unprecedented situation.

When the last of the dockworkers had gone clattering down the gangway and the watchmen had been posted, I climbed back to the bridge. At the end of my watch I went down to my cabin and opened Miss Thomas's letter with dry mouthed, sweaty palmed eager anticipation. It said,

Porthkerry House
Barry,
Glamorganshire
South Wales
9 June 1866

Dear Mr. Smiley,

As soon as my father returned home, Mr. Wilcox came to see him. I do not know what was said, but Father was dreadfully angry with my poor mother and has forbidden me from seeing you or communicating with you again.

My poor, distraught mother has helped me to send this letter. My father has not told my mother what Wilcox has said, but she is blamed for whatever it is Wilcox has complained about.

Mr. Wilcox came to see me after he had spoken to Father, and he was so insufferably smug and conceited that I sent him away with a flea in his ear.

I am sorry to give you such bad news,

Yours sincerely
Mary Thomas

I now knew what the phrase "my heart sank" really meant. I opened the other letter and found it was from Miss Thomas's father. I read it with increasing incredulity.

Porthkerry House
Barry
Glamorganshire
11 June 1866

Third Officer J Smiley
S. S. Earl Canning
Victoria Dock
Liverpool

Sir,

Mr. Wilcox has told me that you behaved in a rude and inebriated fashion at dinner and in consequence caused extreme distress to Mrs. Thomas, my daughter and the other guests. Mr. Wilcox has also advised me that you are the penniless son of a village blacksmith and no fit companion for a lady as refined as my daughter.

I have not consulted Mrs. Thomas about this matter as I do not wish to add to the distress she must already feel for inviting an undesirable person such as you to my house during my absence.

My daughter has been forbidden from communicating with you.

If you are found in this area or make any attempt to communicate with my daughter again, I will take action against you in the courts.

Yours faithfully,
William Thomas. J. P.

I had to read the letter several times before I was able to really grasp the contents.

It was clear that Wilcox had manipulated the truth to his own advantage being confident that a man as autocratic as William Thomas would not consider consulting his wife or any one else about the events of that evening. He, William Thomas, was the man of the house, and he would take all decisions for his family and tell them afterwards what must or must not be done. It was as clear as crystal also, that if I did give

Mr. Thomas grounds for taking me to court, I would have no chance of avoiding whatever legal penalty he chose to inflict. He was a wealthy and important person in the area and a Justice of the Peace as well.

I did not know what to do. He had instructed his daughter not to communicate with me and threatened me with court action if I tried. It seemed as if my dreams of a future including Miss Thomas would never be allowed to germinate. It was a bitter pill to swallow.

After some hours of fruitless, agitated and circular thought, I decided to ask the first mate's advice. He was acting captain, of course, but it would be a long time before I stopped thinking of him as first mate. I went to the captain's cabin, knocked and then opened the door and walked in when I heard him call out, "Enter."

"What do you want, Mr. Smiley?"

"I have received a letter from Mr. Thomas, Miss Mary Thomas's father, and I don't know what to do about it. I would appreciate your advice, Mr. Richards."

I handed over the letter and he read it then studied me for a moment before saying, "Mr. Smiley, I cannot believe that you would have had too much to drink or would have been rude to your hostess. What actually happened?"

I was immensely relieved by his words of understanding and support and described to Mr. Richards what had happened. I also told him what Miss Thomas had written in her letter.

"I recommend you do nothing at the moment. Wilcox is a liar and a troublemaker, but he has Mr. Thomas's ear. All you can do is to wait and see what happens. You should not write as that can only make your situation worse if your letter falls into the wrong hands."

"Aye, sir," was all I could say.

I left the cabin and went to mine and spent a sleepless night worrying about the love I seemed to have lost through the evil and deliberate actions of others.

What a truly horrendous day this had turned out to be, I thought. First of all my father had been relieved of his command and summoned to answer charges of negligence brought by the father of my dead friend, John Evans. I was sure the charges were malicious and realized that Captain Evans must have gone mad through grief to have precipitated this action. Even if Captain Stewart was acquitted, there would be a stain left on Captain Stewart's character and record that unscrupulous people would exploit.

Then there was the revelation that Wilcox had evened the score between us by persuading Mr. Thomas that I had been drunk and insulting to his wife and guests. I could barely contain my anger at the thought. I ground my teeth together to prevent me from shouting out in temper and could barely restrain my fists and feet from striking any object within range. The unfairness was shattering. I was condemned falsely just like my father, but there was no Court of Enquiry to hear my case and demonstrate my innocence to Mr. Thomas.

The dreams of happiness with Miss Thomas that had seemed very promising in my imagination only a little time before as I waited for her letter, now seemed so unattainable that I felt I could not go on with life.

But one has to!

TWELVE

The Enquiry

The first day after the captain handed over command to Mr. Richards was a day of change, as we accustomed ourselves to the new watch pattern and assumed our new and in some cases additional duties. For the crew nothing had changed and the routine of a ship in port continued normally. If any of the crew knew why Captain Stewart was no longer on board, I do not know and being very mindful of Captain Stewart's strictures about discussions, I at least, made certain that they heard nothing from me. All the same, I was puzzled about the reasons for the instruction.

I asked Mr. Richards, when we met on the bridge, "Sir, Captain Stewart said we must not talk about the accident, but I do not understand why we must not. Can you tell me?"

"Are you questioning the order, Mr. Smiley?" Mr. Richards responded sternly.

"Certainly not, sir," I answered quickly. "I will follow Captain Stewart's order exactly, but I would like to know why he made it if you are able to tell me."

"That's right, Mr. Smiley, obey orders at all times. In fact the order issued by Captain Stewart will have come from the President of the Board of Enquiry originally and is intended to prevent collusion. It would be very easy for men living and working on the same ship to discuss and agree between them an account of an event that suited them all, but which was not necessarily the whole truth. At the enquiry you will be asked under oath if you have discussed the events of that dreadful day with anyone since Captain Stewart issued the order banning discussion. If you say you have, you will be cross questioned minutely about who you spoke to, when and about what. The Board could ignore your evidence if they feel another person has influenced it.

Mr. Richards stopped and stared at me for a long uncomfortable time and then said very seriously, "Do you understand now, Mr. Smiley?"

"Aye, sir," was my only possible response.

Mr. Richards started to walk away but turned back and said, "I don't know exactly how the enquiry will be organized but come to the captain's cabin at four bells, and I will tell you all I know. Find the second officer, I mean the acting first mate, and tell him to come as well."

"Aye, sir."

I left the bridge and went in search of Brian Davies, the acting first mate. I found him examining some mooring lines that had been brought up from the cable tier and laid out on the foredeck. The bosun was with him.

"Excuse me, sir."

"What is it, Mr. Smiley?"

"Captain Richards would . . ."

"Who the devil is Captain Rich . . . Oh! I see," he interrupted and then said, "Go on, Mr. Smiley."

"Captain Richards would like to see you in the captain's cabin at four bells, sir. He plans to tell us what he knows about the conduct of a Board of Enquiry."

"Very well," the first mate said, and turning to the bosun added, "You had better come as well, ."

I was dismissed and went below to the mess for my midday meal. In my cabin afterwards, I started to write a letter to Miss Thomas. I had promised her that I would write and I intended to prepare one more letter whilst I considered whether to take notice of her father's ban on communication or not. I wrote,

SS Earl Canning
Victoria Dock
Liverpool

Miss Mary Thomas
Porthkerry House
Barry
Glamorganshire
South Wales

Dear Miss Thomas,

When we docked yesterday, I did hope there would be a letter from you waiting for me and was overjoyed when I was given an envelope addressed in your fair hand.

Because of my duties, it was many hours before I could find the privacy to open it, and when I did so it was in a fever of anticipation. After the warmth with which I was greeted in Wales, I was dumfounded when I read that you had been instructed not to communicate with me again. I could not understand why your father could have taken such action when we haven't even met.

I received a second letter yesterday. It was from your father. Mr. Wilcox has informed him that I was drunk and rude to your mother and the other guests at dinner and clearly Wilcox has turned the truth on its head. Your father has believed what he has been told and decided to prevent us meeting or communicating again. I am considered an unsuitable companion for you and threatened with legal action if I attempt to communicate with you again.

I can only hope your father will discover that Mr. Wilcox has deliberately deceived him and allow me to have the pleasure of your company once more.

Yours sincerely

I also wrote a letter to Mr. Thomas although I was sure he would consign it to his library fire as soon as he realized who had written it. It was brief,

SS Earl Canning
Victoria Dock
Liverpool

Mr. W. Thomas Esq. JP
Porthkerry House
Barry
Glamorganshire
South Wales.

Sir,

I am in receipt of your letter informing me that I may not communicate with Miss Thomas. On the basis of Mr. Wilcox's testimony, you believe I was drunk and rude at a dinner party hosted by Mrs. Thomas and consequently, you consider that I am not a fit companion for Miss Thomas.

You have been misled, sir, and you can verify the truth of my assertion by questioning your wife and the other guests. At an appropriate time I will take action against Mr. Wilcox for his deliberate and calculated libel.

As a fair minded man I hope you will have the courage to place blame where it belongs and lift your ban on my communication with Miss Thomas.

Yours faithfully

At four bells the three of us arrived at the open door to the captain's cabin and went in. Mr. Richards gestured to chairs and went to close the cabin door as we sat down. He looked at us in turn for a moment,

"We are not here to discuss the tragic events that have led to this Board of Enquiry," he said in a calm conversational tone of voice.

"IS THAT CLEAR?" he bellowed in a loud and commanding voice.

We jumped in surprise and then individually we confirmed that we understood.

He went on, "I do not know the composition of the Board of Enquiry Captain Stewart will face, nor it's terms of reference. What I can tell you is based on my experiences at a Board of Enquiry I attended as a casual observer some years ago. I had no role to play and knew none of the participants.

In that instance the chairman of the panel was a retired admiral and his two assistants were both full captains. The various parties to the dispute had retained lawyers to support them, and the proceedings were conducted like a criminal trial with the witnesses for both sides being examined and cross examined by the lawyers. At the end of the enquiry, the chairman presented his report and apportioned guilt or innocence as appropriate, to the parties of the dispute.

It is an ordeal for everyone taking part except for the lawyers and the board members."

He stopped for a moment to look us over, as if searching for our hidden strengths and weaknesses and then went on, "You should not underestimate the seriousness of the situation. If Captain Stewart is found to be guilty of negligence by the Board, then he will lose his master's ticket and his senior position in the Gold Star Line. In all probability he will never be appointed to command a ship again. What is worse is my belief that he can then be tried in the criminal court for causing the deaths of Evans and the others. I don't think he would be charged with murder, for which he could be hanged, but it could be a lesser charge with a long period in prison as a penalty."

Mr. Richards looked directly at me and opened his mouth as if he was about to make a comment only to me but obviously had second thoughts because he closed it again. His final comment was to all of us, "When I receive definite information about the Board of Enquiry, I will ensure you are informed immediately. Please carry on with your duties, gentlemen."

We filed out of the captain's cabin looking dismayed and feeling worried.

In the afternoon we received individual invitations for the next day, to attend at the offices of the solicitors retained by the Gold Star Line to act for Captain Stewart. Mr. Richards was first at ten, Mr. Davies was next at noon, and my appointment was the last one and set at two in the afternoon. Mr. Richards returned on board about midday and went straight to the captain's cabin without a word to anyone. His pale face and bowed head suggested he had been through a difficult time. Mr. Davies still hadn't returned on board before I went ashore to make my way to the solicitor's office.

I set off about thirty minutes before my appointment with Mr. Barnaby Williams of the firm of solicitors called Williams, Henry & Compton. The offices from which this prestigious firm practiced was in Dale Street and reached up a lino covered, dark and dusty staircase. My footsteps, as I climbed the stairs, echoed in the gas lit stairwell, and it felt as if the building was totally uninhabited except for me. On the landing at the head of the first flight of stairs I saw a door. There was a light from inside the offices shining through the frosted glass panel set into the top half of the door. On the glass in a semi circle of black letters was the name William, Henry & Compton and horizontally, lined up with the "W" and the "n" was the word SOLICITORS. I wondered if the upper case lettering made them feel more important.

I knocked and receiving no response, knocked again a little louder, and then opened the door and went in. A balding little man in a dingy frock coat looked up from a ledger. "Mr. Smiley?" he enquired.

"Yes."

And since he worked for a solicitor and needed to be absolutely positive about identifying this stranger he asked, "Ah! Uh! Mr. Jason Smiley?"

I repeated my affirmative.

"To see Mr. Barnaby Williams, I believe."

"Yes."

"I'll just go and see if he is in."

"But he is expecting me at this time. I have an appointment," I said with some asperity.

"I know, sir, but I must be sure he is in before I announce you."

I was beginning to wonder if there was some secret back door that the solicitors could use to slip in and out of the office without their clients seeing them.

The little man could obviously see my increasing bewilderment and probably also sense the growing irritation I felt, because he said in explanation, "I will tell you something in confidence, sir. I must first go and see if Mr. Williams is ready to see you. If he says he is in, then I will announce you. However, if he does not wish to see you, perhaps he has not done what you asked of him or you are a rude and objectionable person, then I will come back and say 'he's out' and invite you to await his return. If you persist in waiting beyond a reasonable time, then I will say 'I am so sorry, sir, but I have to close the office.'

"Then I will make a big pretence of locking up and going home, ushering you out of the office door ahead of me. I will come back after a discrete interval and release the solicitors who were locked in. It's a convenient way of dealing with troublesome clients without offending them."

With the ghost of a wink he said, "I'll just go and see if Mr. Williams is in, sir. Please wait a moment."

He disappeared through a door at the back of the main office and was back in a trice.

"Please come in, sir, Mr. Williams will see you now."

As I followed the little clerk into Mr. Williams's office, I had the distinct impression that the previous fifteen minutes had been a delaying tactic to allow the solicitor to return late, but without appearing rude. I looked but couldn't see a door, but that wasn't conclusive as it could have been disguised as a bookcase or something.

The room was not as gloomy as the rest of the establishment appeared to be. This was a blessing as almost the whole floor of the room was covered with little piles of papers and documents tied with red ribbon. I would certainly have tripped over something had there been the same level of gloom as in the outer office. There were little isolated alleyways of Axminster carpet visible between the piles of papers and I watched with fascination as my guide stepped past obstructing piles of paper as he tacked along and across the visible lanes of carpet towards the big desk set below a window opposite the door. There was a big leather topped table surrounded by six large chairs to the left of the desk. I thought that it would have been quicker to use the piles of papers like stepping-stones across a stream, but perhaps the clients who owned the papers would not have approved. I was introduced to Mr. Williams and my guide disappeared.

Mr. Williams was a slightly bigger version of the little man in the outer office. He was a little taller, a little rounder and certainly hairier, as he had a mop of black hair and a bushy black beard. He had piercing blue eyes set in a wrinkled, ruddy complexioned face, jug handle ears and a snub nose. His clothes, where these were visible, were black and had a wrinkled, lived in look.

Mr. Williams looked me up and down in a speculative way.

He said, "You look a little young to be the key witness in Captain Stewart's defence, Mr. Smiley."

"What do you mean key witness?" I managed to gasp through a throat closing up from panic at the thought and added, "The first mate and the second officer were also there and they are much more experienced than I am."

Mr. Williams looked at me in a pitying way. "Mr. Smiley, please correct me if I am wrong, but as I understand the situation," and raising one finger he said "Mr. Evans handed over his duties as officer of the watch to you when he was ordered to take the boat to the island." A second finger joined the first. "You were officer of the watch when Mr. Evans sailed away." The third finger was raised. "You were alone on the bridge whilst Mr. Evans sailed to the island." Four fingers were erected. "You were officer of the watch and alone when Captain Stewart unexpectedly came back to the bridge, and you witnessed Captain Stewart's discovery of the storm." The thumb joined the four fingers. "You helped Captain Stewart with all the emergency signals." A finger from the other hand was raised to make the sixth digit. "You witnessed the last visible moments of the boat Mr. Evans, the crew, and the surveyors were on before they were overwhelmed and drowned."

I said nothing. There was nothing I could say. It was an accurate summary of the situation that had existed. Eventually, I asked, "What can I do to help Captain Stewart?"

"Tell the truth, Mr. Smiley, and nothing but the truth," was the terse response.

For the rest of the afternoon and well into the evening Mr. Williams led me through the events of a day that I had tried to forget. Simple questions at first, just to ensure the chronology of the events was correct, then more and more detailed questioning and all the time he was writing down my answers in a strange series of symbols. A disengaged part of my brain wondered if it was the shorthand invented by Pitman. Then he started to ask questions that put an interpretation on what I had said that changed the meaning slightly but significantly. A "Yes" or "No" answer to the first two or three such questions made me sound as if I was disagreeing with Captain Stewart's actions, and I became quite annoyed that Mr. Williams was proving to be an opponent rather than a supporter.

He noticed my irritation of course and said, "Mr. Smiley, please believe me when I say that I am here to give Captain Stewart every support I can. I was doing what Captain Evans counsel will try to do. The learned gentleman will expect you to be overawed by your surroundings, as you may indeed be, and he will ask you apparently simple questions. He will ask a series of questions quickly and try to force you into quick responses in the hope that he can trap you into an admission that will go against the captain. I am encouraged that you are quick witted enough to see the dangers in my questions, but we must continue to practice your statement until you cannot be trapped into a damaging admission."

Then he leant back in his chair and stretched his arms above his head and said wearily, "That is enough for tonight, Mr. Smiley, it's late already. Come back at ten in the morning."

He rang a bell on his desk. The little clerk came in from the outer office and escorted me out of Mr. Williams' room, through the outer office and out onto the landing.

"Good night, sir, I'll see you at ten tomorrow morning."

He turned and went back into his gloomy office. The door closed with a thump, and the letters on the glass shivered. I shivered also from the reaction to many long hours of questioning and also to hunger. As Mr. Williams had said, it was late, far too late to get a meal on board, so I would have to try to find a hotel on the way back to the ship at which to buy something. I set off to walk back to the ship, my mind full of thoughts.

As I walked, I remembered the first mate's frightening assessment of the penalties that would be heaped upon Captain Stewart's head if he should be found guilty and then what Mr. Williams had said about me being the key witness in the captain's defence.

The enormity of the responsibility I had to shoulder suddenly struck home, and I was panic stricken at the thought. I would be responsible for my father's future life. He might be freed and prosper or he might be imprisoned and become a broken and unemployable man. And this whole sorry mess had come about because of the mistake made by Sir Algernon Cuthbert Cummings when he sent us to Elphinstone Inlet. How I hated that man for putting my father in this dangerous situation. I walked on, deep in thought and worrying whether my performance in front of the Board of Enquiry could possibly be adequate enough to prove my father's innocence of a charge of negligence.

I found myself at the foot of the gangway, so I went aboard and down to my cabin. I climbed into my bunk with my head full of worries and my belly as empty as a drum. I wondered if I had looked as tired and drawn on my return to the ship as Mr. Richards had earlier.

Next morning after breakfast, I went to Mr. Richards and told him that I had to return to Mr. Williams, the solicitor. I left the ship not long after two bells in the forenoon watch and started walking to Dale Street and the Solicitor's offices. I remember that it was a bright, sunny morning and thinking that it was far too cheerful a day for the business in hand.

Mr. Williams greeted me cordially when I was ushered into his office and invited me to sit down. "First of all Mr. Smiley, you must write a statement describing all the pertinent events of that dreadful day in August 1865. It must be factual and unemotional. The statement will be the official submission of your evidence to the Board of Enquiry and when you sign it, I and one of the other solicitors in this office, will witness your signature. When that is completed we will continue with the review of your evidence and the questioning we started yesterday."

Then he added in a worried tone, "We have precious little time in which to make everything ready."

He led me to the leather-covered table I had seen the previous day.

"Sit down here," and he indicated a chair at the table. On the table in front of the chair was a pile of clean white writing paper, some ink and a selection of new and used pens all neatly arrayed. I pulled a sheet of paper towards me and tried out several of the pens. I selected one that was not only comfortable to use but allowed me to produce neat handwriting. After taking another clean sheet I wrote to Mr. Williams's dictation,

Account of the Fatal Accident that took place on 20 August 1865 in the Elphinstone Inlet.

Prepared by
Third Officer Jason Smiley

from the SS Earl Canning
Liverpool

I then sat and thought for a minute or two to assemble my thoughts and then started to write down a detailed account of that day in August 1865. The discussion with Mr. Williams and the questions posed by him had succeeded in fixing the chronology of the events in my mind to such an extent that the statement seemed to write itself. After the initial few moments for thought, I had not needed to stop again. I took the statement to Mr. Williams as soon as I finished writing and he put down the papers he was studying and read it. As he read, he checked each of my statements against the notes he had made at our previous discussion. I sat and fidgeted, in a fever of apprehension in case he found an omission or some inconsistency or other that would mean rewriting the whole document. It was a great relief when he put it down without comment.

He studied me for a moment and then pointed at the statement and said, "Very well done, Mr. Smiley. It only remains for us to witness your signature, and we can send this document to the Chairman of the Board of Enquiry."

This was quickly achieved, and Mr. Williams then took me through every aspect of my evidence with direct questions, obscure questions and most importantly questions worded to cause confusion to someone under pressure. Many hours later we stopped. Whether it was due to hunger or simple fatigue or both was not important. We had achieved as much that day as we would ever achieve.

I stood up to leave. "Good night, Mr. Williams, thank you for your support and guidance."

"Not at all, Mr. Smiley, but as you now understand, the outcome rests firmly on your young shoulders. I will see you at the enquiry. Good night."

Like the previous evening, I was shown off the premises by the little old clerk, walked down the gloomy echoing staircase and back through the streets of Liverpool to the ship. Once on board I reported my return to Mr. Davies, the acting first mate, who asked, "Is your statement finished, Mr. Smiley?"

"Aye, sir."

"Mine also, but that solicitor Williams asked so many questions and made me so confused, I had to write it three times before it was finished to his satisfaction."

"I didn't have any difficulty, sir. I found Mr. Williams to be very thorough and helpful."

"I suppose it must always be easier for the junior officers who have least responsibility," he remarked, in superior tone of voice, but before I could respond, he added, "The captain left instructions that you were to report to him as soon as you returned aboard. Carry on, Mr. Smiley."

I chose to content myself with a simple "Aye, sir," and left the bridge to report to the captain.

Mr. Richards was in the captain's cabin writing at the desk when I went in to report my return. He handed me an envelope whilst saying, rather unnecessarily I thought, "Ah! Mr. Smiley, you have returned I see. You had better read that."

I took the envelope, slit it open and extracted a single sheet of stiff white paper. I read it and found that I had to report to a conference room in the Corn Exchange building on the following Wednesday at 09.00 to assist the Board of Enquiry in their investigation of the charge of negligence brought against Captain James Stewart, Master of SS Earl Canning. It went on to say that the Chairman of the Board of Enquiry would be Admiral Buchanan with Captains Mountjoy and Royston as advisors.

It was less than two days away, and I experienced a feeling of sheer panic at the thought of the public scrutiny I would face and the responsibility I carried for Captain Stewart's future. I wondered if Mr. Williams had known when the enquiry would convene. Probably he knew unofficially and hadn't mentioned it for that reason. It would certainly explain the intensity with which he questioned and coached me.

Acting Captain Richards leant back in his chair. "This sorry business will be over in a few days. Thank God! How did you manage with Mr. Williams? Has your testimony gone to the Board?"

"I found Mr. Williams very helpful, sir. I finished my statement this morning and the solicitor's clerk was sent to deliver it to the Board's Secretary this afternoon."

"Good. I have been to see Captain Downing, and he has agreed to my suggestion that we work the ship normally tomorrow. The next day, as all the officers will be absent at the same time and for an unknown period, cargo operations will cease. The bosun has not been called to the enquiry, so he will remain on board to ensure the security of the ship and keep the crew busy. He has a long list of repair and renovation items that need attention and a day free of cargo operations will be a good opportunity. I assume the enquiry will be over in one day, but if it goes on into a second day, I will make appropriate arrangements then. Mr. Davies has already been informed of these arrangements. Carry on, Mr. Smiley."

"Aye, sir."

I left the captain's cabin and went to the mess where I was just in time to get something to eat. I was starving hungry, but my stomach was so knotted up with my fearful anticipation of the Enquiry, that I found it difficult to force down more than a few mouthfuls. I went to my cabin, climbed into my bunk and lay in the dark, tired out but unable to sleep as my brain churned over the events of the past few days. I must have slept eventually, as I suddenly woke up from a nightmarish dream shaking with fear and soaked in sweat. In my dream I had watched and listened as my father was hung for the murder of Evans due to my inadequacies at the enquiry.

There was no possibility of more sleep that night, and I lay awake until the confines of my bunk and tiny cabin grew too claustrophobic. I went on deck then and climbed to the bridge in the dawn light and watched the sun rising. It would have been a cheerful and beautiful sight on most days, but it failed to lift the dejected and miserable feeling left after my dream.

The life of a ship goes on regardless of the events surrounding members of the crew. Ruled by the clock as always it was soon time to eat whatever my unsettled stomach would countenance and then take my first watch. My worries and concerns had to be subordinated to the requirements of supervising the ship and ensuring the correct loading of our next cargo.

After a busy day during which I managed successfully to ignore the impending crisis, Mr. Richards called the acting mate and myself to the captain's cabin.

"Captain Downing has arranged for a carriage to come to the ship at seven bells tomorrow morning to take us to the new Cotton Exchange Building. That will be all, gentlemen. Please carry on."

"Aye, sir" we said almost in unison as we left the captain's cabin to continue with our duties. The others didn't seem to be overly concerned about the enquiry, but I at least was fully alive to the situation I faced in a few scant hours. Concentration on the work at hand was no longer a sufficient palliative to mask my feelings. I was frightened of the prospect of public examination by a hostile person, as I had to assume the lawyer representing Captain Evans would be and more particularly of the risk of being proved inadequate in my defence of Captain Stewart. I could only console myself with the thought that I would do my best. It was all I could do and there was no other course.

At the end of cargo loading that day, I went to the mess with a poor appetite and was able to eat very little. I was soon in my cabin but delayed climbing into my bunk for a long time, as I was fearful that a return to sleep would bring a return of the nightmare that had forced me from sleep so violently in the morning. In the end my fatigue overcame my ability to sit up and I climbed into my bunk. I lay there not trying to go to sleep and was startled to find the bridge messenger shaking my shoulder to wake me up. It was four bells on the morning of the Enquiry and I had to get ready to face God only knew what.

My stomach was too nervous to accept much in the way of breakfast, and I have no recollection what I ate so little of. Just before seven bells I went to the gangway wearing my best uniform complete with cap. Everything had been pressed, creased or polished, and I was confident I looked the part of the key witness, even if I didn't feel it.

Mr. Richards and Mr. Davies, also dressed in full uniform, were waiting at the head of the gangway. I was just in time to hear a pale faced acting first mate say confidingly to Mr. Richards, "I couldn't sleep for worrying." Mr. Richards didn't respond, but he looked as though he hadn't slept much either.

With Mr. Richards in the lead, we marched down the gangway in order of seniority and climbed into the waiting carriage. The coachman whipped up his horses, and we set off on our journey as soon as I had closed the door behind my heels. Understandably we sat through the journey in a dour silence, each of us busy with his own individual thoughts. Reviewing what had to be said, worrying about making again, the mistakes that had brought Mr. Williams wrath down on our heads, or perhaps like me, just worrying about the unknown situation I faced. Like a soldier facing battle for the first time.

Worse in the imagination than the reality, provided you are not wounded or killed.

The carriage wheels clattered over the cobble stones in front of the Cotton Exchange Building, and I was surprised to see how many bystanders there were at such an early hour as we pulled up in front of the colonnaded main entrance. We got out of the coach and an audible whisper ran through the crowd as we were correctly identified whilst we walked to the entrance,

"It's the officers from Earl Canning."

Then we were inside the building and a uniformed attendant approached us. He singled out Mr. Richards as the senior and said, "May I know your name, sir."

"We are from the SS Earl Canning. My name is Richards, first mate and these gentlemen are Mr. Davies, Second Officer and the Third Officer, Mr. Smiley. We are called as witnesses at the enquiry."

The attendant consulted an imposing list of names and eventually found ours near to the bottom.

I was curious and asked, "Are all these people witnesses?"

He looked at me as if I was an idiot to be humoured and replied condescendingly,

"Oh! No! Sir! Them's not all witnesses. Most be guests of the Chairman and such, come to see the fun. Better than theatre, sir. It's real life y'see and not playacting. List of witnesses be here." And he pointed to our three names at the bottom of the last page. It was a stark comment upon our status in the forthcoming proceedings.

He turned away to accost some other newcomers.

We stood together, a small isolated group of naval uniforms, in a crowd of people wearing everyday clothes. We were mute in a cacophony of cheerful chatter. This was not the serious judicial atmosphere generated by caring people conscious that a man may soon lose his livelihood and his liberty. It was the sound of people who were anticipating an entertaining and diverting performance.

Davies commented with aptness, but to no one in particular, "Sounds like a theatre crowd just before the curtain rises."

"Aye, so it does. And we're just the small part actors," growled the acting captain and added to no one in particular, "God knows, but I shall be mightily pleased to see the end of this day!" It was a comment both Davies and I agreed with whole heartedly.

I looked around and was just in time to see Captain Evans appear in the hall surrounded by a crowd of people. He was obviously a very popular man here and was treated with great deference, as he progressed towards the far end of the hall. He was ushered through a doorway with a small group of people who detached themselves from the crowd of supporters. I thought I recognized Evans sister but could not be sure as the female figure was so far away. I remembered the venom of her comments at our previous meeting and was very pleased we were no closer.

There was suddenly, a complete and utter silence in the hall, and it seemed as if everyone turned at the same time to face the main entrance door. Captain Stewart marched into the reception area flanked on one side by Captain Downing and on the other by the Company Secretary. Captain Stewart held himself erectly, but his haggard face and exaggeratedly stiff posture showed how much pressure he was under. As they marched along the reception area towards us, the heads of all the people in the crowd turned in unison as they watched. As they marched past us, we saluted but they did not appear to notice. They certainly did not acknowledge the salutes. They disappeared through a door at the opposite end of the hall, and as they did so the chatter resumed and increased in volume until it was much greater than before. Fifteen minutes before nine we made our way into the room where the enquiry was to be held. It was already very full of people and extremely noisy. We had the greatest difficulty forcing our way through the crowd to take our places on the front bench behind the table at which Captain Stewart sat with his supporters and advisors. Behind us was a low railing that separated the onlookers from the participants.

A large table stood on the opposite side of the room. Behind the table and facing us were three chairs, the centre one being considerably more imposing than its partners and set on a low dais. Immediately in front of the main table and making the stem of a Tee was a smaller table with two chairs either side. Men wearing black gowns and white wigs occupied all the chairs. Clerks to the enquiry I assumed.

Immediately in front of me was the big table occupied by Captain Stewart, with Captain Downing and the Company Secretary to his left and two gentlemen in black gowns and wigs on his right. One of Captain Stewart's lawyers looked familiar, but from the back I could not make a definite identification. On the table were some piles of papers and what I took to be legal reference books from the well-worn appearance of the covers and binding. Symmetrically placed in relation to Captain Stewart's table and on the right hand side of the room was another big desk which was occupied by Captain Evans team of three lawyers. They looked quite relaxed and appeared to be enjoying a light hearted conversation. Behind them was a bench similar to the one I was sitting on, and I could see Captain Evans seated in the middle if it. Beyond him sat his daughter, staring fixedly ahead as if her life depended upon whatever it was she stared at. Captain Evans was staring across the room and it was almost possible to feel the hatred in the glances he was directing at Captain Stewart. I thought Captain Evans looked quite deranged.

Between the tables was a lectern. I could not understand why that piece of furniture had been placed there but assumed it was there for a purpose. There was no one to ask anyway.

The room was full to bursting point with people, and it seemed as if every one of them had an acquaintance on the far side of the room with which person contact had to be made immediately. People shouted to be heard, and then other people shouted louder in order to get their message across. And so it went on in an ever increasing bedlam of noise, which culminated in every one shouting and no one hearing. The atmosphere was pure carnival, and if a couple of circus clowns had come pirouetting onto the area between the tables, I do not think the crowd would have seen anything out of place.

Sharply at nine one of the clerks raised a gavel and violently struck the desk with it. Small items on the desk jumped from the impact but no one heard a sound. He raised the gavel again and struck the table four times in succession. The last impact was heard very faintly. He tried again with some greater success and then as the tumult died down a little he struck the table with a crack that echoed around the room and brought a silence born of surprise.

As people started to pay attention, he shouted in a sergeant major's voice "Silence. All stand."

The room quietened and everyone who was sitting stood up. A door in the side of the room opened and three naval officers resplendent in dress uniforms marched to the table and sat down in the chairs provided. In the centre was Admiral Buchan, and sitting as his advisors were Captain Mountjoy on his left and Captain Royston on his right.

The clerk shouted, "This Board of Enquiry into the death of six persons by drowning in the Elphinstone Inlet on 20 August 1865 is now in session. Please be seated."

He immediately started to beat the desk with his gavel to quell the rising tide of noise. He had only a modicum of success. Those few who saw or heard the gesture stopped talking, but the vast majority, who as yet had no real interest in the proceedings, continued to exchange news and gossip.

Admiral Buchan gestured to the clerk of the court who rose majestically to his feet and strode toward the railing in front of the crowd. As he moved forward his black gown billowed out beside him adding the illusion of even greater size to a frame that was in real life more than six feet tall and strongly built to match. The people in the front of the crowd tried to move back as this menacing, funereal figure approached but could not because of the press of noisy unobservant people behind. The clerk of the court halted with a military style stamp of his boots, straightened himself to his full height, raised his black bearded head and in a voice that drowned every other sound in the room shouted,

"SILENCE!"

And there was.

It was the total stunned silence of people whose ear drums have been severely rattled by the unexpected volume of the man's voice. He opened his mouth again before someone else could speak and said clearly and distinctly, "I will not call for silence again. I will send for the constabulary and have this room cleared of all who do not have direct business with the enquiry."

He about turned with the stamping of boots that denoted a lifetime experience as a military man and marched back to his seat in a silence broken only by his footfalls.

Admiral Buchan stood up and turned to the clerk of the court. "Thank you Mr. Tierson."

He turned back to the room and declared the Court of Enquiry open and went on, "This is not a court of law. This is a Board of Enquiry charged with examining the events of 20th August 1865 and determining if Captain Stewart acted correctly or is guilty of negligence. Our duty is to establish the facts. If the charge is proven then it will be up to others to impose penalties or press other charges.

Acting for the plaintiff is Mr. Jonas Jeremiah Q.C. and for the defendant Mr. Barnaby Williams."

And I suddenly recognized the solicitor I had spent so many hours with. The gown and wig had effectively disguised him.

As Admiral Buchan paused for thought, I heard a man behind me say to his colleague, "Evans has brought a Queen's Counsel from London and Stewart has a local man. Poor Stewart is behind before it's started."

My heart sank and my nervous stomach lurched nauseously in sympathy at the opinion the man had expressed.

Admiral Buchan said, "Mr. Williams, if you would be so kind."

And Mr. Williams responded with, "Certainly, sir," and continued, "In the first place I would like to extend to Captain Evans and his wife and daughter our profound sympathy at the untimely death of Third Officer Evans."

"Here, Heres" sounded from various parts of the room. As far as I could detect neither Captain Evans nor his daughter gave an indication that they had heard Mr. Williams's opening remark.

Mr. Williams continued calmly, "When Captain Stewart returned to Liverpool from the voyage in which Third Officer Evans so tragically drowned, together with his crew and the surveyors, he was unable to make the lengthy journey to Caernarfon in North Wales to pay his respects to the family. This was due to the pressing requirements of reporting to the Gold Star Line managers on the recently completed voyage. Captain Stewart decided to send as a substitute, his Third Officer, with express instructions to extend the captain's condolences and to also say that Captain Stewart would attend upon the family in person within a few days. His emissary was treated rudely and sent away, and Captain Stewart himself was not allowed to visit the family as he had intended.

Now, almost a year later, we are gathered here to debate the soundness of the decisions made by Captain Stewart on that fateful day.

I am confident that the Board of Enquiry will find Captain Stewart innocent of the charge of negligence made by a brother master mariner. Whether Captain Stewart will sue Captain Evans for damages due to his defamation is not known to me, but I would recommend such action if consulted."

Mr. Jonas Jeremiah stood up and Mr. Williams sat down at a signal from Admiral Buchan. Mr. Jeremiah responded with a sneering tone in his voice, "It is unlikely that you will be consulted, Mr. Williams, as the evidence against your client is overwhelming. As far as Captain Stewart's emissary is concerned you can hardly be surprised if a snotty-nosed juvenile is treated harshly when he is sent to do a man's work."

To a few sniggers from the crowd behind him, Jonas Jeremiah sat down again, with a pleased and superior expression on his face, and Mr. Williams stood up again. After a pause to adjust his gown, Mr. Williams calmly resumed his opening remarks. "With regard to the first point it is natural that my learned friend Mr. Jonas Jeremiah and I hold opposing views, but this Board of Enquiry will resolve the question of culpability."

'With regard to the second point I find it hard to reconcile the 'snotty nosed juvenile' described with such relish by my learned friend, with the emissary sent to Captain Evans home by Captain Stewart."

Mr. Williams turned to me and said quietly, "Stand up Mr. Smiley."

I stood erect and proud in my Gold Star Line uniform and looked Mr. Jonas Jeremiah directly in the eyes.

"Admiral Buchan," continued Mr. Williams, "This young man was the emissary sent to Captain Evans. I believe you will find it difficult to recognize in this young officer, the 'snotty nosed juvenile' described by Mr. Jeremiah."

I sat down again at a gesture from Mr. Williams, who then wagged an admonitory finger at Jonas Jeremiah and remarked, "I would counsel you to form your own opinions and not expound the opinions of others who may not be very observant."

There were a few more sniggers from the audience and Mr. Jeremiah looked as if he had bitten into a particularly juicy lemon. Admiral Buchan said not a word, but I could see that he was pleased by the way I was turned out and carried myself.

Mr. Williams resumed his presentation, "I will now ask Captain Stewart to describe the events of that day. He will quote from the official ship's log as necessary during his narrative. I will question Captain Stewart at the end of his description and then Mr. Jonas Jeremiah Q.C. will be at liberty to cross examine."

Captain Stewart walked to the lectern and placed the logbook and a copy of his statement side by side on the top. He delivered his account of the events of that day in a strained and sometimes hesitant voice that belied his calm exterior. It was obvious that Captain Stewart was all too aware of the gravity of his situation, and this was having an understandable and certainly undesirable affect. Mr. Williams asked a few questions then gave way to Mr. Jonas Jeremiah for his cross-examination.

Jeremiah had the demeanour of someone who had known exactly what Captain Stewart intended to say and after a few perfunctory questions turned to the Chairman of the Enquiry, "I have no further questions at the moment, but I expect to re-examine Captain Stewart later in the Enquiry."

Mr. Jeremiah Jonas QC sat down, muttered something to one of his companion's, who sniggered and then started inspecting the ceiling as if the proceedings were rather a bore.

Mr. Richards was invited to the lectern next. He explained what had happened from the time he came onto the bridge, a few minutes before the storm struck and was questioned on his evidence by Mr. Williams. Cross examination by Mr. Jeremiah was very brief as he was able to demonstrate that the first mate had little knowledge of events before Third Officer Evans sailed for the island as he was off watch and in his cabin.

Second Officer Brian Davies was next. He approached the lectern, white faced and shaking as if he was facing his executioner and gave his evidence in a weak and unconvincing voice. Even knowing that my ordeal was about to start, I was able to feel some sympathy for someone whose nerves had destroyed his masculinity. I was next and didn't yet know how my body would cope with the stress of public examination. From the cramping pains in my stomach, I feared it would not be very well. I could only pray that I would give a more credible performance than poor Davies.

Brian Davies finished his evidence and answered a few questions from Mr. Williams. Jonas Jeremiah declined to cross examine, saying to Admiral Buchan with out getting up from the seat he reclined in, "I see no point in wasting the time of this Enquiry with a cross examination of such a weak and unconvincing witness."

And then I was on my feet.

As I approached the lectern, I could understand exactly the feelings that had unmanned Brian Davies. I could not have been more frightened if I had been about to be dropped into a pit full of angry cobras. My teeth were clenched so tightly together to stop them chattering that my jaw was beginning to ache. I could only hope the lectern would hide my shaking knees at least from Admiral Buchan.

Mr. Williams materialized on my left side out of the panic induced haze that was beginning to fog my vision and whispered encouragingly in my ear, "It will be easier once you start, Jason."

I found the unexpected use of my Christian name immensely comforting and some of my fear fell away. Mr. Williams turned to Admiral Buchan and explained in his calm way, "Third Officer Smiley was a cadet on the SS Earl Canning when this tragic event occurred. As you know his written testimony has been lodged as an official document of this Enquiry, but before proceeding to review his account of the events of that day, I have a number of introductory questions to ask of him"

He turned back to me, "When did you meet Third Officer Evans?"

"He was the first person I met when I joined the ship as a cadet."

"How did you and he get along?"

"Very well, Sir. We shared the same cabin and as Captain Stewart had made Mr. Evans my teacher and guide, we always shared the same watch. Everything I had learned about the sea and ships up to the time of my friend's death, I had learned from him."

And suddenly the misery caused by his death seemed very close and painful, and it took me a few minutes to recover my composure. Mr. Williams watched until I recovered my poise and then went on. "As time passed by and you became more experienced as a sea officer, I imagine there were times when you and Mr. Evans acted independently. Is that correct?

"Yes, sir."

"On the day of the tragedy it was officially Mr. Evans' watch, and you were shadowing him as usual. Captain Stewart decided that it would be appropriate for Mr. Evans to take the surveyors in the boat whilst you took over the watch."

"Yes, sir."

"As a cadet, Mr. Smiley, had you been on watch on your own previously?"

"Yes, sir."

"Please tell the Board of Enquiry when and where, Mr. Smiley."

"I was alone on watch once in the Indian Ocean whilst on passage to Bombay and three times, including this particular occasion, whilst we were at anchor."

"I'm not a sailor, Mr. Smiley, so please tell me what actions you performed during this particular watch."

"As you know, sir, we were at anchor in the Elphinstone Inlet. From the time Mr. Evans left the bridge, I checked the position of the ship every fifteen minutes by taking bearings on two specific landmarks to ensure the ship was not drifting. At the same time I checked the surrounding water area for local craft and the mountain slopes for signs of local people. Then I checked all around the horizon for any sign of a change in the weather. During this watch I recorded 'No change,' for each item up to the time when Captain Stewart came back to the bridge so unexpectedly. Even then I had seen and heard nothing that would indicate an imminent change in the weather."

"Mr. Evans was already on his way to the island when Captain Stewart came back to the bridge, I assume. Is that correct, Mr. Smiley?"

Before I could answer, there was a stir at the back of the hall that attracted everyone's attention, as someone started to force his way through the crowd towards the front. A black suited man, clutching a hat in one hand and a sheaf of papers in the other, appeared at the railing behind Mr. Jeremiah who stood up, turned and took the papers. Mr. Jeremiah obviously knew what the contents of the papers were, as he turned immediately back towards the board members without even looking at the first word on the first page.

"Admiral Buchan. Just before this Enquiry started Captain Evans received a letter from Bombay that has a considerable bearing on the outcome of this Enquiry. I took the liberty of making verbatim et litteratim transcriptions of the letter. There is one copy for you, Admiral Buchan and one copy for Mr. Williams."

He handed two sheets of paper to the usher who carried one to the Admiral and the other to Mr. Williams. Both of whom immediately started reading the text reproduced below.

SS Blue Horizon
Bombay

Captain Evans
Llandeilo Road
Caernarfon
Wales

Sir,

In accordance with your request, I contacted the office of the Anglo Indian Telegraph Company here in Bombay and asked to speak to one of the surveyors who witnessed the tragic accident in which your son was drowned.

Two days later I received a note from a man called MacAndrew who claimed to have first hand knowledge of the incident. He wrote that he would see me in Bombay and asked for fifty pounds as compensation for travelling expenses. I thought this sum excessive, but knowing how important it is for you to know the truth, I agreed to pay it.

Two days later he came on board in the late afternoon and I interviewed him in front of my first officer. I didn't like the man and but for the fact we were going to sail in a matter of hours would have ejected him from my ship. In the event I gave him the fifty pounds and then posed the questions you had prepared for me and noted that he answered each question without the slightest hesitation. Your questions and the associated answers are shown below.

Question 1. Were you part of the survey party from the Anglo Indian Telegraph Company that went to Elphinstone Inlet?
Answer 1. Yes.

Question 2. How many personnel were there?
Answer 2. Six.

Question 3. What was your position?
Answer 3. Surveyor.

Question 4. On the day of the accident what were the weather conditions?
Answer 4. Initially clear but later very windy.

Question 5. Was it too windy for a small boat to be used?
Answer 5. Yes. That's why there was an accident.

Question 6. In your opinion should the captain have postponed the trip?
Answer 7. Yes. Chief Surveyor told me he had asked for a delay but had been ignored.

I hope these answers will be sufficient to allow you to bring your dispute to a conclusion, although I am very much aware that it will not bring you the comfort of your son.

Yours faithfully

Captain Bertram Rudge
Master
SS Blue Horizon.

Mr. Jeremiah had remained standing whilst the letters were being read and when Admiral Buchan and Mr. Williams indicated they had finished, he resumed his presentation. In a voice full of confidence and condescension he said, "I propose to submit this letter to the Enquiry formally. We would have no objection if Captain Stewart's team request a short adjournment in order to consider this new evidence."

He added and couldn't keep a triumphant note out of his voice,

"Captain Stewart may wish to reconsider his position and save every one a great deal of time and inconvenience."

Mr. Williams stood up with the letter still clutched in his hand and his face was a tapestry of emotions as he considered the implications of what he had read. He squared his shoulders and looking directly at Admiral Buchan said quietly, "We should be grateful for an adjournment to study this document," and sat down.

Admiral Buchan conferred with his advisors and after receiving nods of agreement from both stated, "It is now noon. We will adjourn for lunch and reconvene at two this afternoon. I think that should allow you sufficient time to study this new evidence, Mr. Williams?"

"Yes, sir. Thank you, sir."

At a command from the Clerk of the Court everyone stood up. The admiral and his advisors filed out of the room and immediately the noise level reached deafening proportions as every one in the crowd discussed and speculated about the contents of the letter.

Captain Evans and his team made a triumphal exit, and I wondered sourly if I would here trumpets sounding a tune like 'Here the conquering hero comes', but fortunately, the door opened and closed silently.

On our side, Captain Stewart and his supporters and legal advisors left the enquiry room by a side door with us three officers trailing disconsolately in their wake. We went into a side office opposite the enquiry room and found seats round a small table. Mr. Williams handed the letter he had received from Jeremiah to Captain Stewart who read it and lost all colour from his face. Wordlessly, he passed it to Captain Downing, who in turn read it, but without a change of expression and then passed it to the Company Secretary to read.

Captain Downing looked around the table saw me and as he passed me a small purse instructed, "Smiley, you're the junior here, take this money and the carriage and go and purchase what food and drink you can as we will not have time to go to my Club today. We need all the time we have to discuss this letter. It changes everything for the worse."

I stood and left the room. By the time I returned, they had obviously decided how to deal with this new evidence and with the notable exception of Captain Stewart, they settled down to fill their stomachs with the victuals I had bought. I ate also and as no one chose to show me the letter and I did not think to ask to see it, I went back into the enquiry room in total ignorance.

As before the enquiry room was full of people and very noisy, but at the first sound of the clerk's gavel, silence fell. I think they all sensed that a crisis was fast approaching and didn't want to miss a word.

The members of the Board of Enquiry filed in and sat down.

I stood up and walked to the lectern. I was nervous but more under control than in the morning. Mr. Williams' calm questioning, followed by a break for lunch when my stomach didn't prevent me eating, had succeeded in relaxing my nerves. Admiral Buchan nodded to Mr. Williams to continue, but Mr. Jonas Jeremiah rose portentously to his feet, adjusted his wig, fiddled with his cloak and addressed the Board.

"Admiral Buchan. Before the adjournment, Third Officer Smiley was recounting in absurd detail his life as a cadet at anchor on the day when Third Officer Evans, two seamen and three surveyors from the Anglo Indian Telegraph Company, all lost their lives in a tragic, and in my view, avoidable accident. Third Officer Smiley's testimony is now hardly relevant, as we have received at the eleventh hour, important testimony from an eye witness that clearly supports the charge of negligence. Mr. MacAndrew's statements are clear and concise."

"Whose statements?" I asked loudly of the whole room. Mr. Williams, with a face like thunder, although I was unsure whether his anger was directed at Jonas Jeremiah or me, replied as if I should already know this "MacAndrew! He is the surviving surveyor from the Anglo Indian Telegraph Company."

"Give me that letter" I ordered. Mr. Williams frowned at my tone but stepped quickly to the table retrieved the letter from the top of a pile of papers and handed it to me.

I started to read but heard the voice of Jonas Jeremiah, "Admiral Buchan. I insist that . . ."

What he was going to insist on, I do not know, but my voice, aimed directly at Mr. Jonas Jeremiah Q.C. and carrying all the fear, anger and frustration of many past days, whip cracked around the room, "Sit down, sir, and remain quiet." In the ensuing stunned silence I feared that I had gone too far for a junior officer, but Jonas Jeremiah was so surprised he sat down and remained silent whilst I read the letter, as did everyone else as a matter of fact, although they probably all reacted to the angry tone of my voice rather that the words.

I read the whole letter, then held it up as high as I could reach, brandished it in the air until I had everyone's attention, then deliberately let it fall to the floor.

As Mr. Williams stepped forward with a cry of dismay to retrieve it, I ordered, "Let it lie, Mr. Williams. It's worthless. No one by the name of MacAndrew was included in the survey party from Anglo Indian Telegraph Company. Captain Rudge has been hoaxed."

There was pandemonium. Everyone seemed to be shouting at once and through the cacophony of sounds, came the half demented voice of Captain Evans screeching out "Rudge was not deceived. Smiley is trying to deceive you to protect his Captain. Stewart murdered my son and will pay the penalty." And he started to try to force his way through the crush to get at Captain Stewart. He was overpowered with difficulty and carried kicking and screaming from the enquiry room by the ushers with his daughter in attendance. We could hear the screams and shouts fading into the distance. Then a door slammed and the cries of a demented old man were mercifully cut off.

The clerk made good use of his gavel again and brought the noise level down to an acceptable level. The people in the audience were too excited now to be completely quiet.

Admiral Buchan looked at me angrily. "If you, Third Officer Smiley, cannot give me a satisfactory explanation for your unseemly disruption of this Board of Enquiry it will go badly for you. Explain yourself, sir."

"If you look at the letter, sir, I can explain. He was not part of the survey party. There were only five people and their names were McFadden, Carmichael, Ellis, Tomlinson and Davison. Tomlinson and Davison were not on the boat and survived. Third Officer Evans was an experienced small boat sailor and remarked before he untied the boat and set off that it was a lovely day for a sail. I do not know if the Chief Surveyor McFadden made a complaint about the weather. There was no need to postpone the trip, and when I last saw Mr. McFadden he was laughing and joking with Mr. Evans."

Admiral Buchan spoke quietly to his advisors and when they nodded in agreement he remarked, "We have on the one hand the written testimony of MacAndrew witnessed by two responsible ship's officers and on the other the verbal testimony of Third Officer Smiley, which rejects MacAndrew's statements. Before proceeding with the charge against Captain Stewart, it is essential that we resolve the question of the veracity, or otherwise, of MacAndrew's evidence. It is crucial, in my view that the names of the members of the survey party are established and these are not given in any of the statements laid before this enquiry."

When the Admiral stopped speaking there was a profound silence as the principals to the enquiry thought and looked at each other and shrugged their shoulders at each other, as they realized they could not propose a solution to the impasse.

I was also racking my brains without success until I remembered my diary.

Still standing at the lectern I spoke to Admiral Buchan without further thought or hesitation.

"Sir, may I speak?"

"Proceed. Mr. Smiley."

"Sir, whilst I was a cadet, Captain Stewart insisted that I wrote a daily journal and recorded everything that occurred. He said it would be good practice for writing a ship's log when I became a captain myself. The captain or first mate read my journal every week and questioned me about my entries to ensure I completely understood what I had written. They initialled my journal after the last entry each time. I'm sure I would have recorded the details of the survey party."

"Where are these journals now?"

"Under my bunk locked in my sea chest, sir."

"You can get them this afternoon?"

"Easily Sir, if Captain Downing permits me to use the company carriage."

Captain Downing nodded his agreement.

At this point Mr. Jonas Jeremiah Q.C. stood up and glared at the Admiral. "I object. How can we prove he hasn't falsified the records by the time he comes back to this hall. He'll do anything for his captain."

Admiral took the point but dealt with it positively "You said the box is locked, Mr. Smiley. Where is the key?"

"Here Sir, it's the only one."

"Very well, give it to me."

I walked to the big table and handed the key to the Admiral. He looked towards the door at the side of the room and called out in a commanding voice "Corporal."

"Sir," said a voice and a smartly turned out marine marched to the table and came to rigid attention with a crash of boots as he saluted.

The Admiral acknowledged the salute and ordered, "Corporal, take two men and escort Mr. Smiley to his ship. Collect his sea chest and bring it and Mr. Smiley back here. On no account is Mr. Smiley to touch the chest. Is that clear?"

"Yes, sir," and the corporal saluted again, left turned with a scrape and stamp of his boots and marched noisily out of the room. As I followed the corporal, I heard Admiral Buchan announce an adjournment for one hour. The Board of Enquiry would reconvene at four.

With my marine escort, I travelled quickly to the ship in the carriage, and they retrieved my sea chest from under my bunk whilst I waited in the companionway outside. We drove quickly back to the Cotton Exchange where the box was laid on the clerk's table in front of Admiral Buchan's chair. Two marines stood on guard until the enquiry resumed.

At four exactly and in a hush of expectation, the admiral and his two captain advisors once more marched into the enquiry room and took their places. Mr. Williams, Mr. Jeremiah and I were called to stand in front of the desk.

Admiral Buchan looked at Mr. Jeremiah. "The corporal of marines reported to me that Mr. Smiley has not touched the box. Please confirm that the box is locked."

"It is, Admiral," Mr. Jeremiah reported after tugging at the lid.

"Here is the key, Mr. Smiley. Unlock and open the box, get out your journals and lay them out here. Then stand back."

"Aye, sir."

I opened the box and after a moment of rummaging started to pull my journals out from under the clothes I had placed in the box. I laid all the journals out in a line on the desk in front of Admiral Buchan.

Mr. Williams and Mr. Jeremiah started at opposite ends of the row of journals and started to look for the one that covered the days prior to the 20th August. Mr. Jeremiah found the correct journal and handed it to Admiral Buchan opened to the correct page.

Admiral Buchan read out, "12th August 1865. The survey party from Anglo Indian Telegraph Company have come on board and are using N0.1 hatch cover as their temporary home. There are five people. McFadden is the chief surveyor. Carmichael and Ellis are surveyors and Tomlinson and Davison are the chainmen."

A very subdued looking Mr. Jeremiah looked at Admiral Buchan and stated in a subdued voice, "It is obvious now that MacAndrew was an impostor and Captain Rudge was deceived. The letter we have received is clearly inadmissible as evidence."

Admiral Buchan read on through the journal, and after a few minutes he stopped and after calling for silence he said, "I wish you all to hear part of this entry made on 20th August 1865 by Cadet Smiley."

He stood up and cleared his throat. His voice clearly reached the back of the room when he read out the words I had written so many months before.

He said, "I quote 'Third Officer Evans sailed for the island with the survey party. He said it was a lovely day for a sail and I was quite envious. I stayed on board to complete the anchor watch on the bridge. Conditions stable. Blue sky; no cloud, wind Force 3 to 4 southerly, ship lying to anchor with no sign of drifting. Captain in his cabin and other officers off watch and presumed asleep. Captain returned to the bridge and was very concerned about something. Didn't say anything but picked up a telescope and started to scan around the horizon. Seeing this, I looked also but could see no change since I made my last observation about ten minutes before. The Captain suddenly gesticulated, snapped the telescope shut, jumped to the whistle lanyard and blew the emergency signal. He blew the signal twice more, rang the engine room telegraph to standby and ordered me to hoist flags 'U' over 'K' over 'X', which I did as quickly as possible. . . .'"

Admiral Buchan stopped reading and put down my journal. He thought for a moment or two and then beckoned to Captain Stewart to come up to the desk.

"Captain Stewart this court of Enquiry was convened because someone considered you had been negligent in the discharge of your duties. What I have read in the journal written by Cadet Smiley tallies in every respect with the accounts I have read in the ship's log and in your signed statement. The journals could not have been falsified, as they would not have been produced in evidence if the letter from MacAndrew, about which nothing was known before midday today, had not been introduced. In my opinion you have displayed exemplary seamanship and should never have been accused of negligence. I will make that clear in my report."

Admiral Buchan said, "You are free to go, Captain, and I wish you success. This Board of Enquiry is closed." He held out his hand and as Captain Stewart grasped it he said, "I'm very pleased to see you a free man Captain."

"Thank you, Admiral," was all that Captain Stewart was able to articulate at that moment.

And that was that. It was over and my father had been exonerated. I was very pleased and proud that I had been able to help clear his name.

Now I could decide what to do with the letters I had written all those days ago.

End of Volume One

Contact author John Milton Langdon
or order more copies of this book at

TATE PUBLISHING, LLC

127 East Trade Center Terrace
Mustang, Oklahoma 73064

(888) 361 - 9473

Tate Publishing, LLC

www.tatepublishing.com